Lingerie
Tea

SCEPTRE

Also by Sylvia Mulholland

Woman's Work

Lingerie
Tea

SYLVIA MULHOLLAND

SCEPTRE

First published in 1998 by Hodder and Stoughton
A division of Hodder Headline PLC
A Sceptre Book

10 9 8 7 6 5 4 3 2 1

British Library Cataloguing in Publication Data

ISBN 0 340 67484 9

Typeset by Palimpsest Book Production Limited,
Polmont, Stirlingshire
Printed and bound in Great Britain by
Mackays of Chatham PLC, Chatham, Kent

Hodder and Stoughton
A division of Hodder Headline PLC
338 Euston Road
London NW1 3BH

For Gabrielle, Thelma
and two Alexandras

ACKNOWLEDGEMENTS ∫

I wish to thank Carol Shields for her generosity of time and spirit in the midst of literary awards.

'Love and scandal are the best sweeteners of tea' – Henry Fielding

The Invitation

I 5

From a corner of the boardroom, a grandfather clock struck the half-hour. All Victorian scrolls and furls, it had once intimidated clients in the dark-panelled foyer of Bragg, Banks and Biltmore when the law firm was founded in 1910. The clock was now an anachronism – a gloomy, black-walnut reminder of the days when all lawyers were men and the law was a jealous mistress. Its pendulum swung in a silent, well-oiled arc as Claire Cunningham, Gillian Lawrence and Shelagh Tyler arrived for the morning partners' meeting that had been called at very short notice.

Claire pressed a series of lozenge-shaped wall switches and the women were washed in the halogen glow of a dozen low-hanging lights. Shelagh, petite but always striking, was in a close-fitting chemical-yellow suit, the drama of it enhanced by contrasting patent leather shoes and bag, as glossy black as Shelagh's hair. Her clothing often featured large decorative zippers in improbable places: at the wrist, over one or both breasts, up the back of the skirt. Today's suit had only one: industrial-strength, on a front panel of the skirt. It was partially unzipped, its glittering nickel teeth splaying apart in a wicked grin at mid-thigh.

Gillian was in her usual anti-law firm attire: a peasant-style smocked blouse and longish print skirt. A wide woven shawl, hemmed with a row of tiny brass bells, was gathered and draped over one shoulder. 'I only work here because I need the money,' her clothing seemed to convey. 'This is not really me – here on Bay Street . . . "lawyers' row".' Her shawl seemed a nuisance, for she was continually readjusting it or shrugging to keep it in

3 •

place. My partners, my friends, Claire thought. Good lawyers both, but still . . . a bit hard to take so early in the morning. With her own shoulder-length brown hair (a style she'd worn since the early eighties) and oatmeal linen suit, Claire wondered if she were the only normal one. Or was it just that she lacked a sense of personal style, as one or two wardrobe consultants had suggested over the years? 'Well, ladies,' she said, 'looks like we have our choice of chairs. Take any one you want, so long as it's green.'

'Aniline-dyed leather,' Gillian observed.

'Whoopee cushions,' Shelagh added.

There were twelve of the jade green chairs, smartly pulled up around the oval conference table, as if waiting for serious business to begin. Though the chairs were elegant and inviting, they were also an expensive mistake. The cushions were so soft and plumply stuffed that they vibrated with an embarrassing leather flatulence as each was occupied.

Handbags and briefcases thumped on to the carpet, pens and reading glasses clattered on the flecked surface of the granite table top. On a sideboard, coffee and hot water, muffins, juice and mineral water had been set out by the firm's hospitality hostess.

'Either of you ever think what an appropriate term "bored-room" is?' Gillian said, strolling over to assess the muffin selection. Bran, banana, cranberry. How had cranberries – horrid bitter things, hardly tolerable even at Thanksgiving – become a staple of the corporate diet? She stifled a yawn, filled a cup with hot water and poked a tea bag into it.

'I was thinking how stuffy it is in here,' Claire said, 'and wondering how many times the air's been recycled.'

Shelagh drummed her flame-coloured nails on the tabletop, looking peeved. 'It's past eight-thirty. I want to know why the boys are late. Or, more to the point, why are the three of us always early?'

'Because we're women,' Claire said, 'and our mothers taught us that it's rude to be late.'

'Maybe they're expecting us to get breakfast served up.' Gillian sat down beside Claire with a small sound of breaking wind. Apparently impervious to it (the chairs had ceased to be a source of amusement in the firm), she reorganized her tinkling shawl and took a sip of tea.

'It looks as though we don't have enough to do,' Shelagh worried. 'If we were busy we'd be late for this meeting, maybe not show up at all. What if the *real* meeting is going on somewhere else right now? And this is just a dummy meeting, to throw us off the scent?'

Claire, lacking the energy to respond to one of Shelagh's 'skirts-versus-suits' paranoid fantasies, opened her briefcase and took out the morning paper that, remarkably (given the frantic effort it had taken to get her out of the house and at the office by 8.30), she'd remembered to stuff into it. The front page of the paper was splashed with a story about a lawyer who'd been killed, falling from a subway platform into the path of an oncoming train. He'd been showing off, the paper reported, walking *on his hands* along the yellow dotted line that passengers were supposed to stand clear of. A macho thing. He'd been an athlete in college. Triathlon. Claire pushed the paper towards Shelagh. 'Did you read about this guy? How horrible.'

'They think he was a jumper,' Shelagh said. 'His ex-wife was into him big-time for support and he had a string of mistresses after his balls. But my money says he was pushed. And I bet his partners had his files divied up before he hit the tracks.'

'Okay, so how do you explain the absence of loose change?' Gillian interjected. 'Here's a guy walking upside down – and *nothing* drops out of his pockets? No keys, no coins, no subway tokens? No breath mints? That's what it says in the paper – there was *nothing* found at the scene. Men always have stuff in their pockets.'

'So?'

'So it was obviously a suicide. A guy who was going to kill himself by walking upside down would clear out his pockets first, wouldn't he?'

'So would a guy who was going to show off that way,' Claire argued. 'And he was out with a bunch of lawyers,' Shelagh said. 'What do you *think* happened to all the loose change?' Really, she thought, Gillian was capable of taking the most incredible tangents. What was even more amazing, however, was that Gillian was speaking to Shelagh. As a result of a tiff (according to Claire, who acted as interpreter, Gillian believed Shelagh had undermined her to a client by an oblique and sarcastic reference to Gillian's 'creative pursuits'), Gillian had been ignoring Shelagh for more than a week.

'Maybe that lawyer just fell over the edge,' Claire said. 'A simple accident. I can see myself slipping on to the subway tracks. I wouldn't even have to be walking on my hands. I would just drop over. Distracted, totally unaware of where I was or what I was doing . . . The kids would be running around, up and down the platform, chasing each other. Screaming and laughing. Maybe the dog would be there too.' Claire swallowed. The horror of the imagined scene caused a tightness in her chest, bringing with it a stab of heartburn – the same torment she'd suffered so often while pregnant with first Harry then Molly. 'I've always got too much on my mind. It's having little kids that does it.'

Shelagh rested her forehead on her hands, hoping Claire would resist the urge to launch into her usual lament about working mothers who do too much.

'I went to a psychiatrist once,' Claire continued. 'I told him I was possessed by gremlins or had early-onset Alzheimer's. I can't seem to remember anything. If someone asks me how my weekend was, on a Monday morning, I honestly can't recall. I just gape at them. What weekend? I want to ask. So anyway, this shrink told me that Winston Churchill, not once in his entire life, drew his own bath.'

Shelagh raised her eyebrows; Gillian frowned. 'So?' they said together.

'Okay, it took me a while to get his point, too. You see, if I had people waiting on me – servants and so on – I could accomplish a lot more than I do. And I wouldn't feel so frantic, as if my life's getting away from me all the time. I'm *not* Winston Churchill. And I not only have to draw my own bath but the baths of several others. And baths are the easy part.'

'I thought you had a nanny,' Gillian said.

'Maybe he preferred showers. Old Winston.' Shelagh shifted in her chair, hoping the conversation would move away from children or the history of the bathtub in England – a subject Gillian would surely seize upon with delight. She heaved a giant sigh to indicate that, in her view, there was nothing else worth saying about either topic. 'It's 8.45,' she said, 'and here we sit, wasting time. In the pink ghetto as usual.'

'We are not pink-ghettoized because our offices are on the north wall,' Gillian said. 'I wish you'd stop saying that.'

'No, you wish the pink ghetto didn't exist. If it didn't, I wouldn't have to say it, would I?'

Claire was thinking how unpleasant it was being trapped between Shelagh and Gillian when they were sniping at one another. But at least they were talking – which was better than the big chill. Soon it might be Claire's turn to be put in the deep freeze over some careless comment or chance remark. What an uneasy triumvirate the three of them made, she reflected, their feelings swinging, often several times a day, from empathy to envy to enmity, then back again, depending on who considered herself slighted by whom. The silent treatment, however, only worked with women. On a man, the effect of it was zero, at least in the workplace. Men either didn't notice when they were being snubbed by a woman, or didn't care. Or were actually grateful for the silence.

'Well, girls,' Shelagh said, 'I'd love to sit here yakking all day about loose change and Winston Churchill and what-not, but I've got work to do.' She pushed back her chair, preparing to leave, just as Pete Johnson and Dan Chatwell entered the boardroom. Then Sandy Krupnik and Alexander Spears arrived to settle noisily into the leather chairs, followed by the firm's Managing Partner, Rick Durham. A lot of bustling and clinking of glassware ensued as the lawyers poured coffee or juice and picked over the selection of muffins. Tough, cold, tasteless, Shelagh grumbled to herself. That had to be the most unrealistic part of *L A Law*: those breakfast meetings with the big budget Danishes that started off every episode. At the Triple B. Ranch (as she liked to call the firm) they'd be lucky to see a greasy carton of doughnut holes.

Gillian finished her tea, then spent a few moments surveying the five neckties in the room. Rick's cookie-patterned raw silk was an eyebrow raiser, but he'd knotted it, predictably, in a conservative Shelby – small, precise, balanced – the wide front part forming a perfect, centred dimple. Beside him, Pete Johnson seemed to be strangling in a too-tight Nicole Miller silk that he couldn't have picked out himself. He was a fine lawyer, but definitely from the shallow end of the gene pool, fashion-wise. Sandy Krupnik, as round and bright as a new button, was playing it safe with a diagonal that made Gillian think of bank reconciliations; and Dan Chatwell, tense and flushed and much too pretty for Gillian's taste, was in a corporate kamikaze: an insipid floral tied in a Four-in-Hand. Someone should tell him . . . a floral could do nothing to advance his career.

Ross Owen, who'd been the last to arrive, wore a tie that was tasteful if uninspired: navy, white and burgundy pin-points. The crispness of its pattern contrasted with the rather sloppy Windsor knot he'd tied, as it did with his rumpled, out-of-season grey flannels. Only Alexander Spears wore a tie that Gillian might have been proud to wear herself: an intricately woven paisley in royal blue and teal silk. Alexander (or the woman who had been with him when he got dressed that morning) had tied it in a Half-Windsor. It was the knot of royalty, never extreme, always in good taste. Too bad the same could not be said of Alexander.

Gillian wondered who had picked out each of the ties around the boardroom table. The men themselves? Their wives? Mothers? In Ross Owen's case, was it Shelagh? If she herself wore neckties, Gillian reflected, if the only pizzazz in her everyday work attire was a single splash at her collar, she would be sure to make a statement with it, using all sorts of intriguing found materials: fish nets from the beach, strips of sixties Mary Quant tights, a bunch of Isadora's sparkly neon sneaker laces.

Beside her, Claire was worrying that the next day was her 'duty day' at Molly's co-op play school and that she would have to take the morning off work to slouch around with several other mums in sweatsuits, wiping small noses and bums and arbitrating pre-schoolers' disputes. She pulled her diary from her briefcase and wrote 'snack' at the top of a clean page. 'Juice?' she wrote next to it. Which was it she was supposed to bring? Should she bring both, to be on the safe side? And be sure not to let the other mothers down? She looked up to meet the eyes of Alexander Spears, the man who'd hired her eight years earlier. Though she was well qualified, Claire had known, intuitively, that Alexander's personal interest in her was what got her the job. How could he have predicted that she would show up for her first day of work, already married to Ben, or that she would promptly balloon to gargantuan proportions with two pregnancies in three years?

Alexander was a gloomy man, the Leonard Cohen of the legal profession. He was a big-time corporate lawyer with a stable of Blue Chip clients that was 'to die for' according to Shelagh. He was also, intriguingly, something of a Renaissance man: a black belt in karate, a published poet, and his watercolours of local flora had won second prize at a juried, province-wide, art show. Despite a small paunch and an undeniable thinning of his hair, there was something compelling about those baleful brown eyes, that prickly personality. Flustered and flattered by his stare – would the man never give up? Did she need to have six kids and boobs to her knees to turn him off? – Claire looked again at her diary and folded over the corner of the page, concealing the words 'snack' and 'juice?'.

Beside her, Shelagh was also feeling unsettled. The biceps of Dan Chatwell, the most junior partner, were practically bursting through the crisp cotton of his shirt, and he looked ready to choke beneath his starched collar. He had to be working out or taking steroids or something, to be bulking up like that. But such a shame about his verbal tics. 'Tickety-boo' was the worst of them; 'kopacetic' a close second – his speech generally was littered with the phonetic equivalent of yellow happy faces. Still . . . there ought to be some creative ways of muzzling him, once she'd gotten him into bed. Pity the boardroom table was too wide to allow for an accidental brushing of Dan's leg. She imagined her sheer-stockinged toes teasing the hem of his trousers, then sliding up his executive-length sock.

But her frisson of sexual interest was quickly shadowed by a cloud of self-doubt. Didn't she already have enough trouble managing Ross Owen? He had been predictably late for the meeting, probably after chauffeuring one of his million kids to some lesson or practice or school. She could feel his eyes on her, longing, caring. How many workplace romances, she wondered glumly, did it take to ruin a career? In her mind, she'd had a liaison with every man in that boardroom – dreaming about them all at one time or another – as well as the mailroom boy, the bicycle couriers, the lilliputian man in the white coat who came around periodically to check the air quality in her office, and the loose-jointed pony-tailed youth who tended the firm's office plants.

Shelagh's interest in these men would usually dissipate as soon as she saw them the morning after she'd dreamt of them, and she would cringe at the workings of her subconscious, so obviously crazed with lust. Occasionally, though, a sexual attraction persisted to the point where she was moved to do something about it. The last time that happened, Ross Owen had left his wife and kids for her. That note under her desk blotter! That shaky handwriting telling her he was at the Holiday Inn! She glanced at him, guiltily, reading the questions in his eyes: What did you do last night after I left? What are you doing tonight? Questions that he, still very much encumbered with Marcia and the children (despite being holed up, more or less permanently, in a bachelor apartment in the east end), had no right to ask.

'As everyone here should recall,' Rick was saying, tapping his coffee mug with his pen, 'this is the time of year when we have to start planning our annual tie party.'

Was *this* all the meeting was to be about? Shelagh wondered crossly. The annual tie swap was an affront to the women lawyers at Bragg, Banks and Biltmore. It wasn't that they wanted to be included, it was that the ridiculous boys-will-be-boys bonding thing happened at all. Dozens of ugly and/or out-of-style neckties, otherwise destined for the goodwill stores, were dug out of closets and trunks and piled on the boardroom table. Then a lot of drunken fun ensued as prizes were awarded – for the most outrageously ugly, the one with the least number of natural fibres, the most banal – and the owner roasted for his bad taste in having acquired the tie in the first place. The luckless ties were then tried on and traded, the idea being that even the worst losers would find a new home by the end of the evening, only to surface again the following year for another round of sartorial hilarity. Shelagh grasped the sleeve of Claire's jacket. 'I can't believe they're doing this. Are we supposed to pay for this stupid flight? *And* a Boston hotel?'

'What flight? What hotel?' Claire's attention had wandered.

The cookie pattern on Rick's tie had started her stomach rumbling, reminding her that there was nothing in her kitchen she could take for a nursery-school snack. If snack was really what she was required to bring tomorrow . . .

'The flight to their idiotic tie swap,' Shelagh scowled. 'Weren't you listening? A *Boston Tie Party*. It's totally irresponsible!'

'We've been able to charter a small private plane at an attractive rate,' Rick was saying, 'from one of our good clients, Bert King. Those we can't fit in can fly economy to Boston. We've booked it for the long weekend in August. And we'll be inviting some other clients along – catch a Red Sox game while we're there. It's a great business-development tool.'

'A Boston Tie Party!' Dan enthused. 'And what if the ties nobody wants get dumped into Boston Harbour?'

'The city of Boston will fine us for a polyester-acetate spill.' Sandy smiled. 'I'm from the States – I know how they think down there. We'll be in litigation for thirty years.' The idea of a polyester spill – not to mention a thirty-year law-suit – was greeted by a spray of congratulatory (male) laughter.

'Great party idea, Rick!' said Pete Johnson.

'Super!' Ross added, his eyes still on Shelagh.

'Bonus points for the Rick-Meister!' added Dan.

Rick cleared his throat, affecting an expression of humility, and fondled his necktie. 'But on a more serious note,' he said, 'we all need to examine our business-development tools. Each of us should have a tool kit – and keep those tools good and sharp.' The others struggled with this metaphor, for a few moments, until Rick continued: 'The Executive Committee is also of the view that the women partners should consider doing something similar to the Boston Tie Party – for female clients.'

'Like what?' Shelagh said drily. 'An old girdle swap?'

'Pantyhose might be another idea.' Claire didn't look up, aware of Alexander's eyes on her again and imagining that her pantyhose was a subject he was considering with some relish.

'You know,' Rick said, 'that's just the kind of negative attitude that keeps us from becoming first-rate, and from growing the way we should. This firm is almost a hundred years old. And it looks it.'

'Speak for yourself,' Shelagh said, patting her hair, and was rewarded by snickers from around the table.

'Laugh all you want, but we're stagnating. We've got to do more in this area, move into the twenty-first century, promote like hell.'

'Excuse me, but what about my breast cancer breakfast?' Shelagh demanded. 'The fundraiser? You seem to be forgetting that. It was extremely successful.'

Rick coloured. Words such as 'breast' were known to thrill and embarrass him; even when followed by downers like 'cancer'. 'Boobs', he could handle; 'hooters', 'melons' and 'knockers' were fair game. But anatomical correctness . . . ? He cleared his throat. 'Well, okay,' he conceded, 'except for Shelagh, who has done some very good promotional work for women's . . . health causes in the past months, we just aren't doing enough. Boutique firms like ours are being swallowed up. The competition's strangling us.'

'But not with old neckties and girdles, surely?' Gillian said.

'Rick, you're leaving out the most important part of our weekend plan.' Alexander Spears looked piqued.

Rick frowned, then managed a smile, his face travelling through the brief range of expressions of which it was capable. 'Yes, of course, Alex. Sorry.' He tapped his coffee mug with his pen again. 'The Boston Tie Party will also serve as a forum for a special celebration. A stag.' The other partners looked at each other, surprised. 'But I'll let Alex tell you about it.' Rick sat down abruptly. The leather of his chair protested.

'Believe it or not,' Alexander said glumly, 'I've decided to tie the knot.'

'Who is she?'

'Do we know her?'

'Have you asked her?'

'You know her, you know her.' He looked defensively around the table, his long fingers caressing the silk of his tie. Claire stared at him, startled. But I'm *very* married, Alex, she wanted to laugh, embarrassed. With two kids! 'And of course I've asked her.' He scowled. 'What sort of idiot would be making a wedding announcement if he hadn't?'

Claire gazed out the boardroom window, her ears hot. Gillian was marvelling that such an unpleasant person as Alex could be as successful as he was, but Shelagh merely regarded him through half-closed eyes, waiting.

'And some of you may find this difficult to believe,' he said, 'but she has actually said yes.' He paused. 'I'm going to marry Anna.'

'Our Anna?'

'You're kidding!'

'The *articling* student?'

'When?'

'October.'

'Jesus,' Shelagh breathed.

Claire was now totally intrigued by a tiny scuff mark on the heel of her linen pump. 'I knew buying this colour was a mistake,' she muttered. 'I'll *never* get it clean.'

Gillian poked her. 'Somebody better congratulate Alex.'

'You do it!'

'He's your friend!'

Claire hesitated for a moment, then took a deep breath. 'Well! I think this is just wonderful news!' She shoved back her chair, swept her hair from her face and leaned across the table to pump Alexander's hand. 'And October is a perfect time for a wedding. Not too hot, not too cold.'

'It's Randy Sandler's birthday.' Alexander pressed her hand in return. 'The fifth.' He let go of her hand.

'Sorry?'

'Sandler,' Shelagh said, *sotto voce*. 'Left winger. New York Rangers.'

'Oh. Great!' Claire nodded. 'So you'll be married on the fifth – a famous ball player's birthday.'

'Hockey!' Shelagh hissed.

'Well,' Claire babbled on, 'I can't think of a better day. We'll have a party too – a shower for Anna – the girls, that is. You men go have your tie party and we'll have a tea. In September. At my house. A lingerie shower – we'll have a lingerie tea!'

Shelagh put her face in her hands.

'Hey, can I come?' Rick laughed. 'It sounds a lot more interesting than neckties.'

Alexander was fixing Claire with another of his looks. 'We – Anna and I – appreciate this.'

'No, please, don't thank me. It's the least I can do. I mean, this is such great news. Just great.' She fell back into her seat and the cushion let out an enthusiastic Bronx cheer.

'You've said "great" about a thousand times,' Shelagh said.

'I think we have some bubbly stuff in the cabinet over here.' Rick bounced to his feet. 'Champagne and orange juice. Let's all have a drink to this outstanding news. And, Claire – think about some female clients you could invite to your tea. Make a list. We'll talk.'

Shelagh groaned as the conversation quickly dissolved into a chorus of congratulations: 'you lucky dog', 'you bastard', 'you old hound'. Backs were slapped, a cork popped and glasses clinked. Alexander announced that it was not too early for a real drink, in his opinion, and a bottle of single-malt Scotch appeared, along with an ice bucket and tongs. 'We better stand up and join in the toasting,' Claire said, to no one in particular.

'A lingerie tea?' Shelagh complained. 'You expect us to go out and buy split-crotch panties for Anna's dirty weekend with Alexander Spears?'

'It's not a dirty weekend – it's a dirty life. They're getting married, remember?'

'I'll believe that when I see it.'

'You won't see it,' Gillian said. 'They likely won't invite you.'

Shelagh snorted. 'And this silly tea idea of yours, Claire . . . You must see how terribly regressive it is? You're setting the women's movement back at least five decades.'

'More like three,' Gillian said. 'It's a sort of sixties thing to do. Like hero sandwiches, tail-gate picnics, Tupperware parties.'

'How satisfying it must be to be so exact,' Shelagh sighed.

'It's not, actually. It's a perfectionism I wish I could get rid of.' Gillian drew her shawl around her and the row of brass bells tinkled.

'So, what do you two radical feminists think would be appropriate for Anna?' Claire asked irritably. 'A law-book shower? Cross pens? Mont Blancs?'

'How about nothing?' said Gillian. 'No shower at all.'

'Nothing would get my vote,' Shelagh agreed. 'You're in a state of shock, Claire. You've had the hots for Alex for years and you can't have been ready for this. You should honestly evaluate your reasons for offering to do this idiotic tea. Think it through for a minute – in detail. Anna . . . dirty underwear . . . a bunch of old ladies. Our *clients*.'

'*Sexy* underwear,' Gillian said, 'not dirty. There's a difference.'

'It's too ghastly to contemplate,' Shelagh continued. 'But there's time to back out. You could change your mind right now. Just go up to Alex and tell him you don't know what you were thinking when you blurted out your underwear-tea idea. It's a hormonal thing, you could say. Because you're a working mother. You get on these hormonal roller-coasters – and can't seem to get off.'

'Just part of your general confusion,' Gillian added. 'Tell him you thought you were back in 1963 there for a moment, since you've got too much on your mind – your practice, the house, the kids, the dog. Tell him your Winston Churchill bath story.'

Gillian and Shelagh exchanged knowing looks, liking each other a lot just then.

'I have *never* had the hots for Alexander Spears,' Claire said. 'He's always been after me, if you really want the truth. And I've been married for eight years, a fact you two seem to be forgetting.'

'Oh, we're not forgetting that at all.' Shelagh and Gillian got up to join the men, nodding and smiling infuriatingly. Claire would not speak to either of them ever again, she resolved, not if they wore split-crotch panties on their heads and crawled over shredded business cards. Just look at them! So smug. They wouldn't even be speaking to each other if it weren't for her, coming between them, breaking the ice and forcing them to put aside their appalling pettiness.

'Claire?' Rick called to her, champagne bottle raised high, 'What can I pour you?'

From the other side of the boardroom table, Shelagh threw Claire a challenging look. 'Perhaps a little sour-grape wine might be appropriate,' she said.

'Or at least something *fumée*,' Gillian added.

'We shouldn't make fun.'

'No.'
'It's the shock.'
'Absolutely.'
Rick shrugged, as if to say 'Women!' and, grinning broadly, filled a coffee mug with champagne and orange juice.

For months and years later Claire would remember this meeting and marvel at how casually she had sat there, thinking about cookies and juice, only half listening to the debate about the Boston Tie Party, then falling suddenly down the rabbit hole, bumping along on a nauseating tumble of wounded sexual pride and revenge fantasies about her partners and so-called friends.

That's where it had all started, on that June afternoon, in that boardroom in the clouds. There was the newspaper with its awful story of the subway hand-walker; the joke about dumping ties into Boston Harbour; then Alexander's startling announcement followed by Claire's own incomprehensibly stupid response.

She should have had a premonition, right then, that it was going to be a bad summer for lawyers. And in retrospect, over time, it would seem to her as though she had.

2 ∫

'Jealous? *Moi*? What an absurd idea.' With a short laugh, Claire
continued the argument with Gillian and Shelagh, in her head,
as she drove home. 'It's pathetic, really. After so many women
in so many years . . . that Alexander seriously expects to find
lasting happiness with a woman – a girl, actually – who is, what?
Half his age? If that.' This, of course, would be Shelagh's cue
to be tiresome and point out that Ben, Claire's husband, was
considerably younger than Claire, which would be Claire's cue
to remind Shelagh that seven years was hardly a *generation*; and
then Gillian would be equally annoying and remind everyone of
the time the mailroom boy mistook Ben's photograph, in Claire's
office, as being one of Claire's son. Honestly! She sniffed, waiting
at a red light. In truth, she felt *sorry* for Alex and Anna. What
could they possibly have to say to each other, once the sex
was over? She pressed her foot down, hard, on the accelerator.
Actually, she thought, with a lift of her chin, Alex was probably
getting exactly what he deserved. Over the years, he hadn't
always been a very nice person. In fact, he'd been a shit.

Although Claire had expected to find herself in many awkward
situations with Alex after she started to work at the firm – given
his obvious personal interest in her, no such awkwardness ever
arose. In fact, Alex seemed, abruptly, to have wheeled around to
point his smoking barrel at other, more readily attainable targets:
secretaries, articling students – all of them single. Whether he
considered marriage vows too sacred to be tampered with, or
married women just a headache (since the firm was constantly
being replenished with younger, fresher game), Claire didn't
know. Only the occasional smouldering look from him betrayed

some residue of sexual interest in her over the years. Not that she'd sought out those looks. Or anything more. Not even during that horrible period when Ben had that 'thing' for a certain scrub nurse, a thing that never progressed beyond a friendly tussle on a stray med-cart . . . or so he said.

It was Gillian and Shelagh, actually, who'd had the unpleasant run-ins with Alexander, during their early years as associate lawyers. But surprisingly (since both women were 'available' at the time) the encounters had had nothing to do with sex.

'It's a little poem in a little magazine.' Alexander had barely glanced at the book Gillian thrust under his nose, her pale eyes gleaming moonstones of hurt and anger. 'Are you going to make a big deal out of it?' A little poem perhaps, but it was *hers*. Gillian had been in a state of disbelief since opening *Toadhole Quarterly*, behind her desk, a few minutes earlier. 'What's in there isn't yours anyway,' Alexander continued. 'It's totally different from what you wrote. Obviously, you haven't even read it.' Although he was sitting behind his desk at the time, Alexander still seemed to tower intimidatingly over Gillian – not an experience she was used to, being a very tall woman.

'You made minor changes,' she'd protested, 'a few words.'

'I changed a lot. Enough to make it mine.'

Gillian shook her head emphatically. 'You stole it! You infringed my copyright! How can you sit there and deny it?'

Safe behind the polished sweep of his desk – uncluttered but for a neat stack of multi-coloured files – Alexander scratched the back of his neck, then began cleaning his nails with the point of a letter opener he took from a desk drawer. 'You're up for partnership next year, aren't you?' he said mildly.

Gillian was silent for a moment. 'This is a threat. Isn't it? How can you be so low?'

'I don't threaten people,' Alex said. 'I'm simply pointing out that what's published in this little magazine – which nobody reads, by the way, except for people who are published in it and maybe their mothers – is not the poem you showed me. It's not yours, Gillian. That part you had in there about the threshing machine? I took it out.'

'That was two lines!'

'And the junk about the bits and pieces of your mind scattered all over the floor? Also gone. *Toadhole* never would have published your poem. Too many whacko concepts from flower-power days, if you want my opinion.'

'I don't.'

'You had a reasonably interesting idea, a theme, and that's the only thing I used. I don't need to tell you, since you work in a related field, that there's no copyright in an idea. Or ask your buddy Claire – she'll confirm that for you. It's not protectable. You'd better review that little ditty very carefully before you run around crying that I infringed your copyright. Besides, I'll deny I ever saw any of your writing.'

He paused, for the first time looking unsure of himself. Despite his many shortcomings, Gillian realized, lying was not quite second nature to him. 'No one will ever believe your complaint. And even if they did, there are some in this firm – I shouldn't have to remind you – who won't think poetry-writing will do a hell of a lot for our bottom line. Why aren't you spending your free time promoting the firm? Giving speeches, writing papers? What are you doing with free time to begin with? You're an *associate*. We partners are supposed to be living off your backs – and don't bother repeating that because I'll deny I ever said it. But those are the questions that will be asked. And quite reasonably, I think, speaking as a partner here.'

Satisfied with the condition of his fingernails, Alexander replaced the letter opener, took a fountain pen from his drawer and, affecting a lawyerly frown, began making notes on the inside cover of a file. For a few moments, Gillian's heavy breathing and the scratching of Alexander's pen were the only sounds in the dead air of his office. Gillian remained in her chair, radiating rage. 'Go do something billable,' Alex finally said, eyes still on his file, 'and I'll try and forget we had this absurd conversation.'

'I *trusted* you to read my work!' Gillian was trembling like a chihuahua. She was an ankle-biter – albeit a gigantic one – that's what Alexander had to be thinking. If he were thinking about her at all. His brain seemed to have switched over to other, weightier, matters. But then, abruptly, he stopped his note-making, looked up and pointed his pen at her. 'People who write anything are dying to have their stuff read. They're desperate. I've done you a favour by showing where that sort of pathetic neediness will get you, though it might be a while before you get around to thanking me.'

Suppressing an urge to lunge for his infuriating pen and assault him with it, Gillian clutched *Toadhole Quarterly* to her chest, stomped out of his office and down the carpeted hall to fling herself into a chair by Shelagh's desk.

'What a shit! The man's topsoil. Compost.' Shelagh handed her a tissue.

'I'll sue that bastard for copyright infringement! I bet he's never written an original line in his life. All those wonderful poems he's supposedly had published? I bet he stole them from women who trusted him.'

'You *trusted* him? Didn't anyone ever tell you never to trust a lawyer? Or a man?' Shelagh paused, allowing Gillian to consider these questions. 'And you can't sue him. What are your damages? How much would this magazine, or whatever it is, have paid you for your poem?'

'A free copy.'

'One copy?' Shelagh took the book from Gillian. 'Of *Toadhole Quarterly*? What is it? Some witchcraft thing?'

'Of course not. It's very well-respected in literary circles.'

But not in the real world, is it? Shelagh thought. She said: 'It's not as if Alex has stolen your big moment, though, your Andy Warhol five minutes of fame. Is it?'

'Fifteen minutes. Warhol said fifteen.'

'Whatever.' Shelagh studied Gillian, frowning. 'Let's put your hurt feelings aside – and I'm not down-playing them at all. You have a perfect right to want to twist Alex's balls off, but let's try and be practical. Who actually reads this sort of thing?' She scanned the cover, the table of contents, then opened *Toadhole Quarterly* to Alexander's poem. '"The Granary Floor"? That's the one?'

'He even stole my title!' Gillian was out of her chair. 'I'll get punitive damages. I'll file a complaint with the Law Society . . .'

'Sit down!' Shelagh closed her office door. Gillian sat. 'Do you have some kind of death wish for your career? Don't even fantasize about the Law Society, or the courts. Not if you ever want to work in this town again. Alex Spears knows everyone.

Think about it. Where would it get you? Say he settles with you for a thousand bucks maybe, just to shut you up. And suppose you get some erratum notice in *Toadstool Press*, acknowledging that you are the real author of this poem –'

'*Toad*hole. *Quarterly*.'

'What's a toadhole?'

'How should I know? Do I look like an amphibian?'

Shelagh seemed to appraise her for a moment. 'Okay,' she said finally, 'so then what? You feel vindicated for about a day and then you're free to be a starving poet for the rest of your life. What firm's going to hire you after such a scandal? You'll be known as the poetry-writing ding-bat associate who took a senior partner to court and blew the whistle with the Law Society for some petty squabble over a poem. You might get a job in a legal-aid clinic doing civil rights claims, or go on the talk-show circuit telling everyone how the big bad Bay Street lawyer cribbed "The Granary Floor". But how long is that going to hold the public's interest? Who's going to care? And what happens after that? Wake up and smell the *latte*. You've almost got your partnership here. Think how hard you've worked, how you've struggled to get here and stay here. What's one lousy little poem? It's not *The Odyssey* after all, is it?'

'If it was so lousy, why would he steal it?' Gillian clenched her fists and glared at Shelagh, her eyes glistening.

'Okay, okay. So it's a good poem, maybe a great one, practically *The Iliad*. You can write others. And if you can't, you weren't meant to be a poet. Am I right? Spears might actually have done you a favour, like he said. Look at it that way.'

Gillian stared out through Shelagh's window at the expanse of mottled sky and the office towers beyond, blinking rapidly, trying to decide if Shelagh's advice constituted a betrayal. 'I thought he was a kindred spirit. I was amazed by his – his depth. We went out, had some wine at a bistro, talked about writing for hours.'

'Did he get into your pants? Did he try?'

'It wasn't like that.' Gillian scowled, not wanting to admit that Alexander hadn't made a move on her, not even a half-hearted gesture for the sake of politeness. She was regretting having turned to Shelagh for support; would have much preferred Claire, but she was out having her dog dewormed or her kids deloused or something. 'I thought he and I could be great friends.'

'*Never* assume you can be friends with a man.' Shelagh held out a fresh tissue. 'You've got to forget about this . . . incident and get on with your life. Focus on revenge fantasies. That's what keeps me sane.'

Gillian blew her nose, her eyes pink. 'I do have a novel I've been working on – I should be concentrating on that, I suppose.'

'A novel! Now you're talking something we can work with, something you can sell! It'll probably be a blockbuster, make millions for you. What's it about?'

'A dentist.'

'Oh.'

'And his sexual misadventures. It's about his wife too – she's a lawyer. With an insurance company.'

'So. What else did you and Alex talk about that night at the bistro? Anything interesting?'

'What do you mean?'

'You know . . . how the firm's doing, what new business is coming in . . . what kind of a raise they're likely to give us poor overworked associates. Things like that.'

Gillian stood up abruptly. 'We talked about the most interesting thing I can possibly imagine. My writing!' Her shoulders were up around her ears and she had flushed to a deep purple. Her fists were still clenched.

At that moment, another of the associate lawyers – a woman who had since left the firm – rapped briefly on the door and stuck her head into Shelagh's office. 'You wouldn't have a Shower-in-a-Sack you could spare, would you? I've got a heavy date – right after work. No time to get home to freshen up.'

'You buy Shower-in-a-Sack?' Gillian glared at Shelagh, her face draining of colour. 'After what it cost my father? After it *killed* him?'

'Oops,' the associate said. 'Did I say something wrong?'

'I don't actually *buy* it,' Shelagh said. 'I was given a case of them last Christmas, by someone I barely know, and –' But Gillian was already on her way out of Shelagh's office.

'Look, I'm really sorry. Hey! Don't go away mad. Gillian, wait! Come back!'

Shelagh and the other associate stood in the office doorway, watching Gillian lope down the carpeted corridor, flinging her hair from side to side, even stumbling once. It was doubtful that she would ever recognize the favour Shelagh had just done her; would remember only that she had sided with Alexander – and that she'd done something even more unforgivable: confessed to having used Shower-in-a-Sack: that handy moist towelette impregnated with those marvellous chemicals that made a girl feel so . . . fresh. For a few days, Gillian would slam doors and drawers whenever Shelagh was around, but eventually she would settle down and take up origami or limerick-writing in her office, or get a scare over a missed patent-filing date – and that would distract her long enough to forget about hating Shelagh. These things were always just a matter of time.

'Why is she so mad about Shower-in-a-Sack?' the associate asked, interrupting Shelagh's thoughts.

'Didn't you know? Her father invented it, supposedly. But he screwed up somehow – didn't file the patent on time, whatever. Got bad legal advice. And then when the thing started doing millions in annual sales – I guess it pushed him over the edge.'

'Really?'

'Offed himself somehow.' Shelagh looked away.

'God! And I just blundered in and asked for one.'

'None of us knows how true any of it is, really, but we don't like to press for details.'

'I guess not.'

'No.'

'But how else is a businesswoman supposed to get through a day? Go from meeting to meeting, then out for dinner, without Shower-in-a-Sack?'

'I know, I know . . . Or a man, for that matter.'

'I don't know what we did without it. It's like faxes or instant cash machines – a brilliant invention.'

'Especially for us Bay Street hacks.'

'Everybody uses Shower-in-a-Sack.'

'We should write a jingle,' Shelagh sighed, her eyes on the corridor down which Gillian had disappeared. 'We at the firm try not to rub her nose in it. If you're going to use Shower-in-a-Sack – as we all do – keep them in your desk drawer. And don't ever mention . . . those four words. I'll get you a couple.' She sighed again as she turned back into her office. Poor old Gilly, she thought.

Shelagh had reason to recall her own advice about Alexander Spears a few months later, as, feeling much less in control, she herself confronted him.

'It's a little file for a little client,' he'd said. 'Are you going to make a big deal out of it?' He leaned back in one of Shelagh's client chairs and put a foot up on her desk.

'Actually, I *am* going to make a big deal out of it,' she said evenly, despite the pandemonium of profanities going off in her brain. 'I've been babysitting this client for two years. I've gone out to his meat-packing plant, put on a hairnet, a hard hat, and sloshed through trays of chemicals wearing hip waders to watch his hams being boned. I put together that last prospectus for him and wrote down two-thirds of my account to give him a break.'

'So? You should be glad to get rid of him. He's a leech.'

'He's planning a leveraged buy-out, moving into sausages big time. It's going to be lots more than lunch meat. We're talking capicollo, pepper butts, mortadella. This is not a *little* file. His company's about to take off.'

'You don't know that. Nobody's got a crystal ball.'

'I do know it, and so do you. Otherwise you wouldn't want the file.' Shelagh leaned back in her desk chair, arms crossed protectively over the beige legal folder. 'By the way, Alex – there's a sale sticker on the sole of your shoe.' She dropped her voice. 'I thought you should know.'

Slowly, Alexander took his foot down from Shelagh's desk. 'You listen to me. I brought this client into the firm and now I'm taking him back. I wasn't going to tell you this, but since you're so hormonally overcharged, I have no choice. He's asked that I personally supervise the new deal. He thinks you're inappropriately friendly. You've been making him uncomfortable.' Alexander's eyes flickered over Shelagh's décolletage. 'He's married.'

'What are you talking about?' She straightened up in her chair, adjusting her shoulder pads and lapels. 'We had lunch a couple of times. Business lunches. I have zero personal interest in him.'

'He says you made suggestive comments.'

'Like what?'

'I didn't ask. The guy was embarrassed enough. I'm only interested in damage control at this point. You're off the file. We don't need the Law Society on us for sexual harassment of clients. So you can either hand over that file now, or I'll have Rick Durham fire off an e-mail to you. Your choice.'

'Bastard!' Claire had sympathized, after motioning to the bartender for drink refills, a short time later.

'You believe him, don't you?'

'Of course not. At least, I know you didn't intend any sort of come-on to your client. It's just your way of being friendly.'

'So you *do* believe him!'

'That's not what I said. I only meant that, well, sometimes you might come across in a way that you're not even aware of. It's a question of perception. Some men are threatened by attractive and assertive women. And you are a very sexy woman . . . who practically exudes power. It's pheromones or something.'

Shelagh snorted, rattled the ice cubes in her glass and took a hearty swallow. 'There's been no client complaint. There's nothing going on here beyond Alex Spears taking over a file that he knows is going to put him way over the top with fees before year end.'

'He *is* a senior partner, though.' How contemptible I am, Claire thought. 'Not that that makes it right,' she added as she looked around, helplessly. Shelagh would never forgive her. 'I'm so glad I don't have to compete with him for corporate work,' she finished lamely. 'It must be unbearably stressful.'

'Thanks. For all your support.' Shelagh ordered a double single malt from the waiter.

'Come on,' Claire said. 'We've all known that Alex is a prick from day one. Look what he did to Gillian.'

'Well, he likes you.' Shelagh looked at Claire through bleary, accusing eyes. 'Anyone can see that.'

'I honestly don't know why. If that's true. We barely speak to each other.' Claire was trying to get a glimpse of her watch in the soupy light of the lounge.

'You have to go, don't you?'

'No, I can stay as long as you need to talk. I'll just have to call our nanny – make sure she's not running off somewhere tonight. Did you notice a telephone when we came in?'

'Forget it. You run along. Your kids will be waiting for you. I've got nothing else to say anyway. I'm going to sit here and get shit-faced. I don't need an audience.'

'If you're sure . . .'

'I'm sure. Scram.'

'I don't feel as though I've done you much good . . .'

Shelagh didn't say anything.

'But there is one thing I have to know before I go.'

'What?'

'Did Alex really have a sale sticker on the bottom of his shoe?'

'No.' Shelagh sniffed, threw back her head and downed the rest of her single malt.

'Great put-down, though.'

'I thought so.' They both laughed, then Claire squeezed Shelagh's hand, murmuring more apologies before hurrying out into the daylight, anxiously checking her watch again.

Though they'd shared that laugh on parting, Claire had known that Shelagh would interpret her lack of support as a betrayal. In fact, Shelagh didn't speak to her for several days, rushing past Claire's office without sticking her head in to say 'hi', pretending to wind her watch whenever she passed Claire in the hall, using the washroom for the handicapped to avoid coming face to face in the ladies' room.

But although Claire fully expected to be the next one to go head to head with Alexander Spears, it hadn't happened. So far.

A lingerie tea for Alexander's bride-to-be, Claire marvelled now, as she rounded the corner of her street and the Cunninghams' ridiculously large house loomed before her. What could possibly have been going through her mind? What sort of mid-life early-summer lunacy had possessed her?

But she was, just then, prevented from fully considering the prospect of an exchange of intimate laundry with a bunch of women she barely knew because Cannon, the German Shepherd, was barrelling across the front lawn, all flashing teeth and hackles and outraged canine sensibilities, alerting the neighbourhood that an intruder was in its midst. Stupid dog. Weren't they supposed to become attuned to their master's presence, recognize the car and come bounding out with tongue-lolling, carpet-wetting joy? Instead, every morning and evening, Claire feared for her life, wondering if Cannon would realize, in time, that she *lived* there in the house. And resist the urge to tear her apart.

3 ∫

Ross would have the children from Friday night until Sunday morning, leaving the unpalatable butt-end of the weekend – Sunday afternoon and evening – for Shelagh. On Saturday night, Marcia was throwing a fortieth birthday party for herself, complete with striped marquee, a dance band and fishing boats filled with oysters on the half-shell. Gone was the Marcia Owen who kicked in cupboard doors at the mention of her husband's name, and who called every night at 2 a.m. to scream abuse at him until 4. She was blossoming, Marcia was. In the six months since Ross had moved out, she'd dropped twenty pounds, obtained her driver's licence, begun her master's degree in community planning, and started an affair with her therapist. Ross Owen, it seemed, was the last person she wanted back in her life.

Shelagh woke early on Sunday, feeling an electrical charge of excitement, until she remembered what day it was and that there was nothing to be excited about. In fact, there was every indication the day would be a trying one. She had agreed, reluctantly, to have dinner with Ross and his parents in Wallaceburg – a small town about an hour's drive west of Toronto. She'd never met the senior Owens, and never had the slightest desire to. Ross's children, on the other hand, she'd desperately wanted to meet, back when things were going well between her and Ross. It hardly seemed to matter any more whether she met them or didn't. Now, six months after the day Ross had practically knocked Shelagh out of her chair with his desperate note, their relationship was wheezing its final gasp. Even sex between them had deteriorated into a somewhat silly sadomasochism. Shelagh was fed up with playing schoolmarm to an errant schoolboy Ross.

The starched apron was stiff and uncomfortable, for one thing, and those wire-rimmed spectacles gave her a headache. They could even, she sometimes thought, be the cause of the brain tumour she imagined she might have.

She'd worked out a number of creative excuses – some outlandish enough to be believable – to avoid going to Wallaceburg, but in the end decided that Ross's hurt feelings would take too much out of her, and that he'd only reschedule the dinner any way. She wasn't quite mentally braced for the big *fin de l'affaire de coeur* talk with him; and it wouldn't kill her, she reasoned, to have a good meal with a kindly old couple in the country. It might even be a pleasant summer outing. And why disappoint poor Mrs Owen, who hardly ever got to see her son and was probably excited about meeting Shelagh? On the other hand, she worried, was it fair to the dear old thing? What if Mrs Owen fell in love with her and embraced her wholeheartedly as her new daughter-in-law? The shock, when Shelagh finally ended the relationship with Ross, might well do her in. Why, the poor soul would still be trying to come to terms with what Ross had done . . . walking out on Marcia like that . . . and of course the children.

When he first showed her pictures of his kids, Shelagh had assumed he had a dozen. The plastic photo fold had unravelled down the length of his arm as if he were a street hawker displaying stolen watches. But he had only five, he confessed, looking sheepish. Only! What sort of lunatic in this day and age had five kids? Shelagh had marvelled. As it turned out, there might as well have been a dozen, for all the money and energy Ross had left over for her. Economizing was always on his mind: it was either a birthday gift for Shelagh or a retainer for Lou-Anne's teeth; dinner out with Shelagh or new winter boots for little Obie. Of course, Shelagh always smiled, she understood, the kids had to come first. And after all, she made a good living, with no one to support but herself. As for Ross's energy, there had seemed to be a surplus of it at the beginning, especially during that first night at The Breakers, outside the frozen village of Thamesford, where he'd banged away with more vigour than the metal sign that creaked and swung in the icy wind outside their rattling motel window.

And what had they become after such a promising night of sexual and barometric upheaval? A sort of situation comedy. Only it wasn't funny. Except maybe to Marcia.

In her ensuite bathroom, Shelagh shrugged into an oversized robe (some man's) and took a tiny amber bottle from the medicine cabinet. Dotting the clear odourless liquid at strategic 'fatigue points' on her face, using the eye dropper that came with the bottle, she was freshly annoyed with herself. The liquid cost about two dollars a drop, when you worked it out – a calculation she wished she hadn't bothered to make. She'd applied those drops with the same degree of precision she used to fuck up her life, for the recommended thirty days, anticipating the moment when her wrinkles and lines would 'magically disappear'. Now, at day forty-five, she peered closely at her reflection in the mirror. The only thing that seemed to have disappeared, so far, was her money, though using the colourless liquid had produced an interesting side effect: pimples. 'Isn't that fabulous?' the salesgirl had squealed when Shelagh went back to complain. 'Your skin is like a teenager's again!' Fabulous? Shelagh didn't want to be a teenager again; at least she didn't want the worst aspects of adolescence back. What other ghastly side effects would this mysterious chemical produce? Would she soon get the urge to stuff her bra with tissues? To make out in the back seat of a '69 Mustang?

She tugged gently at the skin around her eyes, wondering what effect a face lift would have, or even something less drastic: a bit of strategic lasering, for example. Cheek, breast or buttock implants were another idea, but she'd recently read a report that certain kinds of implants could make swooshing and gurgling noises at high altitudes. Such a tiresome inconvenience that would be when she had to fly off to some exotic locale with a handsome male companion: gurgling from both sets of cheeks *and* from beneath her blouse. Not that she had a handsome male companion. Or that she was going anywhere. Ross travelled a lot, but not with her. He had a number of out-of-town clients, mostly financial institutions in various cities throughout southern Ontario, who expected him on-site with legal advice on a regular basis. The only good thing about his frequent travelling was that Ross knew all the back roads and secluded motels throughout the province, which came in handy for sneaking around with Shelagh and avoiding Marcia and anyone from Bragg, Banks and Biltmore.

Taking a half-moon-shaped case from the medicine cabinet (she would die if anyone saw it there in her bathroom – of course they'd assume it contained an upper or lower plate), Shelagh lifted out two u-shaped trays into which she squirted a substance that looked and smelled like contraceptive jelly. Then she fitted the cold sticky devices over the slightly uneven rows of her teeth. The gel stung and burned and made her drool. Her lips distended by the plastic trays, like a prize fighter about to enter the ring, she grabbed a paper towel from the kitchen, then turned on the television and settled on to the chesterfield, dabbing the balled-up towel to her mouth, determined to leave on the tooth-whitening goo for the recommended twenty minutes.

She'd bought the product one morning at 3 a.m. (after being impressed by the demonstration on an infomercial), calling in her credit-card number to a friendly operator in Wichita or Hoboken or wherever those people were who stayed up all night taking orders for The Perfect Smile. Now, her head throbbing from the night before (too much red wine, consumed alone, in her condo), she found that managing the drool from The Perfect Smile was demanding almost more dexterity than she was capable of. Twenty minutes would be a struggle. As soon as the trays were out of her mouth, she meant to have a cigarette. She was glad she'd started smoking again. It gave her a method for killing herself. Though it would probably be too slow, ultimately.

Discouraged, she noted that it wasn't yet nine o'clock. She considered the alternatives she had to amuse herself for the six hours before Ross came to pick her up. She could do nothing. Or she could go into the office for a few hours, see if anyone was around, do nothing but look busy, or even actually do some work. Or she could do her laundry, vacuum her condo, scour all the appliances. It wasn't true that a girl's best friends were diamonds. Nor were they cigarettes, dope or booze. A single girl's best friends were Pine Sol, cleaning rags and coin laundries, for it was those things that would always be there for her in the end.

She spat some more drool into her paper towel, thinking again about Ross and how hard it was to imagine a less suitable man for her. But then, attracting unsuitable men was her speciality, from her first love – a bearded seminary student who used her to test his commitment to the priesthood – to the bisexual actor whose only memorable role was Lady Bracknell. (Shelagh could still recite the handbag speech, complete with affronted inflections, exactly as Christopher had done it.) So Ross, with a wife and five kids ranging in age from dirty diapers to sulking adolescence, had to be the culmination of her life's search. In the words of Lady Bracknell, Shelagh had 'formed an alliance with a parcel'. A whole mail bag of parcels, actually – Her Majesty's truck load, in fact. She sighed and spat again. A good man wasn't just hard to find – it was an oxymoron.

And if it was unsuitable men she was after, Bragg, Banks and Biltmore was certainly the place for her. She mentally flipped through the men of the firm, as though each was a playing card; reshuffling the dog-eared pack, mixing up the order, thinking that perhaps one might be mystically revealed to her as a good bet. But even after a fancy riffle shuffle, a couple of professional cuts, the answer always came up the same, like the ace of spades: the card of doom. Her nemesis. Ross Owen.

As for blind dates, Shelagh had had hundreds. And with each she'd put her eye to the peephole of her door to panic at the sight of the man who stood outside on the mat. Except one time. He was a doctor – expensive cashmere jacket, tall, impossibly good-looking. This can't be happening to me! she'd squealed inside her head, eagerly drawing back the dead bolt. And it hadn't. After a single glorious dinner (they'd had so much in common!), he'd never called her again. She called him, of course, several times, but each time he already had plans for the Saturday? Friday? Monday? she was calling about. And the worst of it was that he was a friend of Claire's husband: in fact, Ben and Claire had set Shelagh up with him. Claire very likely knew every humiliating detail of the affair-that-never-was, though she'd been good enough not to talk about it.

Shelagh was thirty-nine: a hair's breadth from forty, the point of no return. Madame Ovary, was how she thought of herself, those dusty eggs sitting on the shelf, cobweb-shrouded, rotting from within. It was a shock when her gynaecologist reminded her that she'd been born with all the eggs she would ever produce: they weren't made fresh each month, as if by chickens on a farm. They were just released, kicked off down the assembly line to disintegrate into dust.

She often wished she'd married someone, no matter how wrong for her, if only for a year, a month, a day. Divorced women had a much easier time hitching up with a new man. It was as if men perceived in them a woman who was sure to know a few tricks about stain removal, throwing dinner parties and keeping up a fellow's interest, sexually speaking. Men didn't view divorcees as failures; they looked upon them as experienced, even exciting. It was so sickeningly unfair.

Shelagh checked the time again, relieved that the drooling twenty minutes of The Perfect Smile were finally up. Back in the bathroom, she spat the gooey trays into the sink, then leered at her reflection, checking the whiteness of her teeth. They weren't any more yellow, at least. Now that she was smoking again, that could be viewed as a modest triumph. And a triumph, no matter how small, was something she desperately needed just then.

Ross's parents clearly didn't think much of Shelagh. In fact, they barely acknowledged her for the first hour of the visit, spent in the living room, during which Ross, Shelagh and Mrs Owen chain-smoked cigarettes and Mr Owen drank rye and ginger ale and sounded off about local politics.

The Owens' country place turned out to be an aluminium-sided bungalow on the fringe of Wallaceburg, far enough from the centre of the village to be inconvenient, but close enough to negate any of the charm usually associated with country life.

Audrey and Derek Owen were English, but not the quaint, dog- and horse-loving, or slightly loony sort Shelagh had hoped to find. There was something sour about them – as if Canada had proven to be thoroughly disappointing. Though after forty years here, Shelagh thought, they ought to be starting to get over it.

Derek's blood pressure had recently shot way up, Mrs Owen announced, implying that it was Ross's fault for abandoning his family and putting his father to so much worry. And for what? She had glanced disapprovingly at Shelagh. Some tart in a zippered trouser-suit, she was clearly thinking behind her small eyes.

'Do you like kidneys, Shelagh?' she asked a while later, after proclaiming that she could use another pair of hands in the kitchen. 'Kidneys on toast was always Ross's favourite. When he lived at home, of course. Knees, he called them. I want knees on toast, Mum. I don't expect Marcia ever bothered with 'em.'

'Actually,' Shelagh smiled thinly, 'I'm not fussy about kidneys. But I've always been a big fan of Spotted Dick. I was hoping you could show me how to do a nice one.'

'Spotted Dick?' Mrs Owen drew herself up and eyed Shelagh with suspicion. 'Too much bloody work, if you ask me.' After that, they abandoned further attempts at conversation, except for when Audrey asked Shelagh what in heaven's name she wanted with all the zippers on her clothing – did they all work? And Shelagh invited her to try one and find out for herself.

To pass the time, when there was nothing on the telly, the elder Owens did jigsaw puzzles. There was a half-finished puzzle on the dining-room table, and completed ones could be found everywhere throughout the house, shellacked and framed on the walls, pressed under glass table tops or embedded in ashtray bottoms. Find ten jigsaws hidden in this room, Shelagh had challenged herself, peering into the master bedroom. She'd counted seven by the time Ross called her to dinner.

Things threatened to liven up only once, when Mrs Owen took a few shots at Marcia. But the topic never gathered much momentum. Ross stood up for his wife, stating that Marcia was doing her best with the heavy load he'd left her to carry and that she wasn't to be picked on, especially when she wasn't there to defend herself. Mrs Owen wanted to know why she was having such bloody great weekend parties if she was suffering so much – a question that was never answered. She then had to content herself with criticizing Ross's children: how Jack was putting on too much weight; how Obie was too old to be in diapers; how Lou-Anne was far too interested in boys. 'You'll have trouble with that one,' she said, darkly, several times over the course of the evening.

No one wanted to go outside. It was a dank oppressive day, with a continual drizzle that became a drilling on the aluminium siding by the end of the meal. Dinner was eaten in the small sweltering kitchen so as not to disturb the jigsaw in the dining room – 5,000 pieces apparently. Mrs Owen said many times that Ross could use some fattening up. Much like his dad, Ross was. She clicked her tongue about her only son living in a bedsit. 'It's a bachelor apartment,' he kept protesting, in response to which, each time, she puffed herself up, reminding him that he was hardly a bachelor, what with five kids and the mortgage on that house that Marcia was using for her parties. Then she complained that Ross wasn't getting proper meals, throwing a sharp look in Shelagh's direction, obviously concluding that her son's money was being squandered on clothes and jewellery for his tarty zippered mistress.

'I knew you'd hate them,' Ross said smugly, as he and Shelagh headed back to the city just after eight. 'I shouldn't have made you go.'

'You didn't make me go. I agreed to go. And they were fine.' Shelagh hesitated. 'Though, I have to admit, I'm not really sure why you wanted me to meet them. Why it was so urgent. I mean, why now? We've been seeing each other for six months. And your parents are still trying to deal with the trauma of you and Marcia splitting up after all these years. So why hit them with me too? The other woman?'

'You're not just the *other woman*.' He looked over at her. 'I'm tired of sneaking around. It's time to air things out. I'm sick of running.'

Air things out? Shelagh thought. What was she? His idea of dirty laundry? 'We're hardly running,' she said. There was another pause. Shelagh licked her lips. 'You're not thinking of making some announcement about us at the firm, are you?'

'What if I am?'

'It would be a bad idea, Ross. And I hope my feelings count for something. Don't do it. Please.' She pressed her lips together, afraid to say anything further. The jeep rumbled along for a few minutes and she wondered, suddenly, what effect such vibrations might have on breast implants, if she someday got them. Could they suddenly fizz up and explode, as a can of pop did after a vigorous shake?

'You're feeling some doubts about us,' Ross said, with another sideways look. 'Aren't you?'

Some doubts? *Some doubts*? 'You might say that,' Shelagh agreed carefully.

'You're thinking that we've got nothing between us any more. Except sex.'

'Well, no. That wasn't what I was thinking – not exactly.'

'So what, then?'

'I was wondering – whether you and Marcia – whether there was any hope . . . You know what I mean. After so many years together, so many children. To throw it all away like this just seems so . . .'

'You want me to go back to her?'

Everything inside Shelagh was screaming YES, but she couldn't bring herself to say it. Though she could hardly deny it. So she didn't say anything, just twisted her mouth to one side and looked nonplussed, leaning her head against the vibrating passenger-side window of Ross's Pathfinder.

'I'll save you having to answer that, Shelagh, because I'm never going back to Marcia. I'd take the kids, though – in a second. I want you to meet them. In a couple of weeks, when things have settled down a bit more . . . I was thinking of something casual. Going to McDonald's, maybe meeting you there – it would seem like a coincidence. A natural thing to happen.'

'I don't eat at McDonald's.'

'But you get the idea. I wouldn't want the kids to feel like it was all planned. That would be too stressful. For everyone.' Another sideways glance. Shelagh wished he'd keep his eyes on the road. 'But maybe there's not much point now . . . Is that what you're telling me?'

Ross's eyebrows quivered, as they always did when he was being earnest. It was something Shelagh had found intriguing about him, initially – those shaggy expressive brows. Now she wanted to shave them, pluck them, stick them down to his forehead with duct tape. She studied his profile for a moment. He looked – she cringed as her mind flailed around to produce the worst adjective she could possibly come up with – pussy-whipped. Even the way he was dressed clearly indicated a man who had abandoned all interest in his appearance. Though it was July, he was wearing grey flannels, with a sports jacket handed down from his brother-in-law. Before Ross left Marcia, Shelagh had tried to dress him on the sly, sneaking him elegant gifts from time to time: silk ties, cotton shirts, sweaters (he gave her stuffed animals), hoping Marcia wouldn't notice and demand to see the bills. What the heck? Shelagh had told herself. I've got the money and no one else to spend it on. For a while it had been fun shopping for Ross. She'd loved the feeling that those who saw her – the salesgirls, other shoppers – would assume she was married, that she *belonged* to someone. But other lawyers in the firm soon started to notice, quizzing Ross (sometimes cruelly) about his sudden sense of style. It was only a matter of time before Marcia got around to looking at her husband and began to ask the same questions.

Now that Ross was free, Shelagh had often thought about continuing to shop for him, mostly to preserve that feeling of being part of something bigger than herself. But, after two pairs of dress socks and some jungle-patterned boxers, she'd abandoned the practice as being just too pathetic. And, frankly, Ross never seemed to notice what he had on, several times passing Shelagh's gifts along to his kids – the cashmere sweater, for example, that Lou-Anne put in the wash and shrank to a pulpy mass that now wouldn't even fit little Obie.

'I think you and I have always had an uphill battle,' Shelagh began slowly, gazing at the boring scenery whizzing past. 'I think we were doomed from the start. I should have left you alone, Ross. I made a mistake. You were a – a challenge to me, big game. You had a wife and family. I'm so ashamed of myself. I can't tell you –'

'Well, don't. My situation was intolerable. You're the best thing that could have happened to me.' He reached out and clamped a hand on Shelagh's knee. 'You did me a big favour by coming on to me the way you did. You were a catalyst. You helped me face up to things, put my life in order. Marcia and I had nothing between us. Only the kids. It's better this way. The kids are doing great, and Marcia and I have our own lives now; we're not tearing each other apart any more. So quit feeling guilty. And stop talking about it. I'm not going to let you destroy my memories of the last six months. So just shut up, okay?'

Since Shelagh had nothing else to say anyway, she closed her eyes and pretended to sleep. Ross took his hand off her knee and pressed down hard on the accelerator, driving uncharacteristically fast on the rain-greased highway, changing lanes with barely a glance in his sideview mirror. It occurred to Shelagh that he might be losing his mind after the strain of recent months; and that dinner with his parents, followed by their discussion in the jeep, might be enough to push him over the edge. Perhaps he meant to end it right then and there for both of them, crashing his Pathfinder through the expressway's guardrails.

'Ross?' she said, keeping her eyes closed. No answer. 'We can talk about this later. Tomorrow.' Still no answer. 'I mean, we haven't exactly had the greatest evening. Maybe we should sleep on everything, see how we feel tomorrow.' Silence. 'Ross?' She opened her eyes to look at him.

'Don't talk, okay? Don't say any more right now.'

'You don't even want to gossip? About the firm? Alexander and Anna?'

'No.'

'Claire's insane tea-party plan?'

'I'd rather put on some music.'

'The Mikado?'

'If that's all right with you.'

'Fine.'

'It reminds me of those first nights – with you.'

'Yes.' Shelagh frowned. 'It was the only CD you had. I never understood why you wouldn't buy a few more. With all the driving you do. Just for variety.'

'I didn't want any more. Plus, I didn't have any money for CDs.'

'No. Of course you didn't. Jeremy needed new skis.'

> On a tree by a river a little tomtit
> Sang 'Willow, titwillow, tit willow!'
> And I said to him, 'Dicky-bird, why do you sit
> Singing Willow, titwillow, tit willow!'

Shelagh just sighed heavily and leaned her head back on the headrest, letting the jeep's vibrations rattle further troubling thoughts from her brain for the remainder of the trip home.

B.M. Bradley looked like a bit like a billy goat, Gillian reflected, with his pointy white beard, hooded eyes and perpetually inquisitive expression. From where she was lying on his scratchy polyester sheets, with his waterbed undulating beneath her, she could see him watching Homes Plus – the local real estate channel. Houses, condos, duplexes and apartments popped on to the screen for fifteen seconds, just long enough to be described in wildly euphemistic terms by an ebullient voice-over. 'This fabulous property won't last long! Call the people who care! Call Rocco Monteleone *now* to view this exclusive *pied à terre*.'

'*Pied à terre*!' B.M. hooted. 'They don't even know what a *pied à terre* is.' He did a double-take at Gillian, as if startled to realize she was still there in his bed. 'Come and watch this with me.' He slapped the chesterfield cushion beside him, raising a small cloud of dust. 'You've got to see some of these places.' The picture on the screen changed again. 'God! How can people live like this? What appalling bad taste. Look, look – flock-covered headboards.' Another picture. 'And these slobs didn't even bother to pick up their *shorts* before their bedroom was photographed. They don't care if their underwear is syndicated across the country.'

'It's not syndicated,' Gillian said, 'it's local cable. Though I hate to nit-pick.' Hate to nit-pick? Nit-picking was her life. If it wasn't for nitpicking, she'd be out of a job. She yawned and rubbed her eyes. She'd hardly slept at all, in the heat, in B.M.'s uncomfortable bed. His apartment overlooked the street car turnaround, and the incessant screeching and moaning of ancient unoiled brakes had given her nightmares. She really hadn't intended to spend the weekend in B.M. Bradley's *pied à terre*. Fine example she was setting for Isadora. Her one comfort lay in knowing that her daughter wouldn't have worried. If she'd noticed Gillian's absence. If she'd come home herself.

'Seriously, you should spend some time watching this channel,' B.M. said. 'You're the one who's looking for a new house. We could get you an agent and start going around to see some. It'd be a howl.'

'I said I was thinking about moving. I haven't made a decision.'

'We could snoop through all sorts of dives – and big shacks too – peek into closets and drawers. It would help your writing.'

'Assuming my writing needs help, I don't think snooping through some strangers' drawers would do the trick.'

'Excuse me?' B.M.'s expression was one of hurt surprise. 'Where else do you think writers get material for their novels? Make it up? No. From life. They get it from real life. Tacky and horrible and miserable and so very *there*, in our faces, if we'd only just *look*. We need to see angel stone, faux terrazzo floors, little black jockey lawn ornaments. As writers we get too insulated – detached from reality.'

'I am quite sufficiently attached, thank you.'

'You are less so than anyone I know.' B.M. turned his gaze back to the TV screen. 'If you think about it, you'll understand what I'm saying. Get yourself a real estate agent. It would be a blast.'

'I'd rather get a literary agent.'

B.M. paused. 'I'm working on that. I told you.'

'Sure.' Gillian could see her manuscript – *At Whit's End* – in the same plastic shopping bag it had been when she brought it to B.M. a month earlier. And it was in the same place she'd put it: on the floor, leaning against a chrome leg of a kitchen chair, beside the table that also served as B.M.'s writing desk. He'd promised to 'put a bug' in the ear of his editor, set something up for Gillian, call a couple of hot young agents. But he had to read her book first. B.M. Bradley was a *name* in the literary community; he couldn't just go off half-cocked, recommending *any* old first novel could he? Even for someone with whom he had become *intime*. Of course, Gillian had agreed; of course she'd assumed he would read her book before he could recommend it to anyone.

She was a prostitute for her art, she thought now, watching a fly settle on the shopping bag, crawl up its handle, and disappear inside. Though, to be fair, she hadn't read any of B.M.'s books either, not all the way through. The last one she'd tried had begun with a septuagenarian procrastinating about masturbating. And his poetry was equally inaccessible, at least to her.

'Hey, Gilly,' B.M. said, 'you haven't told me about any fun patents lately.'

Gillian sighed and pulled the sheet over her head. 'I did a hose clamp the other day.'

'Bo-ring.'

'A blasting wheel and blades.'

'Nix.'

'Then there was the heavy-water sludge removal system.'

'Ix-nay. I'm talking great inventions. The really wacky stuff. Like . . . what's my favourite one?'

'A harness for facilitating conjugal relations between a very short man and a very tall woman.' God! She was tired of talking about that.

'So why don't inventors come up with inspired stuff like that any more?'

'The cost of a search and prototype is a lot more than most inventors have. There are no patrons any more.' She pulled the sheet away, bundling it into a scratchy pile at the foot of B.M.'s bed. 'My clients invent practical things that stink and clog and need oil. I wish you'd accept that. You're always trying to romanticize what I do for a living . . .'

'You romanticize what your father did.'

'My father was a brilliant inventor who was *cheated* out of his greatest invention. He got bad legal advice. It destroyed his life. There was nothing romantic about it. Even his trade-mark got ripped off.'

'Shower-in-a-Sack?'

'How dare you goad me with . . . those words?' Gillian struggled to get out of B.M.'s waterbed and grabbed her tie-dyed, permanently wrinkled Carpathian gypsy skirt, the peasant blouse and the shawl with the tiny brass bells.

'Gilly, don't get so mad. I would never use that – product.'

'No?' The brass bells jingled furiously as Gillian dressed.

'No. I'm a stinky guy and I like it that way.'

'Well, ten million others don't. Annually. So why not you? Give another five bucks to the giant conglomerate that ripped off my father. What does it matter? Dad's dead. He doesn't care any more.'

'I heard someone's come up with a competing product. Bath-in-a-Bag.'

'So?'

'So, I thought it might cheer you up to know that.'

'It doesn't. And speaking of inventions, I don't want to see me or my dad or my clients popping up in any of your books, okay?'

'But you can put me in yours – I've always said so.'

'I don't need to put you in mine. I happen to have an imagination.' The truth was, Gillian considered B.M. to have serious shortcomings as character material. The most interesting thing about him was actually his son. B.M. had been married. and divorced twice, the son being the child of his first marriage. The son's name was Rod. He was a huge hulking brute who was about to leave Canada to play hockey in Scotland. Rod Bradley was an aggressive left winger, a goon. He scared the shit out of his father who viewed him as an alien being, a genetic throw-back to the Neanderthal side of his first wife's family.

'I have to go,' Gillian said. 'I want to see my daughter before the weekend is over.' She yanked her Himalayan mountain tote out from under B.M.'s large snoring ginger tom, on a filthy area rug beside the bed.

'Ah, but does the enigmatic Isadora desire to see thee?' When Gillian didn't answer, B.M. rolled off the end of the couch and bounced to his feet. 'You're pissed off because I haven't read your novel. Admit it. All writers are super-sensitive. Come on.' He unwound the shawl from around her shoulders. 'Let's go back to bed and talk about *feelings*.'

'No.'

'Well, sit down at least. Please.'

Gillian perched petulantly on the waterbed's frame as B.M. dragged a kitchen chair over to sit facing her. *At Whit's End*, suddenly deprived of all support, thunked over on to the floor.

'I *will* read your book, Gillian. It's at the very top of my very long to-do list. I've finally got some free time. My new novel's got a sagging middle, apparently. I don't even know why I wrote the damned thing. I got drunk with my publisher and the bugger talked me into doing it. So that's your first lesson – don't go boozing with your publisher.'

Gillian nodded, slightly mollified that B.M. seemed to assume she'd some day have her own publisher and be able to say 'my publisher thinks' or 'my publisher wants'.

'I've been told not to touch my book until I sit down with my editor. So I've got time. I'm wildly excited about reading your book. You know how much fun it is to anticipate a great read?'

Gillian did know.

'It's the same feeling I get when I realize you're going to spend the night with me.'

Could have fooled me. Gillian avoided his eyes.

'Only I wish you hadn't made your protagonist a dentist,' B.M. said, pulling on his beard. 'Makes me think of pain. I don't like pain.'

'Really,' Gillian said thoughtfully. 'Maybe that root canal scene is a bit over-the-top. Too technical . . . I suppose I didn't need to describe all those instruments in so much detail . . .'

'Makes me think of Nazis.' B.M. leaned out of his chair and, pressing one hairy cheek to Gillian's, tried to grasp her ear between his teeth. 'But then you'd have a best-seller on your hands. And we wouldn't want that. Talk shows, book signings . . .'

'Maybe I could re-tool my hero,' she continued, pushing B.M. back into his chair, 'turn him into a florist or something. I could just use the Search and Replace keys on my computer –'

'No – still too painful. All that sawing and snipping and twisting of florists' wire and tape, those tiny green screams.' B.M.'s golden eyes looked longingly into hers as he touched her lips with a nicotine-stained finger. 'Gilly?'

'What.'

'I really want to fuck you.'

Once again, Gillian looked away.

'Well, I'd like to take another shot at it, at least.'

*   *   *

Gillian had met B.M. Bradley at a fundraiser for redundant journalists in a decrepit pool hall called Ball's Hall of Spherical Arts. For ten dollars, literary groupies got to pit their snooker skills against the writer of their choice, and purchase their books at a discount. Gillian could buy books well enough – she bought one by each of the ten authors at the fundraiser. As for the game, she'd once filed a patent for a pool-cue chalk holder but, while that led to an in-depth investigation into the tips of pool cues, the chalky compound that went on to them and the various holders available on the market, it did nothing to improve her skills.

She recalled that evening as being a headachey one: full of cigarette and marijuana smoke, the clack and spin of shiny balls and endless blather, while she stood awkwardly balancing an armload of hardcover books and trying to sip some unpleasantly grapey white wine from a plastic cup.

'You're very pretty,' someone said and, turning around, Gillian recognized the writer B.M. Bradley. Not that she'd ever read any of his poetry or novels – he just seemed to be everywhere those days: organizing events for literary causes, writing columns and reviews in the local papers or promoting his own books. She'd looked at him guardedly. At five foot nine with thinning red hair, eyes the colour of polar ice and a slight overbite, Gillian might conceivably be called interesting, or unusual, or even striking. But pretty?

'Might I sign this for you?' B.M. had slid his novel out from the pile in Gillian's arms, obliging her to stack the rest on the rail of a snooker table and dig through her shoulder bag in search of a pen. 'Why can't I possess a writing instrument such as this?' he'd asked mournfully, rolling the slim silver pen between his plump fingers.

'Because you don't earn six figures.' This was the remark that, in retrospect, Gillian imagined did the most to inflame B.M.'s interest in her. In fact, she had a theory, now, that B.M. stood for 'Buy Me'.

'To whom shall I dedicate this?' He'd turned the book over and regarded the cover, his smooth pink lips puckering with consternation. 'It's not one of my favourites. I made the mistake of getting drunk one night with my publisher.'

Gillian recognized her cue to reassure him of his talent by

commenting on his earlier novels and noting her particular favourite, but she was trying to imagine a publisher talking *her* into doing anything – except withholding further unsolicited manuscripts. She'd replied only: ' "To Gillian". With a G.'

'Gorgeous!'

What a phoney, she'd thought. Still, he had been published several times. It couldn't hurt to get to know him. And so B.M. Bradley had become a sort of habit, filling (however inadequately at times) Gillian's desperate need to talk about writing as well as her need for occasional (also inadequate) sex.

In the small kitchen of number seven Sidney Street, Gillian's daughter Isadora was drinking herbal tea, her face obscured by a trashy romance novel. *Bring On The Night* it was called.

Funny, Gillian thought, how often the word 'night' appeared in the titles of the books Isadora bought by the boxful at a used book store, then sold back after she had read them. *Blame it on the Night, Queen of the Night*. Those she couldn't re-sell, she simply threw out. As well as romance novels, she read pulpy trash about modern-day vampires and werewolves. Those too had 'night' frequently in the title. *Children of the Night* had been lying on the floor in the front hall when Gillian came in, its cover warped, its spine broken. Despite her resolve not to pick up after her daughter, Gillian stooped to rescue the book. She'd always had a reverence for books – literature actually – and though she disapproved of her daughter reading *Children of the Night*, it was still a book, and reading it had to be better than surfing the Net.

She glanced at the cover of the bodice-ripper her daughter was now reading. Bodices were certainly getting skimpier. It was more like bustier-ripper, or merry widow-ripper. None of those frothy, lace-encrusted things were like the undergarments Gillian possessed; they were found in the drawers of women with normal sex lives.

'I'm surprised you're up so early,' she said, pouring filtered water from a large blue-tinted dispenser into the kettle.

'I never went to bed.'

'What did you do all night?'

'Read.'

'I can remember when I was your age.' Gillian smiled. 'I used to stay up all night reading. Or writing in my diary.'

Isadora did not comment on this. 'Pancake from hell,' was all she said, without looking up from her book.

'You made pancakes?' Fearfully, Gillian looked at the stove, expecting a blackened frying pan, blobs of batter on the counter, grease splatters on the wall.

'I meant your make-up.'

'No one wears pancake any more.'

'Exactly.'

Gillian frowned at her reflection in the side of the toaster. Perhaps she had laid her foundation on a bit thick – the fluorescent bulb in B.M.'s bathroom had been going, flickering in a maddening way – while she was doing her make-up. Foundation. What a word. Laid on with a trowel in a vain attempt to prop up a landslide.

'And you might want to, like, rethink the hair?'

'I spent twenty minutes on this do.' Twenty minutes trying to rearrange and stick it into place over the thinning spot dead centre above her nose; ten hairs doing the work of thousands. How Gillian wished for the misery of a bad hair day, she who had a bad hair life. Isadora, on the other hand, had inherited her father's hair: masses of heavy, coarse, red-gold waves, approximately the colour and texture of a Golden Retriever's. 'So what would you do if you had my hair?' Gillian asked, conversationally, 'Since you're such an expert?'

Isadora's eyes, the pallid colour of peeled grapes, blinked at her above the contorted lovers on her book cover. 'You mean, before or after I killed myself?'

The boiling water spattered as Gillian filled her mug. Spooning instant coffee into it, she wondered when it was that her daughter had first begun to despise her; when her make-up and hairstyle had ceased to be a source of delight and been transformed into objects of Isadora's contempt. At least she hadn't made any acid remarks about her clothes today, Gillian thought. Her clothing was getting funkier, though she disliked that word, as it suggested, to her, personal hygiene problems. Essentially, she was dressing younger: beads, scarves, cheap costume jewellery, short suede granny boots. It occurred to her occasionally that she might not look artsy and interesting at all, but only faintly ridiculous: a forty-two-year-old patent lawyer done up like an adolescent, or a bag lady. Women writers dressed that way, and artists, judging from the few Gillian had actually met. Army boots and short filmy chiffon miniskirts, misshapen hats, bad posture and cigarettes were *de rigueur*. (The poor posture was about the only thing Gillian had a leg up on.) In weak moments, she studied book-jacket photos of women writers, trying to imitate their expressions: slightly sneering, pouty, some of them verging on hostile. The best ones looked sly: as though they knew something their readers didn't. Like how to get published.

So far, no one at Bragg, Banks and Biltmore had commented that Gillian's clothing was becoming too peculiar for Bay Street, though perhaps they meant to. She could imagine Claire and Shelagh whispering in the ladies' room. '*Somebody* has to tell her. We're supposed to be her friends!'

Her silver bangles jangled as she stirred some gone-off milk into her coffee. Dressing was a way of expressing herself, one Gillian needed as she patiently went about her business of searching and drafting patents, with their rigid rules on timing and formalities, their secret arcane vocabulary: words like chamfer, detent, gudgeon and spline. Luckily, she got to meet, and talk to, a number of totally wacky inventors as part of her job: if she'd had nothing to do but draft patents all day she would have put a gun to her head years ago. She had a lot of empathy for those creative types who somehow found their way into her 56th floor office to seek her advice. Many of them reminded her – often painfully – of her father. And, just like many of them, she too had toiled away in obscurity to create a product – *At Whit's End* – that nobody seemed to want.

Gillian always believed she was destined to live two parallel lives: one that got down to business, got a job, gave birth to and raised a child, and looked after the prosaic details of living; the other headed for greatness. Though, at forty-two, she was beginning to wonder how long greatness was going to take to thrust itself upon her, or, even worse, what she would do if it didn't. At what point, she often worried, did one give up and concede that it was never going to?

'So I guess you were at B.M.'s for the last two nights?' Isadora said, still apparently engrossed in her novel.

'Yes – I left a message for you on the machine.'

'So what's the guy's real name, anyway?'

'I've never asked him.' Gillian looked thoughtful, not sure she should put forward her 'Buy Me' theory. The weekend with him had cost her a bottle of expensive aftershave. ('I've never,' B.M. said, his billy goat eyes pleading, 'had to buy my own cologne.') 'Probably, he has some ghastly given names,' Gillian said. 'Barnaby Methuselah, Beauregard Melville. That's what writers often do – use their initials. P.G. Wodehouse was actually Pelham Granville Wodehouse.'

'Whose house?'

'Wodehouse. He wrote the Wooster and Jeeves books. You and I watched that series on PBS. Last winter.'

Isadora just shook her head and sank back into *Bring On The Night*.

'Are you angry about something today?' Gillian asked.

'No. Why do I always have to be angry about something?'

'That's what I'd like to know.'

'Mother – can't you just give it a rest? I want to finish my book.'

'Why don't you come with me and visit B.M. some time? I think you'd enjoy meeting him, since you're so interested in books. He's been published a lot.'

'Only in Canada,' Isadora sniffed. 'When I get published it's going to be in the States.'

'Don't you think you'd better write something first?' Gillian stole a glance at her daughter, wondering if Isadora was on drugs (why was she always sniffing like that?), debating whether to probe deeper to find out what was going on. Isadora was too old (or too young) for raging hormones, so that couldn't be it.

Gillian tried not to view her daughter as a disappointment; Isadora had simply turned out a little differently from what Gillian might have expected. But life was like that. 'Well,' she said, knowing she was on a downward spiral but somehow unable to stop, 'why not make good use of a whole Sunday of free time? Start writing that bestseller of yours, clean up your room. Or get some fresh air, maybe go to the library and get something decent to read.'

Isadora's answer was to sigh wearily.

'You'll never guess what's up at the firm,' Gillian said.

No response.

'Claire Cunningham is having a tea – a lingerie tea. You know,' she continued, hoping to pique her daughter's curiosity, 'it's where a whole bunch of women get together and give dirty underwear to the bride-to-be.'

'Who wants dirty underwear?'

'Sexy,' Gillian laughed. 'I meant sexy.'

'Sounds disgusting. I hope no one ever does that to me.'

'But it's such a bizarre idea. I mean, nobody has tea parties any more. Don't you think it's sort of outrageous?'

'No.'

'And the woman who's getting married is our articling student. Remember her from the picnic? Anna? She's quite gorgeous. But a bit snooty.'

'No.'

'And here's the scandal – she's marrying Alexander Spears.'

Isadora frowned. 'You mean that jerk-off who tries to bonk every skirt that comes into the office?'

Except this skirt, Gillian reflected. But she said: 'That's him.' She was pleased that Isadora had apparently listened to something Gillian had told her about Bragg, Banks and Biltmore. Even if it was only about Alex Spears and his carryings on.

'I think assholes like him should be castrated and pissed upon,' Isadora pronounced. Hoisting herself up from the kitchen table, she clomped in her wooden clogs past her mother to grab her jacket from a hook on the wall. 'I'm going out.'

'Will you be home for supper?'

'Don't know.'

'Need some cash?'

'Sure. Goes without saying.' Isadora looked down at the floor as Gillian took her wallet from her tote bag and pushed some bills into her daughter's hand.

'Well, see you when you get back,' Gillian said. 'Hey, I love you!' she added as the door slammed shut after Isadora. Don't let your last words be bad ones: that was Gillian's motto. What had her last words been to Jerry? 'You don't look so sick to me.' She'd been annoyed with him for keeping her awake with his sniffling and hacking and shaking of the thermometer and pacing the length of the bedroom. They'd just got Isadora to sleep; Gillian had been completely without sympathy for her husband and what she thought was just a bad cold and typical male self-pity and helplessness.

Isadora probably had every right to be angry, Gillian thought now, growing up without a father, living at number seven Sidney Street her whole life. Anyone could tell from the address that it was a down-at-heels one. It was hard to imagine a row of smart town houses with shiny brass knockers and letter boxes on a street called Sidney Street. The town planners must have run out of names by the time they noticed the short cul-de-sac – not much more than a lane – that butted up against the underbelly of the Gardener Expressway. They would have looked at each other, stumped, then at the clerk who was filling his paper cup at the water cooler. Light bulbs would have gone off in municipal planning heads. Of course! They would call it *Sidney* Street!

All day and all night the bright yellow sign of the Speedy Auto Glass shop, across the street, beamed in through the front windows of number seven. Gillian knew that the counter man in there, and all her neighbours, were puzzled about why a lawyer would choose to live in their midst. Gone off in the head, they probably concluded. Sometimes, she herself wondered why she stayed in Sidney Street, though, practically speaking, it cost her nothing to live there (the small mortgage had been paid off years ago) and it was a tribute to Jerry that she'd stayed in the house he'd worked so hard to renovate. She felt his presence everywhere – from the back door, not hung quite straight, that swelled shut in the summer humidity, to the smear of blood near the skylight where he'd had an accident with a dry-wall knife.

Gillian's mother had cried when they first showed her their new home. 'Where are you going to do your shopping?' she'd wailed, her hot pink mules slap-slapping on the scarred wooden floor as she went anxiously from grimy window to grimy window. 'There isn't even a corner store! Nothing but an auto wrecker!'

'Auto *Glass*,' Jerry corrected her, arms folded, all affronted architectonic sensibilities. 'Shopping!' he'd later complained to Gillian. 'Doesn't your mother have anything else in her head? Doesn't she have any *vision*?' Though he'd been an architect, he hadn't been a very successful one. Not that his buildings ever fell down or anything, but he was strictly a concept man, not so great with technicalities. And after he died so suddenly from that mysterious virus – sliding from 'flu-like symptoms, to a respirator, to a tag on his big toe and being wheeled down to the morgue in less than twenty-four hours – well, Gillian hadn't been able to part with the house. Isadora had been only three at the time.

Maybe it was time to let it go, Gillian reflected, standing in the front window, watching her daughter leaning on a lamp post, waiting for a street car to come along. Moving into a fresh new condo might make Isadora feel better about herself. Perhaps the two of them could decorate it, and the project would bring them closer together. Living somewhere that Isadora wasn't ashamed of could motivate her to get a job or go back to school. Lose some weight at least. It was either that or Gillian would be obliged to kick her out, for Isadora's own good. She was, after all, twenty-two.

The street car moaned to a stop and Isadora slouched on board, without a backward glance at sagging little Sidney Street or her mother. Could a condo really be the answer? Gillian wondered. There was something so Shelagh-esque about even the word 'condo'. Wasn't it enough that Gillian worked all day on Bay Street, high up in the clouds, so far removed from the throbbing heart of humanity?

In her wallet, that she still held in her hand, was the scrap of paper she'd found in a fortune cookie in 1983. 'The world is always ready to receive great talent with open arms,' it said. Thinking about it now, it struck her, not for the first time, that perhaps it was not *her* talent to which the cookie, in its inscrutable oriental wisdom, had been referring.

5

By Monday morning, the e-mail of Bragg, Banks and Biltmore was littered with updates on the Boston Tie Party: a list of the lawyers and clients going on Bert King's plane, alternate airlines and flight times, details of the hotel, the ball game. Claire scanned all of these, then quickly clicked on the TRASH icon on her keyboard.

There was only one e-mail message that gave Claire pause, that she couldn't dump immediately, much as she would have liked to. It was from Rick Durham, addressed to her, requesting the names of the clients Claire was planning to invite to the lingerie tea. For a few moments, she indulged herself with some unplesant free associations on this subject; then she filed it away in that crowded corner of her mind reserved for 'things to be dreaded and avoided for as long as possible'. It was ten past nine, time to get out some files and start the process of dividing her day into hours, the hours into six-minute segments, and assigning seven-digit file numbers to each.

More and more frequently, the fact that people asked and paid for her advice filled her with anxiety. *'How the hell should I know what you should do?'* she often felt like demanding. But that would be 'looking down'. Practising law was like tightrope-walking. Once you looked down, you might as well jump. Otherwise, you could probably teeter on forever. Nibbling worriedly on a cranberry muffin, Claire regarded her office, taking some comfort from its soothing decor.

The walls were painted a soft grey, and there was a bukhara rug, patterned in green and plum shades, in front of her desk. A striking, black and white studio portrait of Molly and Harry was prominently displayed on one wall; Molly's fingerpainting, professionally matted and framed, on another. On Claire's bookcase clustered a family of papier mâché spiders Harry had made in pre-school: painted black, covered in silver glitter, with fuzzy black pipe cleaner legs of various lengths.

From the adjoining office, Claire could hear Gillian thumping around, struggling to get out of her Doc Martens and stuff her rather large feet into a pair of pumps: metamorphozing from creative free spirit to Bay Street hack. But Gillian liked her office, she often said, despite its being on lawyers' row. And a location on the gloomy north wall of the firm was actually an advantage. After all, who could get seriously creative in a sunny lake exposure with cheeky catamarans bobbing around on winking waves? Her office was so crammed with board games, medical apparatus and machinery parts that no one seemed to notice her decor: the tatty South American prayer rug on one wall, the antique curio shelf on another. She was having a local artist refinish her desk and book shelves – giving the woman free artistic rein – with results that even Gillian admitted she found perplexing. 'Has the term Spanish bordello ever occurred to you?' Shelagh remarked, arching a brow at the red and black scrollwork that festooned the sides of the furniture. The Executive Committee (Rick, Alex and Pete) was sure to tell Gillian to change it, if any of its members ever got around to looking at it.

Of the three women partners in the firm, it was only Shelagh who complained about her office and the pink ghetto; about how they had been shafted with the lousy real estate, the Baltic Avenue of the firm. There was no sound coming from Shelagh's office now. She'd been in before Claire and gone out again. Claire could understand why she resented being banished (as Shelagh perceived it) to the dead north end of the firm. She was a corporate lawyer, she wanted to be where the action was, near Alex and Rick, the rainmakers: so close she would need foul-weather gear and a sou'wester. And more to the point, as Claire and Gillian had long ago concluded, she wanted to be where the other men were as well.

'Hi there.'

Claire was startled to see Anna standing in the doorway to her office, carrying an armload of legal files. *'Hi there?'* she thought. As if her name were not important enough to recall. Could this casual, offhand greeting have anything to do with Anna's changed status at the firm? 'Well, don't just stand there, come in, come in,' Claire urged. 'Sit down. We heard the exciting news at Friday's meeting.'

'I shouldn't really stay – I'm up to my whazoo in work.' Anna draped her long frame across one of Claire's client chairs and gazed at her with grey eyes that revealed little. Sarcasm perhaps? Antagonism? Casually, she swung one of her legs. A fine kidskin pump dropped to the floor. 'Wonder when the other one will drop,' she said with a slight smile.

Her own smile fixed, Claire noted the expensive detailing of Anna's clothes. Striped in cream and white, the simple summer shift clung to a figure as lean as a runway model's. Had Alexander bought her the dress? Claire wondered. Anna's clothes were the subject of some comment around the firm, and a source of irritation to Shelagh, since the day Anna showed up in a suit identical to hers. 'How does a *student* afford a twenty-five-hundred-dollar Giancarlo Ferre?' she'd ranted to Claire in the ladies' room.

'I have to talk to you,' Anna said. 'Alex told me about the tea party you're planning to throw for me.'

It was her lips, Claire realized, that were Anna's most striking feature. They were juicy and full, and when her mouth relaxed they parted, revealing a hint of buck teeth that suggested innocence and vulnerability. But at the same time, sex. 'I wanted to do something for you,' Claire said, feeling that some explanation for her irrational invitation was expected. On the other hand, she suddenly realized, if she were careful, she just might be able to use this private chat with Anna as a way to get out of giving the wretched tea altogether. She cleared her throat. 'But, I can see that for a young woman like you, the idea's a little – *outré*. A bunch of frowzy older women in hats that reek of moth balls, sipping tea and snapping their upper plates at soggy watercress sandwiches.' She laughed shortly, imagining Shelagh's reaction to being included in that image. 'I bet you and I can come up with something a lot more exciting. Like a Jack and Jill shower. What's the point in excluding the men? Everyone can bring a good Cabernet Sauvignon, get you and Alex started on a decent wine cellar.'

'But I like the underwear idea. I didn't say I don't want lingerie. I do.' Anna's luscious lips were in a full pout now, her grey eyes set.

'Oh. Well. If you *like* the idea . . . I just thought –'

'I say go for it. Definitely. Forget the men – they've got their own thing happening. I'm grateful you want to do something for me. And lingerie is cool. Alex is thrilled – as you can imagine.' She rolled her eyes. 'Men being the simple brain-stem creatures that they are.'

'Yes, well . . .' Claire gave what she thought might pass for a wry smile as she wondered what approach to try next. 'Alex and I go back a long way, you know. He was the one who hired me here at the firm. Years ago.' She hesitated. 'Well – not *that* many.'

'Really?'

'Yes, yes, the good old days,' Claire chuckled.

'I've got to get to the library,' Anna said. 'Could we just talk a bit more about the tea party?'

Why did she have to keep calling it a 'tea party'? As if it were some sand-box social for four year olds. 'Sure,' Claire said, 'what do you want to know?'

'It's a shower, right? The shower is the main event?'

'Yes.'

'But it's not one of those deals where people have to try on stuff and then buy it, is it? Because I'd like my mother to come and she doesn't have a lot of money.'

'Anna, we want to *give* you lingerie. It's a shower, not a sale. We're all so pleased about you and Alex . . . It's time he settled down.' Claire twitched her shirt cuffs, feeling prim and tight-assed. 'But we have another problem – with the tea. You see – Rick Durham thinks I should invite some clients. Women clients.' She made a face.

'Cool.'

'Well, it's not cool, actually. It's a terrible idea.' Claire hesitated. 'But don't bother passing that intelligence along to Rick.'

'Of course not.'

'Or Alex.'

'If you don't want me to.'

'It's just that ' Claire hesitated again '– well, it's hard to imagine a number of our women clients all in the same room. Together. Getting along with each other.' To say nothing of the women lawyers, she added mentally. She made a pyramid with her fingers on her desk top, then studied the effect, avoiding Anna's eyes.

'Why is that?'

'Well, it's like this – I'll give you a simple analogy. You wouldn't invite Coke and Pepsi to the same party where soft drinks were being served, would you?'

'Right. Who'd want to go to a party without booze?'

'Never mind. I'll sort it all out. Somehow. You let me worry about all of that – nonsense – and concentrate on the nonsense that's more fun. Like letting me know what sort of outrageous skimpy garments you'd like – and your size.' Her eyes met Anna's and Claire had a sudden thought: perhaps she could embarrass Anna out of wanting a lingerie tea. How profoundly she regretted the ridiculous idea. Where had she got it from? Some silly women's magazine probably. Most of the stupid notions she'd ever got in her life came from women's magazines: scatter fresh flower petals into your bath water; make a hall table ornament from blown brown hen's eggs; wear a honey and oatmeal face mask to bed.

'I take a size medium,' Anna said. 'I've got a whole drawer full of panties I can't wear because my mother thinks I'm a small. I hate it when they creep up between my cheeks.'

'Wedgies, my sister calls them.' Claire made an attempt at a chuckle.

'So, no thongs either, okay? I save those for the beach.'

'Me too,' Claire said faintly.

'Go to Rio some time if you want to see thongs. Alex had his tongue on the sand the whole time we were there. I had to scrape the grit off every night.'

'Rio. Yes. I've heard that –' She'd been to Rio with Alexander Spears?

'But high-cut panties are good. I like those.' Anna was smiling, apparently not embarrassed a bit. She licked her lovely lips.

'So why don't you give all of this some thought, write everything down, give me a list?' Claire didn't feel like continuing,
item by item, through the intricacies of a lingerie wardrobe with
such an appallingly frank young woman. Thongs? She barely
knew what a thong was!

'Oh, and I prefer silk, of course.'

'Well, who doesn't?'

'I know it's more expensive and a drag to clean, but static cling
makes me crazy. And – you'll laugh at this – but I could really
use some garter belts. Good ones, with lots of snap. Alexander
has a thing for them. We're into some – what do the skin mags
call it? – variations.'

Claire drew in her breath, feeling unpleasantly warm. Was it
embarrassment? Sexual arousal? Or her first hot flash? 'Look,
Anna, I didn't mean to pry into your personal –'

'You'll want my bra size too, I guess?'

'I can't honestly imagine anyone going out and buying you a
bra . . .'

'For the record, I'm a thirty-four B. But don't put it on
e-mail, okay?'

'Of course not.'

'I like short nighties. Long ones get twisted around my waist.
And no black. Alex thinks I look like a hooker in black. Same
goes for red.' She paused, her lips glistening. 'I can't think of
what else . . . Half slips maybe – pretty banal though. And I could
use a chemise or two. Then there's teddies – again silk, not poly.
And I don't have a merry widow, a bustier or a bralette –'

'Or a bagatelle, I suppose.' Claire tossed back her head and
laughed artificially.

'Pardon?'

'Nothing. It's just that our conversation is getting hilarious,
don't you think?'

'No.' Anna looked puzzled.

Claire stood up and moved around to the front of her desk.
'Well, that should just about cover it. No pun intended.' She
made an effort at a smile to indicate an end to the matter.

'You don't want a list of sex toys?'

'I'm sure you and Alexander can manage to get your own –
of those.'

'Fair enough. I wasn't sure about the protocol, how broad an interpretation you were giving the word "lingerie".'

'It doesn't include your contraceptives either,' Claire said.

'Oh, that's not an issue. Alex got himself snipped.'

'Snipped?'

'A vasectomy. It's great. It's had absolutely zero effect on his ability to –'

Claire coughed. 'Excuse me. I really should get some work done . . . The morning's just flying by, it seems.'

'Okay, I'm out of here.' Anna slid out of the chair, stretched her long body and yawned. 'It's sort of a retro thing, isn't it? A lingerie tea. I think it'll be a gas – isn't that what they used to say? Fun things were always a gas . . .' She shifted her files into one arm, freeing a hand to shake Claire's. 'So thanks a lot. I'll get you my mother's address. And if I think of anything else I need, I'll let you know.'

'Great, excellent. Good idea.' Claire sank back into her chair as Anna turned in the doorway to start her runway walk in the direction of the firm's library. Garter belts with zing, silk nighties, sex toys? Well, she had asked for it. Why should she be put out with Anna for being honest? Although, if their positions had been reversed, Claire would have blushed and mumbled that anything at all would be fine, mortified by the thought of her colleagues wandering through lingerie shops puzzling over what she might like to wear in the sack to turn on her man. But then, she was well over forty. And she wasn't about to marry Alexander Spears, was she?

She thought about Ben's chunky figure, rollerblading close alongside her car that morning, following her as she pulled away from the house. She wished he wouldn't do that. She was always terrified that she'd run him over, that his blades would slip under her wheels or he would bump against the car door, ricocheting into the path of an oncoming truck. He'd laughed as he skated along, his boyish round face beaming beneath the shiny black helmet. Ben enjoyed living on the edge, particularly now, as he was closing in on forty. And it was always a lot more fun if he could scare the pants off Claire while he was at it.

She would be meeting him for dinner at their usual place that night. Monday was their night to go out together, have a meal and talk about the kids. Or usually they talked about the kids. Tonight, Claire thought, she might add a few more intriguing subjects to their agenda. Like thongs. And garter belts with zing. Except that it might start giving Ben ideas. Which maybe wasn't altogether such a bad thing.

6

When Ben was in the operating room, he didn't have to think too much about the surgery he was doing. The pondering and planning was over well before he made the first cut. He no longer thought about how many children the patient had, what the patient's life expectancy would be after the surgery, or what it had been before. He wasn't a social worker or chaplain; it wasn't his job to help his patients go gently into that good night. If it came to that.

Surgeons were often said to have a lousy bedside manner, but Ben knew his patients wouldn't want him boo-hooing with them as they waited in the row of steel-sided beds, hairnets on, jewellery off and dentures out, for their names to be chalked up on the OR board. Nor would they want to picture him praying, silently, in the pale chilliness of the operating room, prior to calling for a 'fifteen blade'.

He didn't need mental games to counter the boredom of a long case, as did many surgeons he knew; he didn't rhyme off all the kings of England, or list the varieties of Italian pasta (from *agnelotti* to *ziti*) in his head. Instead, he chatted casually with the residents, the nurses, the anaesthetist – about current films, what their kids were up to, weekend plans. There was usually a top-forty radio station playing and the concentration, the conversation and the volume of the music would ebb and flow, taking its lead from Ben. Sometimes he would exchange dirty jokes with a resident, or meaningful glances with a pretty nurse over the top of his mask: harmless pastimes in which no offence was ever given, or taken. The mask made him feel like a bandit or a pirate – unpredictable, bold – which was how he felt when he was zapping around on his rollerblades.

Normally, Ben paid no attention to the time when he was in surgery, but tonight he was anxious to finish early. His brow furrowed as he nodded to the circulating nurse to dab his forehead, something done far less often than the public assumed from watching doctor shows on TV. What surgeons – male surgeons, of course – really needed was someone to scratch or rearrange their testicles occasionally, but no doctor show had had the balls, yet, to grapple with the issue.

A glance at the OR clock told Ben that he would likely be on time for dinner with his wife. The route to the restaurant was all downhill, and he might get lucky and catch a strong head wind. The Cunninghams' Monday evenings were never very satisfying when Ben arrived late to find Claire staring at the menu, munching on bread sticks and getting drunk on wine when she could have been at the office accomplishing something, being productive. Poor overworked Claire. Ben couldn't wait to present her with his proposal.

'Who says I want to quit work?' Claire said. 'What makes you think that?'

'Because you hate it so much. It's driving you crazy. All those hours you have to bill, the bitchy women, the sexist suits. It's getting to be too much for you. Am I right? Or have you been complaining about something *else*, constantly, since Harry was born?'

'I hardly ever talk about quitting. And I've been practising law for almost twenty years. Why would you think it's too much for me now?'

'You haven't had two kids to deal with for twenty years, on top of your job.'

'I don't deal with them. Francine does. That's why we hired her.'

'Mind of a turnip,' Ben said mildly. 'Do you *really* trust her with Harry and Molly? Now that they're getting older? Or is it something you don't let yourself think about? Even now –' he checked his watch '– I wonder what she's doing. Leaving them alone in the bath while she sneaks out for a smoke . . .'

'Ben, she's been with us for almost three years.'

'That long?'

'We hired her right after Rose-Marie quit.'

'I gained fifteen pounds because of Rose-Marie,' Ben said wistfully. 'That girl sure could cook. How did we ever lose her, anyway?'

'Harry. With the pick-up-sticks. And the one that got stuck up her nose. Don't you remember?'

'Still doesn't seem possible.' Ben shook his head. 'Even anatomically . . . so improbable.'

'It wasn't Harry's fault – he wasn't even aiming them at Rose-Marie. It was a total fluke, something no one could ever replicate – not without a lot of practice anyway. And the amount of blood seemed out of all proportion to the scale of the injury.'

'The Inferior Turbinate is a highly vascularized area.' His eyes met his wife's. 'The inside of the nose.'

'Well, Harry shouldn't have had pick-up-sticks to begin with. He was much too young for them . . . at four.'

'So where'd he get them from?'

'Your mother – because it was your favourite boyhood game. Playing pick-up-sticks gave you the manual dexterity to enable you to become a surgeon.'

'Is that what Prue says?' Ben snorted. 'What a crock!'

'So that's how we lost Rose-Marie. Or at least, that was the proximate cause. She was ready to leave anyway. She wanted to get married, have her own family. And she had that boyfriend . . .'

'A loser.'

'Maybe. But there's a life-cycle with nannies in every household. And Rose-Marie was at the end of hers with us. She was good though, wasn't she? I remember when she started – the first thing she did was go through our spice cabinet, complaining about everything that was wrong with it and our kitchen. We hired her . . . when? About a week after Brita ran off.'

'Hmm.' Ben looked bored.

'You don't think about Brita and wonder what she's up to?'

'No, actually.' Ben glanced over the wine list, his lips pursed. The Cunninghams' first nanny was a subject he obviously did not care to discuss. Brita had almost destroyed their marriage –

certainly threatened it – during the year after Harry was born. 'That's what I mean about Francine,' he finally said. 'I agree with your life-cycle theory. After three years of being a nanny with us, why wouldn't she want to do something else? Get on with her life? She must be twenty-five by now.'

'We don't want her to get on with her life. The kids love her. And why should she leave us? To stand on her feet and be a cashier in a grocery store? Though she might be considering it – she tortures me every day by reading the Help Wanted ads in the paper as I'm getting ready for work. But I think she'll realize she's got a good thing going with us. And it's not as though she's moping around in our basement every night. Since she got her own apartment, she seems to have a very active social life. I can never get her to babysit on a weekend.'

'That's one of my concerns. She's hanging around with a bunch of creeps and dopers – becoming one herself, most likely. She seemed like a nice enough girl when we hired her. A bit naive, maybe . . .'

'She does seem to have – what's the word I want here? – hardened. I've noticed it too.' At one time, Claire had thought it her duty to be more than an employer to Francine, to take her under her wing, set her on the straight and narrow, maybe even send her off to law school after a few years with the Cunninghams. But Francine had deflected any such well-intentioned efforts and Claire had realized that Francine was a project she really didn't need: after all, Molly would be at 'that stage' soon enough. Why would Claire want to go through it all *twice*? 'But I don't think her friends are all that bad,' she added. 'They just like to shock people with their looks. Most of them are from decent homes.' She traced a finger through the condensation on the side of her water glass. 'So what's this all about? Why are you trashing Francine? Don't you trust her all of a sudden? If you don't, we'd better talk about it. The kids are crazy about her, especially Harry. She must be doing something right.'

'You can't honestly expect good judgment from a seven year old?'

They were seated at a table in the cramped dim rear of the restaurant. The airy front section, with the lovely casement windows, was reserved for smokers. They'd had to down-grade their choice of restaurants since Ben started rollerblading because he always showed up for their Monday dinners reeking of sweat, his hair dripping, his nylon sports bag, from which his black helmet dangled, thrown over his shoulder. The rollerblading was her own fault, Claire realized. She shouldn't have needled Ben about his weight, prodding that tough little roll that had accumulated around his waist. Actually, she'd found that roll, like a doughnut or a life preserver, endearing. It had also been a convenient reason for not sleeping with Ben. Now that he was on a diet and rollerblading like mad, he was expecting renewed sexual interest on her part and not what he got: Claire's renewed interest in his disability insurance.

In the still of the night, her eyes would suddenly flutter open and she would stare into the darkness, seeing Ben in the hospital, not in his usual place – the operating theatre – but in intensive care, on a respirator, hooked up with bags and tubes and IV lines. And apart from her own fears for her husband's safety, what would his patients think, already dreading their ordeal in the operating room, to see their surgeon rolling along beneath their hospital windows? 'By the way,' she said, tapping the wine list that Ben still held in his hands, 'the insurance company nurse needs you to pee into a bottle. For your disability insurance. We need to increase it now that you're rollerblading. It's been classified as a "dangerous activity" – like hang gliding. For a man your age.'

'That's ridiculous.'

'Well – when can you see her?'

'Tell her to call my secretary.'

'It's you she needs the pee from.'

'Why don't we order a drink?' Dark half-moons of sweat stained Ben's T-shirt under the arms. He needed a shave. 'Let's get some really good wine tonight. The best in the house – though there's a pretty limited list.'

'So what's the occasion?' Claire asked. Had she forgotten his birthday? Her own? Their anniversary? 'You mean, you forgot to send my mother a birthday card?' Ben had asked her the other day, with a stricken look. It was the same day Claire had forgotten to have his driver's licence renewed. For a while, she had started writing down things she was likely to forget. Almost everything, it seemed, fell into that category: when Cannon and the kids were due for their next vaccinations, what shade hair colouring worked best for her, the date of her last period, where she'd stored the extension cords in the house. All of this she'd recorded in a blue notebook she thought of as *Remembrances of Things Past*. The project lasted only a few days. Claire soon began to forget what she'd meant to write in the book, then where she'd put the book itself.

'The occasion,' Ben was saying, 'is that you've agreed to consider quitting work to stay home with the kids.'

'I never said that.'

'Claire, I make three times what you make. And the cosmetic surgery part of my practice – the very lucrative part – is really taking off. We aren't going to need your income, love. That's what I'm trying to tell you.'

'My pin money, you mean?' As Claire recrossed her legs under the table, her foot struck Ben's sports bag, knocking off his helmet which then clunked to the floor.

'I don't mean your income is insignificant. I'm merely pointing out that if you want the freedom to do other things, you've got it.'

'Well, I don't. At least, I haven't thought about it. Not seriously. Not for years.'

'Well, I'm asking you to. Imagine a life of almost total freedom. You could take courses at the university, entertain more often – like that tea party you're putting on for your girlfriends. I was so proud when you told me you were doing it.'

'*Proud*?' Claire was planning, regrettably, one of the most ludicrous endeavours of her life and he was *proud*? 'They're not my girlfriends,' she said, crossly. 'The whole stupid tea is a business obligation. A development tool – I'm inviting clients.'

'Okay – that's my point exactly. You would be free from business obligations. Forever. You could do anything that interests you, as long as the kids were looked after. They'll both be in school full-time this fall. You could finish decorating the house, start working out, whatever. Wouldn't I love the chance? Think of the possibilities. You could feel like I do, when I'm out on my blades, with the wind in my hair –'

'You wear a helmet.' Claire frowned. 'And if you don't, I need to know why.'

'Okay. You're right, Counsellor. With the wind sweeping, aerodynamically over my helmet.' He looked peeved.

Claire closed her menu. 'You know, I'm really not hungry. I should have stayed at the office – I have so much to do.'

'Wait a minute. I don't get it. You're angry, aren't you? I've waited years for this moment, to be able to make you this offer. How many women would jump at the chance to give up work? But you? You get *offended*. It's incomprehensible. I can't win.'

Claire started to breathe and count, in and out, imagining she was in labour for childbirth. It hadn't done any good then either.

Suddenly, Ben grabbed her hand, entrapping it with his warm paws. His hands were strong but rather small, always immaculately clean; the nails smooth, deeply pink, and filed to even ovals. 'If you don't want to consider quitting from a purely selfish point of view, why don't you think about Harry and Molly? You're yelling a lot, always on at them or Francine, constantly on a short fuse. Your reaction right now is a perfect example of your unpredictable mood swings. A bizarre response, I think, to a well-intentioned suggestion. I can't believe how mad you look. Your face has gone all red, like a tomato.'

Well, Claire thought, still working on her breathing control, wasn't there something to be said for that? At least a tomato was smooth, nicely plump, unlined. She watched his hands, massaging hers. 'I know you're under a lot of stress,' he said, 'but it can't be good for you, or the kids. You should see their little faces when you start to scream.'

'I do not scream. I'm firm with them, that's all.' Not scream? Claire thought back to that morning. She'd had an early meeting again and had been so short of time that she was obliged to put her make-up on in the car. At every red light another bit was added: a stroke of eyeliner here, a smear of lipstick there. God only knew what sort of ridiculous kindergarten drawing of a face she'd had on by the time she met her client. Molly had been eager to do Claire's hair, but Mummy didn't have time. Tearing pink Velcro rollers from her head, Claire had hurried from the bathroom into the bedroom where she rifled through the tangle of her underwear drawer, looking for pantyhose without runs or holes. As she struggled into a pair, she was aware of her daughter still watching her, her sweet apple-cheeked face dark as an approaching storm. 'You can do Mummy's hair tonight, okay, honey?' Claire had said, desperately hoping to avoid a scene. 'You can do a hamster hair-do on me, a duck –'

'Can I do a parrot?'

'Anything you want. But tonight, okay? Not now. Mummy's in a rush this morning.' Mummy's got a headache, Mummy's very busy, Mummy isn't feeling well, Mummy has to go, Mummy hasn't got time. That's all, it seemed, her children ever heard from her. There was a portrait of Claire, framed on their bedroom wall, that Harry had painted when he was five. In it, the wristwatch was the most striking feature: not Claire's lop-sided smile, stringy hair or the half-moon ears that jutted from the sides of her head like orange slices. But she'd had no time for guilt that morning – she would have to remember to write 'feel guilty about Molly' on her 'to do' list for the day. If she could remember where she'd put it. She'd stumbled into a pair of heels, pulled a blouse from a hanger in the closet, sniffed the underarms and decided it would have to do for another wearing.

'Claire?' Francine had yelled from the bottom of the stairs. 'You know the water in the powder room toilet? It's brown.'

'So flush it.'

'I did – but it's still brown. It's grossing me out. And the washing machine won't come on.'

'I can't look at it now. Call me at work. I'll get a plumber – whatever.' She flew down the stairs with her daughter at her heels.

'Can I change the wallpaper in my room so it has dogs on it?' Molly wanted to know.

'No. Sure. I don't know.' Claire pulled open the refrigerator door with so much force that all of the fridge magnets clattered to the floor. 'There's no orange juice. Francine, did you forget to buy OJ?'

'It wasn't on the list.'

'It shouldn't have to be. It's a staple. You should always get it when you do the shopping.'

'Sorry.'

'It's okay. I'll get some later. Forget it.' Claire filled a glass with tap water and shook two tablets from a bottle of Tylenol she'd taken from a kitchen cupboard. The working woman's breakfast. When someone remembered to buy Tylenol.

When she'd arrived at her meeting, the client had, with obvious embarrassment, pointed out that Claire had a pink roller ensnared in her hair. Thank God the client was a woman. A man wouldn't have said anything – if he'd noticed at all – and Claire would have blithely gone around all day like that.

As she studied her husband, and the details of the morning played out in her head, Ben's pager beeped, startling them both. He pressed the button on the side to read the telephone number. 'I have to pop back into the hospital later to check on what one of my residents is doing. But I'm sure you don't want to hear about it.' He grappled for her hand again. 'Now, what were you saying?'

'I was about to start screaming.'

'About?' Ben's eyebrows rose, as if he were preparing to hear a complaint from an unreasonable patient.

The truth, Claire thought, as she looked into his earnest eyes, was that she couldn't bear the thought of being supported. After twenty years of making her own living, she wasn't about to give it up to argue with her husband over every penny. 'You've got a closet full of shoes,' she could imagine him bellowing as he flung open the doors of their walk-in closet (maybe one of the doors flying off its hinges to increase the dramatic effect), 'so would somebody please explain to me why you need *another* pair? In black?'

In fairness, it wasn't Ben's style to bellow. But he would notice, oh yes, when those were his dollars Claire was handing over to the clothing stores. His response was more likely to be that of the careful surgeon, taking the stainless-steel blade approach to the problem (her spending), the cause (her boredom) and the solution (cut it out). Once they were *sharing* one income (and that income was his) she couldn't just go out and buy a new pair of shoes whenever she felt bored or depressed (or both); and he would never understand how a shopping spree could lift her out of her bad mood in the first place. 'Don't you see?'

he would argue, calmly. 'Once you're over that initial high, and the bills come pouring in, you'll be more depressed than ever.'

Eventually, his niggling over every dollar would humiliate and exhaust her until they'd have to part, she realizing what a miserly skinflint she'd married, and he what a giddy spendthrift. By then she'd have blown up like a balloon from overeating, and wouldn't be able to fit into anything but a sloppy sweatsuit. Her hair would be lank and greasy, the roots long and grey.

It wasn't that long ago, Claire thought, that Harry was an infant and Ben was a resident, earning less than Claire's secretary, and moonlighting on weekends by doing house calls. He had a large sign, in eye-popping neon green, that said DOCTOR ON CALL, which he stuck under the wiper blades of their beat-up Mazda's front window. The house-call referral service guaranteed the sign would ward off cops and meter men whenever Ben parked illegally. Claire often joked that they should cruise the streets more slowly, giving her a chance to stick her head out of the window and give a New York cabbie whistle. 'Hey!' she could yell to people on the sidewalk. 'You look like you've got lots wrong with you. The doc's right here. Get out your health card and climb on in!'

Harry, of course, had screamed constantly on those trips, strapped into his car seat like a mental patient in a four-point restraint, spitting out his soother at every red light and stop sign. And they couldn't afford a cell phone back then, so whenever Ben got paged they'd have to drive for miles, searching for a phone booth so he would know where to drive to next. The best calls, they discovered, were from nursing homes. Pronouncing somebody dead was easy, fast and lucrative and, nine times out of ten, there'd be a queue of elderly people in wheelchairs and walkers waiting to see Ben when he was finished. It was difficult not to get cynical about it all.

No, Claire thought, watching as Ben dealt with the waiter who had appeared to take their order, she could never go back to worrying over money. And the children were much better off anyway, weren't they, having a mother who was happy and fulfilled, who enjoyed what she did for a living? 'So,' she said brightly, 'just to change the subject, did you know that Alex Spears has had a vasectomy? And guess what he likes Anna to wear?'

*   *   *

Francine pulled out the baking tray, singeing the tea towel on the oven element. Rocky Road bars, her all-time favourite. This time she'd doubled the chocolate and added more marshmallows.

'Francine? Where's my supper?' Harry demanded. 'I'm starving!' He was in the family room watching *Monster Truckheads*. It was on practically all the time, on several channels. 'We must be ready to launch before the evil Decepticons fly overhead!' cried a gravelly voice.

Molly was upstairs somewhere, doing whatever. Francine hadn't heard from her for a while. She banged the hot tray down on the stove top and yelled in the direction of the stairs: 'Molly? You okay, hon?'

From upstairs, Molly shouted something Francine couldn't make out. So long as she wasn't dead, Francine figured, it didn't much matter what she was doing. Molly was an easy kid. Which was more than she could say for Harry.

'What's for supper?' he yelled.

'Hot dogs!'

'Not again!'

'Well, what *do* you want?'

'Ice cream!'

Francine went into the family room to have a talk with him. 'Cone or cup?' she said.

'Cup.'

'Want me to make you a belly-buster sundae?'

'Sure!'

'But you can't just have that for dinner. It's not healthy. You'll have a couple of Rocky Road bars too.' Back in the kitchen, Francine took a spoon and scooped up a mound of chocolate and marshmallows that was still too hot to cut into bars. 'These are insanely delish,' she said. She took a bite of her toasted bacon and melted cheddar sandwich, then piled ice cream into a bowl, over which she poured chocolate sauce, then sprinkled with coconut, peanuts and butterscotch chips. Bits of coconut lodged under her Chrome-painted acrylic nails. 'Soup's on,' she said, flicking flakes of coconut on to the floor. 'Come and get it!'

'Can I have a pickle too?' Harry asked.

'Bit of a health food nut, are you? Sure you can have a pickle.'

'Do I have to eat that broccoli?' *Monster Truckheads* was at a commercial break so Harry had had time to run into the kitchen.

'Well, your mom left it here for you. But I'm not going to force you . . .'

'All *right*, Francine! You are too *cool*!'

'I know,' Francine took the bowl of steamed broccoli and emptied it into the garberator – an energy-wasting machine that Claire had told her never to use. She switched it on, and she and Harry listened with satisfaction to the voracious churning and gurgling. Harry loved the garberator; it appealed to his destructive nature. He often had nightmares about it. 'Don't tell your mother about this,' Francine said, 'or you know what she'll do? She'll make you dig the broccoli out of there where it's all mushed up with rotten eggs and mouldy cheese and banana peels, and she'll make you eat it. For breakfast.'

'She will not!'

'Don't believe me then.' Francine left the kitchen to stand at the bottom of the stairs. 'Molly! What're you doing up there, girl?' She checked through the pockets of Claire's raincoat that was hanging on a coat tree in the front hall, while she waited for some indication that Molly was still alive. Then she wondered whether Claire had found the Velcro roller in her hair yet. What a howl if she came home with it still there! 'What do you want for supper, Molly?' There was a muffled yell. Francine paused, satisfied. 'And don't forget to wash your hands!' She went back into the kitchen where she took another bite of her sandwich. After that, she dumped a can of Slimfast and a cup of milk into the blender. 'Molly'll come down when she's hungry enough.'

'She's just playing with her dolls or something.' Harry was surveying his meal with satisfaction. 'Can I take this down to the TV room? *Monster Truckheads* is on again.' It was against his mother's rules for the children to take any food out of the kitchen. Or to watch *Monster Truckheads*.

'Okay with me, kid.' Francine buzzed the Slimfast mixture, poured it into a glass and took it over to the table where she settled in to finish her sandwich and flip through the *People* magazine she'd shoplifted from the grocery store. She could have paid for it – or rather, Claire could have – but it was much more satisfying to steal it. Francine's personal groceries, that Claire had paid for but would never know about, were safely in Francine's knapsack, slumped over by the front door. God help her, she smiled, if Claire ever remembered to ask to see the grocery bill. 'Hey, Harry?' she said without interest as she turned the pages of *People*. 'What should I make your sister for supper?'

'Give her a granola bar. That's all she ever eats.'

'Another health food freak,' Francine sighed.

'Francine?' Harry paused on his way out of the kitchen. The spoon dropped from his sundae dish, spattering ice cream and chocolate sauce on to the Italian tiles.

Francine leaned out of her chair to grab a J-cloth from the counter. Claire had some idea about which colour cloth was to be used for kids' faces, which for floors and which for counter tops, but Francine couldn't be bothered with such lunacy. She tossed the J-cloth on to the floor. 'Clean up your mess, kid.'

'I can't. I'll miss *Monster Truckheads*.'

'Well, pick up your spoon at least. You can't eat a sundae without a spoon.'

Harry picked it up and licked it. 'Francine?'

'Yes, dear.'

'I love you.'

Francine glanced up at him from her magazine. 'I know that, Buster Brown. I love you too. Now go eat your supper. You want to grow up big and strong, don't you?'

'Sure.'

'Like your daddy, eh?' Francine smiled. 'Doctor Groovy Rollerblade-Dude.'

7

The Last Millennium Bakery and Cafe was the only place advanced enough in its thinking, and fearful enough of its clientele, to flaunt the city's bylaws and allow unrestricted cigarette smoking. It was decorated with industrial materials: hard rubber flooring, plenty of stainless steel, everything riveted together with bolts big enough to hold up bridges. It was hard-edged, aggressive decor. The waiters were also hard-edged and aggressive, but the service was grindingly slow.

Near the steel-girdered front doors was a sort of community bulletin board where notices were messily tacked.

Rottweiler – 2 yrs old – free to good home. Great with kids.

Drum kit Electronic 7 Dauz pads & kat minikick Alesis D4 & JVC phones stand & pearl kick & throne.

Doc Martens – men's size 10, green, from UK – eight holes.

'I think Claire's losing it.' Francine poked a Cerulean Blue nail into a nearly flattened pack to extract a bent cigarette, lit it off the end of hers and passed it across the beaten-tin table to Isadora. She stuffed the pack into the pocket of her jeans. They were so tight it made Isadora hold her breath, and her stomach hurt just to look at them. On Francine's T-shirt, in bold black letters across her breasts, it said: JUST DO ME!

Isadora couldn't be less interested in whether or not her mother's law partner was 'losing it', but Francine loved to complain about being Claire's kids' nanny, and Isadora was too intimidated by Francine to let on that she was bored.

'I'll give you a perfect example,' Francine continued. 'She's sitting on the can, right? And I'm trying to get the kids to eat this gross Count Chocula cereal, and suddenly she yells out to me do I know how to make tea sandwiches?' She dragged on her cigarette, eyes flickering over Isadora.

'What's a tea sandwich?' An image of a tea bag between two slices of bread floated across Isadora's brain. She sucked hard on the end of her cigarette, trying to get it going properly. Francine had been too quick to pass it to her.

'They're hideous soggy sandwiches filled with cucumbers or watercress, with the crusts cut off. Denture-friendly. You have to eat about two hundred to get full. Sometimes the bread is dyed. Pink, or even green.'

'Green bread?'

'Sick-making or what? Claire's giving this tea because some lawyer is getting married. To a law student. Like, this chick is half his age, right? Maybe less. You heard about them?' The pupils in Francine's eyes dilated with pleasure. 'Claire says he's had a vasectomy, too. Like it's ultra-cool or something. Like nobody's ever had one before.'

'Yeah, I heard about that jerk-off.'

'Anyway, I told Claire I'd never made a tea sandwich in my life and I wasn't about to start, so she could stuff her cucumbers where the sun don't shine.' Francine sniggered. 'Might do her some good, since she and the doc don't make it any more.'

'How do you know that?'

Francine rolled her eyes. 'I get to do their sheets, remember? It's part of my fabulous job. Ben's skid marks in his shorts, the stains on the sheets, condoms under the bed. But like I said – there hasn't been much of that lately. I think it's her, though, who's, like, got the headache every night.'

'And you told her to *stuff* her cucumbers? You said that?'

'Pretty much,' Francine said.

'Man! You're going to get fired.' Isadora gaped in admiration as Francine blew a stream of smoke across the table and looked back at her through half-closed lids that were heavy with copper-coloured shadow.

'Claire won't fire me. She'd never find anyone else to take over those little buggers. Though Molly's okay some of the time.' She regarded the hand that held the cigarette. 'Shit. I don't believe this. I broke a nail. Have you got any nail glue?'

'No, sorry.' Isadora pushed her hands, with their stubby bitten-down nails, under the table.

'I had them just perfect too.'

'I could run over to the drug mart. Get you some glue. I don't mind.'

'Forget it.' Francine slumped behind the menu of The Last Millennium. 'I feel like something humungously fattening today. You?'

'Just a Diet Coke.' Isadora wasn't hungry. She was wondering whether Francine had brought *the book*. She couldn't tell by looking at Francine's knapsack, since it was always bulging and heavy with stuff.

'I could swear I've got a tapeworm,' Francine said after she'd ordered. 'I knew a chick once who had a tapeworm – they had to get it out while she was asleep. Put a bowl of sugar water near her bum. Isn't that the grossest thing you've ever heard?'

'Massively sickening.' Isadora thought that Francine knew a lot of people who'd had interestingly awful things happen to them. She didn't think Francine had a tapeworm though; tapeworms were supposed to make you skinny. Which Francine wasn't. She was also very touchy about that.

Isadora had met Francine two weeks earlier at the Bragg, Banks and Biltmore annual summer picnic. Francine was there because Claire couldn't go and needed someone to take Harry and Molly and she was willing to pay Francine twelve dollars an hour to do it. On a weekend? To a law-firm family picnic? That was danger pay time. Francine had demanded twenty.

Isadora was there because her mother had made such a big deal about her going. She was too old for kiddy picnics, she'd argued, mortified by the thought of hopping around in a sack, or three-legged racing with some four-eyed lawyer. The picnic wasn't just for children, Gillian told her, there would be lots of young people there – some of the firm's associates, a summer student, a few of the younger clients. Tight-asses and geeks was what Isadora had expected. And she hadn't been disappointed.

'You look like you want to be here about as much as I do,' Francine had said, brushing up against Isadora in the crush for hot dogs and hamburgers. 'Want a butt?' She'd held out a flattened cigarette pack.

'My mom's up there.' Isadora indicated the front of the line. 'She'd have a cow if she saw me smoking.'

'Which one is she?'

'The red hair.'

Francine nodded. 'Sure. With the *clothes*. I noticed her right off. Look, why don't you grab a burger and meet me behind the boat house? The kids I'm babysitting want to see the magic show. They won't notice if I take off for a bit. A law firm picnic.' She sighed. 'Can you think of any place more *deadly*? A crematorium, maybe.' She took a last pull on her cigarette, dropped it on to the grass and ground it out with her boot. She was wearing an ankle bracelet with dog tags jingling from it. 'I'm not supposed to smoke around the kids. But since I don't see the rug rats anywhere, I figure they probably don't see me.' She'd laughed at Isadora's expression. 'Don't worry – they're here somewhere. This is an island. They can't just wander off it.'

'They could drown.'

'They're not going to drown. I'm not a *total* fuck up when it comes to looking after kids.' She scratched the back of her neck and fixed her round baby blues on Isadora. 'You look like you could use someone to talk to. Am I right?'

Isadora shrugged.

'Listen, I might be looking for a business partner soon. I could use someone like you. Come on and I'll tell you about it. Behind the boat house. Be there in five.'

'I'm quitting this nanny crap,' Francine said as, gnawing on her ruined nail, she waited for the Super Nacho Meltdown with Triple Sour Cream Overload. 'As soon as my dad comes through with the money. He owes me and my brother a pile, since he never made support payments to my mom when we were growing up. He's been totalling it up all along though, and he says it's a lot and it's really our money. He was afraid

Mom wouldn't spend it on us, which is why he never paid her anything.' She tapped her cigarette on the edge of the ashtray then twirled the burning end to a neat sharp point. 'We hated him for it back then, but he was probably right. I can see Mom blowing it. I might get my dough as early as Christmas – and then hasta-la-beachball nanny crap. He just has to sort some stuff out, cash in some bonds or something.'

'But what about our business?' Isadora said. 'I thought you were going to quit work so we could open the shop – not so you could live on your dad's money.'

'Izzy, relax.' Francine looked down at the food the waiter put in front of her. 'I meant that my old man's money is going to help finance the shop, okay? *Our* shop. It's not all that complicated. Don't go getting stupid on me. I hate stupid people.' She balanced the cigarette on the edge of the ashtray and shovelled up sour cream with a nacho. 'And stop being so paranoid all the time. Want some of this?'

Isadora shook her head, still thinking about the book. Francine was supposed to have borrowed it from a friend of hers who had every weird book ever written: on witchcraft, the spirit world, cannibalism.

'My dad is one very cool dude,' Francine said, licking her fingers, 'except for marrying Midge. What a name. You know what a midge is? It's a bug. A tiny little insect. The kind you can hardly see but that really piss you off. Can you believe anyone naming their kid after an insignificant bug? When I have kids I'm going to make sure they have gorgeous names – at least the girls. Krystal, Amber, Tiffany. And the boys will be Tristan, Blair, Montana. Don't you love that name? I'd give anything to go to Montana. All those cowboys. Or Texas. I hate faggy names for boys. And boring ones. I want to have at least four kids. Two boys and two girls. You want to know how totally groovy my dad is?'

Isadora nodded, her eyes wandering over the banquette to Francine's knapsack. It was made out of some fuzzy fabric, with an Aztec sort of pattern on it, laced with black leather thongs.

'He packs condoms in his suitcase when he goes off on business trips.' Francine watched Isadora, chewing, waiting to see the impact of this information.

'With Midge?'

'Of course not. What would be the point of my story if Midge went? That Midge and my dad use condoms? Give your head a shake.' Francine sighed heavily. 'But if Midge ever saw those rubbers in his suitcase, you know what she'd say? "What do you need those for, honey? I'm not going with you, remember?" That's how stupid she is.'

'Unbelievable.'

'Dumb as a stick. By the way, how much cash have you got so far?'

'I got a twenty today.'

'So the total is what? How much?'

'Eighty-five bucks.'

'We're not going to get very far on that.'

'Well, my mother doesn't just keep money lying around, okay?'

'So take it from her purse.'

'Where do you think I'm getting it from?' Isadora flushed. She'd been expecting gratitude from Francine. Even praise. 'And besides, I've never heard you say how much you've got yourself. And you're the one with the job.'

Francine blinked. 'Okay. I know you're doing your best. But one of the things we've got to buy is an autoclave, so we better start budgeting for it.'

'What's an autoclave?'

'A machine for sterilizing needles and things. Customers are demanding it. It's not like the old days. Now everyone's scared of getting AIDS.'

'So how much does that cost?'

'A lot. But maybe we can lease one. I know some people – I'm looking into it.'

'I thought all this was going to be cheap,' Isadora said, 'to get set up. No big costs – that's what you said.'

'That was before I knew how competitive this business is. Don't get me wrong, this is a very hot thing, very trendy. But you've got to be right up to date with your techniques. Here, I brought that book for you.' She licked the sour cream from her fingers, unlaced the thongs of her knapsack, and pulled out a big book. *Modern Primitives* it was called. Isadora took it eagerly.

'Don't be too shocked by what's in there,' Francine warned. 'We aren't going to jump right into genital piercing or anything. Not at first.'

Isadora opened the book and began turning the pages, mouth open. There was a man hanging by a meat hook through a hole pierced through the skin of his chest; fakirs walking on knife points; women with elongated necks. 'You said tattoos,' Isadora gaped, 'like flowers.'

'That'll be the start. Simple designs, simple piercings. But things have gone way beyond butterflies on butts. There was this story in yesterday's *Star* about a chick who's had mirrors implanted in her face and a guy who's had all his hair replaced with real growing grass.'

Isadora drew back from a photograph of a woman's clitoris studded with a steel ball the size of a marble. 'What do you mean by simple piercings?'

'General rule – if it sticks out, pierce it. If it doesn't, don't.'

'Sticks out?'

'Earlobes, noses, nipples . . . belly buttons – some of 'em. Basically, you don't try to ram a stud through somebody's leg 'cause it'll either get infected or fall out. Or both.'

'What else sticks out?'

Francine shrugged. 'How should I know? I need to do some more research.'

'Dicks?'

Francine's eyes darted sideways. 'Dicks stick out all right. At least when I'm around.' She laughed.

'I'm not sticking a stud through any guy's dick.' Isadora closed the book. 'That's not what we talked about.'

'We have to do piercings. No one wants hearts and ladybugs any more. This isn't the sixties. This isn't flower-goddamned-power. There's a lot of weird shit going down.' She struggled to dig her cigarette pack out of her jeans again. 'Your problem is, you worry too much. If someone comes in and asks for something we don't know how to do, or don't want to do, we just say "Sorry, man, no can do". No one wants to get mutilated. Guys are touchy about what happens to their dicks. Can't imagine why.'

'That's what it looks like to me. Mutilation.' Isadora pushed the book over the table. 'I don't need to borrow this.'

'You should. You should read it. There's a lot of philosophy in here. Altering your physical body is consciousness-raising. A mental control thing. It's very spiritual. I know it's kind of a turn-off when you first see it, but remember, this book is already way out of date. Everything's very sterile now, very state-of-the-art. That's what I was telling you about the autoclave. And you always wear surgical gloves for total protection. Did you know that when you pierce a nose, you don't use an ordinary stud? It's not like an earring stud. It's a screw. If you used an earring-type stud, snot would get trapped around it.'

Isadora thought suddenly, guiltily, about her mother – riding the streetcar in her embarrassing clothes, off to screw that grant-sucking homo of a writer. 'I should be getting home,' she said.

'You're not changing your mind on this?'

'I need to think about it some more.'

'Just read the book. Wrap your head around it. You'll get into it.'

'I don't want to read it.'

'Don't go getting put off before we even start! It's not like we're going to be pinning some guy's butt cheeks together our first day. Though I've heard it's been done. And it worked, too. Unbelievable, eh?'

'I said, I'm going to have to think about it.'

'I can't believe what I'm hearing from you,' Francine bristled. 'Excuse me, but your ingratitude is just a little hard to take.'

Isadora looked uneasily towards the glass and steel doors of The Last Millennium.

'Are you going in with me or not?' Francine demanded. 'I need to know now. There's other people interested if you're not.' Her fingernails tapped a pissed-off staccato on the tin table top.

'I guess so. I think so. But you're throwing a lot of stuff at me that I'm not ready for.'

'Okay.' Francine heaved a deep sigh. 'Fine. Take your time. I can wait. We're looking at next summer anyway. We're too late for this year, since we haven't got our financing together. Nobody gets tattoos in winter. We need bare skin season. We need exposure.' She paused. 'I didn't mean to scare you, okay?

I'm just used to seeing this stuff. I keep forgetting you're not. And that you're a lot younger than me.'

'Three years. Big deal.'

'Oh – I brought you some other good stuff to read.' Francine pummelled her knapsack, then dug deep into it to pull out half a dozen paperbacks. *Wait Until Night, Night Stalkers, The Night Visitors*. 'This one, *Night Visitors*? Don't read it when you're alone. You can keep 'em. I don't need 'em back.' She smiled. 'Look, Izzy, I know it's a bit heavy when you first see some of this.' She picked up *Modern Primitives* and wedged it into the top of her knapsack. 'But what's in here will start looking pretty tame when you see what's really going down these days. Not that we'll do it all. We can just stick to basics, okay? At least for a while. Until we get our sea legs. As my dad used to say.'

She dabbed at her lips with a crumpled napkin, took a cadmium-coloured lipstick from an outside pocket of her knapsack and applied it to her lips without the help of a mirror. Incredibly, it went on perfectly straight: a feat that always impressed Isadora. 'If you want to go slow at first,' Francine added, 'that's cool. Whatever you want is okay with me. We are partners, after all. We're in this together. Right?' She waited, frowning. 'Right?'

'Right,' Isadora said, unhappily. 'I guess so.'

8 ∫

Elfriede was in her garden, feeding her roses, when she remembered that she hadn't telephoned Claire. Reluctantly, she took off her cotton gardening gloves and straw hat and placed them on the grass beside the plastic pail of rose-booster that she'd carefully measured and dissolved in warm water.

Elfriede and Basil Wolaniuk owned a side-split house on the outskirts of a small southwestern Ontario town. Even after thirty years, even though the slender saplings had thickened into trees and the sidewalks settled, then buckled, under the passage of thousands of feet, the Wolaniuks' street – a crescent – had a raw and recent feel to it. Most of the children the Wolaniuk girls had played with had grown up and moved away, their parents gone to condominiums in friendlier climates. A bicycle path (thankfully, too narrow for motorcycles) that divided the Wolaniuks' back yard from their neighbour's, connected the crescent to the last busy street on the northern edge of town: a lifeline of human activity without which Basil and Elfriede might have floated forever on their fragile, crescent moon of a street.

A row of blue spruce shaded the lawn; white petunias and pink geraniums were neatly aligned in circular beds positioned to catch maximum sun. Around Elfriede, the buzz of insects had lulled her into a dreamy reflective state. Until she remembered Claire. She hated to leave her garden, even for a minute. That awful winter! Canada was a country for the young, she'd concluded years ago. But she had survived the winter – her seventieth! – and her reward for suffering through the bitter cold, the treacherous driving, the continual fear of breaking her hip on the icy drive and of Basil dropping dead while shovelling snow, were the roses this summer. Mountbatten, Keepsake, Double Delight. Best ever, she thought with pride. And they started so early this year: barely June when the first bloom appeared.

Two of the rose bushes – the most lovely – had been given to Elfriede by her son-in-law, Ben. They had originally been intended as Mother's Day gifts for Claire – each bush to symbolize one of the Cunninghams' children. But Claire had (so distressingly!) wept at the sight of the burlap bags from which the thorny green stalks sprouted. 'Where am I going to find the time for all that obsessive pruning and spraying and fussing?' she'd wailed. 'I don't even have ten minutes to dig a hole to stick them in – and if I did, I'd throw myself into it!'

'Are you on psychotropic drugs?' was all poor Ben had replied, looking frightened. Then he'd tried to give the roses to his mother. They symbolized *her* two children, he'd explained, patiently, over the phone to Prue. One rose bush represented himself, Benjamin, and the other his sister, Elizabeth. Prue, long ago divorced from Ben's father, lived alone in a tidy, self-contained apartment. 'Oh, honestly, Ben,' Elfriede imagined her protesting, 'I'm long past my gardening days. Why not give them to Elfriede? She would love new roses. She's such a wonderful gardener. But I hope you kept the receipt, dear.' Prue would have been glad of the chance to give her son some practical advice. 'If Elfriede doesn't want them, the nursery will surely take them back. Even if they only give you a credit note. You could get something more suitable for Claire. Something potted. Or artificial.'

Elfriede had heard the details of this story many times from her daughter. It was a story that made her sad, despite the pleasure the rose bushes had given her.

As she walked towards the house (her hip had stopped aching as soon as the warm weather arrived), she paused to check on a crack in a patio stone and pull out a clump of crab grass, delaying the moment when she would have to dial Claire's number.

Phoning her daughter every Sunday was an obligation Elfriede had come to dread. She could never call at the right time, it seemed. If Claire wasn't feeding the children, she was sitting on the toilet or in the middle of some work she'd brought home from the office. Every conversation began with Elfriede asking if she was catching her at a bad time and Claire imply-ing (though of course she never said so) that it was always a bad time at the Cunninghams'. There seemed to be no such thing as a good time when it came to talking to her mother.

But if Elfriede didn't call, the situation would be worse. Claire would feel obliged to call *her*, would worry all afternoon that something was wrong. And when she did call, finally, she would demand to know what had happened. Was Dad ill? Had something happened to the house? Then she would sound aggrieved when Elfriede admitted that everything was fine, she just hadn't yet got around to calling. Once, when Basil had been on the Internet for hours, sharing his thoughts with a student in New Zealand and a book-keeper in Missouri, Claire had called the local police, in a panic over a busy signal that went on for too long and the phone company's advice that there was 'trouble on the line'. The police had been very good about it but Claire had been quite upset, having imagined her parents in the basement, bound up with duct tape. Or worse. She'd seemed almost angry when she was finally reassured that, in fact, Basil and Elfriede had never been better.

The Sunday phoning dilemma was a snarl of guilt and obligation that Claire and Elfriede had been tangled up in since Claire left home for university, neither of them willing to say the words that would set them free.

There was no point in asking Basil to do the phoning. He managed to irritate Claire even more than Elfriede did, endlessly quoting long-dead philosophers when what their daughter needed was a sympathetic ear or some sound advice.

Of course, Elfriede had no idea what Claire's life was really like, as Basil often pointed out. It certainly sounded crazy. Two cars, two children, two careers. That girl Francine. And now a big dog. Claire didn't even have time to enjoy the garden of her beautiful new house. She would never learn the trick of pruning roses – snipping off the finished blooms at an angle, just above a five-leaf (not seven, or three) formation – to force out yet more beautiful blooms. It seemed to be no life, really, what her daughter had.

Inside the house, Basil was listening to Wagner – an unpleasant contrast to the serenity of the garden Elfriede had just left. 'I must call Claire,' she said. 'I won't be able to hear unless you turn that down.'

Basil hoisted himself up from the sofa to retrieve the remote control. 'I might as well turn it off altogether. Wagner was not meant to be background music.' He sighed, settled again on the sofa and opened *The Teachings of Krishnamurti*. Lately he'd been dipping a toe into the twentieth-century thinkers and, liking the philosopher he'd read so far, was inspired to try Indian cooking, asking his wife to find a store that sold ghee and garam masala in their town.

'Darling! How wonderful!' Elfriede cried into the telephone after speaking to Claire for a moment.

Since Basil could never find a pair of frames with a nose pad that fitted comfortably, he used a folded tissue under the bridge of his spectacles. The white tissue hung down on either side of his nose, giving him an eccentric appearance. 'She can't manage with the two children she's got,' he grumbled. 'Now she needs a third? And with that monstrous dog?'

'Claire is giving a tea,' Elfriede said proudly, a few minutes later. 'A real ladies' tea. On *my birthday*! It's such a surprise. So hard to believe. Claire! A tea!' If Elfriede had been told that her daughter was pregnant again – as Basil had imagined – she could hardly have been more pleased.

'A tea party.' With an aggrieved look at his wife, Basil settled deeper into his sofa. Elfriede's teas for her art appreciation group had always annoyed him: tiny sandwiches blanketed by damp tea towels in the refrigerator, the house full of chattering women, the way Elfriede was driven mad by the preparations – the house cleaning, the polishing of silver. And the way she drove Basil mad too: pulling him out of his comfortable chair and away from his music and books, dispatching him to the grocer's to return the milk that wasn't quite fresh, making him slice lemons, dust tea cups, fill sugar bowls.

The whole family had suffered in the cause of Elfriede's entertaining. She was not one of those relaxed women who was overjoyed when others dropped in unannounced, who could throw leftovers together for unexpected guests and plunk a plastic bottle of ketchup on the table when condiments were called for. Elfriede cleaned her house before the cleaning woman came, embarrassed that a stranger might discover (and tell the whole town) that the Wolaniuks actually used their toilets.

'She hasn't got a tea service,' Elfriede worried aloud. 'Or a single tablecloth.'

'As Confucius said: "The superior man cannot be known in little matters, but may be entrusted with great concerns".'

'What will she do? Rent tea cups? She doesn't even have spoons.' Elfriede made a series of fretting sounds as her mind reeled off all the things her daughter would need to put on a tea without bringing shame to the Wolaniuk name. She'd done her best to teach Claire and Christine the skills of gracious entertaining, but her daughters had never shown much interest. 'Oh, Mother,' Claire used to complain, 'why do you bother with teas and dinner parties? It only drives everyone crazy, especially you. Just pay someone else to do it, for heaven's sake.'

'Remember poor Mr Fruitman?' Elfriede said, her eyes bright. 'When he had so many people over for tea? He used one bag for all the cups – he kept dipping it from one into the next.' She chortled at a memory she hadn't examined for years. 'And he re-used the bag *after* the milk and sugar had been added. *After*. Poor Mr Fruitman. He was only trying to economize.'

'Yes,' Basil said, 'one can hardly blame him for that.'

But what if Claire did the same thing? Elfriede suddenly thought, her smile fading. Would she know any better? 'How is Claire going to manage?' she said. 'She's already taken on much too much. That big house. The dog.'

'Don't worry, my dear.' Basil turned a page in his book. 'She will find her way. "There is nothing more pleasant than the tie of host and guest." So said Aeschylus.'

'She's asked me to help.' Spots of high colour had appeared on Elfriede's cheeks. She looked blankly at her husband, her mind elsewhere, even her garden forgotten. Suddenly she was needed, pressed into service again. Basil could never be expected to understand.

'Did you ask if she still has that dampness problem?' he said. 'In her basement? I told her – potassium chloride from any drug store. She never listens.'

Elfriede was not listening either. She was on her way to the dining room where she meant to count her tea spoons. That Claire would need them was a certainty. 'Why don't you put some music on?' she said.

'I had music on. You didn't like it.'

'Not Wagner. Put on something cheerful. Mozart. Or Chopin. I've always loved Chopin – so romantic.'

'A lesser light,' Basil muttered. But he shuffled obligingly to his cabinet of compact discs to select something that would please his wife of almost fifty years, the tissue under the bridge of his spectacles fluttering like a white flag.

Claire replaced the telephone receiver, wondering what she'd done. She *would* have to have picked her mother's birthday as the date for the tea! (How could she have forgotten her mother's birthday?) And so, of course, Elfriede was entitled to be a guest of honour. With such excitement had she pointed out that the date of Claire's tea was also that of her seventieth birthday. A milestone for both of them. Claire considered, but didn't mention, the lingerie aspect.

Their conversation ended the way their conversations usually did: Elfriede about to say something, hesitating, then telling Claire, 'I was about to say something, but I'd better not. It seems I always irritate you.'

'Well,' short laugh, 'don't say it then.'

'All right.' (Same short laugh.) 'I'm learning. By the time you're in your seventies and I'm almost a hundred, we'll understand each other.'

'No, we just won't be able to hear each other.'

'What a blessing.'

'A mercy.'

They shared a final, brief mother-daughter laugh, but it was not without a tinge of disappointment on both sides.

The Complication

9

The small private plane that was to have taken Rick Durham, Pete Johnson, Ross Owen and Sandy Krupnik to Boston was a Beech Turbo Baron. It had twin engines and two propellers. One of its propellers was eventually pulled out of the sludge at the bottom of Lake Ontario and, later, part of a wing. Not much else would ever be recovered.

> ## LAWYERS FIND DAVY JONES LOCKER!
> ## LAW FIRM PLUMMETS INTO LAKE!

screamed two of the evening papers' headlines.

'I was getting ready to go out,' a shaken Shelagh told the young television reporter. 'I wasn't going to bother answering the phone – I was running late as it was – but there was something in the way it was ringing . . . I somehow *knew* it was urgent. One of my clients, I suppose I thought . . . Or some family problem. But I never expected the *police*.' She'd looked steadily into the reporter's eyes, determined to get through the interview without satisfying the nation's lust for *schadenfreude*. She was also determined that no one would ever know what she'd really been doing when the police called: lying on her chesterfield, wearing her ugliest and most comforting flannelette pyjamas, eating Häagen-Dazs straight from the carton and watching an old edition (taped) of *Geraldo: Star-Crossed Cross Dressers*. (Chris is a woman, dressed as a man, who goes out in drag; Pat is a woman, who used to be a man, whose lover is a man who is undergoing a sex change but is about to change his mind and tell us why . . .) A wet cloth was draped across her forehead and she was thinking again that probably she had a brain tumour, the throbbing in her temples was so severe.

The night before, she and Ross had had a tedious debate about whether he should go to Boston. In the first place, he was no jock, he said, and didn't give a fig about baseball. Second, he liked all of his ties, didn't think any of them were particularly ugly, and had no desire to give even one of them away. But the best reason for staying in Toronto was that he could spend the entire weekend with Shelagh. They could finally talk things out – really talk. It was a perfect opportunity, especially as he had a ten-day business trip coming up after that. Of course, he and Shelagh wouldn't be able to go out anywhere . . . He'd never told Marcia who the 'other woman' was, and if they ran into her on some downtown street while Ross was supposed to be in Boston (and, more to the point, avoiding his child-care responsibilities), it could be – well, unpleasant for everyone.

Rage had flared up inside Shelagh like a pan of forgotten grease under a broiler. Stay in her condo all weekend and *talk*? Like two convicts, two mental patients? Not even able to go out for cigarettes without wearing fedoras and mirrored sunglasses? And then Ross (his guilt operating on several levels) would make her put on the pleated chef's hat and paddle his bum with a spatula while they waited for a delivery of order-in food. Her response to his offer to 'stay in' with her for the weekend had been barely articulate, and not very polite. Besides, she told him, Rick would kill him if he didn't go. Out of only six seats, there was one reserved for him on that private plane; it was an honour. Why would he want to piss off their Managing Partner? And insult a major client while he was at it? But she might as well have saved her breath for the pack of cigarettes she would smoke when Ross finally left.

'If I go to Boston it's because *you* don't want me *here*. Not because of Rick bloody Durham!' In her mind, Shelagh could still hear Ross's footsteps clanging down the emergency exit stairs in her building, then see him climbing into his Pathfinder in the guest parking lot, shortly after that remark. The belt of his trench coat had got trapped in the Pathfinder's door as he slammed it shut, and it trailed on the road, like an obedient pet, as the jeep disappeared down King Street.

By the time the police called on Saturday afternoon, however, she was panicking about the empty weekend ahead of her and had leaped to answer the phone, overjoyed that Ross might have changed his mind and decided to stay home after all. She *would* wear the chef's hat, the school-teacher glasses; she would even come up with some exciting new humiliations for him; and she'd been dying for Ho-Lee-Chow order-in food. Had she forgotten to mention that?

'The business and legal community has reacted with predictable shock to the devastating loss of four brilliant legal minds,' the reporter had said, clipping a small microphone on to the lapel of Shelagh's bathrobe. 'Apart from your own personal reaction of obvious grief, can you tell us what effect you think this tragedy will have on Bay Street?'

Shelagh accepted the tissue someone pressed into her hand. 'How can I answer that? I can't even deal with this myself . . . I can't really think . . .'

'Would you expect it to make people take a step back, take a long look at their lifestyles? Lawyers especially?' The reporter's eyes had urged her to agree.

'I suppose so . . . We all work much too hard.' (LOOK HARD AT YOUR LIFESTYLE, SOBBING LAWYER WARNS.) Passers-by gawked at the camera crews and mobile units clogging the circular drive of Shelagh's building and at Shelagh, shivering in her bathrobe under the glare of the mobile unit's lights. The afternoon had just been cooled by a flash thunderstorm, complete with hail, which had compounded the problems faced by police divers out on the lake. 'I'd like to see lawyers spend more time with their families,' she finally said, trying not to think about Ross at that moment, hoping to avoid a meltdown on national TV.

'There's been very little found, so far, of the plane, and the search continues for the bodies. The divers found the site only because of an oil slick on the water.'

'An oil slick . . .'

'Sorry,' the reporter looked embarrassed, listening intently to something coming through his ear-piece. 'I believe that was a gasoline slick. My apologies.'

Shelagh had sighed, looking directly into camera one as she'd been instructed. *Don't* think about Ross. Don't. She squeezed the tissue into a tight ball.

'And it's too early to say whether the police have ruled out foul play.' The reporter paused then, waiting for Shelagh's reaction.

'Foul play?'

'But let's talk for a moment – and we really appreciate your giving this interview – the shock must be devastating – but let's talk about your law firm. Bragg, Banks and Belmore . . .'

'Biltmore.'

'Do you think your firm will be able to recover from this tragedy? In terms of the numbers, I mean. It's a small firm, I understand. Four lawyers must make a pretty big dent in the bottom line. Would that be fair to say?'

Shelagh lifted her chin to face the nation. 'We've survived a lot, our firm. It's over a hundred years old. There are many fine lawyers left. We will come through this. You can be sure of that.'

'Did you know the two businessmen on board? One of them was believed to be the pilot – and a client of Bragg, Banks and Biltmore.'

'Yes. They were both clients of the firm – that's all I can tell you. Look, I can't talk any more. Please. Get these cameras away from me.' (GET OUT OF MY FACE! HYSTERICAL LAWYER SCREAMS AT TV CREW.) She'd yanked the microphone off her bathrobe (whose *was* it?) and, turning her back on the reporter, promptly tripped over a snarl of cables and wires. Then someone was taking her arm, helping her to her feet and towards the front doors of her building.

'Dan!' She'd blinked up at him over the wadded tissue she had pressed to her nose. 'What are you doing here?'

'I was in the neighbourhood. I thought you could use a shoulder.'

'Excuse me.' The reporter was pursuing them, shoving the microphone at Dan. 'Are you also with Bragg, Banks and Biltmore?'

'Yes, but I'm not talking. Except to my partner here.' He eased Shelagh out of the path of the reporter, encouraging her to lean against him, and they shuffled awkwardly towards the doors of the condo complex.

'I don't know what to do,' she moaned, 'I can't get hold of anyone – not Claire, not Gillian. I was the first person the police called. After the families.' She blew her nose and shoved the sodden tissue into the pocket of the bathrobe. 'Thank you for coming, Dan. Oh, look at me! I should have put on something else. Here I am on national TV, in some man's bathrobe. I was just getting ready to go out when the cops called. My dear God –' she pulled out the balled-up tissue again and pressed it into first one eye, then the other '– how are we ever going to get through this?' She clutched Dan's arm as a camera flash popped in her face.

'I'm not sure,' he said.

The building's doorman pulled open the door for them and tipped his cap with a sympathetic smile. He would later give a series of exclusive interviews to a local tabloid, beginning with: LAW FIRM CAN'T SURVIVE! REMAINING LAWYERS AGREE IN CLANDESTINE MEETING.

'You seem much taller,' Shelagh mumbled into Dan's shoulder as they traversed the lobby. 'Up close.'

'Could we go up to your place for a while? I could use a drink.'

'Yes, yes! I don't know how I'm going to make it through the night. Thank God you're here. You absolutely can't leave me now.' (LAWYER ADMITS TO NIGHT TERRORS FOLLOWING FATAL CRASH.) 'What about Alex? Has he heard?'

'Yes. He's hiding out somewhere with Anna. Poor you. You were the only one the media could get hold of.'

'And they were lucky – I was about to go out, as I was telling you.'

'Yes, you mentioned that. Let's get upstairs.'

SURVIVING LAWYERS IN SECRET MIDNIGHT TRYST!

Claire never did hear Shelagh's messages on her answering machine. At the exact time of the crash, she would later calculate, she'd been standing in the playground of a neighbourhood park, trying to keep a fix on Molly who often vanished, with heart-stopping speed, behind pieces of playground equipment, while Harry hung upside down from a spidery network of cables and ropes and yelled: 'What is your will, Oh Evil One?' at Prue, who was sitting in the shade of an enormous leafy elm, reading her library book.

Ben was at the hospital. Though not technically 'on call', he'd gone in to do a consult on a big case – a favour to one of the other surgeons. He would do the case too, in all likelihood, if it was necessary. He had no idea when he'd be back. He'd dug through their untidy clothes closet, searching for a clean set of surgical greens, complaining that no one seemed to do any laundry around there. Claire had nothing planned for entertaining the kids; she'd been counting on Ben to take them for at least a couple of hours. She'd had a hectic week; she needed a break.

She'd leaped out of bed and called the apartment where Francine lived with a fluctuating rabble of roommates, prepared to beg, grovel, whatever it took to persuade her to babysit for a few hours. 'Hi!' Francine's voice cheerfully answered. 'You've reached the nut house. Chief cashew here. We're not home right now but your call is *crucial* to us.' Claire didn't bother to leave a message: by the time Francine got out of bed the day would be over anyway.

'Take the kids somewhere,' Ben said, through his open window, as he backed his car out of the garage (there not being enough time to rollerblade to the hospital). 'Get out and do something with them. It makes the day go a lot faster.'

Claire had stood on the front lawn, still in her nightgown, and watched his car disappear around the corner of their street. From behind the front-door screen, Harry and Molly watched too. The neighbourhood was silent apart from the heavy-artillery in-ground lawn sprinklers that spun and rotated and fired in carefully randomized directions. Most of the neighbours were away, as they were every weekend in summer, as if the prestigious, tree-lined street with its grand ivy-covered houses was something to be escaped from as often as possible.

At Claire's pleading, Prue had reluctantly agreed to help out for a while. She arrived wearing the cantaloupe-coloured jumpsuit she'd worn often over eight consecutive summers: it was faded but clean and freshly-ironed. She had a library book under her arm: *The Bachelor Brothers' Bed & Breakfast*, an account of the titillating tribulations of two men who ran a country inn. Her page was marked by a crewel-embroidery bookmark she'd made in high school. Claire had banned library books from the house because of the number Francine had taken out for the kids and on which large fines had accumulated, or which had simply vanished and had to be paid for. Prue never forgot when her library books were due; she noted the dates on a kitchen wall calendar that also had on it such entries as: 'Lunch, Tuesday – use up hard-boiled egg' and the details of every long-distance call she ever made.

After half an hour in the park, storm clouds had started to gather, rolling in sudden and black off the lake. Claire and Prue quickly gathered up the children, their sand toys and Molly's stroller, and made a dash for the car. As huge leaden drops began to plunk down on to them, Claire installed both kids in their car seats, then turned to tackle the stroller. It was supposed to collapse easily into a compact umbrella shape but Claire had never been able to bend it to her will. The mechanism on it was too complicated: it was either pull up (or press down) on the red latch, at the same time as you squeezed (or pulled apart) the handle release, after which you collapsed (or lifted) the rear axle with your foot.

After several futile efforts, she finally tried to force the thing, still relentlessly maintaining its perky open position, into the trunk. She was soaked through, her clothes translucent, and the trunk lid would not close over the stroller. She swore profusely, doing a small dance of rage on the sidewalk, as Prue smiled encouragingly, waved, and gave a small shrug of helplessness from the front seat of the car.

'I'm sorry, dear,' she said as Claire, her chest heaving, threw herself into the driver's seat and slammed shut the door. 'I have no idea how to manage these expensive imported strollers. Children's things are so different from when Ben and Lizzie were babies.' Prue's library book, fortunately, had stayed nice and dry. 'It must feel wonderful to be able to let it all *hang out* the way you did just then,' she added. 'Makes me realize how repressed our side of the family is.'

The rain soon turned to hail and the four of them sat there

– Claire steaming – waiting for it to stop. The children squealed with delighted terror and asked intelligent questions about hail which neither Claire nor Prue could adequately answer.

'I can't drive in this,' Claire concluded, after five minutes, there being no indication that the storm was about to let up.

'Of course you can't, dear.' Prue opened her book.

In the back seat, Harry and Molly had grown restless and started slapping each other for amusement. Molly, as usual, got the worst of it and was soon screaming, kicking the back of Claire's seat, wailing that her mother didn't care about her or love her any more.

'Dears,' Prue said, replacing her bookmark and placing the book on the dashboard, before turning to kneel on her seat and address her grandchildren. 'Why don't we sing something while we wait for the storm to end? Do you know "Daisy, Daisy"?'

Harry leaned over and pounded Molly in the arm as Prue clapped her hands. '"Oh, you'll look sweet, upon the seat of a bicycle built for two!"' she sang.

Claire closed her eyes.

When the storm was over, Prue stepped out of the car, nimbly avoiding a puddle on the road and, hands on hips, said: 'Now let's see if we can't use the logical approach on this obstinate stroller.' And, of course, proceeded to do exactly that.

Wordlessly, Claire drove across town towards her mother-in-law's apartment. 'What will the three of you do now?' Prue asked.

'I'll take them somewhere else. As soon as I get some dry clothes on.'

'But they've had the whole morning in the park. Why not just stay home? Let them play in their own garden for a while, with the dog. The rain has stopped, it's clearing up quite nicely. All they need is their rubber boots.'

'They're at home all week. We like to show them a good time on the weekend.'

'But I'm sure Francine takes them out a lot. She seems like such an energetic young woman. Why do parents today think children need a mad rushing roller-coaster of fun all the time? Good heavens!'

'Can we go on a roller-coaster?' Molly demanded, checking a sob.

'See what you started?' Claire gave her mother-in-law a look.

'I did not start anything. Don't be silly.'

'A roller-coaster! A roller-coaster!' cried Molly.

'You don't need a roller-coaster, Molly.' Prue turned around in her seat again. 'Ask your mummy to take you home so you can listen to some nice music, or a story on tape. Gosh, I can still remember your daddy wearing those little pyjamas with feet . . . What do you call them?'

'Sleepers,' Claire sighed.

'And sitting in his rocking chair – for hours and hours – just rocking and listening to records of Maurice Evans reading *Winnie the Pooh*.' She looked wistfully through the windshield, hugging *The Bachelor Brothers* to her.

'What's a record?' asked Harry.

'Where's the roller-coaster?' Molly demanded.

After dropping Prue off, Claire drove back across the city to stop in at the house and change before taking the children to L'il Monkeys indoor playground, then to an animal farm (mud, no boots), McDonald's and a video-rental place where Harry picked all the coloured identification tags off the shelves and the manager finally asked them to leave.

It wasn't until after the kids' supper, baths, an unsuccessful (sub-titled) *Adventures of Tin-Tin* video (Prue's recommendation) and five bedtime stories – shortly before ten – that Claire noticed the light on her answering machine. Shelagh had actually left three messages by then: two before the camera crews arrived; one after. But before Claire could rewind the tape to hear them, Molly had fallen out of bed and Claire had sprung to her rescue. A moment later, Harry threw up his Happy Meal and Cannon bayed at the back door to be let in from the yard where, it was later discovered, he'd suffered a serious bout of diarrhoea.

In the end, it was Elfriede who got hold of Claire. She'd heard about the crash on the radio and had been trying all afternoon to reach her. She never liked to bother Claire with messages on her machine. Maybe it would have been better to wait till Sunday, when she made her usual call. But anyway . . . they were talking now, weren't they? It was such a tragedy. Horrible, just horrible. How could a plane simply plunge into the lake? It was a ball of flame, they said. Like Hiroshima. How could such a thing happen? And, she and Claire's dad were worrying, with all those lawyers from Claire's firm dead, was Claire going to lose her job? And what about the one who was getting married in October? Had he been killed too? Was Claire still having the lingerie tea? And, she'd been meaning to ask Claire – had she invited Prue to the tea?

Claire tried to call Shelagh but the line was busy, and there was no answer at Gillian's house. She turned on the radio and both televisions, tuning in different channels on each. In a daze, she wandered through the house, picking up balled-up socks, scented plastic ponies with glittering manes and tails, miniature gargoyles. Finally, at a loss, she got into bed beside Harry and snuggled up against him, one arm around his firm round belly as it gently expanded and contracted. Staring at the wallpaper in the dim light from his night light – the paper was patterned with planes and helicopters – she lay there straining to hear the soothing sound of Ben's car engine over the patter of rain that had suddenly started up again.

Gillian's morning had begun well enough. Isadora was off to a friend's place for the weekend, leaving her with a smorgasbord of uninterrupted time to get a good start on her new novel. But first she'd gone out for a jumbo *cafe latte* and read the book reviews in all the weekend papers. Satisfied that her new one would be far superior to any of those reviewed she'd returned to Sidney Street and made a cheese sandwich for lunch, thinking to keep it in the fridge so as not to waste time preparing it later, when she was deep in the creative process.

While searching for some Dijon mustard she realized that chaos and filth were what was most readily found in her kitchen cupboards. They would soon have cockroaches or rats. She had no choice but to take prophylactic cleaning action immediately.

The first time the phone twittered, Gillian had her nose in a bag of dusty brown leaves that were either ancient oregano or marijuana left over from the seventies. Whatever it was, she had managed to live without using it for a couple of decades. She dropped it into the garbage.

The next time she heard the phone, she'd been trying to get a grip on a slippery mass of rotting onions in a pool of sludge under the kitchen sink. It would be B.M. calling, she supposed, but she was in no mood for the parade of homes he'd recently decided was so *amusant*. Just because he was 'in between books' and had nothing better to do was no reason he should expect to make inroads into her precious creative time.

While she was under the sink, she noticed a slow leak just above the u-bend. The last person to do anything major to the plumbing in the house had been Jerry.

Dear sweet incompetent Jerry, she thought, a few minutes later in the basement, pushing aside skis, winter clothing, and dust-covered cartons of Christmas ornaments, trying to locate the tool box.

Back in the kitchen (twenty minutes with a pipe wrench and a pair of pliers) Gillian finally gave up on the leak. The cupboards! She hadn't finished that job and here she was starting on another. Out came all the food and dishes, off went the stained and crusty vinyl-backed shelf paper. By the time she'd scrubbed and re-papered the shelves (forty minutes to Wal-Mart and back for the paper), organized the dishes and replaced the boxes, cans and jars of food (in alphabetical order), it was half-past three. Far too much time had been spent puzzling over the food organization, she concluded. Lasagna noodles, for example, weren't clearly destined to be shelved with the L's. Perhaps they should be put under P, for 'pasta'. After much pondering, she'd finally decided to alphabetize general categories, and then sub-categorize within them. Bow-tie macaroni was now stored near the far right of the Pasta section (she resisted the desire to create a general sub-category called 'macaroni'), while Lasagna was somewhere near the middle.

It was her obsessive need for organization and precision that had drawn her to the life of a patent lawyer, she reflected morosely; and that same obsessive compulsiveness was now killing her as a writer. It was what made her interested in prosaic types like dentists and their equipment; it was what led her to write about the procedures they performed with painstaking, reader-losing detail. She should have taken up something like philately as a hobby, with its endless categorizing and sub-categorizing; its debates that spanned decades and over which tweedy old men in Argyle sweaters became impassioned, even apoplectic: *was* that a water mark or a pimple on the jowl of George V on the 3-P English issue?

Well, she sighed, whatever she'd done with her day, it was now too late to do much by way of creative writing about dentists or stamp-collecting or anything else.

She changed into a printed chiffon mini-dress, a denim bomber jacket with SAVE THE PLANET embroidered across the back, switched on her telephone answering machine, and took the street car to her favourite book store on Queen Street West where she bought a selection of books on writing: *Use That Writers' Block!*, *What Happened Next?* (all about plotting and structure) and *You Too Can Write A Bestseller!* Then she wandered back along Queen, gazing in the store windows. She'd paused in front of a favourite shop, but was dismayed by what she saw inside. Sanded and stained oak floors, knotty pine cupboards full of silk-screened cushions, reproduction Fiestaware, and sweaters hand-knitted by exploited Bolivians had replaced the fabulously tasteless window art of chains, raw meat and black leather that had been there only weeks before. Gillian looked around her, appalled and frightened. The street was becoming a strip mall, a galleria. Her *mother* would love it!

The real artists, with whatever unique and interesting *objets* they had to sell, must have rushed off to some undisclosed location, leaving faintly ridiculous middle-aged lawyers like Gillian to spend their money in more conventional ways, on more conventional things. Like shelf paper from Wal-Mart.

Her spirits spiralling downwards and her Doc Martens about as comfortable as a pair of cement blocks, she clumped on to an eastbound street car, missing by seconds the first raindrops of a sudden storm. She'd wasted her day cleaning cupboards and thrown away a pile of money on stupid how-to-write books.

She felt a surge of self-loathing as hail, loud as machine-gun fire, pounded on the metal roof of the street car. None of those self-help writing books were written by anyone she'd ever heard of. They were all people like her – losers who couldn't get their novels published.

Dumping her bag on the front hall table, she wrestled impatiently with her boot laces, eager to get to the telephone where the message light was flashing. God! She would gladly talk to anyone right now, she thought, even a computerized sales pitch.

The first message was the only one she heard, as it turned out. It was from B.M.'s literary agent, telling her to come and pick up the manuscript for *At Whit's End* since she didn't have room to store it and honestly couldn't think of a publisher who would find it right for their list. Gillian could perhaps try some of the small presses – but she didn't need an *agent* for that. And if Gillian couldn't pop by to get her manuscript (the agent's voice had risen by this point), well, *At Whit's End* would simply be thrown out. The agent had a small apartment. Storage space was a big problem.

Gillian was amazed by the woman's rancour. Nobody had forced her to take on *At Whit's End*. And, as the agent and B.M. 'went back a long way', she'd supposedly been delighted to have a look at his friend's book. Gillian pushed the Erase button on her machine, deleting the bad-tempered message and, accidentally, whatever else was on the tape. She could guess what those other calls were anyway: silly messages from B.M. that he imagined to be witty, a recorded tantrum of Isadora's, demanding to know why her bank card no longer accessed Gillian's accounts – all messages she could live without hearing.

She took a bottle of tequila from the gleaming, freshly lined cupboard above the fridge, grabbed a glass and flopped down on to the couch. So. Here she was, still with half a weekend to spend however she liked. She could drink, for example. Wasn't that what writers were supposed to do? But how did they ever get any writing done, those famous literary lushes? After two glasses of *vin ordinaire* Gillian's fingers would slip off the keyboard, her mild dyslexia becoming pronounced. And why was it only male writers who drank? She tried, unsuccessfully, to think of a famous woman novelist who was known to be a serious tippler. Most likely, they just didn't talk about it, slipping their flasks out of their décolletages up in their boudoirs.

An hour later, she was still sulking about small presses, her hapless dentist-hero and *At Whit's End*. And, by the time Shelagh reached her, at half-past eleven, Gillian was completely zonked. She grappled for the phone and, upon answering it, was jolted unpleasantly by the realization that someone had popped up in an area of her life where that person had no business being. To what realm of her existence did this disembodied voice belong? This edgy voice complaining that she'd been trying to get hold of Gillian all day?

'It's me.' Pause. 'Shelagh.' Pause. 'Your law partner.'

'You sound funny.'

'Spending the day with cops and reporters will do that to a girl.'

'You've been arrested?' Gillian perked up a little.

'Of course not! Haven't you been watching the news?'

'I never watch the news.'

Gillian could hear Shelagh drawing on a cigarette. 'So, are you sitting down?'

'Lying down. Prone. Unless prone means face down. Which I'm not. Yet.'

'Listen to me, will you? I've got some bad news. Worse than that. Something *devastating*. So tragic –'

'Let me guess . . . it looks like the Jays are gonna throw the World Series?'

'You're drunk.'

'What if I am? It's Saturday – I'm entitled. And I've got to get to bed. I've had a hard day.' Gillian's eyelids drooped. She yawned hugely.

'Listen to me, you fool! You and Claire and I have just become senior partners of Bragg, Banks and Biltmore!' Shelagh waited. 'Are you too much in the jar to understand what I'm telling you? They're dead! Rick, Pete, Sandy and Ross! They've crashed and burned. They never got to Boston. Gillian? Are you still there? Gillian!'

The telephone receiver dropped from Gillian's hand and clunked to the floor. A second later, the tequila glass rolled under the couch where it would remain, home to a dozen dust bunnies, for over a year.

10 ∫

There were three general reasons for holding an inquest. First was to get answers to questions that needed answering. Then there was the community interest – the public's right to know. The third was to obtain recommendations to prevent similar disasters in future. No one argued that an inquest was needed for the Bragg, Banks and Biltmore lawyers, for all three reasons. But even after a four-day hearing, the jury could not say for sure what had made the Beech Baron Turbo plunge into the lake. How were they supposed to conclude anything without physical evidence? There was virtually nothing left of the plane: tiny parts of the control panel (the non-metallic bits), a section of one wing and a single propeller blade. As for the bodies of the four lawyers and the two other men on board, forensic experts agreed that any fragments of the corpses would have bobbed to the surface of the lake and been snapped up by gulls before the search and rescue attempts (made hazardous by the flash summer storm) even got started. The life jackets were also found, floaty bits of a white styrofoam beer cooler, Rick's snazzy waterproof watch, shards of plastic drinking cups . . . None of it of any use.

The best the jury could do was blame the crash on a combination of human error and poor visibility: the usual reasons that small planes crashed. It had been a gloomy morning, with dense clouds squatting low over the lake and a wind rising from the east. The owner and pilot of the Beech Baron Turbo, Bert King – a corporate client of Bragg, Banks and Biltmore – was a loud aggressive type who liked to tell macho stories about near brushes with death while out in the plane: running out of fuel in thunderstorms, flying upside down through fog.

Claire, sitting in the observers' gallery at the inquest, could imagine Bert chuckling as he overloaded the plane with cases of beer, thinking about how he was going to give the four lawyers the scare of their lives. 'All these brewskies better be downed by Boston!' he would have yelled into the wind that whipped across the lake. He would have been half pissed already, had likely been out drinking most of the night before. No one would have challenged Bert, or pointed out that he was in no shape to control a plane. 'The boys' would only have expressed their eagerness to get the Boston Tie Party 'off the ground' or 'to a flying start'. Except for Ross Owen, perhaps. He might have hung back, trying to light a cigarette in the wind and wondering how he could sneak away and on to the ferry to take him back to the city. And Shelagh.

While the Beech Baron Turbo was capable of carrying six, four was the recommended maximum. Bert's co-pilot, another client of the firm, was even less experienced than Bert. They would have ignored the storm warnings coming in at 119.3 megahertz from Pearson International. 'Bunch of wimpy fags,' would have been Bert's opinion of the air traffic controllers. Within thirty seconds of take-off, his drink-sodden brain would have gone into over-drive as the plane shot into dense cloud cover, and Bert's spatial orientation was lost. Without a competent co-pilot, he must have panicked, and become incapable of pulling the plane back on course.

The jury estimated that, spinning downwards, the Beech Baron Turbo hit the lake surface at around 300 miles per hour. And that the six on board were dead within a few seconds of that.

Everyone came away from the inquest unsatisfied. Some new regulations about small-plane safety and improved take-off procedures from the island airport would be put into place, but that was little consolation to the families, friends and law firm left bobbing around in the wreckage.

The relatives of the dead lawyers had organized private funerals, but Alexander Spears, on behalf of Bragg, Banks and Biltmore, arranged for the public memorial service to be held at Metropolitan United Church.

'Choose comfortable shoes. You may be on your feet for a long time today, talking with other mourners . . .' advised *The Survivor's Guide*, a book Claire started reading the day before the service. 'If your eyes are red and swollen from crying or lack of sleep, dab some witch hazel on to cotton wool and apply gently . . . Pack extra tissues in your bag . . .' If she'd managed to read through to the end of the chapter, she would have come to: 'Be sure there is enough gas in all the cars that will be used today.' That might have made her think about having the car cleaned as well, but she'd been interrupted by a call from her father, wanting directions to the church. After taking what Claire thought was an excessively long time to comprehend the location of Metropolitan United, Basil said: ' "There is life only in death. Then death is as life." ' He paused. 'He was a great man, Krishnamurti. I'll bring one of his books for you. His thoughts on death are very profound.'

Claire thanked him for the words of solace – at least, she presumed that's what they were – and invited her parents to come back to the house with her after the service. Then Francine stomped in through the front door, looking sulky and put-upon, obviously peeved at having to work on a Saturday, and dumped her heavy knapsack on the floor. Then Cannon came snarling up from the basement and the children burst, laughing and shouting, out of their rooms to greet Francine.

Claire, Shelagh and Gillian were late for the service. It was Claire's fault, for failing to anticipate the snarl of traffic and then compounding the problem by running out of gas. At least, that was Shelagh's opinion, and she would express it often during the days and weeks that followed.

Claire had offered to do the driving, wanting the others to accompany her. They would need each other for moral support, she'd said; this was a time to stick together, put aside their minor differences. Not that they had any. Not that any of them wouldn't otherwise be put aside.

Gillian, who didn't drive, readily accepted the offer and Shelagh, who mentally calculated the cost of parking and the annoyance of driving around the downtown area on a summer Saturday afternoon, accepted as well.

'Will you look at this?' Shelagh said as they chugged, for the third time, around the church in Claire's car. She was still in a relatively good mood then. 'This is some turn-out, isn't it? I'd never get a crush like this for my funeral.'

'There are *four* dead people here, not just one,' Claire reminded her, thinking that Shelagh could find something to envy just about anywhere.

A carnival atmosphere prevailed in the streets, and the traffic was knotted up for at least a quarter of a mile in all directions. Although Metropolitan United was a magnificent edifice, its location was not the best. A number of pawn-shops with broken neon signs fought for space on one of the bordering streets; ancient, grotty St Michael's Hospital (where Ben had almost taken a job) hulked along another. Transients, rolled in filthy blankets, slept on the edges of the church's tidy lawns, its flower beds overflowing with sweet alyssum, marigolds, cigarette butts and condoms.

As Claire turned the car into its fourth circle and watched the church once again recede in her rear-view, she realized that parking anywhere near it was going to be impossible. The service was scheduled to start at 4 p.m. In exactly three minutes.

'What were you planning to use for a parking spot?' Shelagh finally asked.

'I don't know.'

'Jesus Christ, Claire – it's already four o'clock.'

'We've still got three minutes. Your watch is fast.'

'She's doing her best,' Gillian said.

'We need a contingency plan.' Shelagh's well-manicured nails dug into the car's upholstery as she leaned forward to berate Claire from the back seat.

'We'll make it. Or I could let you both out here. Then all of us won't have to be late.'

'No,' Gillian said. 'We should stick together. You were right, Claire. We're going to need each other.' She was toying nervously with the edge of her hat that was perched, like some large nesting bird, on her lap. It was made of black lacquered straw – an elaborate structure called a cartwheel – and its very broad brim had peekaboo vents cut into it. She'd bought it at a used clothing store called Second Hand Rose. The hat smelled faintly of dog.

Gillian was, of necessity, used to suffering the driving habits of others, and believed she had no business complaining when someone was being good enough to give her a lift, but really, she thought, she would have made better time if she'd walked all the way from Sidney Street. And it would certainly have been less stressful. Not to mention cooler. For some reason, Claire had not had air conditioning installed in her car.

'Christ, it's hot in here,' Shelagh complained as the traffic suddenly cleared and Claire accelerated, feeling a rush of optimism. Then, abruptly, they were forced to stop again. Six long blocks north of Metropolitan United, Claire's gas tank finally ran dry. There was no choice but to park the car – a tow-away zone was the only spot she could find – and walk. Shelagh, in particular, did not accept this gracefully.

'Are you going to swear like that all the way to the church?' Gillian asked her, slamming shut the car door. 'Because if you are, I'm not walking with you.'

'Never mind about me. You've got all you can manage with that hat of yours.' Shelagh slammed her door too. 'And I sure am glad I brought along a Shower-in-a-Sack today!'

Gillian gasped, turned, and marched away down the sidewalk, the brim of her cartwheel hat trembling with anger.

'Shelagh! How could you?' Claire demanded. 'Her father's only been dead for two years!'

'I know, I know. I'm a hideous bitch. What can I say? Hey, Gillian! Wait up! I didn't mean that. I don't even use – *that product*. Never have. I was just mad at Claire and I took it out on you.'

Feeling terribly guilty, Claire walked behind them in silence, clutching her bag to her as if prepared to fend off a physical assault. Her black georgette, bias-cut skirt swirled around her ankles, making walking irritating and hazardous. And by the time they reached the church, she could feel the sharp pinch of a blister on one of her heels, despite the 'comfortable shoes' she'd chosen to wear.

Beside her, Gillian's face was red from rage, the heat and the brisk pace of the walk. Perspiration trickled down her temples and had formed tiny rivulets in the foundation on her upper lip. And Shelagh, Claire saw with dismay, had a melted M&M

chocolate candy smeared across the back of her navy and white silk dress, courtesy of Harry or Molly. She didn't feel like drawing it to Shelagh's attention just then.

'Look,' Claire said, when they were at last climbing the wide stone steps of Metropolitan United, 'I'm sorry, you two – about everything. I meant to get the tank filled yesterday, and have the car cleaned. It just slipped my mind, like most things.'

Neither of the others said anything to make her feel better. Gillian was mentally cursing both Claire and Shelagh, at the same time flooded with sorrow for her father, and wishing for nothing more than a long boozy drink with lots of ice. Shelagh's brain, on the other hand, was completely occupied, working through a detailed plan to murder Claire that had crystallized within seconds of her discovering the M&M smear on her backside.

Six blocks behind them, a tow-truck operator whistled cheerfully as he put the hook on the front bumper of Claire's car.

11

After the bright blast furnace of the August afternoon, Shelagh, Gillian and Claire were momentarily blinded by the dimness inside the ancient cathedral. What a sight they must be, Shelagh thought: stumbling in, squinting like the three blind mice, hot, rumpled and bedraggled. They had to look like a row of demented bridesmaids, unsure of whose wedding they were attending. And that disgraceful car! Vile sticky stuff on the floor, the seats crunchy with crumbs, windows foggy with fingerprints, that melted chocolate that had *ruined* her dress. Surely common decency dictated the cleaning of one's car for the funeral of one's partners? It wasn't something that could ever (forgivably) 'slip one's mind'.

'Amazing Grace' was piping softly through the great organ and all heads turned to watch their entrance. It was obvious, Claire realized, that the service had been delayed to accommodate them: everyone else in the packed church was already seated; the guest book in the foyer already closed.

The first rows of pews were reserved for the lawyers of the firm and the families of the deceased. Alexander Spears sat in the front, by the aisle. With him was Dan Chatwell. Anna sat between them.

Claire slid into the pew, juddering in along the wooden bench to take her place beside Dan. His eyes were closed, his head tilted back; he seemed to be praying. So did Alexander. It struck Claire, suddenly, how alike they were: same well-cut suits, edgy hair cuts and sharp corporate profiles. Dan would be giving the eulogy on behalf of the firm; all the surviving partners had agreed. He had wanted to do it, and no one had felt like arguing. He opened his eyes, gave Claire a sorrowful smile and touched her, briefly, on the arm. Alexander had his hand on Anna's thigh and didn't acknowledge the late arrival of his three women partners.

Taking a deep breath, Claire pulled a tissue from her handbag then dabbed at the perspiration on her upper lip. The church was gratifyingly full. That had to be some comfort to the families. Many of the firm's clients were there, and lawyers from other firms. She recognized several Supreme and High Court justices too.

At the front of the church, positioned among sprays of white lilies and yellow gladioli, were portraits of the dead lawyers. Their painted expressions were stern but sincere – lawyerly in the traditional sense. What handsome, successful men they'd been, Claire thought. What an incalculable loss to their families, friends and, yes, the law. The portraits had been done from photographs – Alexander's idea. An elegant gesture. But it was a shock, being confronted with the faces of the four men. Claire had been trying for days to remember – really remember – what they'd looked like. Though she'd seen them practically every day at work, she somehow hadn't been able to picture any of them accurately in her mind. A flush spread over her face as she dug her fingernails into the palms of her hand and swallowed. Her jaw ached. Crying was allowed, she reminded herself, but once she started, there'd be no stopping her. And she was sure to get everyone else going as well. Buck up, she told herself. No one had more right to cry than the families, and they were holding steady. They'd had to go through the funerals as well.

But Clarie couldn't look at the children. She hoped none of them was going to speak as part of the service. She wouldn't be able to bear it: the clear innocent voice, the sweet face of a child – like Harry's, like Molly's – who would never see his or her daddy again. She would dissolve into a helpless weeping mess on the floor; the caretaker would have to mop her up at the end of the service.

Gillian kept her eyes down, not able to look at anyone at all for the time being. The cavernous church, the enormous crowd, the heavy scent of the lilies, Shelagh's cruel reference to the thing that had killed Gillian's father, all had given her a strong sense of her own mortality. And whenever the realization that she would one day die came over her, it was always a shock; always fresh. She glanced sideways at Claire and Shelagh, seeing them suddenly as though with X-ray eyes: grinning skeletons floating above the pew bench. Her heart pounding with terror, she forced her eyes away. Look at something ordinary. Find some everyday comforting thing. A stronger person. Alexander – dry-eyed, cool and in control – was who she found for reassurance. Though she could never like the man – not after what he'd done to her – he appeared now as a life-affirming force, sitting there with his hand resting possessively on Anna's thigh, too far up to be proper. So carnal, so human. So alive. Anna's dress, Gillian noted, feeling calmer, was one she herself would have been pleased to own: floaty layers of midnight blue chiffon with a glitter of jet at the neck. Anna was even wearing delicate crocheted gloves in the same deep blue as the dress. The sight of her made Gillian feel chunky and ordinary in her bulky linen blouse and dirndl-style skirt. Her hat was all that saved her from looking totally unremarkable: she only hoped whoever was seated behind her would not ask her to remove it. Funeral etiquette would dictate that she comply, unless she could plead religious reasons for keeping her head covered, which, in good conscience, she could not. But perhaps she should remove it anyway, she worried. In the crowded pew it seemed so . . . brimmy. It made her feel like a lamp.

The rector was approaching the pulpit, his black gown flapping officiously behind him. For a young man, he had a surprisingly stiff gait – a poker up his butt, Shelagh would later say. His head was bald on top and what little hair remained hung dispiritedly to his shoulders. Wire-rimmed spectacles perched pedagogically on his nose; on his feet, sandals with criss-crossed leather thongs – Jesus boots, they were called in the sixties. After a bit of fussing with the folds of his gown, he puffed up his chest, gripped the edges of the lectern and gave his audience a baleful stare.

'Before we begin, I must remind everyone that we are in the House of God.' He paused, looking down at them from below brows that joined at the top of his nose. 'Therefore, there must be no taking of pictures during the service.' He paused. 'I'm not going to comment on those few who have arrived late for this important event. It's a busy warm Saturday and I'm sure the traffic is very congested.' His chilly smile took in Claire, Shelagh and Gillian and pinned them there for a moment, making them squirm with embarrassment. 'One of the joys of our Metropolitan United – known to some of us, affectionately, as the Old Met – is that it is located in the beating heart of our wonderful, vibrant city. But there are times when, outside its doors, there is a devil of a traffic jam.' He waited, allowing the congregation a moment to appreciate his wit. 'Now, to those who have arrived late,' his voice reverberated, 'I say only that I am certain no offence was intended and wish to reassure them that none has been taken.' Another sardonic smile; a glint of gold dental work. 'But would the lady in the large black hat kindly remove it during the service so that others may see?'

Gillian glanced around, then, mortified, reached up and yanked off her hat. Her hair would be horridly flattened but she didn't dare fluff it, not with hundreds of eyes on her. Instead, she glared at the rector.

'What an asshole,' Shelagh whispered, giving Gillian's hand a reassuring squeeze.

'Now then,' the rector said, 'I will begin the service in a moment. But first, I would ask all of you to notice something striking.' Gillian crossed her legs self-consciously. He wasn't going to draw attention to her hair! 'And that striking – dare I say, amazing – thing is this. That a well-known Bay Street law firm, in concert with the families of Rick Durham, Ross Owen, Sandy Krupnik and Peter Johnson, has chosen this wonderful historical building, Metropolitan United Church, this magnificent house of worship, in which to remember the four fine men who have so suddenly shuffled off their mortal coils. Look around you, at the person to your left, to your right. How many of you attend church regularly? How many of you have *ever* been inside a church, and I don't mean to attend a wedding or a funeral or a baptism . . . I mean because you have felt the need to talk to God?' He shook his head in disappointment. 'Just as I thought. Not very many.' There was an uneasy clearing of throats. Pews creaked as people rearranged themselves: examining fingernails, adjusting neckties, smoothing skirts and checking watches. 'And as you look around at one another, I want you to ask yourselves *why*.' His voice rang out, accusingly. 'Why have you turned away from the Lord, just when you need Him the *most*? And then I want you to think about it some more. And then again. Ask yourself *why* until it hurts! Until you find the answer which you know in your heart to be the truth!'

From behind Claire came a wheezing sound. It was Mr Biltmore, son of one of the founders of the firm. He was making an adjustment to his hearing aid. Turning it off, Claire thought, if he was smart.

'Would all who can remember the words please rise and join me now in a recitation of the Lord's Prayer?' the rector said. 'Those who cannot remember those inspirational yet comforting words will find them in the front of their hymnals which have been generously donated to the Old Met by the surviving partners of Bragg, Banks and Biltmore.'

How much had these cost the firm? Shelagh wondered, taking up the one in front of her. They were inscribed, on the frontis-piece, in memory of the four deceased. Then she was flooded with shame over her own pettiness. Especially as it was *her* fault that one of them – dear Ross Owen – a man who had *loved* her – was now dead.

'And for those of you who don't know – or have forgotten – what a hymnal is,' the rector continued acidly, 'it's that lovely red-coloured book in front of you in your pew. And I'm sure everyone here must remember what a pew is, since you are all seated in one or another of them.' Another dead silence. Someone cracked his knuckles.

'Where did we find this psycho?' Shelagh whispered to Claire as the congregation rose with a great groaning of wooden benches and rustling of hymnal pages.

'He comes with the church.'

'"Our Father, who art in Heaven,"' Gillian read, her head down and her voice quavering, "'hallowed be Thy name . . ."'

As Claire joined in the prayer, she looked apprehensively around her. She had trouble with funerals and memorials, even when, as here, there was no coffin as tangible evidence of a dead body. Death was a part of life, Ben had reminded her: he saw it virtually every day, in the hospital. Besides, who did she suppose actually *liked* going to funerals? He had promised to try and make it to the service, but Claire knew he wouldn't. He was kicking off a skin cancer clinic that afternoon – an idea his chief of staff thought would boost the hospital's profile in the community. The clinic would be a good source of referral work for Ben and he was expected to demonstrate enthusiasm for it; Rick, Sandy, Peter and Ross, whom Ben had only met a few times, would hardly notice his absence, as he had pointed out.

Basil and Elfriede were sitting a few pews behind Claire. They would have arrived early, to be sure of getting a good parking spot and an unobstructed view in the church.

High above, in the great vaulted ceiling, three puny fans rotated, creating barely a breath of air below, where so many strangers were crushed together, intimately rubbing shoulders, elbows and knees with one another as they prayed. Twelve stained glass windows, composed of thousands of pieces of coloured glass, depicted scenes from the Bible: Moses smashing the tablets; the sermon on the mount. At the top of each was a tiny hinged window that had been pushed open, probably by that rector. Stupid man, Claire thought. If he'd only left the things closed, the church might have retained some of its inherent ancient coolness.

Though Gillian had been a partner, for several years, of the men who had died, she was realizing now how little she knew about any of them. The firm didn't do much socializing. The obligatory Christmas dinner for professionals and staff excluded spouses. There was the annual summer picnic, but it was sporadically attended, and usually only by those with children. This year's picnic had been the last one for her and Isadora, Gillian had decided, after hearing that her daughter had spent much of the time smoking with Claire's nanny behind the boat house. Being a mother herself, Gillian felt obliged to pass this information along to Claire. It gave Gillian an uneasy feeling to know that Francine now despised her for tattling.

B.M. had not been invited to the service; in fact Gillian had specifically told him *not* to come. But it was a public event, he'd argued – anyone was free to walk in off the street. If Gillian was too embarrassed to be seen with him, he would sit in the back and she wouldn't have to let on that she knew him at all. He needed a funeral scene for his next novel; what right did she have to deprive him of material?

Although he finally agreed not to show up, he'd sulked about it, and Gillian didn't trust him. She glanced around, dreading the sight of him pulling on his pointy beard and scribbling in his notebook. ' "For Thine is the kingdom," ' she recited, ' "the power and the glory, for ever and ever. Amen." ' She sat down and was startled to find Isadora suddenly beside her in the pew. 'Oh. Thank you for coming, sweetie. I didn't think you would make it.' She reached out and gripped her daughter's hand in a loving and grateful squeeze.

Looking at her, though, Gillian almost wished she hadn't come. Those jeans! How could she breathe? And that sloppy T-shirt! What was printed across the front? B.U.M.? Gillian coloured with shame, wishing she could put her hat back on and disappear under it. 'You couldn't have put on a dress?' she whispered.

'No.' Isadora slumped in the pew, arms folded defensively across her chest. 'And why am I here, anyway? It's not like you needed more people.'

'Because I asked you to come.' Gillian glanced fearfully at the rector, hoping he hadn't noticed the disturbance in their pew. Isadora's reaction to a public tongue-lashing would surely force Gillian to crawl under a pew. She looked sideways at her daughter. 'What have you done to your ear?' she demanded, forgetting the rector.

'What does it look like?'

'It looks like a dozen holes! Are you crazy? Can they be filled in?'

'Mother, do you want me to leave?'

Yes! Gillian thought. But she said: 'What else have you had pierced?'

'You obviously care a lot about your dead partners, don't you? I don't need this crap.' Isadora hoisted herself to her feet, slouched out of the pew, and shuffled back up the aisle towards the front doors of the church. The rector coughed loudly as the congregation turned to watch her retreat. In the silence, Isadora's chunky denim-clad thighs rubbed together with a sawing sound; her wooden clogs clomped on the worn floor-boards. Gillian gazed up at the ceiling, trying to calm herself by naming the architectural features of it that she knew: transverse arch, formeret, transfolium, archivolt, trefoil.

Claire leaned across Shelagh. 'I just can't wait for Molly to reach that age,' she whispered to Gillian.

'It must be ghastly,' Shelagh nodded sympathetically.

'But she was reaching out. It was a big step for her, and all I could do was criticize!' Gillian's eyes were filling.

'Excuse me?' It was the rector. 'Excuse me? Would it be too much to inquire if all that commotion in the front pew might soon be over?'

'Oh, why don't you go to hell?' Shelagh demanded. The congregation gasped. Shelagh stared at the rector, eyes wide. She hadn't intended for her words to carry like that. They had just popped out. The stifling heat of the church, the stress of being late for the service, the sanctimonious lecturing by the rector, had made her tense and impatient. But all that was no excuse.

Mother of God, thought Claire, her hand to her mouth, exchanging looks with Gillian. Here it comes: fire and brimstone. He's going to damn Shelagh to everlasting hell.

But the rector only cleared his throat as the gathered assembly murmured its disapproval of Shelagh. Obviously, he didn't want to lose their sympathy. Then, holding up his hands for silence, he reminded everyone that emotions were running high and that God's forgiveness would be available to the woman who had blasphemed before Him. He pushed his spectacles further on to his nose and took a pocket watch from beneath his gown. 'Perhaps now would be a good time for all talking to cease, and for us to observe a minute of silence for each of the departed.' His voice seemed to have lost some of its ring of authority. 'I will announce their names in turn and I would ask that all of you reflect on each of them individually – their brilliant careers, their families, hopes and aspirations. And on what they meant to each of you in the context of your own lives. I will begin with Sbitozan Serhiy – known to most of you as Sandy – Krupnik, whose excellent likeness appears to the far left of me.'

'Why not your *right* side first?' demanded a woman across the aisle from the Bragg, Banks and Biltmore lawyers. 'That would be only natural. Who starts with the left? That's my Ross – on the far right. Why not Ross first?'

It was Audrey Owen, Shelagh realized, feeling sick.

12

The rector chose to ignore Audrey, his eyes remaining on his pocket watch. Clearly, he was not going to suffer any further interruptions to his service.

Sandy . . . Sandy, Shelagh said to herself, forcing her thoughts away from Audrey Owen and her own disgraceful conduct. Think about Sandy – Sbitozan Serhiy – Krupnik. She gazed at his portrait, at his round face, his sincere brown eyes. He'd always been an irritation – one of those Gosh-how-are-you go-getter types. An American of Eastern European descent. His eagerness now seemed so touching, so deserving of praise. He'd wanted only to do well, just like anyone else. Shelagh had been sarcastic and spiteful to him on several occasions, but like a joyful (if slow-witted) puppy he always seemed to forgive her, bounding back immediately for more abuse. He'd never married. An elderly lady, who was probably his mother, sat in the pew closest to his portrait, clutching a hymnal, her fingers laced together, lips pressed closed, a black scarf tied over her head.

'Peter Johnson!' The rector seemed to have recovered some enthusiasm for his job.

Across the aisle, Audrey Owen moaned another complaint as Shelagh switched her thoughts over to Pete. He loved fishing, was practically obsessed with it. That fact alone had created a gap in understanding between them that Shelagh had doubted she could ever bridge. Fishing! Sport of morons, the comatose, the (barely) undead. Now it seemed endearing, understandable, a touching human foible. What else did she know about him? He was a loner; his marriage was said to have been on the rocks.

But all of his clients adored him. Shelagh had envied the kind of loyalty Pete seemed to engender in those who retained him. His widow was there in the opposite pew – an odd duck, Shelagh had always thought – dressed in, of all things on an August afternoon, burgundy crushed velvet. There was something wrong with her, though Shelagh couldn't remember what. It was the reason she was having to give up work though she was a biochemist and, apparently, a brilliant researcher. Pete had a young son too, but he wasn't there.

'Ross Owen!'

Shelagh hastily retrieved some tissues from her bag as she prepared to contemplate her dead lover. Then, fearfully, she glanced over at Ross's widow and five children. Behind the granite-faced Marcia, Ross's parents clung together, Mrs Owen sobbing heartily. The youngest of Ross and Marcia's children, Obadiah, looked around with a bright expectant expression, apparently delighted to be in a strange place with lots of new people. Shelagh choked on a sob as pity, shame and dread overwhelmed her. She had taken that boy's father away – first destroying Ross's marriage, then his life. If there really was a hell, there had to be some prime real estate reserved for an unrepentant old sinner like her.

'Richard Durham!'

'That wasn't a full minute!' Aùdrey Owen cried. 'Not a full minute! That was barely thirty seconds! I checked my watch!'

Rick's widow, Jocelyn, and his children – a boy and girl in their twenties – sat cool, blond and impassive in their pew. What amazing composure, Shelagh thought. You might think they were there to watch a boring production for some beneficial society. She turned her gaze to Rick's portrait. In the pose, he was leaning forward, as if anxious to be off to some place else. The artist had managed to capture his essence: Rick the rainmaker, about to dash off to visit clients, roaring around the city in his vintage MG. He was the most energetic man Shelagh had ever known: a top biller, tireless promoter, and Managing Partner for the past six years. Of the four of them, Rick was the one whom she had most deeply admired. She closed her eyes, feeling again the pain of his loss, not only to her personally but to the firm. How would they carry on without his tireless business-development efforts? It almost served them right; they had let him shoulder too much of the load for too long. There was no obvious second in command. Unless . . . unless it was her. Her eyes popped open.

'And now,' the rector continued, 'before the eulogy is delivered, would everyone please rise and join me in one of the most beautiful hymns known to the Christian church – "Nearer My God To Thee". This hymn is of particular relevance to us gathered here today, for it is said to be the last hymn that was played by the orchestra of the *Titanic* as that great ship sank in 1912. So many innocent lives were tragically given up to the waters of the vast Atlantic, just as the four lives commemorated here today have been given up to the waters of Lake Ontario.'

That's a myth, Gillian thought; it's been disproved. The *Titanic*'s band was playing some jazzy tune as their instruments filled up with water. It would serve him right if she stood up and said so, told him off, as Shelagh had done. She was still stinging over his gratuitous humiliation of her daughter and herself.

' "Nearer My God" may be found in your hymnals, at page ten,' the rector announced, gesturing to everyone to rise again.

Claire was trying to remember the last time she'd been in a church. A wedding probably, though she had no idea whose. And when would the next occasion be? Elfriede's funeral? Ben's? (Her own?) Or maybe Molly's wedding. She wasn't sure which idea was the most upsetting. Would Anna and Alexander still be getting married, now that all of this had happened? And would she be expected to host the tea? Most likely they'd decide to put off the wedding; it would be in poor taste to expect the survivors to get cranked up for a big society do, so soon after such a tragedy. Wouldn't it? She watched Alexander's hand, feeling a tingle of envy and sexual arousal. Such carrying on. And at a memorial service. But since when was Alex ever concerned about poor taste? Since when was Anna, for that matter? Claire reflected, recalling the embarrassing conversation she'd had with her about lingerie. Was she wearing anything under that chiffon? Her legs were bare and she wore strappy high-heeled sandals on her feet. A single dew drop of perspiration glittered like a diamond chip on her upper lip as she sang. Claire's skirt and jacket clung to her, steamy, limp and wrinkled. Why were pantyhose so detestably hot in summer, she wondered, when they gave no warmth in winter?

'"Nearer, my God, to Thee, Nearer to Thee!"' The congregation warbled out the last lines of the hymn and everyone sat down again. The rector, apparently satisfied that he had flailed his errant flock into some sort of humiliated order, gathered his gown about him and strode, self-importantly, from the pulpit.

Dan's eulogy was next. He stood up, adjusting his tie and tweaking his jacket into place. From all over the church came scattered snifflings and the sounds of noses being blown, prophylactically, as the assembly prepared itself for a cathartic experience. The pews creaked as backsides settled deeper into them. The only movement of air came from the ineffectual waving of orders of service.

Dan's shiny shoes – obviously new for the occasion – flashed and squeaked as he strode towards the lectern. A sense of expectation hung over the crowd as he took a sip of water and coughed.

'To paraphrase Shakespeare,' he began, 'their lives were gentle, and the elements so mixed up in them that Nature might stand up and say to all the world: *these were men*!' His voice cracked a bit.

Was there some doubt about that? Shelagh wondered, noting how Dan turned his head evenly, from side to side, permitting all members of the congregation to appreciate his superb profile. Well, he had a right to a certain amount of vanity, she supposed. Ross had always disliked Dan, for some reason. Envy, probably. She took a fresh tissue from her bag and dabbed at her nose, careful not to disturb her make-up. Even if Ross hadn't been on that plane, and were alive today, he wouldn't be here beside her, she reflected. He would be in the pew opposite, with Marcia and his children. Where he belonged.

Audrey Owen was not speaking to Marcia, apparently, since getting wind of her daughter-in-law's recent affair with her psychotherapist. It was what had killed Ross, Mrs Owen was telling people; as if he hadn't left Marcia long before, as if he'd pined away from jealousy instead of being the victim of a tragic accident.

'Wherein does greatness lie?' Dan was asking, rhetorically. 'In the head?' A slender finger grazed his temple. 'Or in the heart?' An open palm rested, briefly, on one immaculate lapel of his Armani suit. 'Greatness . . . knows itself.' The dimples on either side of his mouth deepened. 'I know I'm not a very creative guy. I'm afraid I've borrowed a lot from William Shakespeare today.' He bowed his head slightly, as if acknowledging the greatness of the bard and the extent of his own limitations. Claire, Gillian and Shelagh smiled wan encouragement at him from their pew. 'But who else has the words?' he asked. 'The words we may borrow to pay tribute to such men as we, gathered here today, have lost? Who else has the words that may do justice to a sunset?' Amongst the gathering many sad smiles, heads nodding agreement, short sobs. '"Be not afraid of greatness," Shakespeare wrote. "Some are born great, some achieve greatness, others have greatness thrust upon them."' He paused. 'But I would add that still others have greatness torn away from them. Along with their very *lives*!' There was a longer pause as he allowed the impact of his words to sink in. Someone blew his nose violently – a great Canada Goose honk – from the back of the church. Others scrabbled for more tissues. Audrey sobbed openly, loudly, her round shoulders heaving. 'Yes,' said Dan, 'greatness torn away with their very lives. That is what has befallen our most excellent friends, Richard Dusome Durham, Peter Elliot Johnson, Sbitozan Serhiy Krupnik and Ross Makepeace Owen.'

Makepeace? Shelagh looked away.

'Whether you are here today to honour these men as lawyers, or simply as men, you are among friends. Those of us who remain to carry on at Bragg, Banks and Biltmore are with you, and share your enormous grief. We have all lost four trusted friends, four valued counsellors. They can never be replaced.'

'You'll never know! You'll never know!' It was a shriek, the voice torn off in a ragged sob. It was Audrey again. Those whose attention had been wandering in the torpid atmosphere, snapped to appalled attention. Orders of service stopped waving. Audrey leaned over the back of Marcia's pew to jab her daughter-in-law in the shoulder. 'And fat lot *you* cared about my son! Waltzing out on him like that!' She was fanning herself vigorously with a blocky red hymnal and it looked as though she might clobber Marcia with it.

'*He* left *me*, you stupid fool!' Marcia cried, her face scarlet. The congregation drew in a collective breath, horrified. Dan looked as though he'd been slapped.

'Only after *your* carryings on!' Audrey countered, eyes sparkling with fury. 'You pushed him out! He had no choice!'

'You believe what you want – silly old cow! Ross always said you weren't right in the head!'

'That's telling her!' came a man's voice from the rear of the church.

'Not *my* son! He would never, never say that! He was a decent, good man! He adored me! And he was a great father!' Then, clutching for the handkerchief her husband held out to her, she buried her face in his shoulder. 'She killed our Ross!'

If she only knew, Shelagh thought, fumbling desperately in her bag for more tissues as Obadiah began to whine and Dan looked down from his pulpit, his face a mask of tragedy. 'Please, Mrs Owen and Mrs Owen – think of the children. Marcia? Audrey?'

'We don't need your bleedin' input!' Audrey cried. 'We need our Ross back!'

Aghast, Shelagh almost wished for that pompous ass of a rector to climb back into his pulpit and shepherd his flock into peaceful order again.

'Perhaps we should all take a few moments to collect ourselves.' Dan smiled sadly, beatifically, but his hand shook as he reached for the water glass again. 'This is a terrible strain for all of us.' He waited, patiently, clearing his throat and sipping water, for the murmuring in the hall to subside. When it seemed that a further disturbance was unlikely, he continued. 'Now, if you will all permit me – there are some words I would like to say on behalf of those of us who have been left behind.' He fumbled with his notes, obviously flustered. 'I've been talking a lot about greatness here today. As Thackeray wrote – and I'm giving Shakespeare a break now – "To endure is greater than to dare, to ride out hostile fortune, to be daunted by no difficulty and to keep heart when all have lost it . . . Who can say this is not greatness?"' He was rushing his lines a bit, Claire thought, obviously anxious to get through them. Who could blame him? She would have passed out by now if she were the one delivering the eulogy under such conditions. 'Those of us who must now carry on – are we not as great as those we have lost?'

'No! Never! Not like Ross!'

'Oh, for God's sake, Audrey!' With a loud hiccup, Marcia stood up. Her eldest daughter rose too, taking her mother's arm. Together they made an unsteady progress towards the side door of the cathedral. The middle children – two girls and a boy – tried to hang on to a thrashing Obadiah as Marcia moaned something, her words garbled, until at last her voice faded and the great side door of the church swung shut with a soft whump. The middle children looked confused. Then one of the girls burst into tears and was quickly imitated by her sister. Eventually, they all got up and trailed miserably out of the church, after their mother. Gathering her bag and gloves, and clucking loudly, Audrey followed too, prodding her husband along in front of her. The side door creaked open, then thudded shut again. 'Why my Ross? Why him?' came Audrey's strangled question, tiny and helpless. 'Why?'

Why him indeed? Shelagh thought. Because his hideous *mistress* – how she hated that word! – let him know that he would not be welcome in her condo for the weekend, that's why. Because she wanted to go out. Party! Dance! Indulge herself! How Shelagh prayed that the agony of the service would soon be over.

'Now, it used to be,' Dan was saying, 'that greatness was considered exclusively a male domain. Webster, in *The Duchess of Malfi* wrote: "Whether the spirit of greatness *or* of woman reside in him, I know not. I owe him much pity."'

Claire, Shelagh and Gillian exchanged looks.

'Back in Webster's day, it was an either-or equation. If one were great, one could not also be a woman. Fortunately for all of us, things are very different today. The face of the law has changed, and for the better. It certainly has become much prettier.' Beside Claire, Alexander and Anna were panting. Claire frowned, trying to make sense of what Dan was saying.

'Bragg, Banks and Biltmore will carry on – make no mistake about that. From nine partners, we are now but five. And three of us, the *majority* I am proud to say, are women – eager to prove how wrong Webster was. Let us remember that justice, though blind, is always portrayed as a woman. We are privileged to have in our firm three truly great women: Claire Cunningham, Shelagh Tyler and Gillian Lawrence.' He looked expectantly at the pew where they sat.

'Hear hear!' Alexander clapped his large hands together, the sound ringing loudly in the vaulted hall. The organist began to play, softly.

'What are we supposed to do now? Get up and curtsey?' Gillian whispered.

'Don't ask me.' Claire smiled stiffly, turned to the congregation and nodded, then raised a hand in a limp wave.

'Who do you think you are?' Shelagh demanded. 'The Queen Mother?'

Overwhelmed, suddenly, by a surge of courage, Gillian stood up. 'I have a quote too,' she said, her voice startling her with its resonance in the great hall. 'It's from Charlotte Brontë. If you don't mind, Dan. May I?'

'Please.' He smiled down from the pulpit, blinking rapidly.

'Charlotte was writing about someone close to her who had passed away at a very young age.' Gillian swallowed. 'I have to paraphrase a bit.' She took a deep breath. 'I do not weep from a sense of bereavement, but for the wreck of talent, the ruin of promise, the untimely dreary extinction of what were four burning and shining lights.' As abruptly as she'd stood up, Gillian sat down again.

Claire and Shelagh looked at her in surprise. 'That was beautiful,' Claire said.

'Charlotte Brontë had four guys keel over on her?' whispered Shelagh. 'She knew four guys who died young?'

'I *said* I was paraphrasing.' Gillian looked down at her hands. 'I've always loved that quote.'

'That was Gillian Tyler,' Dan said, 'for those who don't know her.'

'*Lawrence*,' Gillian corrected him.

'One of my *great* women partners. Thank you, Gillian.' He lifted his head and calmly regarded the assembly again. 'Although we will never fully recover from the ross of loss – I mean, the loss of Ross –' he flushed brightly '– Rick, Sandy and Peter, we must remember that they died in the service of the law, and in the service of the firm's esteemed clients.'

After a moment of silence, while he stood, eyes closed, looking anguished, he nodded to the organist and the music swelled as he raised his arms and asked everyone to join in a recitation of the twenty-third psalm.

'What? No loaves and fishes?' Shelagh said.

'Those will show up later,' Claire said, 'when that rector comes back to walk on water.'

'Men!' was all Shelagh sighed.

13

In the offices of Bragg, Banks and Biltmore, things looked pretty much as they always had. There were fresh-cut flowers at reception, the coffee dripped through its filter by eight, the cleaners still came around at night with their wheeled canvas carts, dusters and vacuums. Lawyers' shoes were shiny, shirts crisp and monogrammed, stockings run-free and sheer. The man in the white coat continued to drop by to check the quality of the air, and the pony-tailed youth still watered and pruned the plants.

The most perceptible change in the firm was in its sound. The once relentless twitter of telephones, like dozens of exotic birds, had stopped. The air inside the conference rooms was dead, the marble foyer actually echoed when anyone crossed it. People stopped saying 'Thank God it's Friday', on Fridays, though Mondays still brought the usual gloom. There was lots of whispering and the sounds of heavy doors being discreetly closed. No one seemed to find anything funny any more.

A few days after the memorial service Claire, Shelagh and Gillian were in Gillian's office for a quick meeting – at Claire's request. Alex and Dan were out: their secretaries didn't seem to know where they'd gone or when they would be back.

'Ladies,' Claire said, 'I've got some bad news and some worse news. Which do you want first?'

'Let's have the bad,' Shelagh said, 'I need a lift right now.' She was toying with the glittering zipper that ran up the outside of her jacket sleeve, from wrist to elbow. She zipped it up, then down. Up, then down. Her eyes remained on Claire.

'I bet I can guess,' Gillian said. 'Four of our partners have been killed in a plane crash and nobody knows the cause. No, you're right. It's too far-fetched.' She settled into a chair to wait for whatever Claire had to tell them. The collar, cuff and pocket edges of her shirt were strung with rows of teardrop-shaped beads that made a small clattering sound whenever she moved.

'Well – here's the bad news,' Claire began. 'Ross, Sandy, Rick and Peter each had two million dollars' accidental death coverage. With our firm as the beneficiary.'

'That's bad news?' said Gillian.

'Sounds like *fine* news to me!' Shelagh said.

'It would be great news,' said Claire, 'if we could collect it. But there's an exclusion clause in the policy: no more than three partners were allowed to travel together by air.'

'How's that again?' Shelagh didn't really need clarification. In her mind, the memory of the belt of Ross's coat, trailing from his jeep, formed itself into a huge dollar sign, then became a noose which was now available to her for hanging herself.

'Hold on. It can't be that cut and dried,' Gillian protested. 'Nothing in law ever is. We can get around it somehow.' She pressed a hand to her forehead. Claire and Shelagh waited.

'You're not receiving messages from the spirit world, are you?' Shelagh said.

'Shut up. I'm thinking.' Another pause. 'Okay, I've got an idea. The exclusion clause was never drawn to our attention, was it? The insurance company had a duty to highlight that clause – we never read it – there was no disclosure. It's a classic case.'

'We're lawyers,' Claire said drily. 'We can hardly plead that we didn't read the policy.'

Shelagh was now recalling, miserably, the ease with which she might have stopped Ross from going to Boston: a single encouraging word would have done it. Five little Owens with no father, Marcia with no husband, and now the firm (herself included) losing out on *eight million dollars*! She looked briefly at the sky beyond the boardroom window. What would be the best way to do herself in? Pain was out; she was too squeamish. The same could be said for anything messy. How many sleeping pills were left in her bathroom cabinet? Not enough, surely: she'd been popping them like crazy the past few nights.

'Well, how about we argue that they weren't actually *travelling* by air?' Gillian continued. 'I mean, it was hardly what you could call *travelling*, was it? They barely got off the ground, did they, before the plane crashed?' Shelagh and Claire avoided Gillian's eyes. 'Okay, so it's not a great legal argument, but at least I'm trying to find some creative solution.'

'We need you to be smart. Sleazy. Lawyer-like,' Shelagh said. 'Forget creative. But you're right that there must be something we can do to fight this.'

'Of course we'll fight it,' Claire said. 'Alex has already retained the best insurance litigators in the city.'

'You've talked to Alex about this?' Gillian said.

'*Before* talking to *us*?' said Shelagh.

'I did speak with him, yes. Last night. And Dan.' Claire avoided their eyes.

'You got together with Dan and Alexander, *without us*?' Shelagh repeated.

'This is a little hard to take,' Gillian added. She and Shelagh looked at Claire in a hurt silence.

'But I couldn't reach either of you. You should be glad I was around to represent your interests. Gillian, where were you last night? Off at some poetry reading?'

'No.' Gillian thought, guiltily, about where she had been: slumming in the east end with B.M. and an exuberant real estate agent, traipsing through depressing houses where desperate owners pretended to watch television and not notice the three people assessing cupboard and closet space and murmuring about the cost of replacing the broadloom. And that two of those people were taking notes.

'And you.' Claire turned to Shelagh. 'What were you doing? Now that Ross is gone?'

'Ex-*cuse* me? What has Ross got to do with anything?'

'Come on, Shelagh. Everyone's known about you and Ross for months. You must have realized that.'

'Actually, I didn't.' She zipped up her sleeve again.

'Forget Ross for a minute,' Gillian said. 'I want to get to the bottom of this secret meeting Claire had with Dan and Alex. Behind the backs of her two women partners. And friends.'

'It wasn't a *secret meeting*,' Claire said, exasperated. 'Look, I don't need this. I've got a husband who's begging me to quit work. I could just walk out of here right now if I wanted to, forget this whole mess – put it behind me. Live on easy street.'

'Where you are anyway,' Shelagh said.

'So, go for it,' Gillian said. 'I would.' The women looked at each other. No one spoke for a moment.

'Of course I'm not going to quit,' Claire said. 'I didn't mean that. I only wanted you to stop thinking about how far out of joint your noses are and start thinking about the future of this firm. We've got a real opportunity here to turn things around. Bragg and Banks now has five partners, three of us women. It's fair to say this is a woman-driven firm.'

'Don't put it that way,' Shelagh said. 'It reminds me of all those bad jokes about women drivers. Not to mention Dan's speech.'

'It's possible his speech was well-intentioned,' said Gillian. 'That he meant to be supportive.'

'We don't need his support,' Shelagh snapped. 'He needs ours. So what else went on at this meeting?'

'Well, Alex had one request he wanted me to pass on to both of you.' Claire hesitated. 'He wants Anna to join the firm.'

'As what? She's not even a lawyer.'

'As soon as she's called to the bar.'

'That won't be till spring.'

'He wants us to make the offer, so she doesn't go somewhere else, considering the problems we're having here . . .'

'Is the wedding still on?'

'As planned.'

'So will you still be doing the tea?'

'I don't see how I can avoid it.'

'That'll be quite an ugly affair now,' Shelagh said. 'Lots of widows, flapping about in black, like crows.'

'It was always going to be awful,' Claire sighed. 'I don't see that much has changed. And I'll invite a few clients. As Rick wanted me to.'

'Do we have any left?'

'Is an underwear shower really the proper forum?'

'Rick thought it was.'

'So?' said Gillian. 'He's – gone.'

'But I was thinking that maybe he was right. That we should do more business development – any chance we get. It's even more important now that our firm is – sorting itself out. And showers tend to, sort of, draw women together, don't they?'

'They can have that effect,' Gillian said. 'Though I'm not so sure about the one you're planning. It's pretty heavily charged – emotionally speaking.'

'So you'd invite Deborah Ward?' Shelagh said.

'Probably.'

'She hates me, you know. Ever since I went to her company's beach party in a thong. Two years ago.'

'She was just jealous,' Gillian said. 'Look at her body. Look at yours.'

'Doesn't matter. It was bad judgement on my part. Her husband had just dumped her. Her self-confidence was at an all-time low. She'll always despise me.'

'What about Renée Futterman-Cooper-Smith?' Gillian said.

'I'll invite her, probably. But she's got that farm now, spends every minute she can in the country. She probably won't like feeling obliged to drive back into the city on a Sunday . . .'

'Julia Wignall?'

'She's mad at the whole firm. Owes Alex a pile of dough. Something like $85,000.'

'Over ninety days?'

'Over a hundred and twenty,' Claire nodded. 'Then there's Heather Olmstead.'

'She still sends us work?'

'I opened a new file for her yesterday,' Shelagh said. 'But she's a serious feminist – the type of woman who would *hate* Alex for marrying a young student. And she's not exactly the sexy underwear sort . . . I wouldn't think. Though it's a struggle to imagine a female client in her underwear, isn't it? Now a *male* client – that's another story.'

Claire sighed. 'I can't think too much about the tea details right now. It boggles my mind. Soon, I will. I'll have to. But not now.'

'And we want to hear more about your meeting with Dan

and Alex,' Shelagh said. 'Does Dan have any similar requests for hiring lawyers? Maybe he wants his mother admitted to the partnership? Or his dog?'

'Sure, joke. Laugh all you want. But while we're sitting around bitching, what do you suppose they're doing? Dan and Alex?'

'Lunching.' Gillian looked at her watch.

'Power-lunching,' Shelagh said. 'With the firm's clients. They're exchanging jock-itch stories and having a few beers or whacking around squash balls. They're making sure the business stays with them, no matter what happens to the rest of this firm. To us.'

The three women shared a moment of paranoia. Then Gillian's secretary tapped on the door. 'I've got a call on my line for *any partner*. It's *Mrs Owen*!'

'Marcia . . .' Shelagh was suddenly intrigued by the fringe of the prayer rug on Gillian's wall. 'I'm not talking to her.'

'Don't look so spooked,' Gillian told her secretary, 'it's Ross who's dead, not his wife.'

'I'll take the call,' Claire said, 'put her through.'

'Not here. Not on the speaker phone,' Shelagh said. 'You can't.'

'Put her through to my office then. I'll take it in there.'

'You're not going to be able to avoid Marcia Owen forever, you know,' Gillian told Shelagh when Claire had gone. 'She'll be around, picking up Ross's things, straightening out his – affairs.' She gave Shelagh an appraising glance. 'And Claire has a moral and social obligation to invite her to the tea.'

'I don't see why . . .' Shelagh said casually. She lifted a corner of the prayer rug. 'Did you know this thing has bugs, Gillian?'

'It does not!'

'Then how come it's crawling across your wall?'

'Poor Marcia,' Claire said when she returned. 'She sounds terrible. She's hysterical because no one told her about the memorial service.'

'But she was *there*,' Shelagh said. 'She had that big scene with her mother-in-law.'

'Don't you think I know that?'

'It's the shock,' Gillian said. 'The grief. She's gone off the deep end, repressed all memory of the service. Who can blame her, with a mother-in-law like she has? Or maybe she's got total amnesia. No one seems to get total amnesia any more. Remember how common it used to be in films and books? Maybe it's enjoying a resurgence.'

'This is not a film or a book,' Shelagh said.

'I tried to get Marcia to calm down,' said Claire, 'but she was pretty upset. She wants a meeting. I said I'd see her next week.'

'What do you suppose she's after?' Shelagh said.

'I'm sure it has nothing to do with you. She probably has some questions about Ross's estate. Maybe she's found a will. It's not my area but I'm sure I could give her the basics of estate law.'

'Yes,' Shelagh brightened. 'That's probably what she wants. I'll just make a point of being out of the office.'

'You don't suppose Ross left anything to you, do you?' Gillian asked. 'In his will?'

'Look – we had a brief liaison, that's all. Besides, he didn't have much. A big mortgage. Five kids. Lots of orthodontists' bills.'

'You should be prepared, though,' Claire said, 'because it could be pretty awkward for you if he did leave you something.'

'She's got a point,' Gillian said.

What if Ross had indeed left her some *thing*? Shelagh's eyes met Claire's. Something intimate, embarrassing. All his dress-up role-playing sex paraphernalia was gone – she'd bagged it and shoved it down the garbage chute of her condo the day after the memorial service. But what if he got some romantic notion in his head, to leave her his *Mikado* car tape or some other memento of their floundering relationship? Since she'd basically told him they were through? Maybe he'd written her a letter that Marcia would turn up while going through his things.

'Anyway, I'll talk to you more about it after I see Marcia,' Claire said, 'but you ought to be prepared. Otherwise, the only other thing we talked about last night is the four offices . . . Alex wants to go through them on Saturday. He thinks we should all be there.'

'I'm not going through their personal things,' Gillian said. 'I can't even look at those offices, knowing our partners are still out there, somewhere . . . maybe bits of them floating around, bobbing up and down on the waves. A toe, a finger . . .'

'Cut it out,' Shelagh said. 'You're talking crazy.'

'I'm *never* going down to the beach again,' Gillian proclaimed. 'That's all I need – to be sitting there on a rock and see one of Pete Johnson's eyeballs staring up at me from the water . . .'

'Gillian, there aren't any floating body parts,' said Claire. 'You've got to stop having these wild ideas. The bodies are at the bottom of the lake, buried with the wreckage of the plane. Or else there's nothing left of them. Think of it as if they were cremated. Or buried at sea. They aren't going to bob up to the surface. Not ever.'

'I must be losing it,' Gillian sighed. 'It's Isadora's creepy books all over the house . . . vampires, corpses climbing out of the sea . . .'

'Tell her to play with her books outside,' Shelagh advised.

'Ben keeps a human skull on a shelf in the library,' Claire said. 'He's had it since first-year med school. I've been looking at it a lot lately, wondering who it was and what it's doing there between my decorating magazines.'

'I wouldn't be able to sleep in the same house with it,' Gillian said.

'My point is that we're all having morbid thoughts. It's natural. It's common for people to need counselling after a tragedy like this.'

'You've got a good shrink, don't you, Claire?' Shelagh asked.

'Yeah,' Gillian said. 'The Winston Churchill-bath guy.'

'I don't see him any more. And I don't know of any good bereavement counsellors. I'm not used to thinking about death. None of us is. Nobody in this firm has ever done estates work.'

'I've been thinking about that,' Shelagh said, 'about what we do here, about all of our practices. We're going to have to hike up our skirts and think about serious damage control. The good ship Bragg, Banks and Biltmore is springing a hundred leaks. The associates have nothing to do – they leave early every day for the pubs. Resumés are flying all over the city. The word on the street is not good. Sick jokes, mostly.' She paused, frowning. 'Know what I heard yesterday?'

'What?'

'Why did the Bragg and Banks lawyers end up in the lake?'
'Why?'
'Because way down deep, lawyers are really good.'
'I heard a better one. Or should I say worse one,' Gillian said.
'What's the biggest defect with the Beech Baron Turbo?'
Claire and Shelagh shook their heads.
'Not enough passenger space.'
'How sick,' Claire sighed. 'Well, since we're on this tasteless and insensitive topic, what's the definition of a "real shame"?' She waited. 'The crash of the Bragg and Banks plane. What's the definition of a "crying shame"?'
'Don't tell me . . .'
'That one of the seats was empty.'
Each of the women looked away. 'We shouldn't laugh,' Shelagh said, 'we shouldn't even be repeating these. And there were no empty seats.' As I know only too well, she thought. If there were, we'd be collecting eight million dollars right now.
'Well, lawyer-bashing jokes are as old as the profession,' Gillian said. 'And you've got to admit, those aren't half bad – a couple of them.'
'Don't you dare laugh,' said Claire.
'Who's laughing?'
'It's too sick.'
'We must be on the edge.'
'Okay. One last one. What's the new specialty of Bragg, Banks and Biltmore?' Gillian said.
'I give up,' Shelagh said.
'Wait. I know – marine law,' guessed Claire.
'That was too easy,' Shelagh protested.
'*You* didn't get it,' said Gillian.
The three women looked around, daring each other to laugh. 'Well,' Claire sighed, 'we should be relieved about the slow-down of work around here. We couldn't handle the active files of four busy lawyers. Not with our own clients to look after.'
'Without Ross, we're losing – have lost – all the banks and finance companies,' Shelagh said.
'Without Sandy, the securities,' said Gillian.
'Without Rick, the corporate litigation.'
'Without Pete –' Claire paused. 'What did Peter do, anyway?'

Shelagh shrugged. 'I've always wondered.'

'He seemed busy . . .'

'His clients all loved him . . .'

'Something to do with film financing, I thought.'

'Wasn't it computer software?'

'No, tax shelters. I'm quite sure –'

'Oh, well.'

'I suppose we'll find out once we go through his files.'

'God.'

'We have to do it,' Claire said. 'We can't leave their offices untouched, like shrines. Life goes on. The space here is sixty dollars a square foot. We might have to look for an older building – outside the downtown core. And we've got four extra secretaries with nothing to do but gossip and worry about whether their pay cheques are going to bounce. We'll have to let them go, give them all a decent severance package. It'll be tough. Especially since we've got no insurance money coming in . . .' She was looking at Shelagh as she said this.

Shelagh regarded her narrowly. Claire couldn't know that Shelagh had practically stuffed Ross into the plane, pushing the number of partners aboard beyond the permitted maximum. Could she?

'I bet Anna tries to grab one of those big offices,' Gillian said.

'Over my dead body,' Shelagh exclaimed.

'Couldn't you use some other expression?' said Claire.

'Those south-view offices are *ours*. We finally get to move off Baltic Avenue and on to Park Place.'

'Not me. I'm staying put,' said Gillian. 'There's no way I'm going into an office with a lake view. So I can sit there every day watching the water, thinking, wondering.'

'If you're prepared to sit and stare at the water all day, you can find some place else to work,' Shelagh snapped.

'I beg your pardon?'

'We're all going to have to bust our tails or we'll be going down with the others. I'm sorry to put it so bluntly, but honestly, Gillian, there are times when I really have to wonder about you.'

'I've been thinking along those lines too,' Claire said quickly, once again finding herself in the role of peace-maker. 'Not about

Gillian specifically, but about how we're going to survive. We'll have to get down and get dirty. We can't afford to turn away any kind of work. We all got lots of referrals from the four guys. But those aren't going to come in any more. There's no loyalty owed to us just because we still have the firm's name. In fact, it's probably a liability. Bragg, Banks and Biltmore is now synonymous with "disaster" or "death".'

'And we don't do wills and estates.' Shelagh was feeling discouraged, thinking about all the unpalatable types of legal work that could 'come in off the street': personal injury claims, mortgage enforcement; rough and tumble family law cases where husbands threatened to boil their ex-wives' pet budgies, battles over Tupperware – everybody blaming the lawyers. Not to mention the death threats. 'Gillian,' she said, 'you're going to have to get a lot tougher on your inventors. Your receivables are going through the roof.'

'Who are you to look at my receivables?'

'We've got to get serious about our cash flow. No more Haiku-writing during office hours. And you get cash retainers from your inventors or you don't lift a drafting pencil.'

'She's right, I'm afraid,' Claire said.

'But then I might not get any work at all,' Gillian protested. 'Lots of inventors can't afford the up-front costs. They have to wait until their product gets out into the marketplace –'

'Then you'll have to do something else,' Shelagh said. 'Residential real estate, whatever. We're not a bank – remind your clients of that. And if you don't like the lake view from your new southern exposure, keep the blinds down.'

'So what about you? You're pretty good at figuring out how to re-tool everyone else. What are you going to do to survive?'

'I plan to get into business development big time. I'm going to play hard ball, get the work in any way I can. Just like one of the guys. We're all going to have to start thinking like men.'

'Oh, surely we can do better than that?' Claire protested.

'I agree. Let's not get ridiculous,' Gillian added.

'And we can start by getting rid of all the bloody plants around here. The place looks like the rainforest everybody's trying to save. Do you have any idea what the cost of maintenance is on those oxygen-eaters?'

'They *make* oxygen,' Gillian said, 'they don't eat it.'

'And then there's the cut flowers in reception. What's wrong with a few fakes? And what about the free coffee and cookies all day long for the staff? And the abuse that goes on in the mailroom, everyone sticking their personal mail through the postage meter. I've been watching, and it's been quite an eye-opener. We're being bled dry with pilfering – Scotch tape, paper clips, envelopes. A man wouldn't put up with plants and cookies. Ask Alex and Dan. I bet they're thinking exactly as I am.'

'But those little things – coffee and cookies – are what make a workplace human,' Gillian cried.

'Listen, either we shape up around here or we go down with our four dead partners – that's what you get for being human. There's a couple of guys with hairy legs and football cleats who are going to trample us into the mud on the way to the big touchdown. And I think you know who I'm talking about.'

'They certainly seem to be busy . . . Alex and Dan.'

'And don't forget Anna,' Gillian said. 'Lady Macbeth. She's on their side too.'

'She's not saying much these days.'

'Did she ever?'

'Probably lying in the weeds, as Pete would have said, like a pickerel. Or a pike.'

'Well, I've got plans for Anna,' Shelagh said, 'don't you worry about her. And it's no tea party I've got in mind.' She was, of course, making this up. She hadn't any idea at all what should be done about Anna, if anything; had barely had a chance to assess how much of a threat she might be. It didn't seem like the moment, however, to let on that she was experiencing any lack of confidence. Her partners had to be flagellated into some sort of affirmative action.

'We may be getting paranoid,' Claire said, 'about Alex and Dan. We haven't seen them do anything directly against our interests. And okay, maybe Dan got a little carried away with his memorial speech – that women in the law nonsense.'

'That justice is a blind woman crap –'

'But it wasn't a good day for anyone.'

'You've got that right.' Shelagh glanced over at Claire, remembering the melted M&M on the back of her silk dress, the cost of the dry cleaning, and what everyone who saw it must have thought. 'Okay,' she said, 'I agree. I say we try and work with the boys, come up with a business plan, be co-operative. But let's not totally forget that pithy old chestnut . . .'

'Which pithy old chestnut would that be?' asked Gillian.

'Just because you think you're paranoid, doesn't mean someone isn't watching you.'

14

Rick Durham's office looked as though its component parts had been put into a gigantic box, given a vigorous shake, and tossed back into the room. There was little evidence of the efforts his wife Jocelyn had made over the years to decorate it – they'd been about as successful as her attempts to get control of her husband's social and family life. A cheery chintz slipcover (hand-sewn by her, one summer at the Durham family cottage) was almost completely obscured by boxes of court transcripts on an oversized wing chair. Against one wall was an antique roll-top desk, with brass locks and trim, that Jocelyn had expected Rick to use as a mini-bar but had become home only to his gym shorts and squash racquet. A piece of abstract art – a smear of acid yellow acrylic rolled over a sea of soot, too big for the wall it was on – hung crookedly behind his desk.

'Unpleasant though this is,' Alexander said, stepping over a box of files, 'we have an obligation to go through everything that belonged to our partners. The personal stuff goes to the families. Anything related to their law practices, that isn't wanted or needed by clients, stays with the firm. Assuming we still have a firm.'

Dan, kneeling on the floor, began constructing a cardboard carton, reinforcing its seams with clear packing tape. The tape gun shrieked as he dragged it down one side, across the bottom, then up the other side. 'RDD-PERSONAL', he wrote on it. The thick black marker squealed across the top of the box. The others watched in silence, as people with nothing to say to each other will pretend to be enchanted by the activities of a hyperactive child. When the first box was taped and labelled, Dan started on another.

'Look, I don't mind if you want to go through these offices without me,' Gillian said. 'It can't possibly require all of us. This is too cringe-making. I'd really like to beg off . . . if nobody minds?'

'What, exactly, is your problem?' Alexander sighed.

'Well, it just seems like such a horrible invasion of privacy.'

'The dead have no privacy,' he said. 'And you have to be here. You're a partner. Nobody *wants* to do this. You think I wouldn't rather be out at the ball game or off somewhere penning a sonnet?' He and Gillian exchanged looks of extreme dislike.

'Maybe this is harder for some people than others,' Claire said. 'We can do this without Gillian.'

'No,' she said, 'Alex is right. I'll be okay. Office towers aren't the usual places for the paranormal, at least not according to Isadora's books. So –' She rubbed her hands together in an effort to seem business-like, but only managed to appear to be wringing them. She turned to look over Rick's bookshelves that were packed with ragged binders, untidy bundles of papers, law books and a jumble of unrelated objects.

'Everything relates to some case or another,' Shelagh said, picking up a single athletic shoe. 'I remember this – it was a product-liability claim. Something to do with the depth of the treads – some guy who would have been a big basketball star if he hadn't broken his ankle.'

'All of it belongs to clients,' Claire said. 'It's not ours to throw out or give away.'

'What would Jocelyn want with all this junk anyway?' Shelagh said. 'Her house is so perfect.' She pushed aside a plastic coin bank to read the title of a book wedged in behind it. 'So this is where the *Annotated Supreme Court Rules* went. I've been looking for this for a year. I must have asked Rick a hundred times –'

'Check inside the front cover,' Alex said. 'If it's Rick's book, it goes to his family.'

'It's not Rick's. It wasn't Rick's.' Shelagh hesitated. 'It doesn't belong to what Rick was.'

'To Rick's ghost, you might as well say.' Apprehensively,

Gillian took down another book and opened it. 'This one has "Ex Libris Rick Durham" on the book plate. *Persuasion – The Key To Success At Trial*.' Carefully, she placed it in one of the boxes Dan had constructed. 'He was such a good lawyer.'

'Here's another one of his,' Claire said. '*The Art Of Cross-Examination*.' She gazed sadly at the cover. 'He *was* good, wasn't he?'

'One of the best,' Alex said.

'And look!' Shelagh wailed. 'Here's his 'SUE THE BASTARDS' statue. I remember when he got this – a client gave it to him. He treasured it – kept it displayed right here on his shelf. It's even got "To RDD" engraved on the bottom.' She sighed. 'I suppose we do have to do this sorting out. But it seems so soon . . .'

'If we're going to get weepy over every book and knick-knack, we're never going to get finished,' Alex said. 'We've got three more of these offices to do. I feel as badly as you do.' He hesitated. 'I only hope we don't find something that puts us straight into a lawsuit. God knows what we're liable to discover. People keep strange things in their desks. We might stumble across something that would compromise the firm.'

'I don't know about that,' Shelagh said. 'It's hard to imagine a more regular bunch of guys.'

'That's exactly what worries me.' Alex had lost a lot of weight, Claire thought, noting the loose hang of his jeans as he moved around behind Rick's desk. If he really was out power-lunching with clients every day, he wasn't getting much to eat. Either that, or Anna was wasting him with her sexual appetite. The weight loss made him more attractive: there were hollows in his cheeks that were shaded by the blue-black of a five o'clock shadow. On the other hand, in contrast to Dan's buoyant heartiness, he looked pretty debauched. 'People stash stuff in their offices that they can't keep at home,' he said. 'For one reason or another.' Shelagh, lining up Dan's cartons along one wall of the office, made a mental note to take a peek inside Alex's desk drawers some weekend.

'Alex is right.' Dan's marker squealed across another box top. 'We might find something that would embarrass the families. We don't want to add shame to their grief.'

'There seem to be a number of locked drawers around here.

I got the keys from the furniture company. If any don't work, we'll have to call in a locksmith.' Alex pulled a ring of keys out of the pocket of his jeans and tossed it on to Rick's desk. The clank of metal made everyone start. 'Who wants to start on the drawers?'

Dan's tape gun screeched as he taped up another carton. Everyone winced.

'I'll keep going through the books,' Gillian said. 'What's the worst I can find? A flask inside a hollowed out copy of *Great Trial Lawyers*?' She glanced at the lake beyond Rick's windows. 'Anybody mind if I pull down the blinds?' Without waiting for an answer, she scrolled down the grey mesh blind, dropping a gloom over the room that gave it the atmosphere, suddenly, of a rainy day.

'I'll start on the drawers then,' Shelagh said, picking up the keys. 'I can handle it.'

'I'll pack up the personal things,' Gillian said. 'You can stop putting together boxes for a bit. We won't be able to move in here soon.' Besides, she thought, why should you get off so easily? Wouldn't we all like just to tape up cartons all day?

'Yeah, give it a rest,' Shelagh said. 'That screeching is driving me nuts.'

'Sorry.' Dan gave a dimpled smile. 'Nervous energy.'

'Well.' Shelagh took a deep breath. '*Cherchez la femme*, as they say. If Rick had another woman, let's find her.'

'And let's hope it was only a woman,' Alex said gloomily.

15

A few minutes later, Shelagh pulled open the last of Rick's desk drawers. 'I hate to speak ill of the deceased,' she said, 'but our Managing Partner was a pack rat. I feel like I'm playing one of those memory games – how many of these objects will I be able to recall after I close the drawer? There's nothing in here worth keeping – dead felt pens, sticky notes, piles of gum wrappers. A box of cigars . . . I didn't know he smoked. Did anyone think to bring garbage bags? Most of what's in here could just be dumped.'

Gillian offered to run to the kitchen to get some bags and Alexander, selecting the smallest key on the ring, unlocked Rick's credenza doors and slid them open. He frowned. 'Now, why would he keep all these files locked up in here instead of out in his cabinets?'

'A yo-yo, a shoe horn, a jar of loose change . . .' Shelagh continued. 'I guess we give the change to Jocelyn – looks like about twenty bucks' worth.'

'He owed me at least that much,' Alex said, looking over the first few folders he had pulled from the credenza. 'He was always bumming lunch money . . . never seemed to have his wallet on him.'

'And I thought I was the only one he hit up for cash,' Dan said.

'Garbage bags!' Gillian called cheerily.

'Come on over here, Dan,' Alex said. 'I want you to take a look at these.'

'Here,' Shelagh directed Gillian. 'Hold a bag open beside this drawer. I'm making an executive decision. All of it goes.'

'But is it art?' Dan said, looking over Alex's shoulder, his face pale.

'Is what art?' Shelagh looked up, midway through the drawer dump.

'Porno,' Alex sighed. 'All very neatly filed. And labelled. He was an organized guy – I'll say that for Rick.'

'So – what's the big deal?' Claire said. 'If it's porno, just toss it. No one expected him to be a saint.'

'The porno is labelled by *client name*.'

'Those are porno pictures of our *clients*?' Shelagh bounded out from behind the desk, tripping over an empty box in her hurry. 'Let me see that.' She grabbed the file from Dan. 'Hey . . . this is that bank president . . . what's his name?'

'Conrad,' Dan said. 'John David Conrad. Rick's biggest client. He pulled all his work out of here yesterday.'

'So who is this with him? The blonde woman. You can't really see her face but it looks a bit like –'

'Angela,' Alex said. 'Rick's secretary. But at least Conrad's with a human being in that one. Don't bother looking at the rest.'

'Does Angela still work for us?' Claire asked over Shelagh's shoulder. 'I haven't seen her lately.'

'She quit last Friday.'

'Oh.'

'There's no way these could just be fun photos, is there?' Gillian suggested. 'Maybe Rick and his clients were into some kinky stuff together.'

'Rick Durham is notably absent from any of these photos,' Alex said.

'How many of those files are there?' Shelagh asked.

'A dozen, maybe more. Fortunately, all the negatives seem to be here too.'

'Whew,' said Gillian. 'So this was Rick's big business-development tool.'

'And he sure kept it nicely sharpened,' Shelagh said.

'We have to destroy all of these, obviously,' Dan said. 'Don't we?'

'Are we liable, as partners, for Rick's extortion? For his criminal acts? Assuming he was really blackmailing our clients?' Shelagh asked.

'That's what I was wondering,' said Claire. 'What if the firm derived financial benefit from his – activities? We'll have to go back through all of his accounts, see what kind of money he was taking in, compare it to the hours he docketed. Return any he didn't legitimately bill for. But even that won't tell us if he actually *worked* those hours he billed. What a nightmare!'

'And we can't destroy those photos, can we?' Gillian said. 'They're evidence. Of a crime.'

'Why can't we?' Shelagh demanded. 'Rick's dead. Who's left to prosecute?'

The five lawyers looked uneasily at one another.

'I should know the answer to that,' Alex said, 'but I don't.'

'We should all know the answer,' Claire said.

'I'll get Anna to look into it, do some research.'

'We don't want outsiders involved,' Shelagh snapped.

'She's going to be my wife.'

'Well, she's not your wife now.'

'I agree with Shelagh,' Claire said. 'Let's keep Anna out of this. None of it goes beyond this room.'

'We do represent a majority of the partnership here,' Shelagh reminded Alex. 'We three skirts, that is.'

'I'll call the Crown's office on Monday,' he sighed. 'I've got a buddy there I can talk to.'

'This is a very hard thing for me to come to terms with,' Dan said. 'Very hard.' He was sitting on the floor, his head in his hands. 'I respected Rick.'

'We all did,' Claire said.

'But I also owe him my life. If it wasn't for all that work he dumped on me that Friday, I would have been on that plane. If one of the other guys hadn't gone – Ross, for example – who could easily have had some family thing come up . . .'

'Well, he did go,' Shelagh said. 'Nothing came up.' Except his number, she reminded herself, guiltily.

'At least Rick had a sense of humour,' Gillian said, 'filing all these porno pictures in blue folders like he did.'

Alex gave her a look. 'Sure,' he said, 'that's the big consolation prize.'

*   *   *

Sandy Krupnik had been a recent transfer from another Bay Street firm. None of his partners seemed to know much about him. His office was obsessively neat, and therefore unlikely to tell them more, Claire thought.

'Tidy offices spook me,' Gillian said, as the five of them clustered in Sandy's doorway. 'It looks as though he knew he'd never be back.'

'It always looked like this in here. Sandy was a neat freak.' Shelagh pushed past her. 'Come on. This will be easy. Look at his books. They're alphabetically arranged by title. And look here, he's even labelled one shelf as Personal Library.'

'That's what we want,' said Claire. 'It makes our job easy. Who can get weepy when there's no sign of a personality?'

'Sandy had a great personality,' Dan said defensively. 'He was a super guy.'

'I didn't mean it like that,' Claire said. 'Come on, Dan, let's have some of your wonderful cardboard boxes.'

'What about the nail art?' Gillian said. 'I can't believe our firm bought these.' She was contemplating two six-foot-long masonite boards that dominated the walls, each embedded with hundreds of rusty nails of various heights and thicknesses. 'Maybe he was in training to be a fakir.' It brought to mind the number of alarming books Isadora had been carting home lately, all about tattooing and body-piercing and other forms of self-mutilation.

'Whatever,' Shelagh said crossly. 'I think we all agree about their level of artistic merit. I'll phone the art consultant we used. Maybe she'll take them back. Or we could try selling them to a hardware store for parts. Somebody toss me the desk keys.'

Alex hovered at Shelagh's shoulder as she opened the first drawer. 'Looks like a lot of personal files in here,' she said, running her fingers over the tab ends of multi-coloured folders. 'Where was it that Sandy was originally called to the bar?'

'Delaware,' Alex said.

'Also Nevada, I think. Some place hot,' Gillian said.

Shelagh had opened another of the drawers. 'Aspirin, Excedrin, Maalox, Tums, Robaxecet. What's that for?'

'Back pain,' said Claire. 'I can tell you all about back pain.'

Don't bother, Shelagh thought, but she said: 'Sore throat

lozenges, cold tablets, nose spray. Man, this guy was a walking pharmacopoeia.' She held up a plastic pill bottle and peered at its label. 'Some big green bombs in here. Wonder what they're for?'

'I could probably tell you,' Gillian said, 'if you want to toss it over here.'

'Do we really want to find out that Sandy had genital herpes?' Claire said.

'He's got no law degrees in here from anywhere,' Alex said. 'And no paperwork from any of the States. No licences . . . no alumni letters or magazines.'

'I don't keep that sort of thing in my desk,' Claire said. She had picked up two small volumes – one red, one blue – that had been standing upright, obviously intended for display, on Sandy's desk. '*The Military Maxims of Napoleon*,' she read, 'and *Latin For Even More Occasions*.' She opened the book. '"*Veni, vidi, nates calce concidi*".'

'I came, I saw, I kicked some butt?' Gillian asked.

'Bang on,' said Claire. 'I'm impressed.'

'Well, our friend Sbitozan hardly did that,' Shelagh said. 'It's pretty hard to kick ass in corporate securities during a recession.'

'"You should establish your cantonments at the most distant and best protected point from the enemy, especially where a surprise is possible,"' Claire read from the other volume. 'I wonder what a cantonment is?'

'Actually –' Gillian began.

'Never mind,' Shelagh said.

'Let's get back to the lack of diplomas and degrees in Sandy's office here,' Alexander said impatiently.

'It's not so odd,' Claire said. 'I think we're getting paranoid after what we found in Rick's.'

'We know he was licensed to practise here because his licence is on the wall,' Gillian said. 'Framed. Look.' The others turned to look.

'Nobody frames their licence.' Alex frowned. 'Not on Bay Street. That would be like hanging up your high-school diploma.'

'Maybe where he came from they do things differently,' Gillian said. 'You know the States. If you've got it, flaunt it. If you don't blow your own horn, nobody will.'

'But it's not as though he had to prove to anyone here that he was a lawyer . . .' Shelagh began.

'Unless he wasn't,' Gillian laughed.

The room was silent as they considered this very real but unpleasant possibility.

'That was a joke,' Gillian said.

'He was licensed here on the basis of his two State qualifications,' Alexander said.

'Sure. And the Law Society is very careful about who gets licensed,' Gillian said. 'They would have checked him out. Claire's right. We can't get totally paranoid.'

'Well, there are other intriguing documents in here.' Alex plopped a thick file on to the desk top.

'Not –'

'No photos. Just lots of cheque requisitions.' He flipped through a stack of papers. 'All of them for expert-witness fees, all payable to the same numbered company.'

'Witness fees?' Dan said. 'Sandy did corporate securities. He wouldn't have needed expert witnesses for anything . . .'

'Exactly.'

The lawyers gave a collective sigh.

'So he was a con. Is that what we're saying here?'

'A fraud.'

'An embezzler.'

'Probably not even a lawyer.'

'Jesus.'

'That sawed off little bohunk –'

'We're going to have to go through every account he ever sent out, every cheque requisition he ever made,' Alex said. 'Find every penny ever paid to this numbered company.'

'Most of our accounting people have quit,' said Claire. 'They must have been in on it.'

'No telling how much we've lost in profits, and how much our clients have been bilked.'

'Thank God Sandy'd only been with us a year,' Claire said. 'We could have had ten years of dockets and accounts to sift through.'

'Like we do with Rick.'

'We'll have to call in the Law Society.'

'They'll want a forensic accountant to go through everything.'

'How much will *that* cost us?'

'We better call our insurers.'

'I'll do all that tomorrow – maybe Claire can give me a hand,' Alex said. Their eyes met. 'Unless somebody else wants to?'

'No, I'm happy to help . . . anything I can do . . .'

'Speaking of insurance,' Gillian said, 'how's that accidental death exclusion coming along? The eight million we're supposed to get? That would help with all of this, wouldn't it?'

'We're screwed, most likely,' Alex said. 'But I tell you – if those four guys knew about the policy exclusion and went off in that plane anyway, I'd kill them again.' He glared at his remaining partners. 'If just one of those idiots had enough sense of responsibility to have stayed off that plane . . .'

'Well, one of them didn't,' Shelagh snapped, 'so why don't we get on with the other offices and stop talking about it?' Maybe she wouldn't have to kill herself, she reflected, dully. It looked as though Alexander might save her the trouble.

'At least we can count on this office to have no skeletons in its closet,' Dan said.

The others laughed with relief as the last of Ross Owen's drawers was opened. Shelagh laughed hardest of all, having spent the past hour tormented by the fear that they might find something to incriminate her – a pair of silk panties, say (used), in one of Ross's drawers. She could deny ownership, of course, but what if they found something that pointed incontrovertibly to her? Sure, everybody seemed to know about her affair with Ross (a shock, though she should have guessed), but they weren't entitled to humiliating details.

'He sure took enough pictures of his kids,' Dan said, sorting through the things in one of the drawers.

'Oh?' Shelagh said.

'How many did he have again? Six?'

'Five,' she answered, a little too quickly.

'I guess these are the kids at all different ages.' Dan carefully picked the photos out from the rest of the things and piled them neatly on the desk. Some were framed, some weren't; others were in plastic pocket-sized albums or photo folds.

'That's the trouble with children's pictures,' said Claire. 'By the time you get them framed for the office, the kids already look totally different.'

'I'm always trying to take good shots of my nephews,' Dan said. 'I have a heck of a time getting them to hold still, even with auto-focus on my camera. Well,' he sighed, 'there's not much else in here. Some popsicle-stick art . . . a couple of yoghurt containers with glitter and stones stuck all over them.'

'He wasn't here all that much,' Alex said. 'He was always on the road, or off with his kids.'

'He was a real family man, wasn't he?' Dan said. 'That's what's so god-awfully sad about Ross dying . . . those poor little fatherless kids.'

'And look at these sweet lumpy clay things they made,' Gillian said. 'Kids have to go free-form with modelling these days, I guess. Can you imagine how parents would protest if their children came home with ashtrays like we used to make? We even used *asbestos*.' She carried the photographs and children's art over to an empty box and gently placed them inside. 'Marcia will want all these treasures. Maybe we should wrap everything in newspaper so nothing gets broken.'

'The mailroom can do it Monday,' Alex said. 'Let's get going with the rest.' He looked at his watch. 'If we hurry, I can catch the last few innings of the ball game. We've just got one more office to do. But Peter – God love him – was an unmade bed. If anyone's got a roach motel, bring it along.'

'Fishing lures, fishing flies, books on fishing. A rubber salmon.' Claire plopped the fish down on the ink-stained and much-scribbled upon blotter of Pete Johnson's desk.

'That's a Kokanee,' said Dan, 'that salmon.'

'Whatever,' said Shelagh.

'He must have got it out on the west coast.' Dan was still examining the fish. 'Pete was a great fisherman. He won a Small Mouth Bass tournament last year.'

'And here's the prize to prove it.' Gillian was lugging a large trophy of a jumping fish, thickly covered with dust, from Pete's equally dusty bookcase. 'There's more of these fish trophies at the back there.'

'So all these fish-loving manifestations go to Helen?' Claire asked.

'Pete's hobby was a sore spot with her,' Alex replied. 'I'm not sure Helen would want any of it. They'd been separated for almost a year.'

'I didn't know it was that long.' Claire paused. 'That's so sad. I thought Peter'd been looking kind of lost lately – his hair all wild, clothes a mess. As though no one was looking after him.'

'He'd always been that way,' Shelagh said. 'You can't blame Helen.'

Claire took down some books from Pete's shelves. 'He sure had some great reading though: *Bass Myths Exploded, The Scream Of The Reel.*'

'I guess Helen wouldn't let him keep all this at home,' Gillian said. 'Look here – behind his door. There's about a dozen rods, two pairs of rubber boots. Hats, tackle boxes, some kind of net. The cleaners must have hated doing this office.'

'It was an ongoing battle with the union,' Alex said. 'We should give everything to the goodwill store.'

'I wouldn't mind first dibs on this baby.' Dan was casting an imaginary fly with a wooden rod. 'This just might be a genuine Pinky Gillum.'

'If it is, you're not getting it,' Alexander said. 'Whatever has any value will help offset some of our losses. If Helen feels like donating it to the cause. Which she likely won't.'

'Wow,' Dan said. 'Look at this lure. This could be worth a bundle too.'

'Ugh,' Shelagh said. 'Somebody swat that thing.'

'Could be a Bumblepuppy, hand-tied by Theodore Gordon. If it is, it's worth about two grand.'

'Didn't I tell you how much I like feathered buggy things with hooks?' Shelagh said.

'Here's more fishing books,' Claire said. *'Hook 'Em an' Cook 'Em, The Weedy World of The Pickerel, Muskie Masters.* Pretty macho guy, wasn't he?'

'How do you know so much about fishing, Dan?' Gillian was looking over a grey tackle box that she thought might be perfect for storing oil paints and brushes.

'We had lunch together a lot, Pete and I. He used to drool over his catalogues of rare and unusual rods and lures. I guess his enthusiasm was contagious.'

'I wonder if the word "tacky" has its roots in "tackle",' said Gillian, examining a desk clock over which an open-mouthed pickerel leaped.

'We should call in some fish paraphernalia appraisers,' Claire said, 'assuming there is such a thing.'

'I'll find out,' said Dan. 'I've got to know if I'm right about the Pinky Gillum.'

'I'm going to start on the desk so we can all get out of here some time today. Keys.' Shelagh looked around at the others. 'Who's got them?'

'Looks like Pete was a closet snacker.' Dan was peering into the credenza. 'There's got to be a dozen bags of cookies in here.'

'As long as there aren't any dead fish, I'm happy,' Shelagh said.

'Throw it all out.' Claire passed him a garbage bag.

'Chips, nachos, peanuts . . . Some of it almost petrified.'

'Watch out for silverfish,' Gillian said. 'I'm an expert on those.'

For a few moments the room was silent, but for the sounds of fishing gear being moved around and the rustle of foil snack bags being tossed into the garbage. Then Shelagh let out a shriek. 'Oh-my-god! It's alive!' She slammed shut the desk drawer.

'What?'

'Where?'

'In there!' She pointed. 'I can't look. It's a hideous rodent of some kind.'

'Stand back,' Alex warned.

Dan grabbed a fishing net. 'Careful. It might be rabid.'

Cautiously, Alex pulled open the drawer an inch. No one moved. He opened it wider. 'It's not alive,' he said. 'Relax.'

'So? What is it?'

Alex pulled a floppy mass of brown curls from the drawer and tossed it on to the desk. 'A wig,' he said.

'Well, what on earth was Peter doing with a wig in his desk?' Gillian said. 'I mean, he had enough hair.'

'It's a *female* wig,' said Alex. 'And digging a little deeper in here, we find . . . a pair of heels. Size 10 would be my guess.' He placed a pair of mauve suede pumps on the desk. 'There's some kind of slinky dress in here too.'

'Poor old Pete.' Dan shook his head.

'Maybe he used the wig to lure Muskies,' Gillian mused.

'How can you joke about this?' Shelagh moaned. 'We've been partners with a blackmailer, a con man and a transvestite! Is no one in this firm *normal*!'

'I like to think I am,' Alex said drily.

'We don't know that Pete was a transvestite,' Gillian said. 'He could have been a female impersonator.'

'What's the *difference*?' Shelagh demanded. 'He dressed up in women's clothing! God knows where he went in it, or who might have seen him.'

'It happens,' said Alex. 'There were a couple of judges last year, in that big downtown hotel . . .' He was now stacking cartons of books on top of each other. 'Personally, I can leave forever unanswered the question of Peter's sexual preferences. Let's get the cleaners to clear out whatever else is in that drawer – it can all go to Goodwill. Unless one of you girls wants it?'

'Or you do,' said Claire.

'Or Anna does,' Shelagh added.

'Right then.' Dan smiled. 'It looks like a wrap. A few little surprises here and there but nothing we can't handle if we hang tough. Things will be kopacetic soon.'

'Tickety-boo,' said Shelagh.

'So why don't we all head for the nearest bar? Drown our sorrows in a few ales? I know a super watering hole we can walk to from here.'

'I've got to get home, Dan –'

'We've got people coming –'

'I have a date.'

'The ball game –'

'I'll take a rain check.'

A moment later, the five lawyers took one last look around Pete

Johnson's office. Alexander pulled the door closed and Shelagh locked it. No one felt like talking any more. Silently, the partners retrieved handbags and jackets from their respective offices and left the office tower, each heading off, immersed in their own gloomy thoughts, in her or his separate direction.

16 $

Two floors below ground, in the Food Court of the office tower, Claire anxiously scanned the crowds of lunching office workers, hoping to spot Marcia Owen. Her secretary had arranged for them to meet near the Chick 'N' Deli counter at noon. Apparently, Marcia didn't care for fancy restaurants and was only interested in a quick bite. A relaxed atmosphere, and somewhere secluded, would have been more Claire's style, particularly when unpalatable matters (Shelagh?) might be on the table for discussion.

As Claire waited, the harassed short-order staff of the Chick 'N' Deli repeatedly asked what she wanted to eat. 'Still thinking,' she said each time, smiling as she pretended to be interested in the high-gloss menu boards posted over the area where chicken parts were being fried. At twenty past twelve, when there was still no sign of Marcia, Claire was no longer smiling, but she didn't know whether to be annoyed or relieved. In another ten minutes, she thought, she could reasonably assume Marcia wouldn't be coming and leave. Besides, Marcia knew where the firm was – she could always take the elevator upstairs to see Claire – except that Claire had a meeting at two with the legal insurers, so that the person Marcia would likely run into was Shelagh. Claire sighed heavily, cursing her partner and her runaway libido.

Marcia was to be greatly pitied, of course, for losing her husband and the father of her children; but she couldn't have been happy with Ross's philandering, assuming she knew about it, or suspected. Perhaps her life had changed for the better now; maybe Marcia's psychotherapist would turn out to be the good husband that Ross never was. With these optimistic thoughts in mind, Claire managed to find two seats in the shiny Sargasso Sea of round, formica-topped tables, and sat down, her stomach grumbling, to watch people streaming from the escalators and queuing for oriental combo-plates, vegetarian pita pockets, fried chicken or burgers. She preferred to avoid the crowded concourse between twelve and two. The press of bodies, the high-pitched babble of voices, the slow shuffling line-ups for food, irritated her. She was feeling that way now, as she waited for a woman she barely knew, who was extremely (unpardonably) late.

'You wouldn't be Claire Cunningham, would you? I said to myself: That *has* to be her, sitting alone at that table and looking so ticked off.'

'Do I know you? I'm sorry –' Claire half rose from her chair.

'No. But you're about to.'

Claire nodded, waiting for her to say more, wondering whether the woman might be mentally unstable: perhaps concealing, in the folds of her loose cotton shift, a handgun with a single bullet in its chamber, reserved for some, *any*, Bay Street lawyer.

'I should have told your secretary what I look like, so's you could watch out for me. Just tell Claire to look for the fat lady, I should have said. You could hardly miss me. Goodness. Everyone around here is so *skinny*. Though how could you expect me to stay thin, working in a doughnut shop practically my whole life?'

'You're not – fat,' Claire faltered, still wondering, with some anxiety, to whom she was speaking. 'I think there's too much emphasis put on how much women weigh,' she added, lamely.

'Easy for you to say. Look at you. A rake. A stick. No, not even that – a twig. Like Twiggy. Remember her?'

'I've had my ups and downs,' Claire said, bemused by having such a personal discussion with a total stranger. 'And I do watch what I eat. It's not easy . . . with two kids.' At that, her hand was grasped and heartily pumped.

'Look, I'm your lunch date, Grace Owen. And I'm sorry I'm so late. I got totally lost in this underground. They should post a map or something, with everyone tunnelling around like moles. You think anyone would give me directions? No way. Everyone's far too busy to help out a gal from the sticks. It's a mean world down here, isn't it?'

'Your name is *Grace* Owen?'

'Mrs Grace Owen. That's how widows are supposed to call themselves. You'd know that, of course, being a lawyer.' She settled into the moulded plastic chair opposite Claire, her loose shift billowing around her like a small parachute.

'You were Ross's wife?' Claire was trying to recall what she'd learned about bigamy in law school. It was a stretch, going back that far. Something about a form of marriage – it didn't even have to be legal, as long as the deceived party reasonably believed it was. Or maybe the belief didn't even have to be reasonable. Some incense, a bit of hocus pocus, a ring – any small ceremony would be enough to dupe some women, sad to say. She glanced at Grace's left hand, at the plain gold band and modest diamond. 'This is a hard question for me to ask you, Marcia –'

'Grace.'

'Of course.' Claire flushed. 'I don't know why I called you Marcia.'

'You don't, eh?' Grace gave her a sceptical look.

'So, I guess you know about Marcia?'

'Do I know about her? Do I *know* about her! I know so much about her I even know what kind of *bubble bath* she likes. Spring Rain. Ross brought me some once. Like, he wanted both his wives to smell the same. I think that was kind of weird, don't you?'

'A bit.' Claire nodded and studied the face across the table from her: traces of adolescent acne, oversized glasses, hair that hadn't had a proper cut in years. But underneath all of that was a suggestion of good bone structure, and Grace's eyes were large and deep green. She might even have been beautiful, given some care and attention. Was it because of Ross she'd let her appearance slide? And never gone further than a doughnut shop? 'I'd like to get back to the question I was about to ask you,' Claire said carefully, 'and I don't mean to pry or suggest anything . . . untoward. So please don't be offended.'

'You can't offend me. I'm an easy-going gal. Ask anyone.' Grace had taken off her very dirty glasses and was wiping them with a fold of her dress.

'Were you and Ross . . . really married?'

Grace fitted her backside more comfortably into her chair and smiled slightly. 'Of course we were. Signed, sealed and delivered. Licence and all. What kind of girl do you think I am?'

'I didn't – I wasn't –'

'Well, that question was too easy. Ask me another.'

'Why don't we get some lunch?' said Claire.

'Sounds good to me.' Grace rose easily – floated, actually, like a helium balloon – and Claire followed her pillowy form to the end of the queue at the Chick 'N' Deli. 'We've got one of these out in Brighton,' Grace said over her shoulder. 'That's near Kingston, in case you were wondering. It's one of those blink-and-you'll-miss-it pit stops. But it's home. Ross has a client out that way. Which is how I met him. He stopped in for a half-dozen honey-dips one night and the rest is history. I never could get that man to put on any weight, though. And if anything would do it, you'd think it would be doughnuts.'

'Have anything you want to eat, Grace. It's on the firm, of course.'

'We knew Ross had another family back here in the city,' Grace confided, when they were settled again at their table with their half-chickens in baskets. 'And we knew he couldn't always be with us. But we were willing to share. It seemed selfish for one family to claim him all to themselves – he was such a great dad.' She sighed. 'I don't think he meant to do anything wrong, by having two families. I think he just loved kids.'

And wives, Claire thought. And mistresses. 'So, you had children with Ross?' She smiled politely. 'How wonderful.'

'Four. And I have two kids from my first marriage. But they thought Ross was their dad too. I never bothered to tell them different, though I know kids are supposed to be told the truth. But why screw up their little world? It'll get screwed up soon enough anyway. So, who looks after your kids? When you're here at work?'

'We have a – nanny.' Claire frowned. She always had difficulty referring to Francine as a nanny. And now that she had that ring through her bottom lip, those studs in her nostril . . .

'That's the way it is now, I guess, with you working women.

Nannies, *au pairs* and what-not. I bet you've got a cleaning lady too. Probably a gardener. A dog-walker . . .'

'But you work yourself,' Claire said, ignoring the questions about her 'staff'. 'You just told me.'

'Sure, in Horton's. Three shifts a week. My mum takes the kids for me those nights. I only do it because I need the money, believe me.'

They looked at each other for a moment, appraisingly.

'But you met Ross because you worked in that doughnut shop,' Claire finally said. 'You wouldn't have met him otherwise.'

'Yeah,' Grace blinked. 'I met Ross.'

'So how many years have you . . . had you . . . known him?'

'Eleven, this September. I'll show you some pictures.' Grace hoisted her handbag on to her lap. It was one of those crazy quilt patched affairs, made from scraps and ends of leather, crudely zig-zag-stitched together. She dug through it until she found a photo-shop envelope that she handed over to Claire before turning her attention to her chicken. 'Matthew, Jake, Connie and Chuck – they're all Ross's. Just ask me if you want to know who anyone is in any of the pictures.'

Claire looked through the photographs, an agreeable, interested expression on her face, despite her growing alarm. There was Ross, looking a trifle embarrassed – as well he should! – holding a baby up to the camera; Ross steadying a teetering little boy on ice skates; Ross holding a beer and laughing, feet up on a lawn chair, on a wooden deck with potted geraniums behind him, two small girls with gap-toothed grins on his lap.

'That's Caroline,' Grace said proudly, leaning forward and pointing with a french fry. 'And that's Lydia. She looks like Ross, don't you think?'

'Ah,' said Claire, 'yes.'

'Funny, eh? She's not his. Those two monkeys are from my first marriage.'

As Claire continued going through the pictures, she had a disconcerting flashback . . . the weekend . . . Ross's open drawer . . . Dan's question about how many children Ross had, and his comment about the number of photographs as he piled them on the desk . . . the children's artwork that Gillian carefully collected. Now all of it was boxed up and on its way to –

'Mrs Owen?'

'Grace.'

'Did Marcia know about you and your children?'

Grace was steadily grazing, her attention apparently on her chicken, her lips and fingers glistening with grease. 'Ross kept saying he was going to have this big talk with her some day about us but I don't think he ever got around to it. I been waiting for that big talk for eleven years.'

'I have to make a call. It's urgent. Something I forgot to do. Would you excuse me for one minute?'

'Oh, sure, I know.' Grace took a bite and waved a drumstick at Claire. 'You working girls . . . Don't mind me. I've got all the time in the world. I never have any important calls to make. Might as well get rid of my phone, I sometimes think. No one to call anyways, now that Ross is gone.' She looked around her over the Food Court. Her jaw stopped working on the chicken. 'So you go on. Off you go. Scoot. Make your important call.'

Claire stood up, wondering where she could find a telephone in the underground concourse. Or should she try a quick dash upstairs to her office and leave Grace sitting there alone? Though she seemed under control – so far there was no trace of the hysteria that Claire had heard over the phone – she wasn't sure how stable Grace was. And the elevators were so slow between twelve and two. 'Funny,' she said vaguely, 'I suddenly can't think where there's a public phone down here.'

'Over by the john. I saw it when I came in.' Grace pulled the photographs back over the table towards her.

'Don't put those away. I haven't finished admiring them.'

'Sure, sure. They're just kids. Nobody likes looking at pictures of other people's kids. What are you supposed to say? Oh, she's cute. Oh, he looks like his father. And how old is this little guy?'

'I'm not like that. I wasn't bored at all.'

'Just make your call. I'll finish my lunch. I notice you've hardly touched yours. No wonder you're so skinny.'

'I'll just be two seconds. It's important – I'm really sorry.' Claire plunged into the crowd, heading for the sign with the bathroom and telephone symbols. Thankfully, no one was using the phone. 'Gillian,' she said as soon as her call went through, 'I'm so glad you're there.'

'Aren't you supposed to be having lunch with Marcia?'

'Yes – no. I need you to go check the mailroom. For that box that was going out to her today. I'll wait.'

'What's so important?'

'Just go and get it.'

'You won't tell me why I should do this?'

'Look – I'm having lunch with Mrs Owen now.'

'I know. That's what you just said. I think.'

'But not Marcia Owen. With *Grace*. Grace Owen! Oh, Christ!'

'Mother? Sister?'

'His *other wife*!'

There was a silence. 'Oops,' said Gillian.

'And he had *four children* with her.'

'Ross had nine kids?'

'Plus two more who think he was their father.'

'Ross had *eleven* children?'

'That we know of . . .'

'And all those cute kid pictures are being sent out to Marcia –'

'Who *doesn't know* about Grace!'

'Holy shit! Shelagh's going to have a meltdown. Ross, a bigamist. Maybe a polygamist.'

'Gillian – just go check the mailroom, okay?'

Across the Food Court, Claire watched Grace pick listlessly at the last bits of chicken, open her handbag and take out a lipstick and compact. She applied the lipstick, powdered her nose and raked and patted her hair with her fingers. Then she gazed around, waiting for Claire to come back, sipping her Diet Coke.

'It's gone,' Gillian said, back on the line. 'The box went rush courier, first thing.'

'Can we get it back?'

'It was likely delivered hours ago. It left here at nine. God. Poor Marcia.'

'Poor Grace.'

They were silent for a moment. 'Look,' Claire finally said, 'could you put a trace on the box anyway? Maybe Marcia wasn't home when they got there. Maybe – if we're lucky – it's on its way back to the office. Or some Fed Ex place.'

'I'll do what I can.'

*   *   *

'Well now!' Grace said as Claire slid into her chair a moment later. 'I hope whatever it was got sorted out all right?'

'I hope so too. But I somehow doubt it.' She looked uneasily at Grace.

'That's the business world for you. It's very stressful, isn't it? But doughnut shops have their bad moments too, you know. Everything does ... work, husbands, kids. So look, thanks for the lunch. I won't waste much more of your valuable time.'

'You haven't wasted any, Grace.'

'I've pretty well said my piece, I guess. I wanted to meet someone else from Ross's firm. Let you all know that, hey, here I am, right out there in Brighton. In the doughnut shop. Come out and see me some time.'

'We could have gone somewhere nicer for lunch. A good restaurant. Any place you wanted.'

'I like to stick with what I know.' Grace smiled from behind her still-smeary glasses. 'I'm thankful to you for seeing me.'

Claire nodded. 'I don't know how much help I've been. Maybe just talking to someone about it after all these years ... finally being able to let out your secret ... It just shows how poorly we really know one another. I mean, here I am – was – a partner with Ross for years, and I had no idea ...' She looked, hopefully, at Grace. 'You do feel a little better now, don't you? After this talk?'

Grace twisted her mouth to one side. 'A bit. Maybe. But there was one thing I wanted to ask you about. So I guess I better just spit it out.'

'Sure,' Claire smiled uncertainly. 'I'm here to help any way I can.'

Grace leaned forward conspiratorially, her ample breasts pressing on to the table top. 'Well,' she began, 'now that Ross is gone –'

'Yes?'

'I was thinking that I might need a lawyer. To handle things ... the estate – isn't that what it's called?'

'Yes. That seems like a sensible idea.'

'And Marcia, of course – to handle Marcia. I have to expect a bit of fur to fly from that end, don't I?'

'Well, I suppose –'

'At first I was really upset by the accident. Oh, what a dumb thing to say. I was a mess. Totalled. I was sure I'd never get over it. My Ross, somewhere at the bottom of Lake Ontario. And having to tell the kids –'

'I can't imagine.' Claire reached out and put her hand over Grace's plump one. 'I just can't imagine.'

'But then I got mad.' Grace pulled her hand back. 'How would you like to be part of the *other* family? The *other* wife? Not even invited to that big downtown service you guys had for Ross? I had to read about it in the *Whig Standard*.'

'It was a memorial service for all four lawyers. It was mostly only lawyers who went. And boring business types. Quite impersonal, really.'

'Marcia arranged the actual funeral. A small private affair, I guess they called it. But of course I didn't get to go to that either. She was the status wife, the one everybody feels so sorry for now.' Grace's eyes glittered as she picked up a Chick 'N' Deli napkin and dabbed at her upper lip. 'The *other* family never counts for squat. It's Marcia and *her* kids who get all the attention. It's been like that from day one.'

'Grace, please. Be fair. We didn't know about you. No one did, did they?' God, Claire thought, what if Grace and her children *had* shown up at the memorial service? Then she fast-forwarded to Marcia opening the door to the Fed Ex delivery man, signing for the box, taking it into her kitchen, slicing through the packing tape with a paring knife . . . Surprise!

'That's another thing the status family gets,' Grace said, 'protection from the truth. It was all very well for me to know every detail about Marcia and little Obie and the rest of them – I've even seen their pictures. Hundreds of them. But us, out in Brighton? A bunch of nobodies.'

'I'm sure you weren't nobodies to Ross. I'm sure he showed your pictures around . . . probably kept some up in his office . . .'

'Well,' Grace drew herself up, 'I'm not so sure any more.'

'It wasn't easy for Marcia, you know – the service. It was awful, really. You're lucky you weren't there.'

'You mean because of Audrey? That's the one saving grace with being the hidden wife. I never had to be nice to Ross's mother – and neither did my kids. Never got their cheeks pinched by the old lady with bad breath.'

'There! You see?' Claire beamed at her. 'That's a big advantage right there. Huge.'

'They never got Christmas or birthday presents either. Never talked about Grandma and Grandpa. They've only got my mum. Oh, sure, it's a real bonus, never meeting Audrey and Derek. What do they call it? The booby prize? With me as the prize booby.' She gave Claire the look Claire knew she deserved.

'Did Ross have any other – entanglements?' Claire asked gently.

'Is that what we are? An entanglement? Is that a legal term?' Grace zippered her handbag shut and folded her arms over it. 'Fat Grace and her brood from the boonies. You probably wonder what Ross saw in me.'

'I don't wonder that at all. You seem like a wonderful warm person. And what was between you is none of my business anyway.'

'Well, there weren't any other entanglements, as you put it. That I know of, at least.'

Except for Shelagh, Claire thought. How had Ross found the time and energy for three strong-willed women and eleven children? No wonder he'd always looked so wasted and wan.

'What I want to know is, will you take my case? Will you be my lawyer?'

Claire knew she should have anticipated this question, but for some reason she hadn't. 'I don't do estates work,' she said, grateful that she was able to say this truthfully. 'Or family law. And I don't see how I could represent you anyway, Grace. Ross was my partner. And he was a – bigamist.' She felt queasy as she looked at Grace, whose face was settling into a look of angry determination. All those years of feeling shame and the sense of being hidden away; the panic, pain and joy of four births, experienced alone, probably, wondering when – or if – Ross would show up to see each new baby. 'It would be a conflict of interest for me to act for you. Bigamy is, as I'm sure you know, illegal.' How despicable she was, she thought, doling out this preachy, insensitive legal pronouncement.

'Well, which one is the illegal one? That's what I want to know. My marriage to Ross? Or Marcia's?'

'I'm not sure I know. Or that I should say anything about it. I'm in a conflict of interest already, actually.' Claire looked at Grace unhappily. Sure, she thought, hide behind a conflict of interest, you wimp.

'Which one is legal?' Grace spoke carefully, putting small angry spaces between her words.

'Well,' Claire swallowed, 'speaking in generalities, of course, the first marriage would be the valid one – in law. But that doesn't mean you wouldn't have any rights – as mother of Ross's children – even in respect of the two girls from your first marriage, since they thought of Ross as their dad.'

'Lydia and Caroline.'

'You yourself may be entitled to some support – from the estate. You would have all the rights of a common-law wife.'

'Who says I came second?'

'Pardon?'

'What makes you think I'm the common-law wife? How do you know my marriage to Ross was the second one?' Behind her cloudy glasses, Grace's green eyes had become sharp.

'I don't know that,' Claire said warily. 'I have no idea when Ross and Marcia were married, or you and Ross.'

'So it will be pretty interesting to find out, won't it? For inheritance purposes and all that?'

'Yes,' Claire said, 'I suppose so.'

'Has anyone found a will?'

'Not that I've heard.'

'Didn't think so.' Grace settled back in her chair, triumph on her face. 'Ross wasn't that organized.' Around them, the hum of voices in the Food Court had all but disappeared and most of the tables had been cleared, but for some plastic trays and a litter of paper cups and straws. It was almost two o'clock. 'Are you going to eat your chicken?' Grace asked. ''Cause if you're not, I wouldn't mind a hunk of that breast.'

'Is she gone?' Shelagh stuck her head around the edge of Claire's office door. 'Coast clear?'

'She's gone,' Claire said. 'She never came up here.'

'You mean I hid under my desk for nothing?' Looking relieved, Shelagh entered Claire's office and perched on the edge of her desk. She was wearing black leather: pants and a form-fitting jacket over a dazzling white shirt. The ubiquitous zipper was concealed in the front seam of the jacket – there was only a silver ring, pulled halfway down, to suggest its existence and the ease with which she could be undressed. 'What are you doing here?' she said to Gillian who was standing by Claire's window. 'Haven't you got some widget to patent? I want to talk to Claire about Marcia.'

'Too bad Claire didn't see Marcia today,' Gillian said. 'You're a hard person to feel sorry for, you know that, Shelagh? But I do. Well, almost.'

Shelagh adjusted herself on Claire's desk and crossed her legs. There was the creak of leather. 'Really?' she said. 'You feeling sorry for me is not a good sign. What's going on, Claire?'

'Tell her,' Gillian said.

'Well, Shelagh,' Claire began, marvelling at the number of 'careful' conversations she was having that day, 'you were not the only woman in Ross's life. I mean, not the only other woman.'

Shelagh lifted her chin. 'So, who? You?'

'Of course not.'

'A woman named Grace,' Gillian said. 'Grace Owen. Ross had two wives. That we know of.'

'But I was still the only other woman? There was a wife, and another wife. But I was the *other woman*. Right?'

'So far.' Claire frowned. 'It seems that way.'

'Okay,' Shelagh said. 'I can live with that.'

'And his other family had six kids,' Gillian said. 'Four of them Ross's.'

Shelagh nodded, digesting the news. 'Busy guy, wasn't he?'

'Is that all you're going to say?' Claire asked. 'You don't want any details?'

'I don't know. What does she look like? The other wife?'

She should have expected Grace Owen's looks to be Shelagh's main concern, Claire thought.

'So what? A dog? She's a dog? Makes pit stops at every hydrant?'

'Would you feel better or worse if she was?'

'Not sure yet.'

'She's pretty, actually. If she took better care of herself she could really look good. In a girl-next-door kind of way. She lives in the country – some place called Brighton.'

'Brighton?'

'So she says.'

'Ross had a client out that way.'

'That's how he met Grace.'

'In a doughnut shop,' Gillian added, feeling nasty.

'That so?' Shelagh sniffed. 'Doughnuts.'

'You'll probably never have to meet her,' Claire said. 'She wants a lawyer – I told her the firm can't act for her, Ross being what he was . . .'

'You mean, a bigamist?'

'And one of our partners.'

'I'm just wondering about one thing,' Shelagh said, examining her nails. 'In terms of guilt – my own personal guilt. Assuming I have any, of course. Does all of this Grace Owen business now compound it? Or make it less?'

'Makes it less,' Claire said.

'Definitely.' Gillian nodded. 'The guy was top soil. A bigamist. Possibly a polygamist.'

'A Casanova. A Don Juan.'

'Maybe even a Marquis de Sade,' Gillian said.

'Well, it's kind of hard to see Ross in quite that light –' Shelagh coughed, trying not to remember his forays into s & m.

'You were just a pawn in his very sick game,' Claire said. 'He wasn't a well man.'

'You're right. I feel better knowing about Grace. This is good. Good for me. I didn't take Ross away from his wife and kids – he already had another wife and kids to do that.'

'Right.'

'And if he didn't want to go to Boston, he could have gone out to Brighton. Should have, in fact. Not bugged me about staying at my place.'

'Who says he didn't want to go to Boston?' Gillian said.

'I don't know. I didn't say that. Did I say that?'

'Perhaps it's best not to pursue this line of questioning,' Claire said.

'Got to go!' Shelagh creaked to a standing position. 'Time is money, girls. Thanks for the intelligence on Grace. It's been a slice.'

'Ross didn't want to go to Boston,' Gillian said faintly, after she had gone. 'He wanted to stay with Shelagh . . .'

'Eight million dollars!' Claire put her head down on her desk.

The Tea

17 ∫

'For a hostess, the giving of a perfect afternoon tea is without doubt the most theatrical and charming challenge she will ever confront' –
The Delights of Tea

In the tradition established by her mother, the details of the lingerie tea were driving Claire mad, beginning with the invitations. Should she go for the traditional shower invitations (nosegays, fancy parasols, confetti), or for the tea-party type (china cups, lace tablecloths)? There were none that suggested a tea party *and* bridal shower combination, and certainly nothing that hinted at underwear as the supporting theme.

After mulling endlessly over two styles of basic afternoon-tea invitations (having narrowed it down from three), Claire finally decided on a box of Victorian-style pop-ups: an intricately patterned blue and white tea pot that sprang from an embossed background of filigreed paper scattered with forget-me-nots. The cards were packaged in boxes of twelve. She had calculated that there would be at least fifteen women at her tea, give or take a couple due to last-minute regrets or additions, and ignoring for the moment the client dilemma, which could not be ignored for much longer. She would, therefore, require two boxes of invitations. But Paper Pleasures didn't have two.

Sniffling miserably from a messy, late-summer cold, she tried to be patient while the salesgirl checked the stock room of Paper Pleasures, then the drawers under the display racks of cards. There was never anything worthwhile in those drawers, Claire thought irritably, as she blew her streaming nose, waiting for the bad news. Obtaining a second box of Victorian pop-up cards from the supplier would take a few weeks, the salesgirl told her, looking sympathetic. It was also possible that the pop-ups were a discontinued design and that the supplier would not be able to get a second box. Would Claire like her to try another store? Yes, Claire would.

Several calls later, another box was finally located at Paper Pleasures in a distant suburban shopping mall. Oh, for heaven's sake, choose something else, Claire's common sense snapped. But the Victorian pop-ups were so charming, her women's-magazine side argued – such a lovely blue, and that soft white, the combination so like the classic willow pattern china that was enjoying such a resurgence lately.

Though it was barely noon, the summer cold was sapping Claire of her energy: she was already exhausted from the effort of a trip to the library to borrow all available books on the etiquette of tea and recipes for the crustless dainties one was expected to serve. In the back seat of her car were *The Tai Chi of Tea*, *Afternoon Bliss – A Brief Chronicle of Tea in England*, and *Tea Comes of Age* – all background reading – and four cookbooks: the teasingly titled *Love Letters and Lady's Navels*, with its lumpish sister *Black Buns and Basil Butter*, and the prosaically named *Tea Time Cookbook*. The most promising of all, though also the most formidable, was *The Delights of Tea – A Retrospective with Recipes*. Claire had peeked inside to see double column-length recipes for French country prune tart, crystallized violets and rosewater sugar cookies; a hefty index on tea equipment; and a section entitled 'The Proper Setting' that was sure to give her pause. (Did she have one? Could she create one?) This tea business was considerably more complicated than she'd expected. Claire had been allowed to borrow the books only after clearing up her account with the library: paying eight dollars in overdue fines and twelve more as compensation for *Mrs Pig's Bulk Buy* which had not been returned by Francine when it was due the previous spring, and was therefore classified as 'permanently lost' by the library's computer.

'They'll hold the invitations for you until closing time,' the salesgirl was saying as Claire's brain clunked rustily into gear, forcing her to consider the trip to the mall through noon-hour traffic, the parking, the search for Paper Pleasures in a three-level shopping galleria. All for her own stupid vanity. She blew her nose again and poked around in the boxes of pens and sealing wax on the store's counter, waiting for her change. One of the boxes displayed a multicoloured bundle of wedge-shaped felt-pens that were supposed to enable one to create a professional calligraphic effect, without the tedious practice otherwise required. Claire chose a deep blue one to match the invitations, feeling a little cheered. Victorian pop-up cards with calligraphed envelopes. How satisfying!

After picking up the invitations, if she had the time (and energy) she meant to stop in at the party rental place, just to confirm what was available in the afternoon tea department.

'Rent?' Elfriede had exclaimed, during their last Sunday phone conversation. 'I have everything you need – I was just about to clean my silver tea service for you.'

'Oh, Mother, you don't want to be polishing and lugging stuff all the way over here –'

'I won't be lugging. We have a car.'

'But taking all your things out, cleaning everything, and driving two hundred miles . . .' Claire had hoped to keep Elfriede's involvement in the tea to a minimum. Ensuring that her mother was happy and busy (These lemons aren't quite fresh. Haven't you got any silver polish? You aren't going to use *those* cups!) would be more trouble than doing everything herself.

'And there are some things I'll have to rent, that I'm sure you don't have.'

'Like what?' Elfriede's voice was challenging.

'I don't know . . . a samovar.'

'Samovar? Who uses a samovar? We're not in Czarist Russia here.'

'Lemon forks, sugar tongs.' Claire had read aloud from the list the rental place had faxed to her office. 'Bun warmers.'

'I have all that. Don't you remember the teas I used to have for my art appreciation group? Everything just sits here now, gathering dust. I'd like to use it again. Gives me an excuse to shine things up.'

'It's amazing how much I don't have. Even though my cupboards are overflowing.'

'I have dozens of tablecloths, embroidered napkins coming out of my ears – some of them from my mother. Everything is perfect, hardly used.'

'You know, Mother,' Claire had sighed, 'tea for me is a cup and a bag. Maybe a spoon. And I only drink it when I'm sick. Then it's bag in or bag out – that's the only decision.'

'I even have hot water pots. Silver. Beautiful. It's no trouble to polish them. And Dad won't mind driving me.'

'But what will we do with him during the tea?' Basil and his philosophizing, mingling with as many as two dozen women, was a spectre Claire hadn't at that point taken the time to contemplate.

'Oh, he can go out somewhere. A book store. Dad's happy anywhere, as long as he has something to read. But me? I'm not so sure. Aches and pains. You know. It's frightening how the body and mind fall apart.'

Claire sighed. 'Well, falling apart or not, dear, you'll still be the guest of honour at the tea. Since it's your birthday.'

'The guest of honour is the bride-to-be. Not some old woman.'

'You're not some old woman.' Claire and her mother were falling into their usual exhausting conversational pattern.

'You *could* ask me to pour the tea. That's considered quite an honour.'

'Sounds more like work than an honour. But if you want to, of course you should.'

'I'll make one of my lemon loaves. People love my lemon loaf. It's so refreshing.'

'Ah,' said Claire. 'Yes.'

'I have some other recipes . . . Linzertorten, poppyseed cake. You can serve hot savouries too – sausage rolls, scones. But the weather might be too warm, in September.'

'I was thinking about hiring a caterer –'

'For a *tea*?'

'There could be as many as twenty women coming. Maybe more.'

'My art appreciation teas sometimes had thirty. What's the big deal? I always managed. You don't need catering.'

'I work, Mother. Full-time. You didn't.'

'But you have that nanny person.'

'We have Francine.'

'Anyway, tell me – how is everything with your law firm?'

'Not good, if you want the truth. But it seems I still have a job – for the moment, at least. We have to move – to cheaper space.'

'And that poor old woman who made the big scene at the church?'

'I'm sure she's doing as well as can be expected.'

'Things will sort themselves out. Your father probably has some quotation he could give you to pass along to her, poor soul.' Elfriede hesitated. 'Not that you want to hear it.'

'At the moment,' said Claire, 'probably not.'

'I'll tell him to e-mail it to you.'

'Good idea.'

Harry and Molly were still at school when Claire got home from the mall a few hours later. Francine was out too – on her way to pick them up. Grateful for a few minutes to herself, Claire dumped her shopping bags and books on the stairs, retrieved the mail and collapsed with it on the living-room sofa. In amongst the flyers, fast-food coupons and bills was the latest *Katherine's Mail Order* catalogue. *Katherine's* advertised the sort of undergarments that women received as gifts from men but seldom appreciated, feeling then obliged to put them on. (It should have been called *male* order, as Shelagh once said.) A gift from *Katherine's* was usually about as welcome as a new carpet sweeper or (the gift from Basil that had ruined Elfriede's Christmas years ago) an electric carving knife. There were push-up padded satin bras (to make you look like a Shakespearean milk maid!), panties that worked their way up in between one's buttocks, itchy lace body stockings, scanty synthetic sleep wear. The models were often posed against incongruous backgrounds: a Victorian parlour, a skeet-shooting range, a river full of ducks.

But, despite a notable lack of real silk, could there possibly be something in *Katherine's Mail Order* that Anna would like? The prices were reasonable, Claire noted. But could she, possibly, justify buying something for another woman that she herself would not likely wear? The answer occurred to her, with surprising speed. Why not?

At the back of the catalogue was a new section called *Kate's Kosy Kountry*: thick with fly-fishing motifs, plaid flannel robes, drawstring pants and bed socks. In Claire's present state of mucus-filled misery, Kosy Kountry had an undeniable appeal. Comfort over style. Anna would get sick occasionally, just like anyone else. And even if she didn't, wouldn't she appreciate something comfortable to curl up in, by the fire, with Alexander? Maybe at some rustic lodge in winter? Claire turned the pages, impressed by almost everything she saw. Clearly, women were demanding comfort over sexiness, and Katherine had risen to the challenge with her new section.

Claire considered a page of shapeless long johns called 'rompers', longing to crawl into one, then fall into bed and heap the covers on top of herself. Despite the summer heat, her skin prickled with goosebumps – a sure sign of the 'flu. It would be quite a romp for a man, she imagined, to find the woman somewhere in that mountain of brushed flannel. Many might enjoy that sort of pursuit; Alex could well be one of them. (Not that Claire would ever know, or ever want to know, of course.) And then there were the oversized pyjamas with the turtleneck collar, wide ribbed wrist and ankle cuffs; the 'chill-chaser' in soft thermal knit, the blanket-fleece 'lounger' with drawstring hood, front pouch pocket and extra long shirt tail. There was also a battleship grey, strictly hands-off 'Long Jane union suit' with a snap-front placket and no entry point – as far as Claire could tell. Even the model didn't look good in that one. Well. She didn't need to go overboard with the practicality idea. This was, after all, a *lingerie* shower she was throwing. Pretty but comfortable should be her goal. Surely there would be something suitable in *Katherine's*? And buying would be so stress-free: no driving, no trudging through malls . . . All she had to do was call the 800 number, request rush delivery, and *voilà*. The parcel would be Fed-Exed to her doorstep within forty-eight hours. Gift-wrapped. Claire blew her nose with gusto, feeling much better.

She paused at a page where a model with tousled blonde hair pouted before a roaring hearth, one bare foot up on the arm of a horsehair settee. The garment she wore was described as a 'romantic nightdress'. It had lace-trimmed patch pockets, a deep ruffled hem that grazed the floor, and it was made from pure white 'double-brushed flannel'. Anna was sure to love it. Within minutes, Claire had placed her order and paid for it. Done.

Pleased with her efficiency, she flopped back on to the sofa to have a look through the tea books she'd borrowed from the library. *The Delights of Tea* fell open at the dreaded section on proper settings. 'As long as the setting is gracious and elegant,' Claire read, 'the tea party can take place anywhere you wish.' That seemed a bit of a contradiction. She tried to picture a gracious and elegant setting in a barn, a high-school auditorium, a mobile home . . . her own living room. Looking around with freshly critical eyes, she suddenly saw how thrown-together it seemed. No designer had had a hand in it, that was obvious, and yet Claire had always believed she'd managed to 'pull it off'; was forever surprised that guests never asked for the name of her decorator.

All those *objets* she had strategically placed here and there, that were meant to emulate cherished gifts from dear friends, suddenly looked like what they were: dusty clutter. She had no dear cherished friends, she realized, a gust of self-pity blowing over her. And that mill end of gold damask – not enough for curtains or even blinds – that she'd looped over a pole above the bay window . . . if a designer had done that for some decorating magazine, it would have been a 'witty statement'. But swagged by Claire, in her own living room, it looked like a mistake. What sort of bizarre decorating frenzy had made her think throwing remnants of fabric over curtain poles would look smart? She'd been befuddled by all those swatches, wallpaper samples and, each month, a batch of new decorating magazines that made her head whirl with tantalizing, time-consuming possibilities. She'd navigated through snow storms, driving to remote textile mills, discount fabric outlets, antique shops and garage sales for unique decorator accents. She'd learned a whole new vocabulary too: words like jabot, swag and finial. Doors and windows had 'treatments'; things that 'puddled' on the floor were much desired. (The last time there'd been a puddle on her floor,

Claire had slapped Cannon on the backside with a rolled-up newspaper.)

She closed *The Delights of Tea* and contemplated its cover: a silver tea service glowing dully, framed by polished cotton Liberty print curtains with goblet-pleated headings and brass tie-backs. She sighed, realizing she would have to make do with her ungracious, inelegant and all-wrong hodge-podge of a living room. Two weeks was hardly enough time to redecorate.

Discouraged, she turned to *The Tea Time Cookbook*. At least it looked friendly, more accessible. Its cover showed an avalanche of food: solid rib-sticking stuff. 'Ritual and formality should never be allowed to replace the sense of spontaneity and gaiety we strive to achieve,' Claire read in the section called 'Planning Our Tea'. Well, that was some comfort. Spontaneity and gaiety. She would have to remember that.

She closed the book and rested her head against the cushions of the sofa. The gracious setting and food were the least of her problems. The much bigger headache, and the one she'd been trying to avoid since the memorial service, was the guest list. Now that she'd bought twenty-four pop-up invitations and a calligraphy pen, she would be forced to deal with it: the invitations had to go out that week.

Leading the guest list was Elfriede Wolaniuk and, snapping close at her heels, Prue Cunningham – not because she had any interest in teas, or Anna or Claire's firm for that matter, but because she was sure to feel slighted if Elfriede were invited and she were not. Then there were Gillian and Shelagh – Claire's co-conspirators – though they remained adamant that the tea was, essentially, Claire's problem. While Claire liked to pretend that these friends and relatives would be generous and forgiving about her lack of abilities as a giver of teas and showers, it wasn't true. She cared very much what they would think. And Elfriede would feel personally humiliated – a failure as a mother, and Claire a failure as a woman – if Claire screwed up the tea, and *on her seventieth birthday*.

Next was Anna, of course (the wild card), and Anna's mother – both unknown quantities, except for Claire's sense that Anna was somewhat bizarre and unpredictable. Then there was Gillian's daughter, Isadora, who would be sure to add a touch of the macabre. Gillian had asked Claire if she could bring her, for some reason known only to Gillian, and Claire had felt so sorry for her after that unpleasantness in the church that she'd agreed. She doubted Isadora would show up, though: afternoon tea wasn't exactly her scene. She put a mental question mark beside Isadora's name and went on with the list, adding Helen Johnson, Marcia Owen and Jocelyn Durham. As wives of his partners, they had all known Alexander for years and each had, at one time or another, tried to set him up with one or another of their girlfriends. Claire also had to invite Marlene Ruby, the firm's computer systems analyst, who liked to be involved in everything that went on in the firm. Politically, inviting Marlene was a necessity – she was practically holding Bragg and Banks together these days, and offending her by leaving her out of the tea would be a mistake. Claire liked Marlene well enough, and thought she did a good job of managing the most tedious aspects of life in a law firm – deciding who would get the new software or monitor, enduring petty grievances and tiresome questions all day long from lawyers and staff. But it was generally known that Marlene had been having an affair with Rick Durham, for almost a year before his death, that Jocelyn knew or suspected, and that the two women despised each other. What fun to throw them together. Claire sighed wearily.

The next nagging question was what to do about the Owen women. Claire had heard nothing from or about Grace since their lunch, though Marcia was sure to know about her by now. The Fed Ex box of children's photos and artwork had been delivered right on schedule, and Marcia had been home when it arrived. Claire thought uneasily about Grace's sad puffy face and her comment about being a nobody. But it would be inconceivable – not to mention deplorably bad form – for Claire to invite her, with Marcia coming. Cruel and unfair to both of them. Wouldn't it? Even Emily Post could not have dealt with this mess, Claire reflected morosely. Where would it be noted in her famous book on etiquette? Indexed under 'Deceased partner, bigamy of and multiple wives at tea/shower'?

There was Audrey Owen to be considered too. She'd made a fuss at the reception after the memorial service, embracing Alexander, sobbing that he was like a son to her, that Ross had talked so much about him and admired him greatly. She'd congratulated Alex, over and over, on his engagement, her eyes tear-filled. It seemed that Audrey knew him (or thought she knew him) well enough to be offended if she were not invited to the tea, whether she and Marcia were speaking again or not.

So, excluding Grace – Claire sneezed and dabbed her eyes with a tissue – but counting Audrey and herself, how many was that? Thirteen. Bad number. Another sigh. Alexander's mother had already left for her winter home in Florida (thank God) and would be returning only for a few days in October, just for the wedding.

During a prolonged coughing fit, as Claire was desperately searching for cough syrup in her bathroom cabinet, the phone rang. It was Gillian. Isadora wanted to bring a girlfriend to the lingerie tea – was that okay? 'You remember what it's like to be a teenager,' she said, 'they can't even go to the can without taking a friend.'

Isadora was not a teenager, Claire thought, though she was certainly as immature as any. 'Okay,' she said, after another, shorter, coughing fit. 'But tell them no jeans.' She was going to add: 'or any outlandish outfits', until she thought of Gillian, who was sure to appear in one herself. Gillian thanked her profusely, and Claire added another person to her mental guest list, this one with an unknown name. The list was now fourteen – a better number, at least.

One last coughing fit, a violent honk of her nose and a steaming cup of Neo Citran, and Claire finally pulled her sluggish brain around to the most worrisome question of them all. Should she leave the guest list at a nice (manageable?) fourteen, or inflate the list – and the potential for disaster – by adding the most important female clients of Bragg, Banks and Biltmore? She and Gillian and Shelagh had never proceeded beyond the four they had discussed. As clients, would they like each other when trapped together in Claire's living room? Did they already know each other? Had they networked? Would they band together in a corner and spend the whole time complaining about Bragg and Banks' legal accounts (for what else, really, would they have in common), comparing notes and ultimately deciding, in unison, to dump the firm? Would they be appalled by Alex's marrying

Anna? Was it proper to ask clients to buy sexy undergarments for an articling student? Surely not. Perhaps Claire could just invite them over later, for champagne, after she'd had a chance to push the underwear into some potted plants (and possibly, get rid of Anna. And Pruc. Jocelyn and Marlene, and, and . . .)

Totally unsure of herself in the social quagmire she had created, Claire dialled Elfriede's number. If anyone would be able to sort out the horror of the guest-list protocol, it would be her mother.

The next day, Claire found Anna in the small windowless office, behind the photocopier machine, that was referred to in the firm as 'the student ghetto'. It was a grimy, dun-coloured room, with nothing on the walls but a spray of picture hooks (had the firm's art been repossessed? Claire wondered) and some yellow Post-it notes with scribbled messages on them. Anna was reading a bound volume of law reports, a stack of others at her elbow.

'Claire,' she said without expression, pushing back her long fringe of hair to look up from her reading, 'what's doing?'

'I'm surprised to find you in here, with all the empty offices we've got now. Can't we get you one with a window? Have you talked to Alex about it?'

'He's kind of busy right now.' Anna stuck a finger in her book and closed it, inclining her head. She looked tired. 'You want to see me about something? I'm sure you didn't come in here to talk about relocating my office.'

'We need to discuss your shower, actually.' Claire was amazed at how easily intimidated she was by Anna.

'What about it?'

'It's a silly thing, really – but I was thinking about whom to invite, and I realized that you haven't given me a list of your friends and relatives, except for your mother.'

'She can't make it. And there aren't any others.'

'What about the associates here at the firm? Are you friendly with any of them?'

'You mean the ones who have quit? Or the ones who are still looking for other jobs?'

Of course, they had all left the firm, Claire thought, except for one or two who were sure to follow soon. And who could blame them? 'Well then,' she said, 'there are some other women I know who would probably like to be invited, but I'm taking my mother's advice for once. She says it should be your call, since it's your shower. Whatever makes you happy . . .'

Anna shrugged. 'Invite them all.'

'But, you see, some of these women . . . well, don't like each other all that much. I can't think how else to put it. I know it sounds petty –'

'Why don't they like each other?'

'Oh, various reasons. This and that. Over the years people harbour old grudges, you know.'

'I don't.'

'But there are many who do. I'm sure you know that. And I don't want this shower to be a stressful thing for you – a bunch of women spilling hot tea in each other's laps.' Claire laughed shortly, realizing just how likely a scenario that was.

'Don't you think they could pull themselves together? Grow up a bit? I don't mean to sound crass, but the more people you invite, the more lingerie I get, right?'

'Of course. And I want you to get lots of beautiful things.'

'I'm not having any other showers. There's only yours. Our wedding's going to be at City Hall. With just two witnesses. We were planning something bigger . . . before. But we'll just get Dan and somebody else to come – we haven't decided on the other person yet.'

Claire swallowed and smiled, hoping they weren't thinking about asking her. 'Well, big weddings are such a pain,' she said. 'All that fuss, money thrown away. They're no fun for the bride, really. I had one myself, so I know.'

'I think you should invite everybody to the tea. Bitchy women with old grudges don't bother me.' Anna opened her book again. 'I wish I could talk about this all day but I've got a memo to do for Alex that should have been done yesterday. And to tell you the truth, I'm getting sick of the subject of weddings. I don't mean to sound ungrateful – I hope you understand?'

'I do.' Claire sighed. 'I'll use my own judgement for the invitations.'

'I'm sure you'll do a beautiful job. Whatever.' Anna didn't look up again. 'It's your house. If you don't want your Limoges thrown around, fine. Cross some of the dragon-ladies off the guest list. I don't care.'

A Lingerie Tea. Claire carefully penned in the words after the printed word 'Occasion' on the inside top line of one of the Victorian pop-ups. At her elbow was a small mountain – a foothill, really – of wadded tissues and crumpled envelopes on which she had messed up the calligraphy, despite her best efforts.

'Lin-gurr-ee tea,' Harry frowned, his warm breath on the back of Claire's shoulder. 'What's a lin-gurr-ee tea?'

'It's *lingerie*,' Claire explained. 'A French word. It means . . . ladies' underwear. So a lingerie tea is where a woman – a girl actually – an older girl . . . young woman, that is – is getting married.' She hesitated. Harry looked puzzled. Really, Claire thought, when you tried to explain it to a seven-year-old boy, the absurdity of the whole idea became crystal clear. 'And all the other ladies – women – the friends of the bride-to-be, have afternoon tea together and give her surprise gifts of underwear.' She sighed, then smiled at her son. 'That's about it.'

'Surprise gifts of underwear?' Harry repeated. 'Gifts of surprise underwear?' He laughed, exposing all of his dear crooked teeth (those same ones that Claire would take him to several paediatric orthodontists about over the coming year). 'Surprise gifts of underwear!'

When he was in bed, later that night, he started chuckling again. 'Gifts of surprise underwear,' he muttered, snuggling to get comfortable under his blankets. 'Surprise gifts of underwear.' There was another fit of giggles.

'Do you think you could please stop saying that now, honey?' Claire smiled tightly as she turned out the light in his room.

'I'm putting out extra plates in case people lose theirs,' Molly announced. She was busily setting six places at the multicoloured Play School table in the basement. Claire watched with amusement, thinking it odd that her daughter was playing tea suddenly, when she hadn't asked for her tea set in more than a year. It was a Saturday morning – Ben had taken Harry out for hockey skills practice, bundling him up in so much padding and other gear that Claire could hardly imagine the boy being able to move, let alone skate. Why did hockey school have to start in August? She'd felt heartily sorry for Harry, but Ben believed skills practice to be important, one of those character-building things their son needed. And, in fairness, Harry didn't complain all that much, though possibly because he was packed up too tightly to speak.

'We're going to be starving if we don't get some food, soon.' Molly looked pointedly at Claire.

'Okay, honey, I'll cut up some granola bars for you. Pass me one of those plates.'

Molly bustled over with a tiny china plate, then hurried back to the table where she sat down and noisily slurped some water from a tea cup. Then she gargled a mouthful.

'That's not how you drink tea,' Claire said. Not that I'm any kind of expert, she thought. 'Why are you slurping like that, sweetie?'

'Because the animals love it.'

Propped up on gaily-coloured plastic chairs at the table were two stuffed elephants (who were obliged to share a chair despite their size), a grey plush cat and a yellow lion. They seemed to be waiting for the fun to begin. 'My napkin is wet.' Molly held out a soggy balled-up tissue to Claire. 'Can you get me another one?'

Claire, who was still suffering from the summer cold, handed Molly a few tissues from the box she'd been carrying around all morning. 'I'll go and get your food now, okay?'

'Okay.' Molly's hair needed cutting – the poor child could hardly see – and there was a large hole in the toe of one of her pink socks that Claire had, several times, asked Francine to try and mend some day while the kids were at school. Feeling very much the neglectful parent, she climbed the stairs to the kitchen where she cut a granola bar into several sections, then arranged the pieces on the china plate with some chocolate chips and raisins.

When she returned, she found Molly carrying another stack of plates from her toy box to the tea table. 'My beautiful pashas,' she said. 'Pasha means plate, in Spanish. I don't like to say "plates" all the time.'

'Me either,' Claire agreed.

'And my cups. Know what they're called in Spanish?'

Claire shook her head.

'Tashas.'

'I didn't know that.'

'Wait until you see who else is coming to my tea party. Oh! I forgot to give Nala a plate. And the elephants need a cup. They'll have to share one. They suck tea with their trunks.'

Claire smiled, feeling a trifle sorry for the elephants, who seemed to hold a low social position at Molly's basement tea. Could it be the result of their rudimentary table manners? Or were they just friendlier with one another, happy to share their chairs and cups? Molly popped a chocolate chip into her mouth and turned to Claire, peering at her from below her hair. 'This food is great. Would you like a seat? I have extra plates.'

'Well, all right, thank you.'

'Just watch out for the cats. There's two different kinds. One pet cat and one jungle cat. They like to *fight*.' Molly demonstrated with a series of scratching motions.

'Yes,' Claire said, her smile fading, as she squeezed herself into a child-scale arm chair. 'I must remember to watch out for those cats.'

'There's not enough postage on these,' said the woman at the Canada Post Centre.

'Why not? They aren't heavy.'

'They're just over the line. Look at the scale. From forty-five cents, it jumps to eighty-eight. Also they're oversize. It costs more to send oversize envelopes. Twenty cents more for this size.'

'So how much, total?'

'You're going to need another sixty-three cents on each one.' The woman turned on the postage meter which began to whir industriously.

What a shame, Claire thought. She'd found the perfect blue and white stamps – a line-drawn image of Forget-Me-Nots. Now she would have to add another stamp to each envelope. Would she be able to find the right colour? Before she could ask, the postal clerk had pulled a big wet, red and white meter sticker out of the machine and slapped it, crookedly, on to the envelope. Then she did another. As her ham-like hand pulled out more stickers, water flew off the backs of them and across Claire's careful calligraphy, streaking and smearing the names and addresses.

'Wait!' Claire cried. 'I didn't ask you to do that!'

'You need the extra postage,' the woman said, belligerently.

'But look what you're doing! The addresses are smearing. Do you know how long it took me to do those?' She had no replacement envelopes left, having wasted the few extras by making mistakes in addressing the cards, or messing up the calligraphy. That felt pen wasn't quite as simple to use as the pamphlet that came with it promised.

'How was I supposed to know your ink would smear?' The postal clerk shrugged. 'You should have used a better pen.'

'I'd rather you put more stamps on than use that meter.'

'So you'll need a sixty and three ones on each. We're out of twos. And you might have some trouble squeezing them all on – your writing goes pretty high up on these envelopes. You should have written lower down.'

'What colour are the other stamps?'

'Colour?' The clerk stared at Claire with small eyes sunk deep in fat cheeks. What sort of idiot cares about the colour? she was obviously thinking. 'I'd have to look and see what we've got. They're Holocaust memorial stamps – the new sixties. I think they might be black. Or grey. And the one-cent stamps are the Queen. She's orange.'

Black Holocaust memorial stamps? An orange Queen? 'Well,' said Claire, 'I guess you'd better use the meter then. But please, try to be careful. Or maybe you could let me do them?'

'Nope. Federal regulations. I can't let anybody behind this counter who isn't a post-office employee.'

The Canada Post worker applied a little less vigour to the remaining envelopes but none escaped without at least one dribble of water and smear of ink. The women Claire was inviting to the tea would all think she'd been weeping when she'd addressed the envelopes. Well, it wasn't that far from the truth. Included in the brutalized pile that the thick hands of the postal worker shuffled together and tossed into a brown canvas sack, were Victorian pop-up invitations addressed to Audrey and Marcia Owen, Marlene Ruby and Jocelyn Durham, four female clients of the firm (for champagne only, a bit later in the afternoon), Isadora Lawrence, and her mystery guest.

18 ∫

Whenever Gillian found herself in a store as big as a football field, she was gripped by agoraphobic panic. She didn't know which way to turn to locate whatever it was she wanted to buy; she could never even find a store directory. Usually, she avoided monster department stores such as the one she had recently wandered into, since they rarely sold anything unusual enough to interest her. But today she was looking for something, well, ordinary. Dowdy, in fact, might not be too much of a stretch. And if she couldn't find what she wanted here, there was always Marks & Spencer, right across the mall.

Confronted by miles of merchandise: clothing racks that stretched, apparently without beginning or end, in all directions; the chomping metal teeth of half a dozen escalators and the burr of beeping cash registers mingled with the babble and hum of voices, Gillian began to hyperventilate. All the other shoppers seemed to be in a great hurry, confidently bent on buying, knowing what they wanted and where to get it. This was Shelagh's turf, Gillian realized: it would have been smart to have brought her along as a guide.

It was pointless shopping for Anna's shower gift in one of the artsy shops Gillian preferred, not only because she still hadn't worked out exactly where they had moved to, but because Anna was not the sort to appreciate chain-mail panties or ostrich-feather-lined screw-on brassieres. Gillian had recently acquired a few such nonsensical bits of whimsy, in an attempt to tease B.M. out of his sexual torpor; things she hid in a zippered sack under her bed, things she dreaded the thought of Isadora stumbling across.

Freshly resenting Claire for putting her into this frustrating, thankless and embarrassing predicament, Gillian adjusted the Himalayan hiking pack on her back and randomly selected a direction, plunging bravely into the department store's sea of stuff. Her back pack was notably lighter than it had been a few minutes earlier: gone from it were the four copies of the manuscript of *At Whit's End* that she'd dropped off at a post office in the rear of a nearby drugstore. Each manuscript was addressed to a small press that had advertised in *The Writer's Market* as actively seeking first novels, and not expecting the author to pay for the privilege of being published.

B.M. hadn't read *At Whit's End*, and Gillian, having given up hope that he ever would, finally retrieved it from his kitchen – one morning slipping it covertly into her back pack. B.M never mentioned it, if he was even aware of its disappearance. He had a new book of poetry coming out in his publisher's autumn list: *4 A.M. on the Real Estate Channel*. The launch party was scheduled for the weekend after Claire's tea. Due to the economic hard times that had befallen the publishing industry of late, B.M. would be obliged to share the limelight with two other authors: a radio broadcaster who'd written a book on gardening in small city spaces, and a house wife from Shawinigan whose first novel about an endless heat wave and the people-sucking shape-shifters that shimmered out of it was doing enormously well. He didn't know which of them he less wanted to be associated with, B.M. complained; he couldn't imagine what had been going through his publicist's head when he'd set up the joint launch. As the crowning insult, there was going to be a cash bar at the launch, so the turn-out would be small. In his anxiety, B.M. was guzzling Maalox by the gallon, and was more churlishly self-absorbed than ever. The only book now in Gillian's back pack was an autographed copy of *4 A.M. on the Real Estate Channel*. "To Gillian – with a 'G'". She planned to torment B.M. by pretending she hadn't time to read it, though in reality she couldn't wait to find out if it was as genuinely awful as she suspected – and if she and her patent practice were parodied in it.

So. What does one wear to bed with a plagiarist? she asked herself, switching her mind back to the matter at hand, considering Anna and Alex. Just above eye level, not far in the distance, she thought she could make out a row of truncated torsos modelling brassieres. She walked on in that direction and was eventually rewarded by a multitude of silky panties dangling from plastic-clipped hangers, alongside teddies, boxer shorts, bustiers, slips, camisoles, body stockings, even nursing bras – all jammed together on racks, stacked on shelves, or piled into bins marked down for quick sale.

Where on earth should she begin, she who barely gave a thought to what she wore under her own clothes, to the frazzled bras, the greying panties, the pins, the small tears and shot elastics, the limp misshapen undershirts? Anna was Miss Perfect. Soon to become Mrs Perfect. If there was one thing Gillian knew intuitively about her, it was that she would be particular about her underwear; the sort who would wash her pantyhose by hand – using special soap powder for delicate fabrics – hang them up to dry, then *fold* and align them neatly in her bureau drawer, in graduated colour rows ranging from black to palest nude tones. Or maybe she would store them in lace-trimmed lingerie bags, with scented sachets tucked into the corners. Anna was the type who wouldn't leave her apartment unless all her lingerie *matched* – so unlike Gillian who didn't own a single set of matching anything, whose panties, pantyhose and bras were balled up in one gigantic snarl in the sole drawer she had to spare for such things. Apart from that nonsense under the bed, of course.

Gillian paused beside a rack of corset-like things that were supposed to push up and pull in various parts of the female anatomy. They looked appallingly uncomfortable, rubberized and resistant. She had no idea that girdles were back in style. Wouldn't Alex go wild over Anna in one of these iron-maiden jobs? She sniggered. She had to be careful not to cross the line into grotesquely bad taste, she reminded herself. But what the heck. Nobody said it was her job to arouse Alexander Spears. Walking on, she approached a rack of oversized flannel robes. How unattractive they were! Sober taupe and burgundy flannel. Classic British Plaid, said the tag. Spot on, she thought. Perfect for the wheezy old lord of a draughty castle in the Hebrides. Or a bedsit in Wolverhampton above a fish shop. But, come to think of it, one of these robes might be the perfect thing for

Anna. The price was good, and price was definitely a factor. Unlike a kitchen shower, where she could have picked up half a dozen quality tea towels for under twenty dollars, or a wine shower, where a decent Cabernet Sauvignon would be around the same price, it was hard to find anything that could be taken seriously as 'lingerie' for that kind of money. Two pairs of panties maybe, or a pair of tights. And she was going to have to buy a gift for Isadora to bring, and for Isadora's friend. 'She's no one you know,' Isadora had said, in response to Gillian's question. Gillian hadn't pressed.

Of course Isadora would want someone her own age there for moral support, dreading the idea of an afternoon with a bunch of cheek-grasping old biddies in hats and gloves, which was how, Gillian felt sure, Isadora pictured an afternoon tea. (And come to think of it, Gillian thought of it that way herself.) Why had Isadora agreed to go? she wondered. And why had it seemed like such a great idea to ask her along? Some wildly optimistic fantasy about bringing her daughter into the fold, introducing her to the rituals of tea and polite social conversation. Isadora would have a chance to admire Claire's home, the tea table – Claire was sure to knock herself out – and to watch Anna open all the gift bags and boxes and show off the pretty new things in which she would look so fabulous, because she was *slim*. Isadora would surely not miss that point.

Reluctantly, Gillian turned her back on the plaid robes. Much as the idea of buying one amused her, it wouldn't be fair to Isadora. Anna would open box after bag of shimmering satin and frothy lace to reach finally for Gillian's intrusive box, out of which she would pull yards of dour flannel that practically screamed 'bedsit'. And everyone would know, of course, that Gillian had chosen it out of spite, giving Anna the most lumpish thing she could find to even that old poetry-plagiarism score with Alexander. It would also be wasteful, Gillian's practical side reminded her. Why spend good money on something that would be marched straight to the garbage chute in Anna's apartment building, or stuffed under the sofa in Claire's living room?

Maybe, Gillian mused, she should be looking in the nylon or hundred-percent poly departments. What could be more uncomfortable? Good old-fashioned discomfort – the hair-shirt variety – was another possible route to revenge. The garment would *look* good, of course, but would Anna put it on? Not likely. She was not the sort of woman to be lured by the false lustre of polyester. No, the trick was to get something attractive and comfortable enough that Anna would actually wear, but that would also make Alexander's face fall, the night his new bride appeared in it, in the doorway of the bathroom, toothbrush in hand. And not only his face would fall. Gillian would find a perfect dicky-drooper, a willy-wilter. A special gift for Anna. But also for Alex.

Chuckling to herself, she strolled out of 'robes' and into the more remote regions of 'sleepwear'. There was a rack of pyjamas, patterned with pink tea cups on a creamy background of – what was that stuff? Gillian wondered. 'Double-brushed blanket fleece', said the label. It was certainly nicely thick and uncompromising. The pyjamas were wide-cut and boxy. Guests at Claire's tea might easily conclude that Gillian was giving the tea-cup pyjamas to Anna as a souvenir of the shower. No one (except for Shelagh and Claire) would suspect she bought them because they were so *ugly*.

She brushed by a row of nylon nighties that would crackle nicely with static come winter, but a larger white mass had caught her eye. How gruesome, she thought, moving closer to examine the styling of the nightgown pinned and splayed out on a wall board. It was a sorry, incongruous mixture of thick no-nonsense flannel and fussy lace: two materials that could hardly be less happy bedfellows. It was a mongrel of a nightgown, a nightmare of poor design. It was perfect. Gillian studied it, transfixed by every appalling detail. It had a ridiculous flouncy bottom, three absurd patch pockets (more lace), a clown-like floppy bow in the centre of a juvenile Peter Pan collar. It was the epitome of Victorian prudery, as interpreted by some coke-head bargain-store designer. She closed her eyes, feeling a rush of nasty pleasure at the thought of Alexander confounded by cotton, flummoxed by flannel. And yet, no one could accuse Gillian of having purchased it out of a desire for revenge: on some level it might even be considered romantically cosy – so comforting on a cold winter night, a blessed relief from those chilly bits of nothing that

Alex would be expecting Anna to parade in every night for his salacious pleasure.

As she waited in the queue at the cash desk, the snow drift of white flannel piled high over her arm (she'd selected a size medium, knowing it was too big but ready to point out to Anna that wonderfully comfortable things had to be roomy, and that pure cotton was known to shrink a tad in the first wash), Gillian riffled through a bin of sale items. In it she found a bonus, the perfect token gifts from Isadora and her unnamed friend: two pairs of fluffy orange bed socks, with rows of sticky green rubber chevrons on the soles: so *very* helpful in preventing a girl from slipping on the cold tiled floor in the bathroom of a bedsit.

19

Shelagh always made an effort not to appear intimidated or impressed by the doorman at Holt's. He'd been there since she first started shopping at the expensive uptown store, almost two decades ago. She recalled the first time she'd approached those dazzling doors, and how he'd greeted her with unbounded delight, eyebrows raised, arms and doors flung open wide. 'Lovely to see you!' he'd cried, spewing charm as a spigot might spew cheap wine from a cask. Flattered at being recognized and welcomed in such an effusive manner, Shelagh had thought he must have mistaken her for a model, an actress, or one of the city's wealthy elite. But after that first time, she'd noticed that this same ebullient welcome was bestowed on every woman who got within twenty feet of Holt's front door. Fat or thin, attractive or homely, in bad taste or beautifully-dressed, no woman escaped his flattering attention. Why, he would have flung open that door for a bag lady! Shelagh had felt two-timed, cheated-on and resentful, though no one else seemed bothered by his attitude; nor did he appear to notice Shelagh's subsequent snubs. He remained there, winter and summer, year after year, in cold weather topped with a sheared beaver busby as big as those at Buckingham Palace, in summer a smart peaked cap and navy blue blazer with gold buttons that winked saucily in the sun.

Normally, when Shelagh went to Holt's, it was because she had a hot date coming up (rare) or (more likely) because she needed an extravagant purchase to lift her out of whatever depression she was in. Since the plane crash, she'd been shopping at Holt's a lot – which was a concern since her income was spiralling downwards, all partners having agreed to take a twenty per cent reduction in their monthly draws until the firm was out of its red ink.

Still, since no bankruptcy trustee had yet cut up her Holt's card, Shelagh, nose in the air, brushed past the doorman with his hypocritical affection, and strode into her favourite store. She was there for the novel (but never actually sought-after) experience of lingerie-shopping for another woman; to buy something for Anna that would demonstrate Shelagh's excellent taste and generosity. By such an expansive gesture, she also meant to show that she had forgiven Alexander for any unpleasantness between them in the past, and that she was welcoming Anna into the firm. None of which was, of course, true.

As she glided up the escalator, she looked down over the main floor, at the sparkle and gleam of the cut-glass and mirrored surfaces in the cosmetics department. It was with a twinge of longing that she'd passed through it so quickly. She would always adore cosmetics departments, the colour wheels and charts, attractive salesgirls spritzing everyone with the latest perfumes, the 'consultants' in their lab coats always ready with a tester, some cotton balls, and a tantalizing free sample. It was the triumph of hope over experience, she thought; she should, by now simply laugh at all cosmetic manufacturers, their absurd claims, and their pushy sales people.

But the instant she stepped on to the second floor – the lingerie department – her spirits soared. She had spied exactly what she'd pictured as the ideal gift for Anna: a pair of well-tailored pink silk pyjamas. They were elegant, French-seamed and light as air. She imagined, with no small degree of envy, how Anna would slip into that shimmering silk – and out of it – and how she would look in between. One of her long legs would be slung over the arm of a tapestry chaise-longue, the mother-of-pearl buttons of the pyjama top undone, except for one, right in the middle, strategically holding it closed. But only just. She would be talking law with Alexander; perhaps there would be a pair of reading glasses perched on her nose, a stack of *Dominion Law Reports* by one small, shapely foot. Her wheat-coloured hair would be attractively tousled, her pale lips pouting. Alex would be dazzled by her thorough knowledge of her subject, her keen grasp of the issues, her accurate analysis and decisive solution to a legal problem. Overwhelmed by Anna's daunting combination of beauty and brains, he would leap on to the chaise-longue and seize hold of that pyjama top. The fragile button would whizz across the room and he and his new wife would slide down, hungrily kissing each other, on to an Oriental carpet that begged for fornication with every plush and sensuous fibre.

Shelagh cleared her throat, realizing that she'd been panting, took a deep calming breath, and turned over the price tag that hung from a sleeve of the pyjama top. Eleven hundred dollars! Her breathing was suddenly short again.

With an effort, she formed her lips into a blasé smile and strolled over to a rack of silk nighties, cut on the bias, with plunging décolletage and matching bed jackets. Perhaps she should buy Anna a simple nightgown. It had to be less expensive than pyjamas, since there was much less work involved in making it. But those matching, bias-cut bed jackets . . . they were truly exquisite. How was she to resist one of those to go with the nightie? She selected a size small in both and held them to her chest, turning slowly before a three-way mirror.

'So what do you think of the twin set? Gorgeous, isn't it?' A salesgirl had appeared suddenly, as if by Shelagh's having removed something from the rack an alarm had sounded somewhere.

'It's lovely,' she said.

'Have you got the right size?'

'It's not for me. I would probably take a medium . . . This would be a shower gift, actually.'

'Well, aren't you the great friend!'

'Why?' Shelagh smiled apprehensively. 'How much is the set?'

'Fourteen hundred, I think. No, that can't be right.'

'I guess not.' Shelagh laughed as the salesgirl felt around in the neck of the nightgown for the tag.

'It's sixteen ninety-nine.'

'Sixteen *hundred*?'

The salesgirl looked piqued. 'It has French seams. And that

collar – that's all hand-work around it.' She obviously thought the price quite reasonable – ridiculously low, in fact.

'Well, it's far too expensive. I hardly know this woman – the bride-to-be. And I want to buy her a shower gift. Not a mortgage.'

'We have some things on sale at the back of the department –'

'I think I'll just browse a bit.'

The salesgirl twitched the sleeves of several bed jackets into place. 'My name is Gloria, if you need anything.'

And what is it if I don't? Shelagh thought, turning away from Gloria and the twin sets. She *would* find something in silk for Anna. None of that poly nonsense for her. If there was one thing Shelagh had when it came to underthings, it was class. But these prices . . . they gave her palpitations. She had never shopped for lingerie at Holt's. What could she realistically afford to buy Anna? A lingerie bag and liquid soap? A couple of padded satin hangers? A potpourri-stuffed drawer sachet? All niggling impersonal little gifts that would demonstrate only a mean spirit and envy, not at all what she'd wanted to convey.

She paused at a display of 'spa slippers'. They weren't silk, they were terry cloth, with the store's scrolly initial 'H' embroidered in gold across the toes. There was a headband to go with them too: thick terry with a washerwoman knot in centre front. It would take someone like Anna to look good in that, Shelagh thought.

There was plenty of cheap silk to be had in lesser lingerie shops and department stores; Shelagh had turned her nose up at it often enough. But perhaps cotton was a direction in which she could go. It was a natural fibre, and more practical than silk. If the thread count were high enough, cotton could be almost as smooth and luxurious as silk. Terry cloth, though, was probably out of the question. Anna wouldn't care for being dressed in a towel, unless it were one of those single-fold sarong-wrapped jobs twisted around her waist at an exotic Caribbean resort, the kind that dropped to the floor at the slightest touch. With a sigh, Shelagh replaced the spa slippers and headband on the display.

'Did you have your heart set on silk?' Gloria had materialized again at her side. 'I noticed you were turning up your nose at the terry. But what about chenille? We have some luxurious robes I'd love to show you.'

'Chenille reminds me of my grandmother's bedspread. But I might consider a good cotton. Egyptian. Or Irish linen . . .'

'Oh! Well. We have a great promotion going on right now. I'm not really supposed to say anything . . .'

Shelagh brightened, though she was sceptical of this statement. How effective could a promotion be if no one was supposed to know about it? Doubtfully, she followed Gloria out of the designers' section into an adjoining department called Country Casuals. 'I'm not sure this woman I'm buying for is the country type,' she said, thinking of Anna in her pricey, well-tailored work clothes.

'Every woman is the country type,' Gloria pronounced. 'On one level or another. Whether they know it or not.' When they had reached the back of the department, near the change rooms, she turned to Shelagh and smiled. 'Look. These nighties are on sale for eighty-five dollars, this weekend only.'

Shelagh frowned. 'I see. But when I said cotton, I wasn't really thinking of . . . flannel.' She studied the row of fuzzy white sleeves and ruffled hems that hung from the tightly packed rack.

'It's imported double-brushed flannel.' Gloria pulled one of the nightgowns out and held it up for Shelagh. 'It needs a little steaming,' she smoothed her hand over it, 'but we can do that for you in two secs. These just came in yesterday. You'd be the first to get one. They're going to move very quickly.'

'It's not exactly sexy, though, is it?' Shelagh ran her fingers along one of the sleeves. 'Eighty-five dollars . . .'

'An incredible price.'

'It certainly is soft.'

'Soft *and* romantic. What could be more delicious on a cold winter night? Think about it. Your friend and her new husband, curled up by a roaring fire. Him in some, I don't know, plaid boxers or whatever – who really cares what men wear? – but her, your friend, stepping into the glow of the fire, all demure Victorian whiteness and pretend prudery. Look at the depth of this flounce. Stunning, isn't it?'

'Pretend prudery,' Shelagh breathed, enchanted by the picture Gloria was painting with such broad sure strokes. 'I love it.'

'So he, the guy, the husband,' Gloria continued, 'undoes this adorable bow here, then all of these great buttons –' She had to struggle with a couple of them. 'There!' she said at last. 'What fun! Men never like anything they can get into too easily.'

'There must be at least a dozen of those buttons,' Shelagh murmured.

'He'll have a ball taking this off your friend.'

'I wouldn't have thought a flannel nightie was about sex.'

'*Everything* is about sex. I'm sure I don't have to tell *you* that. Did you notice the three pockets? The lace trim? Aren't they *fabulous*? He can slip his condoms in one of these and be all set.'

'He's had a vasectomy,' Shelagh said, marvelling at the frankness of the conversation she was having with this person named Gloria.

'So he tucks something else in there.' Gloria was not one to be easily derailed. 'A penile pump – whatever.' They both laughed, heartily. 'Now let's see if we have a size small. This one's a large.' Gloria stuffed the nightie back among the rest and turned over a number of tags. '*One* small. That's it. You're *so* lucky. All the rest are mediums and larges.'

'Thank God,' Shelagh sighed happily.

'Shall I have it gift wrapped?'

'Please.'

'For a bride. We'll throw in a few sachet crystals, do it up in shower paper, pale blue ribbon. You'll be very pleased. To say nothing of your friend. *And* her new hubby.' She winked at Shelagh.

'Wonderful.'

'Why don't you look around for something for yourself while you wait? You deserve to be spoiled too.'

'I just might do that. Some little thing . . .' Shelagh's thoughts were wandering back to the designer section and a certain pair of silk shell-pink pyjamas.

'If you hang on for a moment, I'll show you a satin robe that will knock your socks off.'

'I'd like that. I could use a sexy new robe.'

'Someone special in your life?'

Shelagh hesitated. 'How can you tell?'

'Something in your eyes . . .'

'And after the robe, perhaps you could show me some sexy little nothings in the men's department?'

'I would *love* to!' Gloria regarded Shelagh with envy and admiration. 'He's a lucky guy, your man.'

'I know.' Shelagh smiled. And maybe some day I'll find the bugger, she added to herself.

20 ∫

'You're not going in that!'

'Why not?'

'For a million reasons. It's totally inappropriate – for a start.'

'*You're* talking to *me* about inappropriate clothing?'

'Yes, I am.' Gillian glared at her daughter.

Isadora looked down at herself. 'So what part, exactly, don't you like?'

'All of it. The chains, that – that chastity belt or whatever that is around your waist. That ripcord thing.' Actually, Gillian was curious to know where her daughter had found such a sublime specimen of kinky bad taste, but now was not the time to ask. 'Please,' she said, 'you can't go to my partner's home dressed like that. Promise me you'll wear a dress? I implore you.'

'Implore? Do you have to be so melodramatic?' Isadora's lower lip protruded. 'Besides, I don't even own a dress – that's only one slight problem with your plan.'

'I'll buy you one. And one for your girlfriend too, if she needs a dress.'

Isadora hesitated. 'Do we get to pick them out?'

'Absolutely.' Gillian swallowed. 'But it has to be something reasonable. Nothing too outrageous.'

'Okay.' Isadora shrugged.

Gillian, who'd just returned from work to be confronted by her overweight daughter in an animal-print cat-suit, jangling all over with what looked like medieval torture devices, picked up her leather-laced yurt mountain bag from where she'd dropped it, only a moment before, in the front hall. 'I can probably give you cash. But I want to see all the receipts. No "final sale" stuff, okay?'

'That's cool.'

Gillian dug down to the bottom of her bag to find her paper wallet. Cranes – Japanese symbol of good luck – swooped across the expanse of rice paper as she unfolded it. 'That's funny, I thought I had a few more twenties in here.' She counted out a series of bills, frowning. 'I went to the cleaners . . . to the liquor store . . . parking was only four dollars . . .'

'Can't you just give me one of your credit cards?'

Gillian looked at her, still puzzling over the small number of twenty-dollar bills in her wallet. 'Well, I suppose I could. I'd have to write you a note of permission to use it . . .' She refolded the wallet and opened a small pocket on the outside of it. 'Let's see . . . credit cards. How about this one?'

'*Sears*?' Isadora's upper lip curled. 'You expect me to find something to wear at *Sears*?'

'Why not? They occasionally have some nice things. Up on the second floor. I was just there the other day. I could go with you, show you where to look. It might be fun.'

'I don't do mother-daughter shopping trips, Mom.' She looked with distaste at the credit card Gillian still held out to her. 'I think it's fair to say, that you and I are not exactly *Sears* types.'

'Well, that's true, I suppose. I don't buy many clothes there.'

'The way you dress is a creative expression of yourself. Isn't that what you've always told me?'

'Yes,' Gillian admitted, 'that's also true.'

'Be an individual, that's what you've pounded into my head, year after year.'

'I've hardly pounded it . . .'

'So why can't I just take your Mastercard? Or Visa?'

'Where were you planning to shop?' Gillian's hand remained protectively over the Japanese cranes.

'I don't know yet . . . I've got a few ideas.'

'But the tea is Sunday.'

'I can shop fast.'

Gillian fingered the gold Mastercard, pondering. 'I get to see the receipts,' she repeated. 'And nothing over two hundred dollars.'

'Each, right? For me and my friend?'

'Yes,' Gillian sighed. 'I suppose it has to be each.'

'I've got no problem with that.'

'Maybe you should get some shoes, too, while you're at it. And if you have time, see if someone can do something with your hair. It'll be more than two hundred then, I suppose. A lot more, probably. Your friend must have her own shoes . . . I won't have to buy those too . . .' Gillian looked worriedly at her daughter.

'I'll try to keep the costs in line. Promise. But maybe I could have a little cash too? In case we go somewhere that doesn't take Mastercard?'

'Like where? Who doesn't take Mastercard?' But Gillian knew the answer to that: all the weird and creepy places she wished she could shop in.

'Don't worry so much.' Isadora patted her mother's arm. 'It'll be some place cheap.'

'Some place cheap won't take returns.'

'Could you just trust me for once?'

Gillian hesitated, looking again at the chain-link contraption around the area where her daughter's waist ought to have been. 'Just try to look half-normal when you're done. Half. That's all I ask. You're an attractive young woman. You have a lovely smile, nice legs . . .'

'Can I go now?' Isadora demanded, as Gillian reluctantly handed over the last few bills from her wallet.

'One last condition.'

'What?'

'You have to take those studs out of your nose. For the tea.'

'I can't. Well, I can, but I don't want to.'

'How about if you leave in just one of them then?'

'Well,' Isadora said, 'it's not that easy. They're screwed in, you know. But I guess I could take most of them out. For a few hours. On Sunday.'

'I'd appreciate that.' The gold card flashed as Gillian handed it over, with a feeling of dread, to her daughter. 'Half-normal, remember.'

'I'll do you proud, Mom. Little white gloves, a veil, the whole get-up.'

'You'll do no such thing!' Gillian laughed nervously.

'You just start thinking about your own outfit and don't worry about us, okay?'

'Please,' Gillian begged. 'Don't embarrass me.' But Isadora made no sign that she had heard. Her cat-suit-clad backside was already swaying up the stairs, chastity belt clanking.

She wouldn't need Isadora to embarrass her, Gillian thought a short time later as she stood, hands on her hips, facing the rat's nest that she called her wardrobe; she might be able to do a proper job of it herself. She dragged a chair across the floor and climbed up on it to access the dark netherworld at the back of the top shelf. 'Heavens! You don't need to bother with a hat!' Claire had said during their last conversation about the tea. 'Just wear whatever's comfortable.'

'If you got it, flaunt it,' Gillian muttered to herself now, stretching high over her head to grasp the cloud of dry cleaners' polyethylene that shrouded her amazing black straw cartwheel. If she could find Jerry's hot glue gun, she planned to stick three rust-coloured roses to the grosgrain band to make the hat look more festive and better coordinate it with her dress. Also, once trimmed with flowers, it was less likely to bring back painful memories of the memorial service to the widows, and Gillian liked to think of herself as a person who was sensitive to such matters.

The dress she had bought for the tea was a fantasy of long, rust-coloured lace, discovered amongst the spandex, the teensy Mary Jane frocks with see-through fish net tops and the fifties candy pink crinolines in a store called F/X. The manager had refused to haggle with Gillian, wouldn't even take ten per cent off the dress, though she'd gone in to try her luck several times over the summer, on each occasion determined to convince him that he would not be able to sell that dress to anyone but her. F/X was an off-the-wall clothing store that didn't belong in the prim and proper commercial zone where Gillian had stumbled across it. With its lop-sided wooden sign (singed around the edges as if some vandal had taken a torch to it), its jaw-grinding music and changing rooms with curtains that didn't quite close, F/X was not going to make it in that zone, despite the number of hot young designers who were represented in its racks.

Ultimately, Gillian got the lace dress for a quarter of its original price, on the weekend the front window of the shop was papered over with giant red banners that announced STORE CLOSING! EVERYTHING MUST GO!!! She had smirked about her victory for weeks.

After unbundling the hat from its polyethylene, she placed it in the centre of her bed, then unzipped the garment bag to take out her tea gown (as she liked to think of it). It consisted of a slim silk sheath over which was layered an entire bolt of lace, pleated, gored, gathered and tucked in the most astonishing ways. When she wore her boots (ecru leather, high buttoned, laced with satin ribbon) the hem of the dress just tickled her ankles, or would have, were it not for the boots. More rusty lace festooned the deep V collar and the edges of the three-quarter-length sleeves. She stood back a bit to admire it. And with the cartwheel hat topping it off, it would be truly amazing. Her resentment over Claire and the lingerie tea had dissipated. Without Claire and her tea, Gillian might never have had the chance to put all these fabulous elements together to make the remarkable fashion statement she was about to make.

'Damn!' Shelagh cursed, as she shuffled across the carpeted floor of her bedroom, dressed only in her terry robe. Would she ever get a chance to wear anything but terrycloth *chez maison*? For example, those shell-pink pyjamas that had just cranked her Visa card over the limit? The ones she hadn't yet bothered to take out of the Holt's bag, since there was no one around to wear them for, and there was no point in getting them dirty just for herself since she'd discovered, while stopped at a red light on her way home, that the damned things had to be dry-cleaned. Who *dry-cleaned* pyjamas, for Christ's sake? But the bother of trying to return the pyjamas – sure to be considered by Holt's as 'intimate apparel' and therefore non-returnable, she could see Gloria's sneer of incredulity already – was more costly to Shelagh's pride than the price of the dry-clean-only pyjamas.

Shelagh hadn't had a man since Ross, except for that brief

unsatisfactory skirmish with Dan Chatwell the night of the plane crash – and that hardly counted, being no more than an act of mutual desperation, and hardly the stuff of romance.

She paced, wearing a path through the pile of her carpeting, her teeth crunching into an antacid tablet. And even when she'd been seeing Ross, half of the time she was not in alluring lingerie but in some ridiculous get-up: Little Red Riding Hood representing the absolute nadir of their relationship. And now, thanks to Claire, she was having to confront that whole wretched part of her past by spending an afternoon not only with Ross's widow, but with his tweedy old stickleback of a mother as well.

'So tell me,' she pictured herself saying to Marcia as she speared a lemon slice, 'what did *you* get to be for Hallowe'en?' Or: 'Did you sew all those great little play outfits Ross used to bring over to my place?' she would politely ask the senior Mrs Owen as she passed her some gone-off milk for her tea.

Shelagh had managed to avoid Audrey at the reception after the memorial service, and Audrey must have been so distraught and busy blaming Marcia for Ross's death, that she hadn't seemed to notice Shelagh, or remember her, on the single occasion when their eyes met. The dinner in Wallaceburg was likely forgotten, as was the fact that Ross had had ANOTHER WOMAN – never mind another wife – before he and Marcia split up. Well, Shelagh's coming eyeball to eyeball with the old haddock over a tray of treacle tarts would likely refresh her memory PDQ. She picked nervously at a pimple on the side of her nose as she pictured the Owen women squaring off, shoulder pad to shoulder pad, wheeling around in formation to tear Shelagh to bits with lemon forks and sugar tongs. It would do them so much cathartic good, wouldn't it? They would share a common enemy, be therapeutically drawn together in their united hatred of *her*.

Crunching another antacid, Shelagh considered again the possibility of not showing up for the tea at all. She could send the gift over to Claire's via bicycle courier, or deposit it in Anna's cubby hole at the office. Surely she could come up with some creative reason for not going? She could really and truly break her leg, for example – jumping off her second-floor balcony might do it. But, knowing Claire, she would offer to swing by in her filthy car (or send Ben, who was sure to remember Shelagh's humiliating blind date with his doctor-friend) and pick her up, crutches and all, so that Shelagh wouldn't have to miss the fun of the tea.

Maybe she could overdose on antacids, if such a thing were possible. Or what if she went in disguise? Put on a wig, a headscarf, dark glasses and a false nose? She could pose as Claire's zany old friend from the west coast.

Get a grip on yourself, she told herself, sharply. If you're going to be the OTHER WOMAN – a title Shelagh had never shrunk from before – or rather, the OTHER OTHER WOMAN (did all of the players know about Grace yet?), go down with your head high, rip some curtains from the windows, grab a few yards of tassels and do it in style. Though white vertical blinds might be difficult to press into service as a tea costume, they would surely be eye-catching, as well as make a great deal of clatter. And the Owen women would simply conclude that Ross's OTHER OTHER WOMAN was a lunatic, possibly dangerous, and leave her alone, jabbing their cake forks in some other, more explosive direction. At each other, for example.

With a discouraged sigh, Shelagh took the bottle of single-malt scotch from the top of her bedroom bureau, then dropped on to her bed to sit, shoulders sagging, in front of the double-mirrored doors of her clothes closet, drinking straight from the bottle. Studying her pathetic, terry-clothed figure, she experienced a wave of self-loathing, followed by a brisk tingle of self-respect. Her beaten-down pride began struggling to get up. Then it *was* up! It was looking around, flexing its atrophied muscles, stretching. Yes! She straightened her shoulders, recapped the bottle, retied the belt of her robe and looked herself in the eye. Why was *she* suddenly the victim in this hideous melodrama? She was supposed to be the *villain*, the one who had led Ross by the nose on a merry chase out of the comfort and security of his two marriages to practically throw him on board the doomed plane. She was Carmen, for God's sake, not Anna Karenina. She'd never before shrunk from what she was, from holding her head up, no matter what she'd done. Shelagh had pride, a great wardrobe, and a fantastic figure, whatever other qualities she might lack as a human being. And those essential assets of hers should always be put to good use.

Pushing back the sleeves of the terry robe (no longer caring whose it was), she got off her bed and flung open her closet doors. When she was finished putting herself together for this wretched tea, not one of those squabbling Owen women would ever be able to ask themselves, or each other, what it was that their dear departed Ross had ever seen in *her*.

21

'Tea murmurs, it never brays. As we sit down to tea, we are transported to an elevated plane – where utter peace prevails. Serenity surrounds us . . .' – The Tai Chi of Tea

'This place looks wild,' Ben said. 'You're going to impress the heck out of everyone.'

'Wild? I don't know what you mean. And I'm not out to impress anyone.'

Not impress anyone? Ben looked at his wife. Who was she kidding? The house was so thick with exotic flowers it looked like a tropical rainforest. And there was all sorts of other nonsense all over, like the lavender heart-shaped soaps and lace-edged hand towels by all the bathroom sinks. (Ben was forbidden to touch those, directed instead to use a rumpled gym towel that Claire had pulled from the laundry hamper and pushed into his hands. Oh, and should he feel the urge for a – well, a bowel movement – perhaps he could hold it until he was out somewhere with the kids?) And what about the china, the silver, the refrigerator sagging from the weight of cream-filled pastries and hundreds of little sandwiches? None of it was meant to *impress*?

'I'm giving a bridal shower for a young woman who won't be having any other showers,' Claire said primly. 'Now, isn't there something you should be doing? Taking the kids out, for a start.'

'I'm going to. But first, I want you to know how proud I am of you.'

She gave a small snort.

'And I think it's great, what you've done here for the tea. One would almost think you were born to it.'

'I was. My mother used to kill herself entertaining. She went into hard labour over every event.' Claire had been vigorously scrubbing the kitchen sink with powdered cleanser and a sponge.

'Well,' Ben said, 'I guess I better grab my gear and hit the road.'

'I wish you wouldn't say things like that,' Claire said. 'In the context of your rollerblading, it's disturbing.'

But Ben was already on his way down the basement stairs, whistling cheerfully. Now it was only a matter of finding his blades. He hoped Claire hadn't moved them; she'd been rearranging furniture for weeks and hiding everything she considered embarrassing or unsightly, most of which, it seemed, belonged to Ben. His mood soured as he realized that his rollerblading equipment had indeed been moved from its usual place beside the furnace. Surely it wasn't necessary for Claire to rearrange the entire *basement* because she was having a few women over for tea? Couldn't she just have closed the door on the mess and left it at that? And if she was going to go to all that trouble cleaning, why hadn't she put flowers down here? And out in the garage, too? He pushed aside his golf bag to see if his blades were behind it, flushed with irritation, perspiring.

Above him, beyond the tangle of exposed electrical wiring and hot water pipes, loosely wrapped in crumbling asbestos insulation (a hazardous situation he was supposed to see to), the front door opened and the floor boards of the hallway protested. Claire's parents. Two very good reasons for hiding out in the basement for as long as possible. The third good reason was Prue who was due to fly in on her broomstick at any moment. Ben was hoping to miss seeing his mother this visit; he didn't feel up to hearing her cluck on about the irresponsibility of a talented surgeon, with two young children, doing something as asinine as rollerblading. She would use that word too: asinine.

After more futile searching, he went back upstairs and stuck his nose in the dining room where Claire and her mother were deep in a worried discussion about whether champagne should be served before the tea, to get people relaxed and talkative, or after – the popping of corks a celebratory background noise as the bride-to-be opened her gifts.

'Of course, in Europe there would be no question of champagne,' Elfriede was saying. 'A tea would never include alcohol. There is a certain order. A way things are done.'

'Well, I for one will be needing a drink,' Claire said, 'probably several.'

'Over here everything is so mixed up. It doesn't seem to matter what you do. Champagne before, champagne after . . . Some people even serve coffee. Can you imagine? At a tea?'

Claire raised her eyebrows and clucked in pretend disgust, thinking about the drip, drip of the Melita coffee maker, ready to start up in the kitchen. 'So, about the booze,' she said, 'think we could do both?'

'Both?'

'Serve it before *and* after the tea?'

'Claire, honey – I know you've got a lot on your mind –'

Mother and daughter turned towards Ben, looking annoyed.

'Any clue where you might have stashed my blades?' he asked.

'Try the useless cupboard.' Claire turned back to Elfriede. 'What about this business of tying a paper plate on to the bride-to-be's head? Should we do it? Is it still done?'

Relieved that the mention of his rollerblades had passed without comment, Ben slipped into the kitchen to peek inside the fridge. Trays, many trays, everything on them covered by damp tea towels in the frigid silence, like so many stiffs laid out in the hospital morgue. He lifted the corner of a towel.

'None of that's for you, Ben!' Claire's voice was sharp from the dining room. He would be taking the kids out for some real food anyway, he thought, closing the refrigerator door: Whoppers and fries and gallons of ketchup. Harry and Molly were in the TV room with Basil who was mesmerizing them with his magic tricks: pretending to chop off their noses and hide them under the sofa cushions. Ben was looking forward to an afternoon with his kids; he was going to show them the time of their lives.

The basement, he thought, as he made his way down the

stairs, heading for the 'useless cupboard', was the only part of the house that seemed half-way normal now. The upstairs smelled like a funeral parlour, and was beginning to look like one too. A woman had swept through the house a week before – a big snooty blonde with hunks of silver jewellery. 'You're doing the flowers for the tea, my wife tells me,' Ben had said pleasantly, having surprised her in the vestibule where she was looking perplexed, turning in slow circles. 'You work for the florist, do you?'

'I'm a *designer*.' She'd given him a look that indicated confusion over what planet he could possibly be from.

Some designer, he'd thought that morning, as a snarl of vegetation attacked him at the bottom of the stairs. It was a humungous display of foliage that poked out in all directions at the same time as it managed to cascade to the floor, balanced on a pedestal affair, draped with a cobwebby fabric that looked vaguely familiar (Prue's old curtains?). He'd given it a mock karate chop – Ben of the jungle, hacking his way through the bush with his machete.

Another source of irritation was the annoying antique tables that had popped up suddenly in very awkward places. Ben had banged his thigh, painfully, against a rickety one in the dining room – startled to find it there when he turned a corner – and all Claire had done was gasp and run to steady the flowers on it before barking at him to be more careful.

In the basement – a man's last true domain – he pushed through a forest of hockey sticks, skis and poles, before stumbling over a stack of child safety gates. Finally, stuck under some dusty track lighting parts, beside an old electric tooth-brush, at the back of the cupboard that he and Claire called 'the useless cupboard' for the quality of the stuff they stored in it, Ben found his back pack. Just because he hadn't used his blades for a couple of weeks was no reason for his wife to assume he'd abandoned them, and to relegate them to the cupboard of contemptible things. Grunting, he dragged out the pack and checked to make sure everything was in it: the black boots with the row of purple wheels, each with POWER inscribed around its circumference, the shiny helmet with the racing stripes down the sides, his Velcro-lined knee, wrist and elbow pads. Wait until the kids got a look at their old dad on his blades, he chuckled. He planned to take them to the parking lot of a new No Frills grocery store that hadn't yet opened. There, with an acre of deserted asphalt laid out before him, he would demonstrate his spins, his dipsy doodles, maybe even shoot a puck around a bit. It would be good to get Harry fired up for the hockey season. The boy was becoming a bit of a wimp, hanging around all day with Molly and Francine.

'Awesome, Dad!' Harry would say, as Molly sat on the curb outside the No Frills, gaping as their (formerly uncool) father whizzed by, swerving and spinning: king of the road, commander of the asphalt. Then, after an all-you-can-eat trip to Burger King, Ben would take them to Sporting Life to get them fitted out with their own rollerblading gear: snazzy pink nylon for Molly, with a Barbie helmet; for Harry, a junior version of his old man's. Ben had mentioned these plans to Claire that morning. 'Oh, Ben, are you sure it's safe?' She'd been counting teaspoons in the kitchen, looking worried. He had considered sweeping her up in his arms and laying her back, in her bathrobe, over the breakfast table, sending her spoons flying, but had ultimately decided against the manoeuvre, being unsure of the reception it would get.

Prue opened the invitation, checking the time of the tea again, even though it was marked in red and circled on the wall calendar in the kitchen. The invitations must have cost a fortune, she thought, imported from England, no less. She wondered why her daughter-in-law hadn't been able to find any to suit her that were made in Canada, and why she had to squander such a lot of money on paper invitations that couldn't be recycled and would only be thrown out. And the postage on the foil-lined envelope – a dollar and eight cents! No wonder Ben and Claire had chronic money problems. The sensible thing would have been simply to telephone everyone. But Claire had a tendency towards ostentation. One only had to remember the wedding. What a lot of fuss! That reminded Prue that Elfriede still owed her copies of several photos from that day, a grudge Prue had nursed for over eight years. Now she would be obliged to spend the afternoon with the woman, making chit-chat about gardens or the grandchildren, enduring Elfriede's complaints that she hardly saw Harry and Molly and how Prue was clearly the favoured grandmother. As if it were somehow *her* fault that Elfriede and Basil lived two hundred miles away from their grandchildren. As if it were *her* fault that the children liked her best.

But Prue had a secret weapon to ward off Elfriede and others with their unwanted social chat: an envelope of photographs, an inch thick, taken at the retirement party for Prue's best friend at work, Maureen Baguley. Practically everyone Prue had ever worked with, in almost thirty years with the Ministry of Labour, was in one or other of those photos. Prue knew a lot about their lives and their grown children's lives (even their parents' lives) and found all of it endlessly fascinating, as she was certain her listeners would.

Before slipping the invitation into her handbag, she wondered again why the ink had run all over the front of the envelope and why Claire was bothering to give this tea party at all. Four in the afternoon was such an inappropriate time to eat, especially rich foods. Prue had already decided that the tea would be her main meal, and that she would do without dinner later. She wouldn't stuff herself, of course (she never did), but she would eat as many of the tea sandwiches as necessary to feel satisfied. She hoped there would be sandwiches: she could hardly be expected to load up on pastries and sweets as her main meal of the day. By way of precaution, she had tucked a tuna sandwich, wrapped in well-washed recycled plastic wrap, into her bag. (She'd gone out for lunch on Friday – a surprise, her supervisor had asked her – and so had been left with the perfectly good sandwich she'd brought in to work, uneaten.) She would be pleased, actually, if Claire didn't serve sandwiches, for then the tuna would not be wasted. She wouldn't be noticed off in a corner eating it, and if anyone asked, she would simply murmur that she had dietary restrictions. No one ever pressed her on such delicate matters, fearing a discussion about her health or religious beliefs.

As for the lingerie aspect of Claire's party, Prue found it more off-putting than the rich food. Why spend so much money on skimpy over-priced things that probably wouldn't suit? (And wouldn't the bride-to-be be happier choosing her own trousseau? Prue couldn't bear the thought of some stranger – or anyone, for that matter – selecting underthings for her.) The young woman's friends could have chipped in to buy the couple something sensible, a Canada Savings Bond, for example, to get their nest egg started. But after making several such helpful suggestions, Prue had given up, deciding not to push. She'd marched instead into Marks & Spencer, to purchase an intimate gift for a woman she had never met, and finally selected something she herself liked: three polyester (silk was too warm) camisoles that came as a boxed set: one nude, one black and one white. They were on the plain side, but were practical and sure to be appreciated, especially come winter when all sensible working women wore camisoles under their blouses. She'd wrapped them in some tissue paper that she'd preserved, carefully pressed between the pages of *The Concise Canadian Encyclopedia*, from her last birthday (ribbon was not necessary), wondering why neither of her children had the sense to buy her a set of camisoles instead of expensive perfume that she never wore (Ben) or costly vouchers for beauty salons that she never used (Elizabeth).

For the tea, Prue had decided to wear her dotted blue Swiss. Though five years old it looked as fresh as on the day she'd bought it. Once dressed, she sat down in a comfortable chair by her front window to read her library book – a biography of Robert Frost – until it was time to go, the boxed camisoles and her handbag leaning against the chair, close by her feet. But the biography was not holding her interest the way she'd hoped, and she sighed as she looked out of her sparkling clean window at the lovely sunny day she was about to waste. She would not know a soul at the tea, aside from Claire and Elfriede, so it was her settled intention to arrive late and leave early. Her daughter-in-law would surely get the message that in future Prue was to be relieved of any duty to attend such extravagant and nonsensical social events.

22

'But the true benefit of afternoon tea is in its propensity to enrich the everyday, gilding a few hours with importance and celebrating the cutting loose of daily demands . . .

On the other hand, more than a few "rain makers" are finding the "power tea" given in big city hotels, with acres of fresh linen and glistening pots of preserves, to be an effective conduit to negotiating and closing a deal' – Tea Comes of Age

Six white pastry boxes, tied with yellow ribbon and fastened with gold seals, were stacked in Claire's refrigerator, surrounded by dark green bottles of French champagne. The boxes were labelled 'triangles', 'checkerboards' or 'pinwheels' so that Claire would know where to find the cucumber triangles with mint butter, for example, when the platter on the table needed replenishing. On the refrigerator shelves above the boxes, draped with spotless tea towels, were several trays – oblong, rectangular and round – on which had been carefully arranged meringue kisses, raspberry-filled Linzer hearts, petits fours iced in the colours of Easter eggs, and Calla Lily cream horns that would be filled at the very last moment so as not to be soggy by the time they were eaten. Claire had made none of these things herself. Apart from her mother's lemon loaf, everything had been supplied by the caterers, who charged extravagantly and by the piece. There was not a single artery-clogging dainty that was priced at less than two dollars and fifty cents. Claire didn't dare tell Elfriede, who would have been shocked and ashamed of her daughter – she who'd always taken pride in the tireless rolling, kneading, mixing and baking required for a proper afternoon tea. Claire hadn't mentioned the cost of those delectables to Ben either.

The china had been delivered a week earlier, each piece securely bundled in bubble-wrap and snuggled in moistened wood shavings and straw. Claire had to buy a surprising number of such pieces, starting with a tea pot. The one she had, that had served the Cunninghams faithfully for years (brought out only once a year, during 'flu season), was squat, practical, a dull wine colour, and had a chip in its lid. It wouldn't do at all, she realized as she took it down from a cupboard: its charmless presence would overpower the delicate blue and white tea table of Claire's imagination. To match the new pot (Regency style), she'd ordered serving trays, a muffin dish (for the hot cinnamon rolls and pecan scones), cake and pastry knives, a multi-tiered sandwich platter, a china bowl for lemon slices and another for sugar cubes. Elfriede brought the sugar tongs, lemon forks and extra spoons, silver hot water pots, and table linen.

Then there were the things that, strictly speaking, Claire didn't really *need* to purchase, such as the unsteady antique tea trolley that had been rolled into the dining room to be graced with a vase of irises and cornflowers. As Anna's gifts were brought in, the flowers would be whisked over to the sideboard to make more room. 'What's the idea behind that thing?' Ben had asked as the delivery men carried the trolley, creaking and protesting, its wooden wheels spinning, up the front walk on the Tuesday before the tea.

'It was a fabulous buy,' Claire informed him. 'The antique store was going out of business.'

'I can see why,' was all he'd replied.

Claire's only excuse for this apparent excess was that she'd been completely seduced by *The Delights of Tea* and the other books from the library. The recipes were time-tested and true, the photos lavish; the comforting, soothing rituals described with such obvious pleasure by their editors. She'd plunged into the subject of afternoon tea the same way she'd approached the study of law or any other subject – with a passion. In a few hours of intense reading, she'd learned a great deal about a world she'd never known existed. 'Go on,' she challenged

Shelagh over lunch one day, 'ask me anything about caddy spoons – from ancient China up to the present. Come on. Try me.' Shelagh had regarded her with narrowed eyes. 'No? Okay. It's a very broad subject – you'd be surprised.'

'Would I?'

'Did you know that a muffineer is often confused with a domed pepper dredger? And that controversy still reigns over the purpose of the centre compartment of a three-section caddy?'

'What do you think I should wear?' Shelagh said, before biting into a bagel. 'To your 'effin lingerie tea?'

Claire drew back a little, at a loss before her friend's aggression. How tragic that Shelagh could not understand what it was like to experience, even vicariously, a world where napkins and embroidered cloths were always snowy, where silver spoons tinkled, ingredients were forever fresh, only the thinnest of bone china would do and the delicacies that were served hot, were always 'pipingly' so. Victorian women wore soft diaphanous gowns to tea, lacy and loose-waisted, without stays (especially when a lover was expected), and callers left embossed calling cards on engraved trays in grand foyers.

'No, I really need to know,' Shelagh pressed. 'I mean, what is the appropriate outfit to wear to one's own execution? No jewellery, I've figured out that much. I remember Marie Antoinette taking off her necklace – or was it Anne Boleyn? – in some movie, before they chopped her head off.'

'What are you talking about? Who?' Claire had said uneasily. 'Marcia and Audrey?'

'You are so smart! You're totally wasted doing intellectual property – or practising law at all.'

'It won't be that bad, Shelagh. They don't even know about you.'

'I had *dinner* with Audrey Owen!' Shelagh had hissed. 'In her aluminium-sided bungalow! In Wallaceburg!'

'Oh, relax.' Claire made an attempt at a breezy laugh. 'Nothing awful's going to happen. Not at *my* tea. It will all be very civilized. Tea envelops all guests in an atmosphere of serenity.'

'Oh, put a lid on it.'

'Lids . . . Another fascinating subject. Take the caddy lid, for example.'

Shelagh glared at her.

'Look, Shelagh, I bet Audrey won't even remember you. So much has happened since you went out there – when? Last year some time?'

'Two months ago.' Shelagh had settled back in the moulded plastic chair in the Food Court and regarded Claire through glittering, half-closed eyes. 'So. Do you think a bullet-proof vest would be over the top? Or simply *de riqueur* for such affairs?'

Claire had learned through her studies that, sadly, afternoon tea had been muscled out as a popular form of home entertaining, during the early sixties, by gatherings such as 'chilli for a crowd', après-ski buffets, the fondue party and the suburban wife-swap. In the opinion of many knowledgeable experts, the tea party, though enjoying something of a resurgence at the moment, had never fully recovered, and perhaps never would.

'So fresh,' Elfriede murmured, after she'd taken a white cardboard box of pinwheel sandwiches from the refrigerator and snipped away the ribbon to inspect them. 'They must have made them this morning – on a Sunday. They are professional, your caterers. Expensive, too, I imagine.' Claire said nothing, just continued tweaking the petals of a single magnificent white rose that floated in a crystal bowl on the kitchen counter near a window. 'These pinwheels are so moist,' Elfriede said, 'I can't imagine how they keep them from drying out.'

'Can't be too fresh, can't be too moist,' Claire sang, giving the bowl a final quarter turn to better show off the perfect rose.

'You know, I would have made everything myself, for the tea. A few cakes, some cookies, small sandwiches. It's nice when people "ooh" and "ah" over goodies you made yourself.'

'I don't have your kind of time, Mother.'

'Ah, yes, you working girls. Everybody works nowadays. It's a shame nobody can afford to stay home.'

'You're beginning to sound like Ben.'

'Well,' Elfriede closed the box. 'I admit, professionals can do things you can't do yourself. They have tricks, special equipment, suppliers.'

Claire gave her mother a loving pat on the arm. 'Your lemon loaf will be a big hit. It looks wonderful. And so do you.'

'Sure, sure. Old, fat.'

Claire paused, wanting Elfriede to know how much she appreciated the trouble she'd gone to, dressing up in a pastel flowered skirt, a pretty silk blouse with a coordinating cotton cardigan, pearls, stockings and low-heeled shoes with gleaming buckles. Her hair had been freshly set and sprayed by the small-town hairdresser who worked from her home near where Basil and Elfriede lived. It would have been done on Saturday; Elfriede would have worn a hair-net to bed on Saturday night to preserve the shape and structure of the hairdo. 'Happy birthday,' Claire said. 'You don't look seventy at all.'

'So what – I look sixty-nine? Or maybe I look eighty? What are you telling me?' Elfriede had her head in the refrigerator by then and was moving around bottles of champagne, muttering.

But Claire didn't hear the question. From where she stood in the kitchen, she could see the front hall and the dining and living rooms. Her tireless shopping, moving of furniture, scrubbing, polishing and efforts to exact some level of cooperation from Ben and Francine, had paid off. She was actually enjoying this last hour of preparation, she realized, thanks mostly to her mother. The lingerie tea was a necessary event; it would draw together her partners and friends with the other women who had suffered so much after the plane crash. It was a sort of ritual cleansing, a way to set the law firm back on course, a readjustment of emotional rheostats. What a remarkably astute and prescient idea! How had it ever occurred to her? For one afternoon, fifteen women, with little in common besides death and a faltering law firm, could talk, laugh, gossip and exclaim over oodles ('oodles', yes – she needed that word right now) of gorgeous lingerie, their heads swirling with champagne bubbles and the aroma of Lapsang Souchong and Darjeeling. They would forget their squabbles and petty differences, cosily wrapped in the comfort and intimacy of an age-old ceremony. Ah, tea!

Claire gazed out through her kitchen window at clusters of Heavenly Blue Morning Glories tumbling over the stone wall that edged the back garden. 'The mere chink of cups and saucers tunes the mind to happy repose' – some profound Victorian had said that. She sighed deeply, awash in feelings of good will and anticipated pleasure.

'You haven't cleaned this tea pot properly,' Elfriede said.

Claire turned from her reverie. 'I just unpacked it new – from the china shop. I assumed it was clean.'

'It's dusty. I never use anything new without washing it first. Even clothes. But never mind, I'll do it.'

'When should we warm up the rolls?'

'Not until people arrive. You don't want them to dry out or get cold.'

'No. Well, I guess I'll leave it to you – you seem to know what you're doing. I'm getting a little tense.'

'I can manage. Don't worry so much.'

'The clients – the businesswomen – are coming later. After the lingerie has been opened – and put away somewhere.'

'But they'll want to see it.'

'No they won't.'

'Yes. Of course they will.'

'Well, I'll worry about that later. Now I'm going to take a final tour of the house, if you don't need my help.' Elfriede waved her daughter out of the kitchen, clicking her tongue.

Climbing the stairs, Claire held up yards of silk chiffon in front of her to keep from tripping. She'd actually found an authentic tea gown in a Yorkville boutique. Her feelings about it fluctuated from embarrassment (this wasn't a costume party!) to a sense that she was gloriously upholding (if not actually resurrecting) the fine old tradition of wearing the proper gown for such an occasion. 'You're not even dressed yet?' her father had frowned, when Claire answered the door. It wasn't all that peculiar a garment, she thought now, nor revealing either. Long and loose, its skirts swept the ground with an air of quiet authority. And it wasn't as though Claire were done up in stays and corsets and bustles, for heaven's sake. She had no white gloves, no parasol, no hat. There was nothing too fussy. She thought she looked rather glamorous, truth be told.

Music, that's what was missing, she suddenly realized – she'd forgotten to select appropriate background music, after Ben had been so unreasonable about hiring the string quartet. No matter, she could quickly find some Vivaldi or the Brandenbergs upstairs in the Cunninghams' collection of compact discs. Why had no record company thought of doing a lingerie-tea CD?

But there was already some noise in the house, coming from somewhere – it penetrated Claire's consciousness just then, quite unpleasantly. Gunfire. Explosions. 'Grimlord has sent one of his new mutants towards the reality barrier!' a voice screamed. She froze, midway up the stairs. 'Ben!' she called, shattering the delicate tea-scented serenity that had, only moments before, surrounded her. 'Why are the kids still here?' It was three-thirty; he'd promised to have them out, and be out himself, by three. What sort of mess were they making down there in the family room? Claire couldn't be expected to go around scrubbing carpets and spraying glass surfaces with window cleaner at the last minute, dressed in a tea gown! 'Ben!' She hurried the rest of the way back down the stairs. From somewhere below, deep in the lower intestine of the house, she heard her husband's voice – faint but loud enough to convey his irritation.

Elfriede met her at the foot of the stairs, wiping a tea cup with a dish towel. 'He says as soon as he finds his nylon jacket, they'll go. Do you know where it is? The children are watching television – they certainly enjoy that programme, but it seems so violent . . .'

'Ben's jacket? Lord knows. What jacket? I have no idea. I have to find some music.' Claire grabbed the skirts of her tea gown again to charge back up the stairs. Rattled now, she hurried from room to room, tweaking bed spreads here, flicking microscopic or imagined bits of dust there. Why was it that she'd come upstairs? she wondered. Then, with a surge of panic, she realized that people could start arriving at any moment.

'Remember, Mother,' she said, breathlessly, back in the kitchen a moment later, 'you're to use only the filtered water, and pour it over the loose tea as soon as it boils, not a moment later. That's what it says in the books. They seem to be unanimous on that point. But not about when the milk should be added. Some say after the tea is poured, some say before. There's quite a debate raging. On several continents.'

'Books!' Elfriede drew her cardigan closer over her shoulders.

'You don't have to tell me how to make a pot of tea.' When she had arrived an hour earlier, carrying her old wicker picnic basket full of table linen, she had found Claire staring helplessly at the dining-room table, a stack of china plates in one hand, a cluster of tea cups in the other. 'I haven't got a clue,' she'd moaned, 'what goes where. Does everyone have tea first? Does the food go in between all this china or behind it? Do we put out sandwiches first and sweet things later? Or does everything just go on the table at once?'

'The first thing is to put on the table cloth,' Elfriede said, firmly. 'I brought you a very good one – my best.'

'Of course. A tablecloth. I'm so stupid. I don't know why I'm feeling so helpless, why it all seems so complicated, why none of it makes sense.'

'I tried to teach you. For years.' Her mother took a damask cloth from the top of her picnic basket and shook it out.

'But it's just a tea. We have to remember that. And try to keep things in perspective.'

'Still, there's a right way to do everything. There's no such thing as *just* a tea or *just* a dinner. Unless you want to live like pigs. Then who cares? Throw everything on the table – ketchup, jars of pickles – what does it matter?' She'd paused. 'You don't have an underpad for this cloth?'

'Do we need one?'

'Luckily, I brought one. Without it, everything clunks on the table. Did Dad leave? The underpad is in the back seat of the car.'

Basil, who was now showing Harry and Molly the trick where he pretended to cut off his finger and glue it back on again, was dispatched to the car for the underpad, then given specific directions to several book stores and to a shop that sold ingredients for Indian cooking. On his way to the front door for the second time, he paused to contemplate the floral display: the tall pedestal table draped with yards of filmy cream-coloured fabric, topped with a mottled blue and white china urn from which heather, thistles and African lilies sprang, and from which English ivy trailed.

'Why do you have a rag over this little table?' he asked his daughter.

'It's not a rag, Father, it's an Edwardian wedding veil. An antique.'

'It looks like those curtains we used to have in the bedroom, doesn't it, Elfriede? On Clark Street?'

'It's not mine,' Claire said tightly. 'It's on loan from the designer.'

'Basil, darling, just go.' His wife pushed him towards the door. 'He always says stupid things he doesn't mean,' she assured Claire when he was gone.

Basil's exit was followed by the women's retreat to the dining room where they had another debate about when to uncork the champagne. Claire had the last word on this, finally: there would be champagne before, during, *and* after the serving of the tea, and it would be appreciated by most of the guests.

'These women are alcoholics?' Elfriede didn't drink herself, not publicly. She sipped sherry though, looking out the lace curtains of her kitchen window, but only after five in the afternoon, and only when certain that her husband had his nose safely in some philosopher.

'They're not alcoholics,' Claire said, thinking that some (if not all) of them might very well be, 'but with the stress of the plane crash and everything that's gone on . . . who could blame them for wanting a nip or two?'

Elfriede nodded sympathetically. 'The widows. Will they all be coming?'

'*Everyone*'s coming. Even clients.' Claire felt her stomach flip over. 'But not till later, thank God.'

'You should be pleased.'

'Yes.' Claire hesitated. 'Of course I am.'

'These flowers are too big for the table. I had a feeling they would be. They almost touch the chandelier. I don't know what that floral person had in her head.' Claire was suddenly aghast by the inappropriate scale of the bouquet: ornamental cabbages and white carnations in a blue-glazed bowl from which blue delphiniums, foxgloves and huge white trumpeting lilies shot up towards the ceiling. 'It looks so . . . aggressive. The way all that spiky stuff jabs into the air.'

'I wouldn't have used delphiniums on a tea table,' Elfriede

said from the kitchen, 'but you insisted on blue. I didn't want to argue.'

'Mummy!' Molly yelled from the hallway. 'Can I pick some of your flowers?'

'No, sweetie, you can't! Ben? Aren't you watching her? What are you doing? Why haven't you all gone yet?'

'We're just leaving,' he said. 'But Molly wants a flower.'

'But that would unbalance the whole arrangement.' Claire darted out from the dining room. 'You kids stay away from Mummy's flowers! Ben, why aren't you taking them out the back door?'

Molly started to cry. 'Oh, come here, darling,' Elfriede said. 'After your mummy's party you can have *all* the pretty flowers you want.'

'But I want one now!'

'Can't she have just one?' Ben said. 'You've got about a thousand here. What difference is one going to make?'

Defeated, Claire approached the daunting display and carefully plucked a daisy head from a section near the wall where she didn't think it would show. 'There. Okay, honey?' She kissed her daughter's plump tear-dampened cheek.

'But I want one of the prickly ones!'

'But this is prickly, sweetheart. See? Ouch, ouch. It's very prickly and pointy.'

'No! The other prickly ones!'

'She means those thistles,' Elfriede said disapprovingly.

'Well, of course she can't have a thistle. You can't have a thistle, darling. It might hurt you.'

'What are thistles doing in a bridal bouquet?' Ben wanted to know. 'They're weeds, aren't they?'

Claire flushed. 'Its not a bridal bouquet. And if you have any questions why don't you ask that idiot designer?' Her stress-o-meter flying off the scale, she hurried back into the dining room. This was followed by scuffling sounds from the hallway, the thunk of Ben's rollerblading bag as it hit the edge of the door frame, Elfriede's warnings and more wails from Molly, who'd apparently managed to grab, and prick her finger on, a thistle. Then Harry complained that he was thirsty and wanted some juice from the kitchen. Finally, the front door slammed, followed, a few seconds later, by several car doors.

Claire sighed and sank into a chair to try and collect herself. She was *not* going to have a stroke over this tea. There was much uncomfortable wetness in the chiffon of her gown, under her arms. She wanted a bath. She wanted to run away. She was already the frazzled hostess, and not a single guest had yet arrived.

Elfriede was back in the kitchen where she was slicing her lemon loaf. Chop, chop, went her knife on the wooden board. 'I won't cut up all of it,' she was saying, 'just a few pieces. People can cut more if they want it. Do you have a pretty knife to put on this plate?'

'All the knives I have are already on the table.' Had that floral person played a sick joke on her? Claire wondered, freshly affronted by the tea-table arrangement. Was tipping expected with floral designers? Should a discreet (plump) white envelope have been slipped to her when she came to do the final touch-ups? Spots of uncertain pink appeared on her cheeks. She was positive now that that floral woman had set out to humiliate her in her own home. But why? Claire had paid her the going rate – what she'd asked for. Could she really have sought such vengeance over something as minor as a neglected gratuity? Could anyone be so vindictive?

'We should put some parsley on the sandwich plates. Have you got parsley?' Elfriede was standing in the kitchen doorway.

'No, Mother. Only people who cook use parsley.'

'A few grapes?'

'No.'

'You must have some paper doilies to put underneath.'

'Mother, I don't. I'm hopelessly inadequate and unprepared as a hostess. Go ahead and say it. Tell me how I've shamed you. On your birthday.' Claire flushed.

'Don't be silly. We'll just have to serve them as they are. Sometimes simplicity is best.'

Naked and shivering, goose-pimpled sandwiches, exposed on a chilly plate with not even a doily for warmth. Why couldn't her mother just come right out and admit that Claire was a social failure? She put her head in her hands. How could a tea be so complicated? Why was she so unable to cope? What would she do when it came to significant events like Molly's wedding? Her parents' funerals?

Then the door bell chimed. Music! Claire had forgotten the music. As she hurried to answer the door, the hem of her tea gown snagged in the hinges of one of the French doors. Impatiently, she yanked it free, causing a small tear in the lavender silk chiffon.

'Guests!' Elfriede called cheerily. 'Claire! Answer the door. I better fill the cream horns.'

23

'The characters of the guests must also be considered. Not everyone can properly appreciate an entertainment as refined as the afternoon tea . . .

Done properly, the afternoon tea should create an atmosphere, not of escape from the world, but of mental and spiritual tranquillity, one that encourages guests to transcend the mundane concerns of the work place, that allows them, and the hostess, to share their innermost selves with one another' – The Tai Chi of Tea

'Gillian! Shelagh!'

'We didn't plan to arrive together,' Shelagh said. 'It just worked out that way.'

'We thought you might need some help – that's why we came early,' Gillian added.

'Well. Come in, come in!' Before any of the neighbours see you, Claire thought, then was immediately ashamed of such an uncharitable thought. Her partners had obviously gone to a lot of trouble putting themselves together for an afternoon tea – a subject of which, in fairness, they knew next to nothing.

'Nice dress.' Gillian gave Claire's gown an envious glance. 'And you found lavender shoes to match! They're incredible!'

'But look at *your* dress,' Claire protested. 'There must be six yards of lace –'

'Ten, but who's counting? I brought you a cake.' Gillian pushed an enormous white Tupperware tray, covered with a translucent dome, at Claire. 'Take it. I've got too much to carry with all these presents.'

'Oh! It's heavier than it looks. Well . . . great! Thank you.'

'Life Celebration Cake. Straight from my hippie days to you. It's loaded with fruit and nuts, even crunchy granola. Jerry's recipe.'

'Sounds fabulous,' Claire said, wondering what she was going to do with the thing, which had to weigh at least five pounds.

Shelagh was inspecting the floral display in the hall. 'Someone's going to kill themselves tripping over this curtain thing.'

'It's not a curtain, it's a veil – Edwardian.'

'Really?' The crown of Gillian's hat grazed the coach lamp that hung from the ceiling as she moved over to get a closer look. 'It's *won*derful!' She fondled the fragile edge of the veil, then took a step back to admire the whole display. 'I'm impressed. Did you do this yourself?'

'I had a designer. She knows Shelagh's mother, actually.'

'Mother's into Ikebana these days. I'd be surprised if they were speaking. She wouldn't really have much in common with a designer who could do . . . this.' Shelagh took in as much of the house, and Claire's clothing, as she could, with a quick appraising glance. 'So, where do we put the presents?'

Then Elfriede appeared, holding the knife she'd been using on her lemon loaf.

'Mother,' Claire said, 'these are two of my partners – Gillian Lawrence and Shelagh Tyler.'

'Yes, I met you both at the memorial service. And I've heard so much about you, of course.'

'All lies,' Shelagh said breezily. 'That is, if it's good things. If it's bad, then it's all true.'

'That's a most interesting suit,' Elfriede said to her. 'It fits you so well. Is that real leopard?'

'Some animal rights nut would have spray-painted me by now if it was.' Shelagh looked brightly at Elfriede. 'So, the gifties go where? I need to dump this box.'

'Look, Mother. Gillian was nice enough to bring us this cake,' Claire said. 'It's called Life Celebration. Could you cut it up for the tea table?' They exchanged looks as Claire handed her the heavy container. Then she took the big, brightly wrapped gift box from Shelagh. 'Ooh. Intriguing. What's inside?'

'Surprise.'

'Here's mine,' Gillian said, thrusting three packages at Claire. 'The big one is from me and these two little ones are from Isadora and her friend. They're coming, but I was afraid they'd forget to bring the gifts so I brought them. Don't ask me why they're in black bags. It was Isadora's idea.'

Shelagh was teetering in her four-inch heels towards the living room, adjusting her elbow-length gloves. 'The place looks great, Claire.'

'And so do you,' Claire said. 'That suit. Those heels.'

'Manolo Blahniks. Aren't they killers? I can hardly stand, let alone walk.'

'And stockings with seams,' Elfriede said, faintly. 'I haven't seen seams since the war –'

'There's a garter belt too,' Shelagh said, without turning around, 'but don't ask to see it. Not before I've had something in the potable department. And I'm not talking Lapsang whatever. I need to sit down. But first I want a quick snoop through the house.' Elfriede trailed after her into the kitchen.

'Can I do anything to help with the tea?' Gillian asked. 'Cut something up? Boil water?'

'Everything's done,' Claire said. 'Relax. Have a seat in the living room. Want me to store your hat?'

'Store it? This is a tea. A hat is *de rigueur, n'est ce pas*?'

'*I* don't have a hat,' Shelagh called from the kitchen. The refrigerator door opened, then closed. Elfriede said something in a low voice.

'I was just about to choose some music,' Claire said.

'Guy Lombardo. Then you can crack open that champagne.' Shelagh minced past her and into the living room where she eased herself on to the sofa beneath the front window. 'I counted twelve bottles in the fridge – that's almost one per person if my math is correct. Let's hope you get some no-shows.'

Gillian had also found her way into the living room, followed by Claire with the pile of gifts.

'I need someone to move the flowers off that tea trolley in the dining room,' Claire said. 'I'm going to use it for the presents.'

'Sorry,' Shelagh said, 'I doubt I can get up. This skirt is cutting off my circulation. Anyone mind if I smoke?' A cigarette and lighter were already in her hands.

'I would prefer it if you didn't,' Claire said, after a pause.

'You're going to make me go *outside*?'

'Mother, could you please find something in the kitchen for Shelagh to use as an ashtray?' Claire watched apprehensively as Gillian moved the flowers off the tea trolley and on to the buffet, mindful of Gillian's hat and of how close it was coming to the chandelier, and Gillian's dress, which was long and stiff and took up a great deal of space around her.

After some clanking of pots and banging of cupboard doors, Elfriede brought out a large white dinner plate from the kitchen. She handed it to Shelagh. The two women exchanged looks. 'Thanks,' Shelagh said.

As Claire put the gifts on the tea trolley, she realized that when she added her own – which was as big and bulky as both Shelagh's and Gillian's – there would be little room for any others. What a coincidence that the three of them had bought Anna something that came in a king-sized box. Lingerie was normally given in tiny gift bags or slim cardboard envelopes – not these great, hulking presents-from-Santa cartons. 'I hope we didn't all get Anna the same thing,' she laughed, deciding to stand her contribution on end, on the floor beside the trolley, allowing more room for everyone else's.

'What time did you tell her to come?' Gillian asked.

'Four.'

'It's after that now.'

'Can't we start on the champagne?' Shelagh asked.

'I thought we should wait until Anna gets here.'

'But the bride-to-be is never on time. I could die of thirst before then.'

'Have a glass of water,' Elfriede told her.

The door bell rang again. 'I'll get it,' Gillian offered.

'Be careful of those flowers in the hall,' Claire called as Gillian and her miles of lace rustled out of the room.

'I don't know what to do with that cake she brought,' Elfriede whispered to Claire. 'No matter how I try to cut it, it falls apart. It's a big mess. Come and see.'

'Would it be rude not to serve it at all?'

'She'll notice. She'll be offended. Of course we have to put it out.'

'We came together.' Jocelyn Durham was striding into the living room with the easy authority of someone who was used to being a Managing Partner's wife. She flashed her large teeth and swung her auburn hair. Behind her cowered Helen Johnson, and beside her Marcia Owen. The three seemed to have rolled into the room like a great cumulus-nimbus cloud: all were dressed in grey, as if their grief had faded since the memorial service and their funeral garb paled along with it. Jocelyn wore a simple sleeveless A-line with a triple strand of pearls around her neck. Helen was in suede – a suit that folded and buckled uncompromisingly as she moved, like so much cardboard. And Marcia, who'd lost more weight since the memorial service, wore a narrow cotton knit with a matching bolero jacket.

'Welcome all!' Claire beamed. 'I'm so glad you could come. We haven't seen you since – the service.'

'We haven't seen each other since the service,' Marcia said.

'Please, everyone, help yourselves to some goodies. There's sandwiches, cakes, all sorts of wonderful fattening things.' The first hurdle – the mention of the memorial service – had been cleared, Claire thought happily.

'I think I'll just visit a while first.' Jocelyn slid on to the sofa beside Shelagh and poked her arm. 'You look great,' she said. 'I love fake leopard. And you've even got a matching bag!'

'So, how've you been, Jocelyn?' Shelagh said through a smoke-ringed smile.

'I've been well, all things considered. There's been a lot to do – tidying up Rick's affairs and what-not. Probating the will was a major pain. I had no idea.'

'You should see the hell people go through when there isn't a will,' Shelagh said. Then she thought that reference to hell was inappropriate, since Rick Durham was sure to be there. The firm was still going through the laborious and expensive process of identifying the sums Rick had brought in through his appalling and devious means. None of which, even if ever 'found' by the Law Society's sniffer dog forensic accountants, could ever be repaid by Bragg, Banks and Biltmore – the firm could barely cover its ongoing expenses these days. And the same went for repaying the legal fees charged by that great con man in the sky, Sbitozan Krupnik. Thank God for legal insurance.

'Where do we put the gifts?' Marcia asked. 'I've got all three here.' Her prominent eyes swept the room, alighted on Shelagh, then goggled along, giving no indication that she recognized her. Shelagh dragged heavily on her cigarette. So, it looked as though no photos of her had been dredged up in Ross's estate. And no one had told Marcia about the affair. She looked sideways at her, trying to assess whether she was safely out of the woods yet, or not. Perhaps Marcia was crueller – and more cunning – than Shelagh gave her credit for. Maybe Marcia was going to let her twist in the wind for a while, for malicious pleasure.

'I'll take those.' Claire was relieved to see that the newly arrived gifts were small: three pretty bags looped with yards of curling ribbon from which pillow-shaped satin drawer sachets dangled.

'Jocelyn did the shopping for all of us,' Helen murmured from behind her hair.

From her seat on the sofa, Shelagh pulled again on her cigarette, eyes still on Marcia. 'Got another butt?' Jocelyn nudged her.

'I was just going to put on some music,' Claire said. 'Anna should be here any minute.'

'Goody.' Jocelyn swung her hair again: once over the left shoulder, once over the right. 'This is so exciting. Wouldn't I love to be getting a load of sexy new things?'

But your husband is dead, Claire thought, marvelling at how well Jocelyn looked, how happy. Not that she should look anything else – she had a right to get over her grief, surely. But so soon? Perhaps she'd already found someone new. Marcia and Helen, on the other hand, looked as subdued as one would expect the recently widowed to look, and they were the ones who'd been separated from their husbands before the crash, not Jocelyn. Helen looked especially miserable, slumped in a corner chair. She'd managed so well to avoid Pete's business obligations while he was alive, she had to be wondering what on earth she was doing here with all these women, now that he was dead. Perhaps whatever illness she had had flared up recently, Claire thought; maybe that's what had taken all the colour from her face.

'Audrey's not here yet, I see,' Marcia said, crossing her legs. 'She and I have patched things up, by the way, everyone will be relieved to know.'

'That's wonderful,' Claire said.

'Strictly for the sake of the children. She *is* their grandmother. I'll never get away from that fact, will I?'

'But she's such a sweet old thing, isn't she?' Helen said. 'So properly English. A classic dear old mum.'

Everyone stared at her, wondering if she could possibly be serious.

'I'm concerned about where *my* daughter is,' said Gillian, who had gone back to occupying a great deal of space by the tea table.

'What a fab hat,' Jocelyn said. 'You wore that to the service, didn't you?'

'I've added the flowers since.' Gillian preened a little as she selected a pale pink and green *petits four* from a silver tray.

'How did you get them to stick?' Jocelyn asked.

'Hot glue gun.' Gillian licked her fingers. 'But I'm irked that I'm the only one wearing a hat here,' she lied. 'What's a tea for, ladies, if not for hats?'

'We'll put one on Anna,' Helen said. 'A paper plate.'

'Oh, no,' Jocelyn moaned. 'I hate that silly custom.'

'I have trouble imagining her tolerating a paper plate and bows on her head,' said Claire.

'We all went through it,' Helen said. 'It's a rite of passage.'

'One we could well do without,' said Claire.

'But she's an articling student,' Marcia protested. 'Students are supposed to put up with indignities aren't they?'

'That was in the old days,' Claire said. 'They have unions now.'

'Well, everything just looks so lovely,' Helen sighed from the depths of her arm chair. 'So many flowers . . .' Her suede suit was buckled up around her ears. 'Is Alex coming? Is he bringing Anna?'

'I don't think so.' Claire frowned. 'But I didn't ask him.'

'Men don't understand things like this,' Jocelyn said. 'Every man I told about this lingerie tea thought we'd all be trying on sexy underwear – modelling it.' She laughed.

'That's right,' Shelagh said. 'They wanted to be invited until they found out that no one would be wearing the stuff. Men are so simple. As if we were all going to strip down and struggle into split-crotch panties.'

'Ooh! Did somebody buy some of those?' Helen asked.

'What are split-crotch panties?' Elfriede murmured. But then the conversation faltered.

Helen smiled sadly and Marcia gazed out of the window, shaking her head.

Claire wondered whether Marcia's affair with her therapist was over. And about her reaction to the Fed-Exed box from the office. Poor Marcia. For the first time, it struck Claire that the doling out of lovely underthings for a pretty young woman about to get married to a sexy and successful older man might strike a painful chord with the women so recently bereaved, and Helen especially, who had to have discovered by now that her husband liked to wear exactly the same sort of frilly frippery that was the subject of this tea. Really, it was monstrously inappropriate, Claire concluded. A kitchen shower would have made more sense. At least it wouldn't have rubbed the widows' noses in the fact that they had no men to wear alluring underwear for. The clock on the living room mantel ticked loudly. Shelagh exhaled twin dragon jets of cigarette smoke through her nostrils, her eyes flickering back to Marcia. 'Well,' Claire said, 'I suppose I'd better go put on that music I keep talking about. Anyone have any requests?'

'It was such a surprise to hear that Alexander was getting married,' Marcia said. 'A shock, really. He'd been seeing a friend of mine, Pauline. She really liked him. When Ross told me that Alex was getting married, I was so thrilled. Naturally, I assumed it was to Pauline. She's such a great person.' The corners of Marcia's mouth turned down further. 'Oh, well,' she sighed, 'I'm happy for him. What's she like, this articling student? Anna?'

'Gorgeous,' said Claire. 'You'll see.'

'I wouldn't say *gorgeous*,' Shelagh said. 'Attractive, I'd call her. At best.'

'Long legs,' Gillian added from her grazing station beside the tea table.

'And very bright,' Claire added. 'She'll be a Supreme Court Justice some day.'

'It's no wonder he dumped Pauline then,' Marcia said. 'She's nothing like that.'

There was an audible, collective sigh in the room as all thoughts turned, sympathetically, to Pauline.

'Shall I pour the tea now?' Elfriede grasped the sleeve of Claire's chiffon gown.

'Well, if you think now is the right time ... You're the authority.'

'Am I the only one who's going to eat anything?' Gillian demanded. 'I feel like a pig over here.'

'Come on, let's forget the damned tea and uncork that champagne,' Shelagh prompted.

'Forget the tea?' Elfriede gasped.

'Now you're talking!' Jocelyn slapped Shelagh on the knee and stood up. 'You stay where you are.'

'I couldn't get up if I tried,' Shelagh confessed.

'There's lots more food,' Elfriede said. 'I was just going to put the rest out. We have some rolls – they're warming up now.'

'I've got enough rolls,' Helen said ruefully, poking at the waistline of her unwieldy suit.

'There goes the door again,' Gillian said. 'It's probably Isadora. I'll get it.'

'I guess I'd better help with the champagne,' Shelagh said, struggling out of the sofa to follow Jocelyn, 'otherwise I'll never get any.'

'Shouldn't we wait for Anna?' Claire asked.

'Anna?' Jocelyn called gaily over her shoulder. 'Who's Anna?'

As Claire was about to pursue them into the kitchen, she was startled by the appearance of Isadora. With her friend. 'Francine?' she said faintly.

'I'm sorry, Claire,' Gillian said from behind the two girls. 'I had no idea.'

'*You're* Isadora's friend?'

'Sure, why not?' Francine grinned.

'Well. What a surprise.'

'We're only the very *best* friends,' Francine said, 'since the picnic, which Izzy's mom can tell you all about, I'm sure.'

'I was only concerned about Claire's children,' Gillian said.

'Sure, sure. It's only natural,' Francine said. 'After all, you're a mom yourself, right?' Her blue eyes took in Gillian's dress, her hat.

'And your hair, Isadora,' Claire said in amazement. 'What are those? Dreadlocks?'

'Corn rows.' Isadora shook her head, making the beads at the end of each tiny braid clatter. 'Mother paid. She said we should get our hair done.'

'Remind me to kill you later,' Gillian told her daughter.

'Do you like our fetching little gloves?' Francine said. Both girls were wearing fingerless crocheted gloves and matching hats – more like doilies – on their heads. 'So *prop-ah* for high tea,' Francine snickered. The studs in both girls' noses glittered. Their dresses were loose, sloppy, tie-dyed prints; on Isadora's feet were oversized suede pumps; Francine wore Doc Martens.

'There's something familiar about those shoes of yours,' Gillian said to her daughter. 'Where did you get them?'

'The Goodwill store. They were cheap.'

The front door opened again, though there had been no ring of the bell. It was Prue. And Audrey Owen. They marched in with authority. Audrey was wearing a hat. 'We need to know where to put the gifts,' Prue said, clutching the boxed camisoles protectively. 'And a safe place for our handbags.'

'It seems so weird to be here without the kids,' Francine mused. 'And the house looks totally different. I guess Doctor Ben took the little gremlins out, eh?'

'I'm really sorry, Claire,' Gillian said, as the girls clomped down the hall, through the living room and towards the tea table. 'They won't stay long. It's their idea of a stupid joke – they're just trying to be funny.'

'It's fine. I'm fine. Don't worry about it.'

'At least they're not in tight jeans.'

'Why don't we grab some champagne?' Claire said. 'Shelagh's right. Who needs tea?'

'Are those clients of ours still coming?' Gillian asked.

'Yes. Well, actually, I hope not, but probably. Later.'

'Later? Is that a good idea? What if we're totally in the jar by then?'

'They will be too,' Claire said. 'I'll make sure of it.'

'There's a man at the door.' Marlene Ruby tapped Claire on the arm, startling her as she was taking the pecan scones from the microwave. 'We got here at the same time. He has a suitcase – he wants to know where he can change.' Marlene was a petite young woman, covered in freckles, dressed in jeans and a flowered shirt. She'd just come from moving computers and files in the office, apologizing for her casual clothes. There was a lot to be done at the firm – systems-wise – to get ready for the move.

Claire put the tray of scones on to the counter, picked up her glass of champagne (her third) and knocked back what was left in it. 'I didn't order any man,' she said.

'Well, why the hell didn't you?' Jocelyn demanded over Marlene's shoulder. 'It's not as though no one around here could use one. Right, Marlene?' The two exchanged looks.

'Perhaps he comes with the sandwiches. He must be from the catering company.' Elfriede regarded Claire and her guests with disapproval. Things seemed to be getting out of hand. People were guzzling champagne, glass after glass, not eating much, breaking corners off sandwiches and cakes, tasting, nibbling like rabbits. Very rude to take something and not finish it. The bride-to-be hadn't arrived and it was after five. No one seemed terribly interested in where she was, nor in drinking tea, though there were three pots of it on the table and Elfriede had been continually refreshing them with hot water, fussing over them, worrying about bitterness. She hadn't sat down for an hour. 'You shouldn't have used the microwave for the scones,' she told Claire. 'They're soggy now. The oven would have been better. At two hundred and fifty degrees.'

'Tell the man to change wherever he wants,' Claire told Marlene, still puzzling over how the catering company had missed telling her about the waiter. 'But make sure he's got the right address. I'm positive I didn't order a waiter.' If he was included with the sandwiches and pastries, shouldn't he have arrived earlier, to help set things up? She refilled her glass with champagne, her hand unsteady, feeling woozy and disorganized.

'Haven't you had enough to drink?' Elfriede said.

'A good tea hostess always gets drunk.' Claire's cheeks were flaming. 'I read that in *The Untold Secrets of Tea*.'

Shelagh brushed past Elfriede to take two more bottles from the refrigerator. 'Now you're getting into the swing of it,' she said.

'You hired a waiter? For a tea?' From her perch on a kitchen stool, Prue frowned at Claire. 'I can't imagine Ben allowing such an extravagance.'

'I make my own money,' Claire said testily. 'Ben doesn't have to approve every dime.'

'She really wants to be taken seriously, doesn't she?' Francine was smirking to Isadora. They were momentarily alone in the dining room. 'Frau Wolaniuk, I mean. Claire's mother.' She put a finger horizontally under her nose and clicked her Doc Martens. 'Heil Hitler or what?'

'She's not a Nazi.'

'German. That's bad enough.'

'I think she said she's Austrian.'

'They were *worse* than the Germans.' Francine sank her teeth into a Linzer heart. 'Yuk.' She made a face, rolled the cookie into a napkin and shoved it behind the floral arrangement on the tea table. 'You should have heard her going on about her book club or whatever it is she belongs to. I felt like saying: So what are you reading these days? *Mein Kampf*? Have you got two million members?'

'Shh! She might hear you.'

'So what?' Francine scowled as she pulled apart a small triangular sandwich and sniffed it suspiciously. 'Gross! There's mint in here. And the cheese is green.' Shaking her head, she put the mangled sandwich back on the platter. 'And how about the Queen Mum out in the kitchen there? She's even worse. Potty, as they say. Getting potted too, along with the rest of them.'

Isadora watched in silence for a moment. What an unpleasant person you are, she thought, not for the first time.

'Look out,' Francine said. 'Here they come.'

Jocelyn and Marlene came into the room carrying plates of sandwiches and tea cakes and sat down to exchange filthy looks with each other across the living room. 'Still battling it out over monitors and mouse pads?' Jocelyn asked, acidly.

Marlene examined a meringue kiss. 'Actually, we're too busy meeting with Revenue Canada and Crown Attorneys,' she said, 'going through our records and files. Maybe they'll want to go through yours too. I'll put in a word for you, if you like.'

'These sandwiches are very rich,' Audrey pronounced, following Elfriede, who was carrying a tray of shrimp pinwheels to the table. 'Loads of butter, I should think.' She took one from the tray and pushed it between her teeth. Audrey's hat was a slightly tatty *peau de soie* pill-box in a wan shade of turquoise.

'Of course, there has to be butter in the sandwiches,' Elfriede said. 'That's how they stay moist.'

'Derek, my husband, would never take sandwiches for his tea. He likes a nice Danish. We get them by the box at the Price Club. They're quite a bargain, when you buy them in the big box like that.'

'I always thought English people made a big fuss over tea,' Elfriede said. 'I know in Innsbruck, the Austrians –'

'Well, I don't know as I'd say we make a big fuss. Derek loves his pudding, of course, when he can get it. But it's too much bloody work for me. And not good for his heart condition neither. Far too rich.' Audrey scanned the tea table, waiting for someone to ask for details about Derek's condition. 'Those cinnamon rolls look quite nice,' she said, when it was apparent that no one was going to. She moved over to help herself to two of them, then gazed around with sharp expectant eyes. 'Now, you look rather familiar for some reason,' she said to Shelagh, who was leaning on the door frame of the kitchen, a full champagne flute in each hand.

'We met at the memorial service,' she said. 'Remember?'

'Well, of course I remember that. But there's something about you –'

'Oh, everybody thinks they've met me before,' Shelagh said gaily. 'I've got one of those faces that gets lost in a crowd.'

'No – that's not it. I'm sure I've met you before.'

'I'm just as sure you haven't.' With a little laugh, Shelagh slipped around the door frame, back into the neutral territory of the kitchen.

'Have I shown you the pictures from my friend's retirement party?' Prue was asking Helen Johnson, as she settled herself on the arm of her chair.

'Now's our chance,' Francine said to Isadora some time later. The two were alone again, this time in the living room: everyone else had drifted back into the kitchen, where it seemed they were going to stay for a while. 'You take that fake leopard job and I'll do this one.' She reached down alongside an arm chair and put her hand into a black vinyl handbag that was leaning against it.

'You expect me to steal from my mother's friends?' Isadora gasped.

'Why not? You steal from your mother. They're all in there getting pissed to the gills. They'll never miss a thing. If you see a new lipstick – one still in a box – grab that too. Get going. There has to be a dozen bags in here. It's an effin' field day.'

'You didn't hear what I said. I'm not taking anything from any of these handbags.'

'What the hell is this? Dope?' Francine held up something lumpy, wrapped in plastic. 'Christ! It's a sandwich. One of these cows brought a sandwich!' She giggled. 'Oh, God!' She stuffed it back. 'It's too funny.'

'My mother is not a cow.'

'Well, okay, I didn't mean your mother specifically. Though I'm not exactly her biggest fan. She tried to get me fired, you know. Telling Claire about you and me at that stupid picnic.'

'That's a lie.'

'She did. She said I wasn't watching the kids. So don't get me started on your old lady.'

'Well, you should have been watching them.'

Francine rolled her eyes. 'Like *you'd* know something about looking after kids. Anyway, forget it. Just get going. There's fat little handbags all over this place.'

'I said, I'm not going to steal from my mother's friends. Or my mother. Not any more. And neither are you.'

'You got any better idea for getting some quick cash? What

do you think we're here for? To munch mint sandwiches? How else are we going to get our business going?'

'There isn't going to be any business.'

'What are you talking about?'

'Not with me anyway.'

'Don't start on that again.' Francine was clawing at the clasp of Prue's change purse. 'You're always saying that.'

'You take anything from any of these handbags and I'm going to call Claire. The police too.'

'You wouldn't dare.'

'Oh, yeah? Why don't you try me?'

'You hideous, ungrateful bitch!'

'Why don't we step outside and discuss it?'

'Did you order doughnuts?' Marlene asked Claire. 'There's a doughnut truck in your driveway.' She had a cup and saucer in one hand, two checkerboard sandwiches in the other, and was looking out through the kitchen window. Francine and Isadora had disappeared somewhere outside.

'Doughnuts?' Claire said.

'I wouldn't think you'd need any more food,' Marlene said, 'especially not doughnuts.'

'I get the feeling Anna's not coming.' Helen looked at her watch. 'It's going on six. That wouldn't be her in a doughnut truck.'

'I better see what they want,' Claire said.

'Now, this fellow here in this picture, holding the cake, is my friend Bob,' Prue was saying to Elfriede. 'It's not a good likeness – he's really much better looking. We used to work together in the unemployment insurance unit. His sister is married to my friend Mary's brother. No. Wait a minute. Maybe it's the other way around. His brother is married to Mary's sister. That's it.'

Elfriede accepted the photograph, reluctantly. 'Oh, yes,' she said, adjusting her glasses. 'Did I tell you today is my birthday?'

'No,' Prue said.

'I'm seventy,' Elfriede said. 'Can you believe it?'

'There's just a few more pictures,' Prue told her. 'Sit down.

You've been working too hard. Let the younger women do the fussing. We've earned the right to put our feet up. You're seventy. A guest of honour. This is a milestone for you. Somewhere in my bag I've got pictures from my friend Joanne's sixty-fifth birthday. It was also a retirement party. So we had quite a time finding the right cake, deciding on what to have written on it . . . Did I tell you about Joanne? She's had a very interesting life. And she's such a toot!'

'Everybody? I need your attention.' Claire looked stricken. A woman in a wild-patterned muumuu loomed large behind her in the hallway. 'I'd like everyone to say hello to Grace.'

'Grace?' Jocelyn smiled and tipped her head to one side. 'Just Grace?'

'Grace Owen,' said Grace.

'Owen?' Audrey said, her eyes bright. 'That's my name.'

'What a coincidence,' Marlene said.

'Are you related to us Owens?' Audrey asked, biting into another cinnamon roll. 'We're originally from Manchester. We live in Wallaceburg now. My Ross lived here, in Toronto –'

'I know exactly where Ross lived,' Grace said, 'and where he didn't. I was his wife.'

'How's that again?' Audrey's mouth, full of partly masticated roll, hung open.

'Excuse me?' said Marcia. She was scowling at both Grace and Audrey. Could it be that she'd never opened that box of photos that was Fed-Exed to her from the office? Claire could only watch, helplessly. 'A good hostess always takes pains to introduce her guests and point out what they have in common before leaving them in each other's company.' Some blasted tea book had said that. Well, she didn't know about taking pains, but she was certainly experiencing some now.

'I said, I was Ross Owen's *wife*,' Grace was saying.

'*I* was Ross Owen's wife,' Marcia said.

'Oh, my,' Elfriede said.

A blob of whipped cream gushed out the side of Gillian's Calla Lily cream horn and plopped on to the kitchen floor.

'*You* invited *Grace Owen*?' Shelagh had come up behind Claire and clutched her arm.

'Well, no, I – Shelagh, let go. You're hurting me.'

'I just got sick of being left out of everything,' Grace said. 'And if your secretary, Claire, hadn't asked me if I was coming . . . I guess I never would have known about this tea, would I?' A soft, tissue-wrapped package crinkled under her arm and she toyed with the ribbon on it. 'It's rude to crash a party – I know that – I'm not a total slob – but personally I think I should have been invited. I know Alex. Sort of. Heard enough about him over the years – from Ross. I heard all about Anna too.'

'You probably know more than we do,' Shelagh said.

'She's not here yet,' Gillian added. 'There seems to be some doubt about whether she's coming.'

'You think you were *married* to Ross?' Marcia demanded.

'I *was* married to Ross.'

'Oh, oh,' Audrey moaned. 'Oh, no!' Claire and Elfriede hurried to help her into a chair.

'Grace, this is unfair,' Claire said. 'She's an old lady.'

'I don't understand!' Audrey wailed. 'How many wives did my son have?'

'Two,' Shelagh said. 'Only two. That we know of.'

'You!' Audrey cried, flinging her head around. 'You were at my home! In the spring.'

Summer, actually, Shelagh thought, looking around for her leopard skin bag, longing for a smoke. 'No – I don't think so, Mrs Owen. You're confusing me with someone else I'm sure.'

'Yes indeed you were there! Ross brought you for supper.'

'Ross took you to meet his *parents*?' Grace said.

'*You* were having an affair with Ross too?' Marcia turned to Shelagh.

'*I* wasn't having an *affair*,' Grace said. 'Look at this wedding ring. Look at my diamond. We were married, Marcia. For over ten years. You've got to face up to it. We have four kids.'

'Children too!' Audrey Owen's tea cup thumped on to the carpet of Claire's living room, the dark stain of tea seeping instantly into the pale fibres.

'More grandchildren!' Jocelyn cried. 'You should be very pleased.'

'I'll get a cloth,' Elfriede said. 'Some soda water. Tea stains never come out if they set.'

Audrey moaned and put her face in her hands. Her hat fell off and rolled across the floor, like a loose tyre thrown from a vehicle that was no longer roadworthy.

'*You* had an *affair* with *Ross*?' Marcia repeated, advancing now on Shelagh.

'It wasn't really what you would call an affair,' she said, backing up towards the dining room.

'Then what was it?'

'You've got to face up to things too, Audrey,' Grace was saying, moving over to her mother-in-law's chair and squatting down beside it, ignoring the spilled tea. 'I'll show you pictures of the kids. They look just like Ross, some of them. Actually, the two that look the most like him aren't his. Isn't that weird? I know it's a shock but you'll be glad, in the end, that everything's out in the open.'

'Why are you so mad at me?' Shelagh said to Marcia. 'At least I wasn't *married* to the guy.'

'You were his law partner!'

'Yeah, well, I learned my lesson, okay? About the company inkwell, not dipping my pen into it and all that.'

'So *you're* the reason he left me? Stuck me alone with five kids?'

'No. Oh, no. I'm sure not. I doubt I was even the catalyst.'

'Like hell you weren't!'

'Ladies, ladies! I need your attention please.' A smoothly shaven, handsome young man suddenly appeared beside Shelagh. He was dressed in black and white satin – an imitation English butler's costume. He held up a ghetto blaster and gave them all a thousand-watt smile. 'Could one of you girls show me where to plug in this boom box?'

'Oh,' said Claire. '*You* brought the music? I was going to select some.' Her head was swimming, nothing was making sense. And the man wasn't wearing shoes! That couldn't be a good sign. And since when did caterers supply music?

'I'm the entertainment,' he said. 'A present from your lovely friend, Anna who, unfortunately, won't be joining us here today.'

'Are you a peeler?' Jocelyn demanded.

He winked. 'You've got that right.'

'You're going to take your clothes off?' Shelagh said.

'You bet your little leopard booties, sister.'

'All *right*!' Jocelyn clapped her hands. 'I'll help you find a plug. Follow me.'

'Now, wait just a minute!' Claire protested.

'*Nein*!' cried Elfriede, waving her arms. '*Nein, nein*!'

Grace and Prue were fanning Audrey with the decorating magazines that had been carefully arranged, by Claire, on the coffee table.

'Everyone, come out into the living room and get comfortable,' Jocelyn called. 'You're out-voted on this one, Claire.'

'Cool.' Isadora had come back in from outside. 'I've never seen a guy strip. Things are really jumpin' now.'

'But it's my *birthday*!' Elfriede cried.

'In that case, honey, I'll sit on your face for free,' the young man laughed.

Elfriede fell back in her chair. 'What does he mean? What is happening here?'

Through the pandemonium, Gillian looked at her daughter, suddenly remembering where she'd seen Isadora's over-sized mauve suede pumps before. They had been in Pete Johnson's desk drawer.

24

*'It is often agreeable to provide some musical entertainment at tea,
but the lady of the house should not ask her amateur guests to
take part. And the hostess . . . unless she is musically-inclined and
wishes to sing the first song, should remain free to devote herself
entirely to the comfort of her guests' – Love Letters and Lady's
Navels*

'*Mein Gott*! The furniture will have to be steam-cleaned.' Elfriede
fiddled anxiously with her necklace.

'And the carpets,' Prue said. She and Elfriede were standing,
half in and half out of the living room where the exotic dancer
(as it turned out the man – whose name was Kenneth – preferred
to be called) had struck a seductive pose by Claire's mantel
and was about to begin his performance. Jocelyn hit the 'play'
button on the ghetto blaster. After a bit of static, a single guitar
strummed, a banjo joined in, then something that sounded like
tap shoes was added. A boisterous bump and grind was soon
rolling from the boom box.

'*I got a souvenir in London!*' warbled the tape. '*Got to hide it
from my mum! Can't declare it at the customs, but I'll have to take
it home!*'

'What a dreadful song,' Audrey wailed from her chair. She'd
followed the others out of the kitchen and was now ensconced
in the most comfortable living-room chair. She appeared to be in
a state of denial about Grace, concentrating instead on the young
man in the butler's suit. 'What's all this about?' she demanded.
'What's going on 'ere? I don't understand.' In her anxiety, she
was dropping her h's.

'Tried to keep it confidential!' the tape went on. *'But the news is leaking out! Got a souvenir in London. There's a lot of it about!'*

'The clap!' Isadora leaned over and shouted in Audrey's ear. 'It's about the clap!'

'What?'

'Gonorrhoea!' Prue exclaimed, wondering who on earth cared about gonorrhoea, now that people had worries like AIDS to contend with.

Kenneth was peeling off his white gloves, moving his hips in a vulgar way and pouting at the women. Then he tossed the gloves, along with his bow tie, into the arrangement of pompom chrysanthemums on Claire's coffee table. Slithering out of first his black satin jacket, then his trousers, he began twirling them over his head. His pelvis thrust back and forth, side to side, grinding and bumping to the music.

'Yes, I've found a bit of London! And I'd like to lose it quick.' He was down to a black waistcoat front, tied around the back, and a white satin, well-stuffed and very tight, g-string. As the women watched, he mounted one of the generous upholstered arms of Claire's love seat to make exaggerated humping motions over it. Boom! Boom! Boom! went the bass drum.

'Got to show it to my doctor, 'cause it isn't going to shrink!'

Elfriede gasped. 'This is too much! How far is he going to go?'

'Let's pull the plug!' Prue called. 'We must!' But she made no move to do so. The fingers of one hand rhythmically stroked the stem of the champagne flute she held in the other. 'He has to be stopped!' Then she too gasped as Kenneth, back on his feet, undid the ties of his fake waistcoat, pulled it off and whirled it around, making it flutter high over his head. His chest glistened with sweat. Cymbals crashed. Everyone started. The ghetto blaster practically leaped off the floor from the force of the vibrations.

Kenneth's g-string swaggered past Audrey, at nose level, so close she could have nipped it with her teeth. She shuddered and drew back. Stiff upper lip, Shelagh thought, glancing at her. Close your eyes and think of England.

'Want to keep it confidential! But the truth is leaking out!'

Then Kenneth was down on the floor, on all fours, making

more doggie-humping motions, after which he rolled over and executed a series of energetic kicks.

'The lamp! Watch out for the lamp!' Claire cried. 'I had it made specially,' she added, faintly.

There was nervous laughter from the women, most of whom sat frozen in their seats, knees tightly together, clutching their tea cups or champagne glasses. Then Audrey rose and staggered out of her chair. Marcia rushed to her side to help her towards the stairs, patting her arm and stroking her hair. Grace watched them go, looking envious.

Suddenly, Kenneth leaped to his feet, shoved his hands into the front of his g-string, and tossed back his head in a paroxysm of pleasure. He looked around the room as he swayed, pelvis gyrating, taking in the women, one by one, from below half-lowered lids. He seemed to be winding down now.

'Got a souvenir in London! There's a lot of it about!' Then he was suddenly on the carpet again, this time on his back, simulating an orgasm, pelvis thrusting towards the ceiling. His bare toes dug divots into Claire's living-room carpet.

'He's actually very fit!' Prue shouted to Elfriede as the cymbals crashed again and the tap-shoeing rhythm on the tape picked up tempo. Her fingers stroked the stem of her glass, faster now. 'He must play professional sport! Or do you think doing this keeps him so fit?'

'He's going too far!' Elfriede wailed. 'We must stop this naked man running around my daughter's living room! On my birthday! *My* birthday!'

The music did, in fact, stop a few seconds later, trickling down to a lone guitar strumming, the same way it had begun. Kenneth jumped to his feet and did an exaggerated bow. A few of the women clapped.

Claire made an attempt at a nonchalant laugh. 'Well! I'm glad you didn't go any further with that, Kenneth.'

'I'm not,' Jocelyn said. 'He was just getting to the good part.'

'We wanted it all off,' Shelagh said.

'Be quiet, you silly person!' Elfriede snapped. 'Nobody wants any more of this obscene –' She struggled to find the right word, but failed.

'Nonsense,' Prue volunteered. 'It's all very interesting, but where is it getting us? In a socio-political sense?'

Kenneth grinned and cantered over to her, fell down on his knees, threw his arms around her legs and wiggled his bum in the air. 'So you're the birthday girl,' he said.

'No, it's me,' Elfriede said. 'It's *my* birthday.'

'Oh, dear.' Prue tried to push him away. The sweat rolled off Kenneth's chin and dripped on to Claire's carpet. The soles of his feet were black.

'Please, please!' Claire said, still trying to laugh and act as though she were terribly amused by this unexpected diversion. 'Thank you. That was very well done. But we should be getting back to our tea now.'

'Tea?' Kenneth looked up from Prue's lap. 'Bummer.' Reluctantly, he released her and got up off the floor.

'The man's an artiste,' Shelagh said.

'*Arriviste* is more like it,' Elfriede said firmly.

'Well, hardly,' said Prue. 'What this man is reduced to, to make a living, is very degrading. Not only to him, but to anyone who watches his ... performance. I think we all feel a little debased right now.'

Grace was wiping her glasses on the hem of her muumuu. 'I don't know about debased, but I've never seen anything quite like it. I think I'm welded to my chair here.'

'Ahem!' said Kenneth. He had stood up again and struck another pose by the mantel. 'I have a note to read to all of you.' He was panting, dripping more sweat on to Claire's broadloom. 'From Anna. Your absentee guest of honour.'

'She didn't come,' Helen said, 'to her own shower.'

'Where is she?' someone else asked.

'I'll read the note in a sec,' Kenneth said. 'Can I get a glass of water first?'

'Water – yes. Get him some water.' Elfriede pushed Marlene in the direction of the kitchen. 'Use a paper cup. By the sink – the dispenser.'

'Would you like a bathrobe or something?' Claire asked, feeling apprehensive about Anna's note and in no great hurry to have it read. 'Or can someone get you your clothes?'

'I need to cool down first.' More panting.

'I've got the water!' Marlene cried.

Kenneth guzzled it noisily, crumpled the cup and tossed it into the fireplace. It landed in a splendid arrangement of shasta daisies and cornflowers that had been placed in the grate by Claire's floral designer. Then, with a weary sigh, he reached into the front of his g-string and took out a folded paper.

'I wouldn't have thought there'd be much room in there for stationery,' Prue said drily.

'Attention, attention!' Kenneth put one bare foot up on the edge of the coffee table. 'I wanted to be an actor once, I'll have everyone know.'

'Did you?' Claire said weakly.

'Yes. Now shut up, lovely. I don't care if this is your house.' He grinned. 'This little ditty appears to be a short verse written by your great friend Anna. The dear departed, you could say.'

'Departed?' someone echoed.

Kenneth cleared his throat again. 'No more interruptions, girls. Okay? Here goes: "I'm in the South of France. I've found a new romance".' He paused, looking around the room with a provocative grin. '"I hope you liked the dance. And keep your underpants."'

'Keep your underpants?' Claire repeated.

'I guess you were all going to give her split-crotch panties or something?'

'We were not!' Prue protested. 'I brought some nice camisoles.'

'Whatever.' Kenneth shrugged. 'I don't know. It sounded pretty kinky to me. Oh – there's a P.S. here. It says: "I'm sure you will all get, if not what you need, exactly what you deserve." Anyone want to keep the note?' He held out the paper to Claire, eyebrows raised. 'Souvenir?'

'No. Thank you.'

'Okay then.' With a shrug, Kenneth crumpled the note and sent it through the air to join the paper cup in the shasta daisies.

'Does this mean that she and Alex aren't getting married?' Helen asked.

'That would seem to be the gist of it,' Shelagh said.

'I wonder if Alex knows,' said Marcia.

'Well, ta-ta, ladies.' Evidently bored with his audience, Kenneth yawned and began collecting the bits of his costume from the various pieces of furniture.

'Your performance was very good,' Helen told him.

'Thanks.' He strutted past her to retrieve his ghetto blaster, blowing her a kiss on the way. 'I'll just pop upstairs and change, if that's all right with you?' He turned to give Claire a long look. 'And by the way, gratuities *are* the norm for these things. Whenever you get your handbags out.'

'Well, sure,' Claire said. 'Fine. We'll pass the hat.'

'Not mine you're not,' Gillian said, touching the brim of her cartwheel.

'There are lots of bedrooms upstairs,' Claire told Kenneth. 'Use any one you want.'

Elfriede frowned a warning at her, meaning to indicate that someone should accompany him to make sure he didn't steal anything. Claire ignored the look. 'Well,' she said. 'Can I get anyone something else to eat? More to drink?'

'I wonder how much he charged for that performance?' Prue said. 'It's been paid for, I should hope. Or will this Anna person be sending you a bill now?'

'When do we open the presents?' Jocelyn asked. 'If Anna's not coming and she's not marrying Alex, then we get to keep the things we brought, right?'

'Well, I guess so,' Claire said uncertainly. Emily Post, she thought, where are you now? I need to look up 'Showers, absence of bride-to-be, and distribution of underwear'.

'Wouldn't it be more fun to mix them all up?' Gillian said.

'Sure,' Jocelyn agreed, 'let's mix them up. No gift tags. Just like grab bags.'

'Great idea!' Shelagh said.

'Who's going to wear the paper-plate hat?' Marlene said. 'I brought one.'

'Why don't you wear it yourself?' Jocelyn said. 'It would suit you.'

'I'm wondering whether we should call Alex and tell him about all of this. Marcia's right. What if he doesn't know?' Claire sat down abruptly on the edge of the love seat.

'Don't sit there,' Elfriede cautioned. 'That's where that man was doing his business.'

'If Anna's taken off for France, and found someone else, I'm sure Alex has figured out that there's not going to be a wedding,' Shelagh said. 'He's a quick read – Alexander.'

'It could even have been his idea, sending her away. He's been so depressed lately,' Gillian added.

'Hey, Anna owes me a memo,' Shelagh said. 'This means we don't have a student any more.'

'Surely that's the least of our worries?' Gillian said.

From upstairs, Audrey's voice, raised in anger, could be heard. Then a car pulled into the driveway, several doors were slammed, the front door of the house was opened, followed by a terrific crash. Everyone gasped. 'Well, what the hell?' an aggrieved male voice complained from the hallway. There was a dragging, thumping sound. 'It's Ben!' Claire jumped up. Her chiffon gown had lost all its oomph and floated dispiritedly about her. The rip in the side of it had doubled in size. So had the arcs of sweat under each arm.

'Am I too late for tea, ladies?' Ben filled the entrance to the living room, his face beaming. 'I tripped over that curtain thing in the hall. I told you it was nuts to put it there, Claire, with all those flowers on top of it. An accident waiting to happen. I'd clean it up but as you can see,' he attempted to wave a crutch, clumsily, at them, 'I don't have a free hand.'

'Where are the kids? What happened?'

'The kids are fine. They're fooling around in the ambulance.' With that, the peculiar warbling shriek of an ambulance siren ripped through the room. 'The driver's a good guy – he likes kids. But there's some doughnut truck blocking our front walk. Did you know that?'

'But your leg, Ben,' Prue said. 'Whatever happened?'

'Little rollerblading incident – nothing serious.' He thunked into the room on his crutches. His right leg was encased in dazzling white plaster from big toe to hip. 'You girls can all sign my cast if you want.' He was wearing a pair of shorts fashioned from some surgical greens that had been cut off above the knee. 'I caught my wheels in a sewer grate or something. Didn't even see it coming. My guess is I've got an anterior cruciate ligament tear – partial. I'll get it scoped on Tuesday. The resident didn't have a clue what to do. I don't know what that emergency department is coming to.' The ambulance siren warbled again outside.

'I'll bring the children in,' Elfriede said. 'That ambulance can't stay there. What will the neighbours think? And with that doughnut truck beside it?'

'So, how come you girls aren't trying on all the sexy under-wear?' Ben asked. 'Isn't that the point of this shindig?'

'Benjamin,' Prue said, 'I'd like to hear more about this so-called *incident*. I can't believe you're still doing something as asinine as rollerblading.'

'Oh, now, Mother – it's only a partial ligament tear. No big deal.'

'But you're in a body cast!'

'It's not a body cast. It's a full-leg cast.'

'How long does it have to stay on?'

'Eight weeks or so.'

'Will you be able to work?'

'Yes, yes, Mother. I'll manage.'

'Because all that lost income –'

Squealing and shouting, Harry and Molly then hurled them-selves into the room, followed by an out-of-breath Elfriede. 'Children,' she begged. 'Please! No running!'

Then Cannon barrelled across the room, barking sharply, hairy tail thrashing wildly, and loped into the kitchen after the kids, his nails skittering on the Italian tiles.

'Isn't Dad's cast cool?' Harry yelled. 'They had to cut off his pants to put it on! His knee was big as a football! Hey, Mom! Can we have some of these cakes?'

'Harry, please!' Elfriede cried. 'Your father's had a terrible accident.' As she passed Claire she muttered: 'And such a mess in the hall. I told you, you should have done the flowers yourself. Then you would have had some control.'

'So where's the bride-to-be?' Ben asked.

'She's not coming,' said Claire.

'Isn't she supposed to be here?'

'Of course she's supposed to be here!'

'Take it easy, Claire,' Shelagh said, 'the man's been wounded in battle.'

'I'll put on the TV for the kids.' Ben hobbled towards the

kitchen, grunting with exertion. 'I like that *Monster Truckheads* – maybe it's on now. You girls get on with your tea.'

'I can't believe this is my party,' Claire said. 'I can't take any more.'

'It's very difficult, entertaining well,' Jocelyn said sympathetically. 'Some of us never achieve it. We can't all be Martha Stewart.'

Claire put her face in her hands, her shoulders slumped.

'Look, Claire, cheer up. Things are working out well,' Marcia said. 'Grace and I are actually talking. See?'

Cautiously, Claire looked at them through the cracks between her fingers. The two Mrs Owens (junior) were sitting side by side on the sofa.

'We may never be best buddies,' Grace said, 'but it's not like we've got nothing in common.'

Someone passed Claire a linen napkin with a crocheted lace edge. She blew her nose. 'Well, good. That's wonderful that you're talking to each other.' She sniffed. 'But poor Alexander – what about him? He's been left standing at the altar.'

'He'll probably be relieved,' Helen said. 'Plenty of women would kill for a man like him. Anna's too young anyway. It wouldn't have worked. I can't wait to tell Pauline.'

'I know someone he might like,' Marcia added. 'A terrific person.'

'Me too,' Marlene said.

'That man wants to be paid – that person who took off 'is clothes.' The small bulk of Audrey Owen, her grey fringe of hair standing out from her head as if she'd been electrocuted, appeared suddenly. 'That dreadful man who took off 'is clothes. He scared me 'alf to death. There I was, 'aving a quiet lie down – because of 'im, I might add – and 'e barges, *naked*, straight into my room wanting to know where 'is bloody clothes 'ave got to. 'E's in the kitchen, making a right bloody pig of 'imself now. I'd put a stop to it if I was you, Claire. But, as I say, it's your 'ouse.'

'Why should we pay him? We didn't order his services.' Prue looked around for her handbag, then grabbed it and clutched it to her breast. 'I'll speak to my son – Ben will know how to deal with this.'

Then Claire's father was in the room, carrying bags of groceries from an Indian food store. 'Why aren't you lovely women modelling your fancy underthings?' he asked.

'Dad!' Claire moaned, as Elfriede clucked in disapproval.

'There's a big mess in your hall. Did you know? Somebody broke the vase.'

'I'll clean it up,' Marlene offered. 'I don't mind. Just show me where you keep your garbage bags and rags.'

'You're not going to clean,' Claire protested, 'you're a guest.'

'Somebody should pick up the broken glass,' Isadora said. Everyone looked at her, surprised to hear from her. 'The kids could hurt themselves. I don't mind doing it.'

Gillian beamed at her, radiating maternal pride.

'Let's get on with opening the sexy underwear,' Jocelyn said.

'If one more person says "sexy underwear" today, I'm going to vomit,' Claire said.

'You should vomit anyway,' said Shelagh. 'You're entitled.'

'You know your dog?' Isadora said, popping her head back into the living room. 'I think he's had an accident.'

Then the doorbell rang.

'Clients!' Shelagh hissed.

Claire slumped over the arm of her chair. 'No, please.'

'It's your party,' Gillian reminded her, 'you can cry if you want to.'

By seven o'clock, the September sun was slanting in through kitchen windows, still gleaming from Claire's diligent cleaning earlier in the week. She, Gillian and Shelagh sat at the table. The living room – littered with boxes, tissue, satin sachets and ribbons only minutes before – now seemed much as it had always been, though bits of highly scented sachet crystals would remain embedded in Claire's broadloom for months. Most of the guests had gone. So had Gillian's cartwheel hat. Cannon was generally considered to be the villain of that particular piece. There was no trial.

Prue had insisted that she not be forced to trade gifts, snatching her box of camisoles from the pile of presents, protesting that she was too old for a grab-bag exchange and didn't see why she should have to go home with something she couldn't wear and didn't want when she was quite content with what she herself had bought. Elfriede, too, expressed an interest in keeping her dozen Swiss cotton handkerchiefs, as a small birthday present to herself, as something she'd always wanted.

The three double-brushed flannel nightgowns had been reshuffled and somehow managed to find their way back to Claire, Shelagh and Gillian. A blizzard of snowy flannel was piled over the back of the kitchen chairs they now occupied.

Jocelyn had taken home a red satin garter belt that had been, surprisingly, a gift from Audrey; Helen Johnson got a set of five thong bikinis in stretch lace bought by Marcia; and Marlene was very gracious about the polyester sleep shirt that Grace had brought to the tea. The two pairs of sticky-soled bed socks went to Audrey who'd pronounced them very practical and exactly what she'd been meaning to get herself before winter set in. And Isadora had expressed delight with the stretch satin slip, in a wild animal print, bought at Holt's by Jocelyn. Grace got a lingerie bag and three pillow-shaped satin sachets from Marlene and she'd never had anything so pretty and feminine, she'd said. Marcia, who was definitely 'seeing' her therapist again, was totally thrilled, she said, with the cotton gauze nightie with the embroidered sweetheart neckline that Helen Johnson had brought to the tea.

The three Mrs Owens were out on Claire's deck, talking and smoking. So much smoke was rising from the deck, in fact, that it looked as though they were grilling something out there on the barbecue. Apart from the Owen women and Gillian and Shelagh, only Isadora had stayed after the others left. She was sitting on the kitchen counter top, watching her mother and her mother's friends, from time to time picking at bits of whatever food was in easy reach. 'Lingerie teas are a blast from the past,' she said mildly.

'Don't remind me,' Claire groaned. 'I'm trying to forget this ever happened.'

'And your cake is good, Mother,' Isadora added.

'It was your father's favourite.'

'Life Celebration Cake.'

'I've told you we called it that?'

'You may have mentioned it. The odd thousand times.'

Ben had gone upstairs to elevate his leg and Elfriede and Basil had taken Harry and Molly to Sher-E-Punjab for dinner. It was time they were exposed to the cuisine of other cultures, Basil had announced, as they were leaving.

'I'm trying to picture myself in white flannel,' Shelagh sighed. 'I must have been out of my mind. From Holt's too. Can you believe it? Flannel is one thing – okay, maybe it has its moments – but this pure-as-the-driven-snow *white*?'

'I'm still trying to figure out how all of us managed to buy *exactly* the same thing for Anna,' Claire said.

'And worse, how we've managed to end up stuck with them,' Gillian added.

'Anna would have hated them,' Shelagh said. 'I see that now.'

'Probably,' Claire said.

'They're so *ugly*,' Gillian said.

'Do you really think so?' Claire said. 'I wasn't sure. I was sick when I bought it. The 'flu.'

'Trust us,' Shelagh said.

'They're hideous.'

'Just don't try to palm them off on me,' Isadora said.

'You mean, you don't want to trade that sexy little animal print for a bolt of cosy but romantic flannel?' Shelagh said.

'What if you get sick some day?' Gillian said. 'Get a head cold or something? Wouldn't you like to snuggle up in one of these?'

'I'd rather die,' Isadora said, with the confidence in her own immortality, so typical of the young.

'Hey, where did Francine go?' Claire said. 'She came with you.'

'I fired her. You won't be seeing her again.'

'You *fired* my *nanny*?'

'You *fired Claire's nanny*?' Gillian repeated.

'She's not the kind of person you should have looking after Harry and Molly.' Isadora turned to pick at her mother's cake again.

'Hold on. Are you going to explain this, Isadora?' Gillian said.

'If I were Claire, I wouldn't want the details. But she can ask if she wants.'

'But I need someone to help with the kids while I'm at work,' Claire said. 'And Ben will be like a third child. He won't be on his feet for weeks.'

'Take some time off,' Shelagh said. 'It's not like we're swamped at the office.'

'She's got a point,' Gillian said.

'Or you could hire me,' Isadora said, 'to be your nanny.'

'You?' Gillian said. 'You don't like children.'

'How do you know?' Isadora flushed. 'Did you ever ask me?'

'Well, no.'

'I happen to love kids.'

'You do?'

'I couldn't look after them for very long, though. I've signed up for some courses in January. At a community college.'

'You have?'

'I'll be working with disaffected teens.'

'Since when do you know words like disaffected?' Gillian said.

'I thought you *were* a disaffected teen?' said Shelagh.

'I'm not sure I could hire my best friend's daughter,' Claire said. She was thinking about how often, and unashamedly, she and Ben bickered, and of how she tore through the house most mornings, half-dressed, yelling at the kids. 'I don't think you'd like working for me.'

'Just till you find someone else then?'

Claire sighed. 'I bet the kids would like you . . .' They might not even be able to distinguish Isadora from Francine, she thought. Certainly, with that stud in her nose . . .

'You think of me as your best friend?' Gillian said, faintly.

'Sure I do.' Claire looked at her, realizing, with a slight shock, that it was true. 'Both you and Shelagh.'

'You do?' Shelagh said.

'Yes. I do.'

Shelagh got up to fling her arms around Claire's neck. 'That's so sweet! I'm going to howl!'

'We're all drunk, obviously,' Claire said, her words muffled by the fake leopard fabric of Shelagh's suit.

'Don't I get a hug?' Gillian asked.

'I think I'll get going now,' Isadora said, sliding off the counter top and easing towards the screen door of the kitchen.

'So how come you didn't serve my cake if I'm your best friend?' Gillian demanded, as she and Claire hugged each other.

'Yeah,' said Shelagh, 'why didn't you serve her cake?'

'We did serve her cake. Ask my mother.'

'Nobody ate it, then. Is that it?'

'Nobody ate anything! Did you see the tea table?'

'But all the booze is gone,' Shelagh said.

'I'm sure I can find some more around here somewhere. We could sample Ben's precious single-malt scotch collection – so long as he stays passed out upstairs. We'll be able to hear him coming, at least. He can't sneak up on us – with those crutches.' Poor Ben, Claire thought. Even though his rollerblading was idiotic she felt very sorry for him.

'There isn't any of Ben's booze left,' Shelagh said. 'Our clients drank it. I had to give them *something*. They were incensed when they found out that the champagne was all gone.'

'Oh God,' said Claire. 'I can't even remember them coming. Who showed up? All four?'

'Julia, Deborah, Renée –'

'Heather?'

'Heather too. They arrived *en masse*. Right about the time your dog –'

'Never mind.' Claire closed her eyes.

'Forget it,' Gillian said. 'They were very good about – everything.'

'They were?'

'Sure. They wanted to know why everyone seemed so fucked up. And where the bride-to-be was. They gave out lots of tissues and sympathy. Renée even helped with the dog's – you know.'

'And then they drank all of your husband's booze,' Shelagh said. 'And left.'

'Did they know each other before this?'

'Absolutely,' Shelagh said. 'They network like crazy. Corporate types, you know.' She laughed, then sniffed. 'They might forgive us. Being women. I'm sure each one of them

has suffered through some sort of social –' she hesitated –
'disaster.'

'It's true,' Claire sighed. 'I don't even mind you saying so.'

'Yes, well, we can thank our dear departed Richard for the
inspired idea of inviting clients in the first place,' Shelagh said.

'So let's move on. It's not your fault, Claire. Let's drink to
Rick,' Gillian said.

'We're out of booze, remember?' said Claire.

'I've got another idea, then,' Gillian said. 'Why don't we have
a pyjama party? We can wear our flannel nighties and eat Life
Celebration Cake.'

'Oh, sure,' Shelagh said, 'and do each other's hair, and write
on Ben's cast. Give me a break!'

'Come on, it would be a riot,' Gillian said.

'You've got to be kidding,' Shelagh said. 'I'm not putting on
that ridiculous mass of flouncy polyester.'

'It's one hundred percent virgin cotton,' Gillian said.

'Worse! Infinitely! I'm not nearly looped enough.'

'Now I know I'm out of here,' Isadora said. 'See you tomorrow, Claire. I'll be here at eight.' The screen door banged
after her.

As if on cue, Gillian and Claire each grabbed a double-brushed
flannel nightgown from a chair back and, smiling wickedly,
advanced on Shelagh. 'Get your camera, Claire,' Gillian said,
'this will definitely be one for the Bragg and Banks bulletin
board.'

'There isn't one,' Shelagh said, nervously backing away from
them, 'it's been repossessed. We only got to keep the tacks.'

'Good,' Claire said, 'we could use something to help hold you
down.'

And Afterwards . . .

25 ∫

Barney's Oyster Pit didn't really exist, Claire concluded, as she tramped along the street where she hoped it was located. She was heading east, this time, on foot. She'd given up on going west – but not until she'd reached the old mental hospital, and the street car turnaround. She passed a Goodwill store, a few bright blue garbage dumpsters, a row of neglected yellow brick warehouses – most of them with shattered upperstorey windows. As unlikely a district, it seemed, for a trendy oyster bar as the one she'd just left. Barney's was not only the hottest mix and mingle singles' joint in the city but was also, according to Shelagh, staffed by gorgeous out-of-work actors. Unless Shelagh had managed to catch the eye of one of them, and unless he was paying her a lot of flattering attention right now, she was sure to be in a foul mood. Claire was almost an hour late by the time she finally found Barney's weather-beaten sign, with the dim orange lamp glimmering dully above it.

'Malpeque, Pemaquid, Canaquette,' Shelagh said calmly as Claire reached her at the bar, apologies ready. 'Cotuit.'

'Pardon?'

'I've been sitting here so long I've become intimately acquainted with all varieties of these slimy little suckers.' She inclined her head in the direction of the display behind the bar where huge white oval platters of oysters on the half-shell shimmered. 'But they all taste the same – like slimy bum wad.' She gave Claire a chilly smile.

'Sorry, sorry . . . I went the wrong way on Queen. I was sure you said this place was west of Yonge.'

'You know how much I hate sitting alone at a bar.'

'Yes,' Claire sighed.

'People think I'm a loser – that I've been stood up by some *man*.' The long, curved, snakelike counter in front of her was cluttered with shredded cocktail napkins and snapped swizzle sticks. 'I quit smoking, so I can't even have a butt to help me look like I don't care that I've been stood up. Which I haven't been.'

'Nobody thinks that. I should have written down the phone number of this place but it wouldn't have helped because my cell phone just bleeped out on me. I guess I forgot to charge the battery.'

'Shit happens.' Shelagh was remembering a certain gas tank.

'And it's hardly well-márked, this place. That rotten little fishy sign – that tiny lamp.'

'Sure, I know. And your kids had you rattled.'

'Ben had a late case, and we don't have a nanny any more, as you've probably heard.'

Shelagh, slightly mollified by the prospect of hearing the details of Isadora's failure as a nanny, patted a bar stool. 'So sit. I'm surprised the doc lets you out at all.'

'At least I got here before Gillian.' Claire settled on to the stool beside Shelagh and looked around with obvious pleasure. 'I can't believe I'm out!' She inhaled the atmosphere of the restaurant. 'God, it's good to get out. Look at all these hard-working business types. Suits . . . ties . . . high-heeled shoes. Silk, cashmere, cigar smoke. Someone should bottle this air. I miss seeing the men, you know – the good suits, the haircuts. I long for the bracing scent of a fine aftershave in a crowded elevator.'

'I knew you wouldn't be able to stand staying home,' Shelagh said smugly. 'Not for long.'

'But I'm feeling much better about the kids. I'm getting to know their teachers, some of the other parents . . . I used to scream at them in the morning when I left for work and scream at them at night when I got home –'

'And now you scream at them all day. Excellent. Congratulations.'

'It's a temporary leave of absence.'

'So when are you planning your come-back? We could use you. We're getting busy. Very busy. We've got no one who does your type of work ... those trade-marks and what-not. We have to send it out. To other firms. I can't tell you how that kills me. Like a knife in the heart. After all we've been through ...'

'I still have to sort out some things. What if I get to like being a lunching lady?'

'You won't. There aren't enough others out there like you to lunch with. Besides, without a job you'll have nothing to talk about. No office gossip, workplace romances. You won't be able to complain about stress 'cause no one who works will have any time for that. You get to stay home, they'll think – what stress have you got to complain about? So, think it over. Seriously. Like I said, we could use another body.' Shelagh picked her teeth with a red swizzle stick. '*Your* body.'

'At Spears, Tyler and Chatwell ... It must feel good, having your name up there on the masthead.'

'It could be Spears, Tyler, Chatwell and Cunningham.'

'I think it would be Cunningham and Tyler, in that case.'

'Tyler and Cunningham.'

'Okay – but we drop Chatwell. That much we agree on.'

'Even Spears is in doubt. He wants to retire in a couple of years – but you know him. He's so morose. He's been talking about retiring since I first met him.'

'I saw him! I *know* I saw him!' Gillian was suddenly overwhelming them in a sea of blue satin. 'I was standing there by the front door, looking at all those pictures of champion oyster shuckers, and who walks right past me but Sandy Krupnik!'

'Get out of here,' Shelagh said.

'He did! I swear it was him. He looked me right in the eye and then he turned and ran.'

Any man would have, Shelagh thought, after being given the eye by this behemoth in blue. And what was that on her head? Could it really be a turban? So much for attracting any normal guys this evening. She sighed, looked at her watch. Won't you ever grow up, Gillian? she wondered.

'I tried to follow him but he gave me the slip. Took off down an alley.'

Shelagh gave her a look. 'And I thought we'd successfully pulled you through your spook stage.'

'Why don't you sit down?' Claire said. 'You've had a terrible shock. Have a drink.'

'You don't believe me.' Gillian shook her head. 'That's so predictable. I'm very disappointed in both of you.'

'A lot of men could be mistaken for Sandy,' said Claire. 'He wasn't all that distinctive. Short balding lawyer with glasses.'

'So they're not dead! I knew it!' Gillian lifted off her turban, realized there was not enough room for it on the bar, then put it back on her head.

'The inquest was pretty conclusive,' Claire said. 'No one survived.'

'But it's not like any of those guys had *no reason* to disappear, is it? They were all *up to* something.'

'And it's not like none of us have had this thought before,' Shelagh added.

'Well, I don't know where this type of thinking is going to get us,' Claire said. 'I for one am not going to spend the rest of my life searching every face in every crowd for those four.'

'You should forget it, Gillian,' Shelagh said. 'I know you're a wing-nut and all that, but that wasn't Sandy Krupnik you saw out there on the street. If he were still alive, he wouldn't have the nerve to parade past popular Toronto bars at happy hour. He'd want to stay hidden, wouldn't he? He'd be lying low in the Bahamas or someplace. Enjoying his embezzled money or whatever he'd be living on – with a new girlfriend.'

Gillian was silent for a few moments, frowning. 'Okay – nobody believes me. But I have a strong sense that those four guys are still around. And I know who I just saw.'

'Okay, you know who you saw,' Claire patted her hand. 'Let's have a drink and talk about your clothes. What is that? A kimono?'

'It's inspired by the kimono.' Gillian said. 'I have a great new client – a very hot designer. She's doing really well. This is hers, what I'm wearing. I'm filing three industrial design applications for her tomorrow.'

'Really,' Shelagh said, drily.

'Let's get those drinks,' Claire said. 'I'm free for the night, out on the town, and we haven't seen each other for what? Six months? We have to celebrate our new lives.'

'It hasn't been six months,' Shelagh said. 'I saw you two at Christmas.'

'Still, considering we used to see each other every day, that's a long time.'

'A virtual eternity.' Gillian was rearranging her clothing again. 'After the rough and tumble excitement of the legal profession, life must be pretty dull for you, Claire,' she said, finally settling on the bar stool. 'No more whining clients, accounts receivable over ninety days. But I've discovered that I can live without all that. I still see the same goofy inventors. Only the stress level is lower.'

'What's the name of your organization again?'

'The Newton Centre. We just got a grant that's going to keep us going for a few years. I enjoy my clients much more now that I don't have to worry about whether they're going to pay my bills for protecting their inventions. And I do more market research, more cheerleading. Rah-rah stuff.'

'Is deep-sixing ever one of the options for these inventions?' Shelagh asked.

'Oh, for sure.' Gillian looked around happily, apparently taking no offence at the remark. 'So, Claire, tell us the truth. How do you like being a housewife?'

'Home-maker,' Shelagh corrected her.

'Woman who works not-outside the home,' said Claire. She laughed, shortly. 'It's not such a bad life. I'm in control of it. At least, I think I am.'

'Except for the money,' Shelagh said. 'Small point.'

'Ben's being better about sharing one income than I gave him credit for.'

'Still. It's not like having your own, is it?'

'But I know what my kids are doing, I know where everything is in my house. Well, almost everything. Nothing gets broken during the day, nothing disappears.'

'That was just because Francine was living with you,' Shelagh said.

'She stole things from Isadora too,' Gillian said. 'She was bad news.'

'Well, thank God the kids survived. Harry adored her. But I'm not so sure about Molly. I think she had Francine's number.'

'She's got a body-piercing studio, did you know?' Gillian said, looking over the bar list – a small wooden plank – of exotic beers. 'With a guy from LA. In a mall somewhere. Apparently they're very busy. Isadora hears from her occasionally.'

'More often than you'd like, I bet.'

'This is true.'

'And how is your man, Gillian?' Shelagh asked. 'That writer?'

'We don't speak. He stole one of my poems. It showed up in his new anthology.' She continued to peruse the beer plank. 'I might try this Japanese stuff – the Sapporo draft. What are you two drinking?'

'Champagne for me,' Claire said.

'Sure,' said Shelagh. 'Champagne. You should have it too, Gillian. To celebrate B.M. Bradley crawling out of your life.'

'Oozing,' said Claire. 'Leaving damp slug-like trails – like Boo Radley in *To Kill A Mockingbird*.'

'Anyway, let me finish the story,' Gillian continued. 'He didn't know "The Granary Floor" was mine, he says. He thought it was Alexander Spears'.'

'He copied that same one from *Toadstool Quarterly*?' Claire said.

'And he's going to get away with it, isn't he? I mean, Alexander certainly isn't going to do anything about it, since he plagiarized it from me.'

'What about *Toadstool*?' Claire said.

'*Toad Hole.*'

'Why don't *they* take some action?'

'They're history. The government yanked their grant. Fiscal restraint. You know.'

'Well, look,' Shelagh said, 'at least now you know B.M. is a bottom feeder with no talent.'

'I always knew that.'

'You're lucky you had it confirmed again.'

'Just like I was lucky that Alexander stole my poem in the first place?'

'I was only trying to make you feel better when I said that,' Shelagh said. 'You were ready to ruin your career over it.'

'Oh, I don't care any more. You were right. It was one lousy little poem. Though in Brad Bradley's collection, it sparkles like a jewel. That's what one reviewer said.'

'B.M.'s name is Bradley Bradley?' Shelagh asked.

'Yes. But here come the drinks. Forget B.M. I have something real to celebrate.' She waited as the glasses were placed in front of them, the champagne uncorked. 'My novel's going to be published.'

'The one about the dentist?'

'Who's publishing it?'

'A small press. Tiny actually. They're just getting started – only one other title so far.'

'Would we have heard of them?' Claire asked.

'They don't have a great name.' Gillian laughed, a little embarrassed. 'Guttersnipe Press.' She avoided her friends' eyes.

'Guttersnipe?' Shelagh said.

'Who cares what it's called?' Claire said. 'You're being *published*! That's what counts!'

'It's a great accomplishment,' Shelagh said. 'And I mean that sincerely.'

'Well, thank you. I have to admit it wasn't the deal I'd hoped for. I always fantasized about some giant New York publisher, flying me down for lunch at Le Cirque . . . life-size cardboard cut-outs of me in every book-store window, that type of thing.'

'You're far too literary,' Claire said. 'You don't do shlock.'

'And, unfortunately, you'll probably never get rich either,' Shelagh said.

'I know. A dentist isn't the sexiest of topics. And the book's no *War and Peace*, but I can live with that.'

'You'll probably win the Booker,' Claire said.

'Not unless it's published in England.'

'The Pulitzer then.' Shelagh raised her glass.

'You have to be American.'

'Okay,' Claire said, 'the Governor General's Award.'

Gillian twirled the stem of her glass. 'I wouldn't refuse.'

'Think of the prestige.' Shelagh raised her glass again, doing a good impression of enthusiasm. 'To Gillian's book and the GG Award!'

'To *Whit's End*,' said Claire.

'And, more good news: Shower-in-a-Sack's going under.' Gillian gave her friends a wicked smile. 'Class action suit. The combination of active ingredients – I won't bore you with the details – in the impregnated towelette makes hair fall out in patches.'

'No!'

'Yes.' Her smile grew more wicked. '*Pubic* hair,' she added. 'And the patchy fall-out appears to be permanent. In the odd, unlucky person.' She rested her elbows on the bar and sighed happily. 'But there's enough of them to make up a class action. So. There is a God. And justice.'

'And she's always portrayed as a woman,' Claire said. 'Let's not forget.'

'Or Dan's speech. How could we ever forget that?'

'That was some day.' The three clinked glasses and reflected, for a moment, upon the day of the memorial service.

'Anyway,' Gillian said, 'Isadora's doing okay at college – not exactly straight A's but okay. She's in a course for helping developmentally handicapped teens. It's more her style than . . . minding young children.' She didn't look at Claire.

'She did her best,' Claire said. 'Harry and Molly liked her. They still ask about her.'

'That's okay, Claire. You don't have to be nice. I know she royally screwed up.'

'Not badly. I mean, nobody was hurt – that's the main thing. We just had a good scare. That mall is pretty big, to try and find two little kids, when you're in a panic . . .' Claire swallowed, trying not to think about that day that had a lot to do with her decision to take some time off work, to think about staying home – if not on a permanent basis, then at least until the children were older.

'But enough about me and Isadora,' Gillian said. 'What about you, Shelagh? Any new man on the scene?'

'In fact, there is someone.'

'Dan!' Claire said. 'I knew it.'

'Don't be ridiculous.'

'Who, then?'

'Alexander? I always thought you might take a run at him,' Claire said carefully.

'I'm way too old for him. He's dating a twenty-one year old – a veterinary student.'

'How much would you have to say to a twenty-one year old?'

'I don't know that talking is a big part of their relationship.'

'We had a long boozy lunch, Alex and I. Just before I left the firm.'

'Oh, yeah?' Shelagh said, cautiously, not wanting Claire to clam up and deprive them of further details.

'So did he finally confess his undying lust for you?' Gillian demanded.

'Actually, he seemed to want to mope about Anna, mostly. How no one had ever made him feel such searing jealousy before.'

'Searing jealousy? He said that?'

'How hot she made him – how every man that saw her had his tongue on the floor.'

'He never talked about you?'

'Oh sure. I was always the salve, the balm in his life.'

'The what?'

'Whenever he looked at me, he saw a beautiful woman who had it all – blooming in pregnancy, then gorgeous kids, career, fabulous home, a balanced happy life. A dog.' She made a face. 'I was the sort of woman he could never hope to attain.'

'What did you say to that? "Just try me"?'

'I said I'd never thought of myself as a salve. Or a liniment for that matter.'

'That's telling him,' said Gillian.

'Then he asked me to go to bed with him.'

'No way!' Shelagh said enviously. 'Just like that?'

'I told him I was happily married, that I liked staying at home with my kids – for now – and that I was not interested in destroying my family for a night in the sack with him. You know what he said? "They're little kids in a little life. Why make such a big deal out of it? I wasn't proposing marriage, Claire."'

'Well, no one ever expected Alex to be a prince,' Shelagh said. 'He's from that never-hurts-to-ask school of sexual advancement.'

'So I hope you threw a drink in his face?' Gillian said.

'I should have. But I'm such a wimp. I just walked out of the restaurant and left him with the tab. I was an idiot for going – I don't even know why I did. Curiosity, I suppose, after all these years of believing he was panting after me. I did it for my own ego. It served me right, me with my "little life".'

'I only work with the man,' Shelagh said. 'He's a good lawyer. What can I say?'

'I wonder if he's published any poetry lately?' Gillian said.

'Who cares? I don't ask about that. But getting back to me – you two didn't let me say a word about my love life.'

'So, who is he?' Claire said. 'A lawyer?'

'God, no.'

'What does he do?'

'He's in transportation.'

'A pilot? That's sexy,' Gillian said.

'You think I'd go for a pilot after what happened last summer?'

'What then?' Claire said. 'Shipping magnate?'

'Don't tell us he's a trucker,' Gillian said. 'Does he own his own rig at least?'

'What if he was? I don't see that what Tristan does for a living should matter so much.'

'Tristan?'

'So you're not going to tell us anything about him?'

'He's in the courier business, if you must know.'

'Well, that sounds good,' Claire said. 'Couriers seem to be busy these days. So he has his own company?'

'He *is* a courier, actually.' Shelagh lifted her chin. 'Bicycle.'

'One of those wild guys who rides around in Spandex?' Claire said. 'With dreadlocks and walkie-talkies?'

'It's a whole creepy underground culture,' said Gillian.

'You know something?' Shelagh scowled. 'You two are occupation snobs.'

Gillian looked hurt. 'I was being *complimentary*.'

'Tristan happens to have a PhD in mechanical engineering. He's young and sexy and smart. For the moment, he's chosen to be a bicycle courier. And I respect him for that.'

'Well, naturally,' Claire said.

'Who wouldn't?' added Gillian.

'He's also in incredible shape.'

'I guess he would be – with all that peddling.'

There was an uncomfortable few moments. The three women looked over to study the chalked blackboard menu on the wall.

'I know what I want,' Shelagh said. 'But then, I've had more time to consider the menu, since you were both so late.'

'Don't rush us,' said Gillian. 'I saw a ghost, remember? I'm still rattled.'

'It's all the same stuff up there. Oysters. We'll just order a pile. Stewed Quahogs sound nicely gross.' Shelagh tapped her nails impatiently on the bar, then gazed at the waiters (cute, with those snappy white towels around their waists) then over towards the entrance where a number of live lobsters were floating dreamily in a tank, under a rushing waterfall. The place certainly was hopping, she thought, for a Tuesday night. It had to be the spring weather that was bringing everyone out. She watched the people coming and going, pausing near the entrance to look over the framed photos, mounted oysters, the wall maps of famous oyster bays. 'I wish I had a cigarette right now, let me tell you. But while we're on morbid subjects, ghosts and what-not . . . you two remember that subway hand-walker? The guy who was killed last summer? His firm is folding. He was a key player. Without him the firm's fallen apart. It's sad. They've been around forever.'

'So? They'll just regroup and open up again under a new name,' Gillian said.

'Yeah,' Shelagh said. 'Like we did. After our wonderful women clients dumped us.'

'Well, who can blame them? I'm sure they thought we were all insane. Would you want a firm of lunatics working on your files?'

'Never trust a client,' Shelagh said. 'Or a woman.'

'Come on now,' said Claire. 'I think it's fair to say that we three trust each other.'

'It's not like we've got all that much to lose, is it?' Gillian said.

'But still, we do.' Claire looked at the others. 'Don't we?'

'Yeah.'

'For sure.'

'But it's true what Gillian was saying.' Shelagh said, 'We lawyers are very resilient. Like the cockroach, we adapt. We'll outlive any nuclear holocaust. Lawyers and cockroaches.'

'Thank you for sharing that thought with us,' said Gillian.

'You know what I'd really like right now?' Claire said. 'A good strong cup of tea.'

'This is an oyster bar,' Shelagh said. 'They aren't going to serve you *tea*. And we want to party. You can't have *Lapsang Souchong*.'

'I was thinking of Gunpowder Green. After all, you only live once.'

'And you might as well do it dangerously. Walk on the wild side a bit,' Gillian agreed. 'If the lady wants Gunpowder Green, we'll go find her some.'

'Speak for yourself,' said Shelagh. 'I'm staying. It looks like the waiters are changing shifts. That means new blood.'

'Did somebody say they served shark here?' Gillian said.

'No,' Claire said, 'but it looks like it can be had.' She and Gillian laughed, clinked glasses and verbally abused Shelagh until she too had to laugh.

'Bottoms up, mates,' she said.

'Down the hatch.'

'Here's mud in your eye.'

'To absent friends.'

'Absent friends.'
'And may they stay there.'
'I'll drink to that.'
'Hear hear.'